My Path to Greatness

A novel

David Sahatdjian

My Path to Greatness
David Sahatdjian

ISBN: 979-8-9916245-0-3 (hardcover edition)
ISBN: 979-8-9916245-1-0 (paperback edition)
ISBN: 979-8-9916245-2-7 (ebook edition)

Extract on page 230 from Ginsberg, Allen, 1926-1997. Howl and Other Poems. San Francisco: City Lights Pocket Bookshop, 1956.

For my family

Contents

Part 1

In the Long Before

Long before I came to any knowledge of Jane Thayer or fully embraced that I wasn't among the brightest stars in the firmament and long before my parents and older siblings made themselves invisible on the earth, there is my childhood room overlooking Broadway, along which the cars and trucks and buses of the city are given the right of way to race along, not as they please but within the guidelines of the traffic lights installed to impose a kind of order, a sorrow suffusing me that the trolleys cannot be there too in the time that I have come into but had to be retired in the relentless current of change the world has not found a way to resist.

Before the bad people came we lived in a palace bigger than any ocean, with rooms that sparkled. Rings inlaid with precious jewels adorned our fingers and necklaces lustrous with pearls encircled Momma's neck and the radiance of springtime was ours to enjoy without ceasing and frankincense and myrrh were at our disposal. In chariots we rode and slept in bowers of bliss and drank the milk and honey of the land.

"Don't exaggerate, my son. But yes, how beautiful it was," Momma says, while braiding her long brown hair by the full-length mirror in the vestibule.

"Why did the bad people come?" I ask.

"Because there is iniquity in this world. There always has been and always will be, until Jesus returns, like a thief in the night," Momma says.

"What is iniquity and why would he come like a thief in the night?" You can always ask Momma a question, and the answers she gives are all her own.

"Iniquity is when the heart lives without Jesus and is filled with dark purpose. Thieves will always live for surprise. And Jesus too will be a big surprise. And so you must be ready for him with a soul whiter than snow when the clouds part and Judgment Day arrives."

Momma is on fire for the Lord and says Jesus wants *me* for a sunbeam.

Momma sleeps in a big mahogany bed, in the room next to mine. When I wet my own bed and the warm pee turns cold in the night, I go to her and lie next to her warmth. There is the endless softness of Momma in which to lose myself and the hardness of my father on the other side. In the morning I wake in their bed to find him staring down at me, his arm across my chest like an iron bar. He is smiling, as if I am an insect he had pinned and is now closely examining. It is everything for me not to struggle, though I can feel a sense of panic rising. Smiling or not, my father's face, with that big nose full of hairs, has the dark purpose Momma spoke about.

"Are you my good son?" my father asks, as if he has some doubt.

"I am," I say.

"You are what, my son?"

Though I feel my own smile giving way and a scream coming, I manage to say, "Your good son."

"And does my good son want to get up?"

"No," I say. I must not say yes, yes, please let me run off to the open spaces where you are least and even not at all. Please let me go into the life of freedom I must have before your violence erupts. Please do not trap me here forever so I can never live. Because if the panic that is beginning to rise is allowed to show, the consequences will have to be severe. The iron bar will press harder against my small chest and the smile will vanish from my father's ancient face and the extermination process will have to begin.

And there it is, his arm lifted like those zebra-striped crossing barriers in front of railroad tracks.

My father is saying there is a price for Momma's bed, and the price could be my *life.*

My father is not my father. I say to myself I am Momma's son, her Svenska pojke, as she calls me. I can wear the blue and yellow and white of Sweden and not be burdened with the blackness of the land of rats from which my father comes.

The truth is, if I am to go back to the beginning, at which I can never seem to arrive, I was in Momma's room before I was in the room next to hers. A cot had been placed behind her bed, where I was to sleep. I would lay there, my head bursting with sums I could not manage—long division and multiplication and all the rest. A sinking feeling would come over me that would cause me to cry and cry, as if I were falling into a hole from which I could never escape while life moved on, leaving me behind and all alone.

"Trust in the Lord Jesus," Momma said. "He will take care of your every need. The nighttime is Jesus time, my son. All time is Jesus time, my son."

My older sister Naomi's voice rises in song. Another older sister, Rachel, accompanies her on the upright, with sheet music as her guide. They have broken through. They have brought the world into our crowded apartment. They have brought the light. To hear them summons a rush of excitement but I am not to draw near them. Their smiles are not so much friendly as fierce. A fire burns in them.

And there is fire in my oldest sister Hannah when Naomi and Rachel go against her with words. "Poor Hannah. Have you ever seen such big feet? They're bigger than Daddy's…Daddy is Hannah's boyfriend…" The two of them scratch and punch and try to pull out Hannah's hair and Hannah does the same to them. "I'll kill you witches," Hannah screams.

Rachel wears her hair in a long braid, the same as Momma makes using the full-length mirror by the front door. Momma combs out her hair before braiding and wrapping it around her head. But Rachel allows the braid to hang down, thick and long, like Rapunzel. She comes home cradling a stack of schoolbooks against her chest, holding tight to her treasure. The room she shares with Naomi is like no other in the world. She sleeps on a sea of books, four or five deep on the floor, with her eyes open on their pages. To Rachel this is not disorder but proof of plenty. Momma is proud of Rachel as her shining star.

Bessie Floxley lives on 125th Street, just east of Broadway and the elevated subway line. She lets me climb in and out of her ground-level window and takes me through the swinging doors of the tavern down the block, where everyone knows her name and I can play on the sawdust-strewn floor.

Bessie is old and alone in her apartment and her life. She is warm in the way that Momma is warm but she can never be Momma. When she becomes ill, Momma takes me and my older brother Luke and younger sister Vera to visit her on Wards Island, in the East River. An overwhelming stench meets us as we enter the huge enclosed space and stare at the endless rows of beds and the dying people lying in them. That people can be thrown together, with no privacy, in such a way. And though I am astonished that Momma has brought us to this space reserved for the suffering, she explains herself, saying it is only right that we should all say goodbye to dear Bessie.

Come nightfall and under its cover, Naomi and Rachel go to the movies down at the Nemo Theater on One Hundred Tenth Street and Broadway and the Loew's Theater three blocks farther south, though Momma says moving images of that kind are worldly and a sin.

Not only does Rachel want the world, but the world wants her, too. She has been *chosen*. She will be going to college well beyond Manhattan. That the college is famous for its excellence is more than my mind or any mind should be asked to bear.

Naomi doesn't go to college. She has a change in her life that requires Idlewild Airport. The propellers are whirling on the tarmac so she can prepare to get married. There is a family out in Chicago waiting to see who she is. The marriage takes place when Naomi returns. Naomi wears a gown of white to show that she is new. Some world beyond where I stand is going on. Naomi getting married does not bring the same happiness as Rachel going off to college. The wedding photos show too many people wearing too many clothes in too small a room. The wedding photos are confining. They do not let me breathe.

Chuck is Naomi's husband. It is a name that requires big teeth. His army jeep overturned in France, causing him to drink all the wine the country had to offer. But now his mind is equipped for the study of science at Columbia University, where he is earning something called a doctorate.

Momma has given Naomi and Chuck room 9C3. They both have conditions that require this room. So Chuck can be productive as a husband, he nightly sits in the lobby in one of Auntie Eve's upholstered armchairs. He is there to guard the security of her furniture so it does not disappear and to be a witness to everyone entering and leaving the building during the hours of sleep. While on duty he talks in a crabby voice, seeking to snare people with his song of lamentation. His face says things have been done to him of which he barely knows how to speak. Several bottles of wine, the kind that have no cork in them, are to the side of the chair. He has a way of reaching down and turning the cap left and right on the bottle without removing it just so he knows the drink is at hand. Complicated interaction with his cigarettes is also going on. He lights up a Pall Mall and draws on it slowly, making the burning tip to glow. The night is a time for his reflection, and the wine and the smoke work together so he can be orderly in his mind and his life.

Chuck walks with his chest out. Naomi says he is a cut above the rest with the science power of his mind.

"Wine is a mocker; strong drink is raging," Momma says. "It saps the strength of the living, deceiving the drinker as to its real intent, and sends him to an early grave. It is a spirit bent on evil, my son. You must listen to me when I speak. Never let it be that my words mean nothing to your ears. Have I not told you about my father back on the farm in Sweden, and how my mother would send me out into the snow to find him, and when I did, how I would smash the bottles he drank from against the rocks before getting him home so the cold could not terminate him from this earth? Have I not told you how I followed my mother's instruction in the spirit of anguished love in which she gave it?"

Naomi is my pretty sister of darkness. In the lobby she also appears, singing her Judy Garland songs at a fever pitch to the tenants as they come and go. Naomi would be a star of stage and screen and apart from the fire and brimstone base on which she was bred if she only could.

Momma says it is the doctors' fault that Naomi cries and passes out, so the ambulance has to come. Momma says the doctors give her pills she doesn't need.

"Listen, little Flathead. I just want you to know that my husband, Chuck, is a big strong man, a real man. He's the one to keep you in line, so don't try getting fresh with me or giving me any trouble, because you can believe he will give you all you need and don't want if you do." So Naomi says to me from the dark place where her mind goes.

Chuck does not come to our apartment. He made my father get up the one time he did. My father pursued Chuck out the door with his smacking hand high above his head.

The room I was given after Naomi and Rachel left has a window with a screen so I cannot fall down onto Broadway. The election trucks of the men who would be president roll past, festooned in red and white and blue bunting. The music of America plays over a loudspeaker so the right people will be chosen to run the country and no one will get hurt in the chaos that would otherwise ensue.

Auntie Eve came from Sweden to put us here in the building. Auntie Eve has a fine mind, Momma says of her older sister. Sweden, if you don't know, is north of Europe and has people in it whose eyes are blue and hair is blond, like the colors of its flag. Sweden is where the lingonberries grow, the same lingonberries Momma places on the pancakes that she has me take to Miss Hansen some mornings.

"Run on your long legs now, while the pancakes are still warm," she says.

Miss Hansen has the same room as mine, only on the third floor. With her beaked nose, she is like a big bird. Already, at eight in the morning, she is standing in her smock at the easel with a paintbrush in her hand. Some of her framed watercolors hang in the lobby next to verses of scripture Auntie Eve has hung for all to see as they are coming and going from their rooms so they know where they are.

Momma says that when my grandfather died, there was no reason for Auntie Eve to stay on the farm. The snowstorms blew in all the time and it was dark for so long and there was America, beckoning like a warm fire. America took Auntie Eve in and gave her a job as head nurse at the local hospital before she purchased the building where my family came to live. And America would have given Auntie Eve more, only people were mean to her. They took away what was rightfully hers in a way they weren't supposed to do.

"They reviled her, my son," Momma said.

"Reviled?"

"They scorned her. They heaped on her abuse. They treated her like dirt beneath their feet."

"But why?"

"Because she was a Christian and walked with the Lord and they didn't, not even the ones who said they did. The Crucifixion is not a one-time thing. Your aunt is a saint. She did not die on the cross at Calvary but in her own heart to the aspiration that it had created, and yet she got to live again in the renewal of the spirit. Because no one can kill the Christ. No one. The Christ lives and lives and lives, and it avails water nothing should it seek to extinguish that flame."

Momma is a roaring river named Conviction sweeping you along.

There is another window. It looks out on a small yard. Momma put no screen on the window because the yard is level with my room, and so I could not fall and fall and fall to the death that can come to those who fall a greater distance. From the floors above bags of garbage arrive, making a popping sound as they break open in the yard. Momma says it is the lazybones upstairs who can't bother to deposit their trash in the incinerator, though no one knows exactly who they are.

Tenants arrive from all over the world: the Indians, the Sikhs, the Pakistanis, the Koreans, the Chinese, many with mathematical minds that can also do science. They are here to get the education they need to make their countries work in the way that they should, with modern bridges and roadways and trucks that can drive over them full of rampaging purpose. They are here in the full state of their ambition, Momma says.

Momma sends me out into the yard with a broom and a shovel and a big box to sweep and sweep so order can be restored. I sweep long and I sweep hard, with the efficiency I am capable of showing, while practicing heads-up vigilance against the gifts the air-mailers routinely send. Nothing means as much to me as a good sweep, so the yard can be restored and my mind can be at peace that order has prevailed.

My childhood is my own. It is where I rest and find the nourishment that I can.

My brother Luke is loud and does not know to put caution into his ways. My father hits him hard with his hands of death and my oldest sister Hannah, older even than Naomi and Rachel, does the same. They hit him in the bottom bunk of the bed in which we sleep. They hit and hit, beating his rebellion in the night without a thought to what it will look like in the day.

At night Momma comes to me in her endless softness and with her love, and though she is not in white, she is always in raiment of white when she appears in my mind. She is Momma, walking with me and talking with me and calling me her very own; Momma, without whom I would have to die and with whom I can live and live so long as she keeps seeing me above the clamor of the world that she says has sometimes to take her away. Every night she says that prayer I cannot say to myself. "Now I lay me down to sleep, the Lord I pray my soul to keep. If he should come before I wake, the Lord I hope my soul to take," her spoken words moving me further into her softness.

If Momma says we must not fall into worldliness because Jesus could come like a thief in the night, then Pastor Odachenko, at the downtown tabernacle, says it differently: "We must be lucrative in the Lord," those words some of the few that linger among the many of his that disappear.

All children wishing to stay alive should have ears for their fathers when they come through the door. Always mine are alert to the sound of my father's footsteps as I lie in bed. In the distance can I sense him approaching on streets foggy and desolate, his alone-ness fully preserved. On his huge feet are wingtip shoes, and his big body is clothed with a Robert Hall suit ("When the values go up, up, up/ and the prices go down, down, down/ Robert Hall this season will show you the reason/ High quality! Economy!"). A wide tie, a heavy overcoat, a fedora—these too are the apparel of my father, who wishes to show himself in the garb of prosperity. My father is an Armenian, with all that can ever mean.

My father is also a walking man. Momma says walking brings my father the peace that passes all understanding. He is in the apartment now. His footsteps come nearer and nearer. Have I done something today to deserve him? Are annihilating impulses once again ruling his land? Or will he go to the other room across the hall, where Momma sleeps in sweet peace with an aura of light all around her?

And yes, the love of Momma pulls my father to her. He has no need to vanquish me on this night. I have not made him to get up, which is his dire warning to all concerned that the danger threshold has been reached.

It is not nothing to fall asleep in a room overlooking Broadway. Nightly will a fast-moving light lap the ceiling before moving to the center, where it thickens and descends to the floor in a ghostly luminous shape. "Er-ra-ra man, er-ra-ra man," it shouts, driving me from my bed and through all the rooms of the dark apartment in a state too terrified to call out. What can stop the tormenting pursuit by the er-ra-ra man, so close to touching me so that I will have to die?

In the morning I am allowed to wake to the brightness of the sun pouring in from the east without the roll of thunder or the parting of the sky. The throne of judgment has not appeared, the roll had not been called way up yonder, the fire that burns hot and everlasting is not upon my skin in the forevermore of hell. Surely mercy has a chance of following me *all* the days of my life.

"Your mother is my rock. I have no idea what would have happened to me if I had not found her," my father says at the breakfast table. The burner is on under the coffee pot and the smell of Savarin regular grind coffee, from the red can, is strong. Soon the coffee is percolating. In the deep sink, black metal showing under the worn away enamel, my father has washed cups and plates.

My father is tired. He has traveled long and hard from his place of birth and will never go back. My father shuns other Armenians while maintaining old country ways in hanging rugs on the bedroom wall.

Momma comes to the table in a white terrycloth robe. Her brown hair, which later she will braid, hangs down, and her eyes look smaller with her face free of glasses.

"Eisenhower is the only answer. This other man, Stevenson, he does not understand the world," my father says, his white chest hairs visible in the V of his dark green robe and his nose curving down toward his mouth "He is too friendly toward the Communists, who would take everything from us, including God."

"Is that so?" Words like these Momma speaks in reply. Both my father and my mother read the Bible. My father also reads the *New York Times*. Momma depends on him to explain the world. Both my father and Momma wear deep rich Republican blue. The Republican Party is the Bluecoats of the Civil War and Abraham Lincoln and Grant's Tomb. It is the granite with which buildings of worth and substance are built. It is the Grand Old Party on which the country was founded. It is a time I do not know but wish I did. The past is where you can be alone with your life.

Momma pours heavy cream from a half-pint container into her coffee, creating a warm and friendly brown, and sips from the china cup that is for her alone, an indication that Momma knows finery when she wants to. In the corner, where my father sits in his black wicker chair, the toaster is busy. Nothing in the world is better than rye toast drenched with butter and topped with strawberry jam. Nothing.

"I have great fear for the country if the Democrats win. They don't mean the country well."

"I see," Momma says, as if her eyes are being opened. She says the same many mornings.

Momma met my father in Central Park, where he was out walking. He came here from Boston after wandering through France. Momma seeks to make him someone I can see as she does.

On the wall behind us is a photo of my father and mother in the long ago. They are sitting on a hill. My father has his jacket off and is wearing a shirt and tie. My mother is wearing a dress and the sweetness of her smile is showing in her face.

"How did you sleep, Hannah?" Momma asks. Hannah, my oldest sister, has come from the room outside the apartment where she now lives. The table is small and Hannah is big, and so she sits apart. She is dressed to meet the world at the office where she sometimes works.

"Who cares how I slept?" Hannah replies, the light of laughter far away from her.

"Ushtah, Hannah. Must you speak in such a way?" Momma says.

"I'll talk any way I please."

"Can we not be reasonable?" Momma seeking to draw from the well of understanding she says must be in all of us.

"Just leave me alone."

"Hannah, do you know where you are?" my father says, pausing the toast-making operation.

"I know where I am. Do you know where you are?" Hannah says right back, not caring any which way for my father's cautioning words but frying the air with her sound.

"Are you trying to aggravate me?" My father has sent Hannah a message.

"When are you not aggravated?"

"Hannah, please. Do you wish me to be ill?" Momma pleads.

"Will I be made to get up?" my father asks.

Can Hannah be so reckless? Does she not know that violence, once unleashed, can never stop?

"Don't you so much as put a hand on me. I'll have the police on you if you do," Hannah shouts.

"The police? Do you not know that in my country you would be stoned to death for talking in such a way to your father?"

"We're not in your goddamn country," Hannah answers back, rising from her chair.

Truly does Hannah make my father get up. Truly does he give chase to my fleeing sister, Hannah streaking for the front door with my father right behind her in his bathrobe. His right hand is held in the high, pulverizing smacking position that the most serious offenses call for. But suppose, as in the stuff of dreams, the front door does not open? Suppose it shows the contrary spirit that the inanimate can summon and remains viciously locked and the hard smacks begin? Suppose Momma, screaming and imploring, falls down dying while pursuing her mission of mercy? What is this terror that has visited the earth to make my knees go weak and my breath to flee so not even a gasp is possible?

But the door is not hostile to Hannah's well-being; it does not thwart her in her moment of need; it opens easily for her escape. And yet, for those of us who remain, the vibrations that have been set forth last into eternity.

"Your father has a condition as well as a fine mind. He cannot handle stress," Momma later says. "The Virginian, The Californian, The Iowan, The Texan. The names of the downtown restaurants where your father has worked as an expert cashier are many. Your father could have a book written about him. Your father could be a book. He has that kind of mind, and the noble attributes that only the afflicted can possess. That is why the restaurants always, always take him back after he has stormed out, even after the light of reason has not shone and curbed his angry excesses. Because a condition is a condition and demands respect for its own existence. Your sister is ruled by her own fire and has been on this earth for a long, long time. Have you heard of the Great Depression, my son, when the whole world had not one nickel? In this time was she born. We had no building such as now to live in, but only a basement dwelling, and in truth in a basement was the whole world dwelling. Your father was out of work because no jobs were to be had. I have never been afraid of a little dirt, my son. I grew up on a farm and know the smells of animals as well as those of the lilac bush. My hands are rough and my spirit is strong and the world has nothing that I want. Into the poverty that gripped the nation was Hannah born, with your father having to watch over her while I worked as a maid for a Park Avenue Jewish couple. No one has fine minds like the Jews have fine minds. That is why Jesus was a Jew, my son, because only a Jew could bring the light of love into the world in the way that he did. It was for your father to administer to her needs before Auntie Eve could rise triumphant and call us to be with her."

"Hannah is mean."

"She only appears so because she is lost to her own love. She is like your father. She too has a condition. She cannot handle stress."

"And Naomi and Rachel are mean."

"It is possible that Naomi is seeking to work a dark magic on Rachel and to taint the pure whiteness of her soul," Momma says.

"What dark magic?"

"That is an unfolding we must continue to watch," Momma only says.

Momma. The way she can lift me up with her words but also defeat me.

The next morning my father sits at the breakfast table as if nothing has happened the day before to make him get up. The arrival of Hannah brings no new storm. She is cheerful, as if her mood is regulated by some inner clock that takes her from darkness to sunlight. My father speaks about Red China. It has no business being part of the

United Nations because of its redness, he is saying, when Auntie Eve appears from her ground-floor apartment. She is as gaunt as my mother is stout, her dress hanging on her meager frame. She comes like the wind, as Momma says, causing loose papers to fly in the air and hot coffee to turn cold. "Maya, I have need of you." Auntie Eve's eyes are on Momma alone. A giant building has risen out of the earth and they must tend to it now, right now. Momma excuses herself from the table. In the next room Momma allows the collaboration to commence in a language foreign to my father's ear.

My father is not made to get up by Auntie Eve's whirlwind intrusion. If he is annoyed, he does not say. Instead he summons understanding of what he owes to both Momma and Auntie Eve for the shelter that the building provides. My father puts on his thick reading glasses and reaches on the shelf behind him for a slender pamphlet from the great A. A. Allen and his ministry of faith. The literature of eternal life is right at hand. Month after month he receives these pamphlets, printed in red or blue ink, so he can have the fortification he needs for the life he lives.

The cars and trucks are everywhere, not just on Broadway. They tear down the side streets as well, forcing you to stay on the sidewalk and to say "Please" before crossing. Momma says these are the rules of the world, and the consequences of disobedience are severe. A yellow Studebaker, built low to the ground and with a canvas top, comes for me when I dash into the street. Halfway under a parked car the Studebaker knocks me and has a mind to go on its way. A simple truth is this: The cars of New York City show no mercy. They have patience on their side in waiting for the time when they can strike.

Some men carry me home and lay me in Momma's bed, and Momma comes to visit when she can, as she has the building to attend to, and all the commotions it can manufacture. A book of fairy tales is given to me as my reward for living and a golden bell to keep me safe when ringing or not.

My sister, Vera, shares the room with Luke and me. Momma has placed a little cot at a right angle to our bunk bed for my sister. At bedtime she holds her leelah, a strip from an old blanket, to her nose.

Momma has Luke and Vera and me bathe together. Momma often asks if I have moved my bowels but never in the bathtub. And yet I thrill to the shrieks my kaka summons. Surprise waits around every corner, and I am there to deliver it. I am powerful upon the earth when I do.

"Daddy, Daddy, Johan smacked me," Vera Severa cries out, in our room, where we sit on the floor. Having heard the call, my father responds. "Have I been made to get up? Have you chosen to aggravate me?" When I do not and cannot answer I feel his annihilating power on my face.

Father, do you know what you have done? Do you see the betrayal profound that you have taken her side without prior questioning? Do you see the alliance you have made that will allow me no room to breathe? But my father sees only that his action was just. He has given himself to Vera Severa for all time and given her face reason to adopt the malevolent smile of triumph that shall also, for all time, be with her.

Once again, I am Momma's son. My father cannot be with me where I am going. Gone must be Armenia and all its primitive punishments, gone all the hairs on all those hairy bodies, gone all the torturing names with their ongoing consonants. I must approximate the land of Sweden as it manifests in blond hair and tanned skin and the blue and yellow of its flag. Father, I am leaving you now. I commit you to your own devices. I cleave myself clean. Nothing attaches. *Nothing.*

The school is Episcopal, Momma says, explaining that the word means it is not one thing or the other, neither Protestant nor Catholic, but something in between, and that you can tell the emptiness of a religion by the clerical adornments and rituals that it embraces. Momma says God is a lightning bolt upon her mind and body, and so neither saints nor finery is needed. Still, Momma says, a misguided heart is not the same as a bad heart, but that in any case I am not to allow the black-robed nuns who run the school to take me away from Jesus.

Vera and I make it to the front steps of the school before racing back up the hill and into the building, where we find Momma, who has gone beyond us into her day and is speaking with a woman inquiring about a room. "What is this foolishness? You go back there right now," Momma says, flashing iron where I had known only pillow softness.

The school stands across from the welfare hotel, where only Negroes seem to live. The block is quiet and even-tempered except for this one stretch, as if we have been walking in sunlight and now are in a place of dark shadows, Negro men and women and children leaning out of windows with rotted sashes shouting down to others hanging out on the stoop in a riot of sound all through the day and the night.

Momma saying, "I have a job. Why don't they? I'm not afraid of a little dirt. Lazy bones living off the money the city gives them." Momma means the welfare checks that she says let the Negroes remain idle all through the day with their liquor and their noise and their violence.

The school is where I begin to learn my place in the order of things. Momma is patient with me that my grades are not good. "There are many ways to be a shining star," she says, seeking to ease my hurt that my world is out of control because I have fallen behind. I cry that I should have to be stupid in the world because I cannot correctly answer the questions on the arithmetic test that Sister Mary Christabel had sprung or that my penmanship reveals the poor quality of my mind, the letters of my words lacking a consistency or flourish pleasing to the eye, or that, in the matter of art, I show myself a copycat, drawing the patterns of classmates on the stiff colored paper I have been given because I could not summon any patterns of my own.

That I should be so low in my own estimation, but Momma says, "The lamentation of a child and all human beings has its basis in comparison; you must not succumb to such folly," seeking to give me buoyancy in the dark waters into which I have been plunged.

Beyond the school's reach, I go to the very top, shimmying up a streetlamp pole and onto its extension as Momma looks on in horror. A son in red high-top Keds and a polo shirt and jeans dangling high, high above, showing Momma what he can do.

At the school the boys enter the girls' cloakroom to sniff Alison Pauley's overcoat, so longing are they to be near her blondness. And yet it is not for me to show my interest in her though other boys, like Johnny Lacy and Edward Macy, do just that in making her their own.

In the basement cafeteria, Alison Pauley and Johnny Lacy and Edward Macy talk about a birthday party to which she has invited them. They and others talk about the same party some days later, and the fun they have had. I have been established in the place I need to be outside their realm, and the pain is astonishing.

In truth, I have been to the homes of Johnny Lacy and Edward Macy. The apartments they live in are beyond understanding, with modern furniture and complicated draperies and kitchens with spotless surfaces and dazzling appliances. I am left stricken by the comparisons Momma has warned me not to make.

And they have young fathers who work for corporations and wear expensive suits and walk with one hand in their front pocket in the way that men of power are supposed to walk. And, in turn, these fathers have taught their sons to walk with one hand in a front pocket so they can be proud to call them their sons. And their fathers do not come from Armenia but from America, and do not have last names that are disorderly and strange and afflicted with consecutive consonants. Johnny Lacy and Edward Macy do not have to say where they are from because their names say where they are from. They do not have to hear the titters on that first day of school when Sister Mary Christabel takes the roll call.

Nor do Johnny Lacy and Edward Macy have mothers who are old when they were born. And their mothers do not wear the man-shaped shoes that she wears or the rubber stockings she needs to ease the pain of her varicose veins.

"Momma, no," I gasp, when Johnny Lacy and Edward Macy come calling. She does not see the smirks the sight of our living room brings to their faces: linoleum instead of carpeting, a sofa that is really a bed with a spread thrown over it and a couple of pillows placed against the wall, an old TV, and cluttered surfaces. I rush from the dining room and the cardboard box where I have been trying to find a matching pair of socks and push them back out the door and say to her, "Momma, don't ever ever do that again. Momma, do you know who they are and what they can *do?*" How their tongues can shape and deliver the word "pigsty" that day and for the rest of the week, and soon that same word will be on the tongue of Alison Pauley and all those Johnny Lacy and Edward Macy have claimed for their own.

But Momma has a mind that protects from the laughter of Johnny Lacy and Edward Macy. Or maybe Momma does understand, and I have no need to tell her what she already knows. "Oh, if I only had the time, we would have such a beautiful home," she says, as if she is visioning that other life of order right then and there. Some song of wistful longing can rise sometimes from Momma, and when we hear it, we know once again that Momma is careworn with the burdens of this earth.

Though Alison Pauley has been claimed by Johnny Lacy and Edward Macy, my mind will not let go of the possibility that I can be with her, too. But for that to happen, I would have to be with her alone, beyond the confines of the classroom, where I am contained and reduced and not as I want to be. And so I wait for her across the street and up the hill from the school, my heart beating wildly, as wildly as it ever has since, and I hear the voice in my mind saying, "Do you know what you are doing? Can you not just go home?" But I cannot go home, not with Alison Pauley in my mind the way she is, with that golden hair that represents the bounty of America. And now here Alison Pauley is, climbing the hill in her blue parka and blue jumper and white blouse and knee socks, but I cannot go to her. All the words I had thought I would speak I cannot speak because the very sight of her is like cold water on my face, awakening me to the reality of who she is and who I am, with certainty established as to why she is on one side of the street while I remain on the other. For this reason do I just have to let Alison Pauley walk on by.

But that defeat does not mean that my mind loses its focus on Alison Pauley, or that hope does not revive that I could have her more in my life than she is. The day comes that the girls are walking up the stairs single file from their cloakroom and I jump out from behind the door and kiss Alison Pauley on the cheek. Some of the girls scream and others burst out laughing but Alison Pauley looks at me as if I have burned her with a match. And so I flee to some unused room where I can be away from the punishing stares. But even alone they are with me, saying I have taken something that was not mine to take.

Hours pass. I sit at the back of the classroom, where I lift the top of my desk and pretend to be busy organizing my books in the small space so I can hide my face. My stolen kiss has not brought me any closer to Alison Pauley. I can see that it has done the opposite. Now she is more claimed by Johnny Lacy and Edward Macy than ever.

Sister Mary Christabel silences the room with her entrance. After taking attendance, she says, "Johan Manootdjian will now stand and tell the class why he kissed Alison Pauley." Her pale face framed within the headpiece seems to quiver, and her eyes project a cold anger.

"I don't know," I say.

"Speak louder, please," Sister Mary Christabel says.

"I don't know," I say again.

"That is not a satisfactory answer."

"Because I had to."

"Because you had to?"

"Because I don't know."

"Tell us the truth."

"I don't know."

"You may sit down," Sister Mary Christabel says.

The school day comes to an end, and Johnny Lacy and Edward Macy are waiting for me outside.

"That was so crazy what you did," Johnny Lacy says.

"It sure was," Edward Macy adds.

Though one has red hair and the other black, and one is chubby and the other thin, they stand as one, and I feel outside of whatever connection they have made.

There is a building called the House of Order right across from my own. It rises no higher but shows a rebuking posture, with its cleaner face and window frames freshly painted to keep them from rotting. It has hedges along its margins and a recessed entranceway and uniformed doormen who stand inside a marble lobby with soft chairs set out in which you can sit and know all the peace that is to be found in this world. It is not a building with striving immigrants or the sad and lonely elderly but men and women with families and the hope of America in their bright faces.

Langley Farmer lives in the House of Order. Like me, he is skinny and blond. Within minutes of seeing him with Luke, the two of us are streaking down the hill and into Riverside Park. Still, I cannot outrun the guilt I feel that Luke has been left behind, but if I have been wicked, then let me be wicked and bear the full consequences.

On Dead Man's Hill, in the park's lower drive, we roam with our broomstick M1 rifles. On our bellies, amid the small stone markers for the dead, we pick off Kraut snipers and lob grenades into pillboxes. Kazing. Kazing. Pow. Pow.

Langley Farmer's father is gone, electrocuted in the basement of their country home. His mother has faded blond hair and eyes that speak their terror. On the eleventh floor of the House of Order they live, behind a heavy door that closes with authority on the stillness of the landing. In the kitchen is a sparkling white sink with its enamel intact. A curtain of yellow happiness hangs over the window, the sun kissing the white tabletop. In the entire apartment not a single cockroach. Even the closets have the stamp of order, with linens and clothes neatly arranged. Langley Farmer's room has a single bed and a desk and an illuminated Rand McNally globe of the world. From his window, you can look down on Broadway and see the narrow island in the middle of the boulevard full of trees and the garage across the street, with its Esso sign, and the old people's home on the opposite corner.

A third person, his mother's mother, lives in that apartment. She looks tiny in the armchair she sits in. Though Momma has me keep my hair short, I have begun curling strands of it so a lock will hang down over my forehead. Langley Farmer's grandmother says, "Are you trying to be a girl? Is that what you're trying to be?" The smile she shows me seems at odds with the harsh words she has spoken. Only later do I understand that the smile goes with her words and is meant to make them sharper. She is like my sister Naomi that way, smiling while she word smacks.

"No," I say, smiling back to show that I am not hurt, though I am hurt to the point of being destroyed, the way I can be when someone speaks to me as Langley Farmer's grandmother has.

"Then don't try to act like one," she says, with that same smile, to ensure that I am dead.

An unmistakable smell causes me to look down. The sole of the Keds sneaker on my right foot is caked with dog doo. I have tracked it all over the carpet. Only when I see what I have done do Langley Farmer and his mother and grandmother see as well. In seeing the doo they are seeing me, seeing that all I can offer them is doo and more doo. I untie my smeared sneaker and run out the door holding it and down the eleven flights of stairs and out past the uniformed doorman back to my side of the street and my family's building, like a rat disappearing into a hole.

Tall Tommy is the building handyman. Momma can count on him to replace blown fuses or burst pipes or repair broken light fixtures. Tall Tommy can do just about anything. The room he lives in, 2C3, is big enough for his single bed and a chair and a fridge and a small stove.

"Look at him. He goes right for the meat. Doesn't pay any attention to the vegetables," Tall Tommy says of me to my brother, after heating beef stew from a can in a pot, as if he is noting something important that I will have to correct in future. For drinks, he mixes Seven-Up with Welch's grape juice.

"Maybe this will put a little hair on his balls," Tall Tommy also says to Luke after handing me the drink, as if there is no need to speak to me directly. Or maybe it is his way of making his words more important, that I should have to hear myself spoken about instead of to. Tall Tommy's annoyance does not destroy me. And as for what Tall Tommy says the delicious drink can do, the word "balls" is naked and horrifying, and in combination with the word "hair" makes me recoil. Hairiness is what my father and all Armenians are afflicted with, and I have been born under the Swedish sun.

"I think there is something wrong with your brother. I think he is a little girl," Tall Tommy also says that night. I have been sitting on his lap, and his warmth against my bottom makes me want to stay there forever. Luke laughs, the way he can, when Tall Tommy finds fault with me. Tall Tommy taking the time we had together that I was so much liking, and then saying what he does in the way that he does. Again the shame finds and owns me until it doesn't.

Tall Tommy's Labrador, Biff, leads the way into the night. Down the hill we go, past the welfare hotel, fallen into silence and only the feel of sullenness calling attention to itself, and the now dark school building. On Riverside Drive, we rest by the base of a statue of a Polish hero who helped America to be free. And though there are cars in violation of the stillness of the dark, their headlights so bright and the rapid revolutions of their tires so persisting, they cannot take away from the peace of what Riverside Drive is, with the roadway and the bank of orderly buildings and the iron fence and warm lights of the street lamps and the traffic lights and all that people have made existing with the green grass and the trees in a way that doesn't result in sadness. The smell of damp earth rises and Tall Tommy taps tobacco from a small canvas pouch into thin paper, which he then rolls tight and smokes, the smell of that lit cigarette adding to my delirium. It is only that I want, in that moment, to be there forever with Tall Tommy and my brother and Biff, romping through the fallen leaves of autumn.

North along the top drive of Riverside Park we walk on the bridle path beside a low retaining wall. Then, as if Tall Tommy has heard the call of the Hudson River farther west and the glittering lights on the New Jersey shore, the Spry sign glowing a devil's red, we take the curving stairs down into the lower level of the park, past Dead Man's Hill, where Langley Farmer and I left so many Germans dead and dying. Only now, without the safety of daylight,

I am aware of the danger that loud talk and careless movement can bring, because this is New York City, where things happen on every corner, the cold steel of a thrusting blade and all the rest. So now it is I, though young in my years, who is with the innocents, Tall Tommy and Luke not grasping what violence can await.

We come to open flatland, the frenzied cars racing along the West Side Highway with that violence all their own. Tall Tommy shines a flashlight on a spring with drinkable water and has us cup our hands to draw from it. He shows us grass that is not grass but wild scallions, with the onion-like smell abundant when he pulls the shoots from the soil and holds them to our noses. He has us gather fallen limbs and twigs for kindling so we can make a roaring fire on which to roast marshmallows, all charred on the outside and gooey inside, and eat them off our sharpened sticks.

Tall Tommy has brought us into a world that connects to other worlds: cars pulled north by the magnetic attraction of the George Washington Bridge, shining silver in the night, and beyond the bridge to the country that awaits, where now Rachel is; and the river traffic heads that way as well, away from the salt water deep of the Atlantic Ocean. And there is the Chevrolet advertisement mounted on a billboard over the meatpacking plant on One Hundred Twenty-fifth Street, causing an indescribable fever of longing.

"I want to show you boys something, so you will know the fake from the real McCoy. Are you ready?" Tall Tommy asks, the fire now dwindled to embers.

"Ready for what?" I ask, but Tall Tommy has already begun to walk away with Biff now back on the leash across the exit road from the highway. On the other side he lifts Biff and swings his legs over a railing and disappears down an embankment. From below he shines the flashlight so we can find our way through the thick brush. At the bottom of the embankment we pass through an opening in the wire fence and now stand on level ground where a roadbed of rock ballast and three sets of tracks have been laid. Across from them are the highway and the river.

"Should we be here?" Luke asks, and I am thinking the same, but Tall Tommy just sits on a rail and pulls out his harmonica and plays "Home on the Range." I know the words, and they and the tune make it the slowest, saddest song I have ever heard. Then Tall Tommy produces from another pocket a green pint bottle, the kind that my brother-in-law Chuck carries around, and swigs from it.

"That's good, fellas, that's real good. Makes the night into day."

"How does it do that?" I ask.

"Someday you'll find out," Tall Tommy says.

"Momma says—"

"Momma says what?" Tall Tommy says.

"Nothing," I say.

Tall Tommy has a gleam in his eyes that hadn't been there before. "You're a momma's boy. That's why you like to sit on my lap. But that's all right. Someday I'll teach you what a man needs to know. I'll be going back to my avocado farm in California. And I'll send for you boys so you can grow up real good."

"When will that be?" Luke asks.

"Well, you both need to be patient."

There is a tunnel just a short ways south of us into which the tracks disappear. You can look down into it through the grates set into the meadow on the lower level of the park. The smell of diesel smoke rises through those grates when the trains rumble past. The penetrating sound of a train whistle turns us toward the tunnel's mouth. There, in the distance, we can see the light coming closer, its beam spreading outward onto the tunnel's walls.

The whistle sounds again, and then a third time, as the train bears down. Luke and I step back but Tall Tommy raises up only slowly off the rail. By now Biff is tugging frantically on the leash and barking. Tall Tommy gives way only a foot while holding tight to Biff, as if he doesn't want the train to think he is afraid, while the boxcars of America rollick past: the Wabash; Atchison, Topeka, and Santa Fe; Erie Lackawanna; Bangor and Maine; Rock Island Line; Southern Pacific; Illinois Central; the Seaboard Line; and all the rest, displaying the might of America and finally the fading red lights of the caboose as the train continues toward the George Washington Bridge and beyond.

Grabbing us by our shirts, and thrusting his pale face close, Tall Tommy says, "Now do you understand, boys? Now do you?"

While lying in bed that night, I hear the driver of the *New York Times* truck shout "Yo" and then a bale of wire-bound papers thud to the pavement in front of the luncheonette. I think of the life on the street, and how I am away from it for now, and of Tall Tommy's avocado farm in California, and what a wonderful thing that would be to live on such a farm, particularly in California, the word itself summoning some new sweet pain of longing, as if it really is a land of the golden sun, with a light achingly beautiful and peculiar to that place alone. And I think about me wanting to be a girl, according to Tall Tommy, and how that can't be true. But mostly I think of that New York Central twin-engine diesel, with the red decal front and center below the engine's beam, and the train's rumbling resolve, saying, I am here, from the tunnel I have come in all my overwhelming strength that clears your mind of everything else it could ever think.

I'm going to tell you something, but only if you promise to keep it secret."

And so I promise.

"The government sent me here on a top-secret mission. As soon as I can wrap it up, I'll be heading back to my avocado farm." So Tall Tommy says to me when I am alone with him. He looks scared and even ashamed, as if he knows he is lying but can't help himself. Please don't hurt me, his worried face is saying. I must care for and protect Tall Tommy, he is saying.

Alcibiades Ghent has a room on the second floor as well, though in a different compartment than where Tall Tommy lives. Alcibiades is mine alone. I go to his room without Luke. Alcibiades lets me sit on his bed in the afternoon watching *Hopalong Cassidy* in his black outfit ride his horse, Topper, and sling the lead.

Alcibiades says he has a beautiful two-wheeler bicycle with a red frame and thick tires stored in the basement. He says he will make a gift of the bicycle to me and that I will be seen as a young prince throughout the neighborhood when I ride it.

Alcibiades does not watch *Hopalong Cassidy* with me on his black and white TV. He is busy throwing darts at the target board on the wall. The darts have long needle-like tips and a heavy metal barrel and plastic tail fins. Alcibiades stands with his legs slightly spread and throws them with a short, compact right-hand motion.

When a week and then two pass and I have not yet received the bicycle, I ask Alcibiades when it will be mine.

Alcibiades kneels so his eyes can be level with mine and takes firm hold of both my arms. His eyes are like two big black pools.

"Do you know what the name *Alcibiades* means?"

"No," I say.

"Alcibiades means *truth*. That's what it means. So when I say something to you, it will always be true. Always. Do you understand?"

"Yes," I say.

"The bicycle can only come when you have been good enough for it to come, as only a very good boy should have the privilege of riding such a bicycle."

"Good enough?" I say, fearful now that the bicycle might never be mine.

Alcibiades goes back to his darts. "Roberts comes set, he goes into his windup, he delivers…Roberts brushes the batter back off the plate with a high, hard one…Roberts is painting the black… Roberts is demonstrating his pitching artistry…" In this way does Alcibiades now speak, not telling me who Roberts is.

"Are you ready for the Major Leagues?" Alcibiades continues. He comes between me and the television set. "Well, are you?" Anger is now written large on his face, leaving me to understand that I am in the center of his mind and not on the sidelines of his strange activity. "This is America, Bub. A man has to earn his keep. Otherwise he doesn't appreciate it. So are you ready to earn that beautiful red bicycle?"

I can only nod.

Alcibiades pulls me from the chair and positions me to the side of the dart board and has me take a batting stance. "Hands high and your weight on your back leg, so you can spring into the pitch the way you wicked batters always try to do. Because you're out to drive the ball over the fence, to take away my bread and butter. You see, there you go, trying to crowd the plate and get an edge."

When he goes into his windup I close my eyes. The dart is silent in the air and sinks into the cork.

"Strike one," Alcibiades says.

Then it is ball one and ball two and then strike two and then there is a loud knocking at the door. Alcibiades puts his index finger to his lips, should I have any thought of calling out. But then a key enters the lock and the lock turns and the door opens and there is Momma with folded sheets and pillowcases and a towel over her arm. There isn't a lock in the building Momma doesn't have a key for so she can distribute fresh linens to the tenants each week. "My goodness, are you here, Mr. Ghent? And my Lord, is that you, Johan?" Because Momma is on full alert that goodness might not be prevailing, she does not wait for Alcibiades to explain. "What is the meaning of this? Run along now, Johan" she says, keeping her eyes fixed on Alcibiades.

That night Momma comes to me. "I do not want you in that man's room." Momma says to me.

"Yes, Momma," I say.

"I do not have a good feeling about that man," Momma says. "Are you listening to me or do my words mean nothing?"

"I'm listening, Momma."

"Has he made any trouble for you, my son?"

"What trouble?"

"Has he been normal with you, my son?"

"He has me stand next to the dart board while he throws darts," I say.

"He does what?"

"He says this is America, Bub. A man has to earn his keep."

"What is this foolishness you are speaking now?"

"He says I have to do what he wants if I am to have his red bicycle."

"Bicycle?" Momma says.

"The bicycle he has stored in the basement, Momma."

"I see," Momma says, but nothing more.

Momma has disposed of Alcibiades Ghent to a place where I can see him no more. Another man now occupies the room. Luigi Santibelli is here to assist Auntie Eve with her enterprise. He has come from Sicily with white hairs on his tanned chest and has set up a shop in the basement where he can reupholster the padded chairs of Auntie Eve and make all her furniture shine with the varnishes and shellacs and polishes he applies. The joy that explodes from Luigi's face is not unending. There are whispers that he has split a policeman's skull.

Luigi Santibelli does not throw darts or come set before going into his delivery or say "bub." Instead, Luigi says to Luke and me, "Oh what no good sumbitches you a gonna be" and to me only he says, "How is your little dickie?" laughing with the tears streaming from his eyes, and "How is your auntie, the old pussy." The word *dickie* hits me so I am paralyzed as he jabs at my private place, and it is not for him to be speaking of Auntie Eve in such a way, as if she were no more than her private part. Still, nothing can long get in the way of the love that I am feeling. Because those words he speaks have no bearing on his light.

Sometimes, like now, Luigi's face is bound with the purpose his work has given him. He is bringing a table back to life, sanding where the surface is troubled. Later he will heal the wounded spot with potions that smell so good.

Once, back in Sicily, Luigi was up in the branches of a tree, where he had taken refuge from the wolves gathered below to feast on him. He had a rifle, but only a small supply of ammunition, and so he would have to take careful aim. Bang. With a single shot a wolf fell dead. And then, bang, and another wolf fell dead, shot between its yellow eyes. And when two more fell dead, such was Luigi's marksman's eye, the wolves slinked off, cowed and defeated.

The thought was worrisome that the wolves would wait so patiently to have their bad breath mouths on Luigi. Worse was to imagine what could have happened if Luigi hadn't had a rifle, or if the rifle jammed, or if he had shot and missed the wolves, or if the wolves had had more staying power—if night had come and Luigi were still in the tree and now more wolves had arrived. How would he keep from falling asleep and out of the tree? And what if the wind and the rain and hunger came and there the wolves still were? No, no, this was a world to watch out for where wolves could have such a fixed intent.

Beyond the small basement shop is a territory I forbid myself to go, a wilderness of piled-high chairs and tables, a chaos of unsettling clutter.

Luigi reaches into the pockets of his baggy pants for dollar bills and sends me to the meat store for sausages, which he slices with a pocket knife and places flat on the small grill. Nothing is as good as a Luigi sausage on a roll with mustard, nothing on this earth.

"Letta go," Luigi says.

Momma is happy that a Coney Island outing is in store for us with Luigi. But Vera cannot come. Momma doesn't have to tell us why. It is because Luigi says things like "little dickie" and "old pussy" and lets his hands go where they do not belong.

Harry Frug's radio and TV store stands on the corner and there is Mr. Debray's hosiery store right next door. Harry Frug has the face of a bulldog and Mr. Debray has the face of a man from France. He removes delicate stockings from the tissues of thin boxes for the women of the Upper West Side and holds them up for their inspection. The softly insistent words he speaks sound like silver, the color of his hair. The Drago shoe store one door down smells of leather and polish. Inside Mr. Delfonico takes nails from his mouth and drives them with a hammer into the heel of a shoe on the last. Mr. Delfonico is back after being away for a week, an angry Negro woman from down the block having struck him in the eye with the heel of her shoe in a dispute over the cost of the repair. And there is the luncheonette, where the men of the building gather at night for their newspapers, and Ralston's Clothiers, where the Columbia University students come for their Ivy League outfits; and the bakery, where Luke and Vera and I can go for free ends of bread from the slicer. What a rackety vibration the slicer makes, and what work it does with rye and pumpernickel and whole wheat, too, making even slices for the world to see. And we come to the Robin Dell restaurant, where each table has a tomato-shaped dispenser with which to splatter the hamburgers that taste so good with ketchup that makes them even better. Toward the end of the block are the meat store and the produce store and the tiny jewelry shop; and the Bon Ton dry cleaners on the corner. All these stores are there, and all of them have meaning to my life for the order they provide.

And on One Hundred and Twelfth Street and One Hundred Eleventh Street are there stores as well: the Royal King dry cleaners, in direct competition with the cleaners just across the street; and the Happy Garden Chinese restaurant; and Riverside Hardware, where Auntie Eve has an account; and in that same building above the store the Puerto Rican barbers, where Momma sends Luke and me, so we can look American with our hair cut short; and on the far corner, the Chase Manhattan Bank, where Auntie Eve and Momma deposit the rent money they receive.

Over a bridge does the train slowly rumble, and as I look down I am afraid in a way that does not allow me to speak. The bridge will buckle and the train, with its heavy weight, will plunge and we will drown. No one should place his faith in the supposed certainty of steel, not when it takes you so high up and the ocean is waiting. New Utrecht Avenue, Stillwell Avenue—Brooklyn has burst the bounds of comprehension and order. What can Twenty-Fifth Avenue possibly mean when in Manhattan there is only a Fifth Avenue and nothing higher than a Twelfth Avenue and what is that to join a name to a number and call it Bay Fiftieth Street?

On the ramp down to street level tattooed vendors hawk white sailor caps, but the salty smell of the ocean draws us across Surf Avenue. Soon we are under the boardwalk on cool rippled sand, dappled light filtering down through the slats, before encountering the scorching heat of the unshielded sands beyond. Children are batting beach balls the many colors of Joseph's coat into the air. Under beach umbrellas with poles sunk in the sand old men with breasts and sagging flesh lounge in folding chairs. And there in the distance mere specks in the shimmering air become, as they draw closer, boys with black boxes strapped to their backs containing their ice cream cargo kept cool by dry ice.

The sun casts my shadow on the sand, so distressingly thin in comparison with Luke's. Boys with strong, sun-darkened bodies whip past, hair plastered to their well-shaped heads and their bathing trunks clinging after a dip in the ocean. I am not like them, I think, staring at the wet footprints they have left behind. My knees are knobby; my flesh is tired, like that of old people.

Luigi is made for the beach. His round body soaks in the sun. Luke and he go where I cannot, far out beyond the breakers. The lifeguard stands in his tower and blows his whistle. At the water's edge I stand, the surf coming and going, leaving my feet deep in the wet sand.

Now the lifeguard is down from his perch and at the water's edge, blowing his whistle again and again and motioning with his arms, directing his blast not at the bathers in water to their waists but at Luigi and Luke, who have gone beyond where safety is to be found. How sleekly powerful the lifeguard's body. How perfect his shadow.

It is not Luigi's way to be reined in. "Whassa matter that you a blowa the whistle like that? Why you do-a that? Why?" he says, pulling up and retying his brown trunks as he comes dripping from the surf.

"It's a safety regulation," the boy says.

"No tella me about safety. I coma to beacha to swim," Luigi says.

"But that's my job."

"My life-a not a your job. Your life-a is a your a job. Capisce?" Now is Luigi gesturing, his right forearm up and his right hand moving back and forth. And now is a scowl on his face that darkens it and places him beyond any use for words.

A crowd has gathered, drawn by the fuss, but disperses when the lifeguard, sensing danger, returns to his station.

Luke and I take a short walk. "He gets really angry. I was scared he was going to hit the lifeguard," I say.

"Don't be so scared," Luke says, staring out at the horizon.

"Letta go, you no-a good sumabitches," Luigi says, when we return. He is back in the sun where no dark shadow can find him. Hot dogs and French fries in paper cones, sprinkled with salt and doused with ketchup, await us on the boardwalk, and cotton candy like a woman's teased hair, and candied apples. The rides are endless that Luigi pays for, the terror of the Tornado and the Cyclone as the cogwheel pulls our string of cars to the top before the plunge that causes our stomachs to drop and then bracing ourselves as the cars tear around the curves. Surely there will come a time when the track doesn't hold or a beam falls across our path. We ride the Whip and go-carts and bumper cars. When there is congestion, tall young men with open shirts jump aboard and guide us free.

And then to Forty-second Street we go, only now it is evening, and Luke and I wear sailor hats Luigi has bought for us. We are part of the slow-moving crowd passing under movie marquees, one after another, extending out over the sidewalk for the entire block, the cool air a balm for our burnt skin. My eyes go, as if magnetized, to the stilettos in the store windows and mannequins of women in black and red and purple undergarments. And above it all a stream of news on the neon message board banding the New York Times Building. Such worldliness as the world had never seen, I can hear Momma say.

Whassa matta? You a sick? Why you-a no-a eat?" Luigi says. "You-a all skin and-a bones."

Luigi has dragged me to the shame place with his disapproval, and redness far redder than the sun has turned my skin floods my face. Luigi has seen what I saw in my shadow on the sand, that it will be best for me to cover up lest my meagerness show itself to the world.

That night, even the touch of a sheet is too much for our burning skin, but Momma comes and coats our burns with calamine lotion. "There is one sun for the world, my sons, but another for the children of hell. One burns hot and the other hotter."

So Momma says, leaving us to contemplate our iniquities, and the wrath to come.

It is Sunday. The smell of lamb roasting in the oven is everywhere. Even with my door closed, I can sense my father is home. "The world has failed your father to the point that he has no desire to reap its sinful harvest. This is a place that all of us must come to," Momma says. My father sits in his corner in the dining room reading *Abundant Life,* a magazine by the faith healer Oral Roberts, from Tulsa, Oklahoma.

Out on Broadway, Frenchie the Algerian is lassoing fire hydrants with a long, thick rope while riding his bike without hands. He is Frenchie because he speaks with a French accent. He is twice our size and strong. Then the thick rope comes down over me and he pulls it tight around my chest.

"Where you go?" Frenchie says, having dismounted from his bike.

"We're going to church," I say.

"You know what I do to some kid the other day?"

"No," I say.

"I pop out his eye with my thumb. I don't do that to you because you and your brother are my friends."

He brings his face close to mine. He is like a dog, sniffing me as well as seeing me. He has thick lips and sad eyes and brown skin.

"Did he really do that?" Vera asks, after Frenchie removes the rope and rides off.

"Maybe. He's pretty scary," Luke says.

I wear my white sailor suit and Luke his navy blue. Vera is in a white dress.

"It's the store that smells good," Vera says, of the Jewish deli on One Hundred Eleventh Street. The vent blows out warm air smelling of corned beef and pastrami. On the next block we stop at the toy store, where we buy comic books and candy. Behind the counter stands Mr. Dolphus. He has a pockmarked face and stares down at us from a great height.

We ride the express train to Thirty-fourth Street, and downstairs enter the arcade of Pennsylvania Station. At the east end is a florist's shop, with rhododendron leaves such as are set out in our lobby by Auntie Eve, and an array of flowers. A concession stand draws us with the aroma of roasted nuts, freshly squeezed orange juice, and candied Macintosh apples. Behind the row of ticket windows for the Long Island Railroad is a bathroom without doors that features an electric drier, while beyond the arcade awaits a vast concourse with marble columns and wrought iron grillwork and giant windows through which light pours as if from Heaven itself. And through gates can you go to the Pennsylvania Railroad, its burgundy-colored and pinstriped trains with the overhead electrical connectors pulling sleek coach cars of the same color that you want to live and die in.

The trains beckon us to worlds beyond, that our world cannot be a part of, not on this day, not where we are headed.

A Nedicks serves up franks on a toasted bun with sweet pickle relish and an orange drink with a sharper, more synthetic taste than pure orange juice could ever have. Lobsters are still alive in the dark waters of the tank in the deli window next door, and in the window of the closed Doubleday bookstore hardcover books with jackets are on display. Another hot dog stand, the Royster, stands lonelier and more subdued than Nedicks, while across from it is a long, narrow restaurant and bar. The lower panel of the window is of ribbed, opaque glass, as if you are not meant to see the drinkers inside. And before we can even come to it is an alcove with an escalator mounting to the Greyhound Bus Station.

At the other end, the life in the arcade begins to wane. Seed packets in cardboard boxes are on display outside another florist shop, and a wide and dreary staircase leads up to the IND Eighth Avenue trains. Bearing right, we take a downward path that shows no sign of commerce or people but only desolation without end. Everything is the loneliness of steel girders and tiled walls and iron fencing in this forlorn stretch. Now the silence penetrates our bones that we are walking where no one else is, first straight ahead and then to our left, the expanse of the arcade and the bounty of life behind us in this shrunken, secluded space.

A long set of steep steps take us to the exit. Momma will be making that same ascent, all on her own, so she can be present for the afternoon service at the tabernacle. The thought of her mounting higher and higher only to lose her footing and fall backward, down and down, brings paralyzing dread. Do you know the consequence for a skull when it impacts with a concrete step? The horror of it, Momma lying in agony in her own blood?

In the middle of the long block, and high above it, the giant electric cross suspended by brackets from the church wall beckons those to the east and the west to contemplate what Momma calls the emblem of suffering and pain and get right with the Lord Jesus before he comes again. Occupying the entire other side of the block is the gray granite mass of the General Post Office, and even now, on the Sabbath, are postal trucks entering and leaving the giant loading bays. And if we turn and look back, what do we see but another structure of strength, the Pennsylvania Railroad Station, with its columns rising over Eighth Avenue and one after another of the yellow cabs of New York City emerging from its carriage way into the flow of traffic.

The church has creaky floors and wainscoted walls and ammonia cakes in the bathroom urinals strong enough to snap me briefly out of my afternoon drowsiness. In the passageway to the large room on the ground floor, where our Sunday school classes are held, wall racks hold small white and manila envelopes in which we can make a contribution to the missionaries of the world. Those missionaries are in Africa and Asia and many other places, spreading the message of the Christ Jesus's love and being, as Momma says, fishers of men. The church has doors I have never been through. From one of them comes Sister Henry, so much in the image of my mother that I have to look twice to be sure it isn't her.

Sister Henry gathers our group at the back of the room: Stinky Maldonado and Eddie Goyco and Reuben Alvado and Willie Peterson and Peanuts Kozinski and Kenny and Johnny Jones, who say they are brothers though one is blond and the other is half Chinese. Lieutenant Martin Delmonico teaches Luke's class in a smaller room. Sometimes Lieutenant Delmonico has to run out of the church and down the street to uphold the law, his hand on the holstered gun he wears with his suits at all times.

Momma has given each of us a leather-bound pocket version of the King James Bible. The paper is gold-edged and fine, and the print is small. Sister Henry has us turn in our Bibles to the Book of Daniel, from which we take turns reading. But nothing in the reading about Shadrach, Meshach, and Abednego, nor Daniel's gift of prophecy that he hopes will save him from the wrath of King Nebuchadnezzar can keep my attention on the words and what they are signifying. Soon I am fast asleep on the bench, overcome by Momma's lunch and the big, moist salty pretzel I bought in Pennsylvania Station. When I awake, Kenny and Johnny Jones are chanting the books of the Bible. They fly through Habakkuk and Haggai and Malachi and First and Second Thessalonians, and when they have gone through them all, from Genesis to the Book of Revelation, they then do the same thing back to front, causing Sister Henry to exclaim that they are indeed sunbeams for Jesus.

After Sunday school, Luke and Vera and I walk west to Ninth Avenue. On the way we pass a building beyond understanding. It shows a face of clean brickwork and the metal guards on the windows say serious work is done there by hard and industrious people, those with slide rules and mathematical minds. The deep-set loading bay, empty now of trucks, cries out its forlorn status, reeking of some time gone by of which I may not have been a part but should have been.

We cross over Ninth Avenue and come to a wall, beyond which we stare down at the sprawling grid of tracks on which the trains come and go from Pennsylvania Station, and the overhead wires that power those trains. Vera too stares down so she too can see what power really is, before heading up to the Whelan's Drugstore on Thirty-fourth and Ninth.

Dolly is working the counter in a white uniform that can barely contain her and with a smile she cannot suppress. The ice cream sundaes she creates rise above their glass containers: three scoops of vanilla ice cream coated with Hershey's chocolate syrup and topped with sprinkles and nuts, and a maraschino cherry to make her work complete. I do not tell Dolly all that is happening in my mind: that she might have to die and die because of the glaze of makeup upon her happy face and her other worldly ways outside the tabernacle.

I am just happy for the light she shines and the ice cream sundaes she delivers.

High up on a shelf, out of easy reach, are suitcases for those in need of travel. They are Whelan's suitcases, at prices people can afford. In the racks are paperback books and greeting cards shout from the aisles and Whitman's samplers are loudly prominent on the shelves. Whelan's is a store that stands upon the earth in many places, and the tabernacle cannot contain it.

There, in the distance, is Momma coming toward us as we return to the tabernacle. All alone she walks in the sunlight, free from the shadow of the building that burdens her. She wears her brown dress with the white polka dots and rubber stockings to give her legs support and her man's shoes to give her the comfort that she needs. And Momma hasn't fallen down and down those many steps from the subway. No, no, no. Momma has walked up and up and up. And now she is walking slowly and within herself, as if the spaces outside—the post office and the small rooming houses—are things of the world she needn't bother herself about on this, the Sabbath.

Hanging from the balcony, where we sit, are the flags of many countries—the tricolor of France and the red and white and green of Italy and the Union Jack of Great Britain. And Momma has seen to it that the blue and yellow flag of Sweden is displayed, but no one has hung the flag of Armenia, if ever there was one, which could only be the blackest black.

On the platform where Pastor Odachenko stands is he looking down on those in the pews below, but from the side balcony where we sit is Momma looking down at him. Momma doesn't say of Pastor Odachenko that he looks or sounds magnificent in the Lord, though it is clear he thinks so, arrayed in his dark blue suit and red tie and with his head of salt-and-pepper hair, the words of his ministry gathering within him as he stands in his black leather shoes that shine with the very best and on his face the satisfaction with what he is about to say before he has even said it.

Pastor Odachenko doesn't start with thunder but with murmured words that rise slowly, as if his mind were first set to musing. "Brethren, I am crying in the Lord. Crying. I am crying in the Lord. Do you all know what it means to be crying in the Lord? Have not you all, in your loneliness, your sickness, your bereavement, been crying in the Lord? Did not Jonah cry in the Lord? And Job, with his boils, did he too not cry in the Lord? Oh, my brothers and sisters, to be lost at the feet of the Lord's wisdom and then to be found in that very same place. Oh, my brothers. Oh, my sisters. Jesus, Jesus, Jesus."

Jesus. Like salt water taffy does he pull the first syllable before he sling-shots the fat wad of the second.

"Hush," Momma says, her face full of concentration, when we squirm in our seats. "Hush now."

Pastor Odachenko's mother sits upright behind her son. Her shoes and stockings are white. Her dress is white. Her skin and hair are white, as if she is saying that purity itself is present in her on the earth and that she will be watchful for any speck of sinful dirt that dare approach.

Behind Sister Odachenko is the baptismal font where the children who are willing to have the Christ Jesus are lowered by her son into the holy water. And behind the font is a mural of the Garden of Gethsemane, where Jesus has to find some calm before the Roman soldiers come to take him from this earth.

There are hymns to be sung. "There Will be Showers of Blessings" and "In the Garden," Momma's favorite, and "Bringing in the Sheaves," and all the hymns that testify to the goodness of the Lord. If we lean over the balcony, we can see Nino, with his head of black hair and his teeth as white as the ivory keys of the grand piano he plays. Nino's teeth so very big in his mouth that sometimes they are all you can see.

Nino has won a scholarship to the Juilliard School of Music. The world has chosen him. Some commotion starts in my mind at the thought of Nino going forth into his new life, some happiness, as for my sister Rachel, but also some tormented wondering as to how he can go out to the worldly Juilliard world without it being called a Judas Iscariot betrayal of the world he has here.

The words of Pastor Odachenko now going up, down, flying all around. Pastor Odachenko preaching with *conviction*. Now, in the congregation below, Lorraine Hansen has caught fire, spewing words the world can find no meaning in, her voice loud not with lamentation but with tear-summoning ecstasy, her body doing the herky-jerk, as if she has stepped on a live wire. And there, looking down, is poor Pastor Odachenko, his word flow stalled at the pulpit. It is not a small thing for the passion-wracked Lorraine Hansen to interrupt the disappearing words of Pastor Odachenko.

When Lorraine Hansen has settled back into her seat, softly weeping, and Pastor Odachenko has once more fired up, now Momma is led to stand and speak in the tongues of the angels, her sound spreading throughout the tabernacle, like a long freight rumbling past a crossing, and Pastor Odachenko can do nothing more than smile as he endures this new obstruction to his word flow. But Momma is not caring about Pastor Odachenko. Momma, come back, Momma, come back to me now. Come back with the attention that you must show. This I say within the confines of my own mind, sensing Momma must not be interfered with when she has gone away. And Luke and Vera hold their silence, too. The Lord has her and she has the Lord and there is no room for Luke or Vera or me in their ongoing interaction. We have been here before with her tears and her vocalizing and the spasms of her visited body. We have seen it come and go, and yet now, as if it never has happened before, I am afraid the fever will not come and go but never run its course.

But it does break and Momma does come back, the vessel of her being has been filled. Not that you would know her state of ecstasy at first, seeing her weepy and spent, like Lorraine Hansen before her—no good for listening, no good for anything but sitting with herself in the aftermath of the Lord.

The words of Pastor Odachenko have resumed. Faster and faster, and ceaselessly, like giant waves crashing down over me before receding like the tide, taking their meaning with it.

Drowsy again, I slide onto the floor and curl up under the pew on the scratchy carpet liner. But it isn't long before another voice is heard. "Liar. Cheat. Fornicator. You who lies down with the whores on Eighth Avenue and who guzzles whiskey and smokes cigars in the saloons on Eighth Avenue. He's a hypocrite, ladies and gentleman. A hypocrite." A man is standing in the balcony opposite ours and pointing an accusing finger down at Pastor Odachenko.

"Ushtah," Momma says, a word she reserves for nose-picking and other habits she finds disgusting.

Two church officers in suits and ties are now moving toward Pastor Odachenko's tormentor. They approach not with wrath but in sorrow. Do they not know that they are in the danger zone? The man, tall and strong, can stab them in their faces and throw them from the balcony, overcoming their combined strength with his hysteria. But he doesn't even struggle when they each take an arm and lead him away. And soon Pastor Odachenko is flying once again, slapping his open Bible and brandishing it in his right hand, saying, "The word has come. Jesus. Jesus is the word. Let there be no backsliding among us, my brothers and sisters, lest the fiery pit be our final destination," all his words once more set out on their pathway to disappearance.

The sky is the gray of the post office across the street, but though the sun has gone away, Momma has the warmth of her own sun. "Let us go for some normal food," she says, leading us to the Automat on the corner. The lady at the booth takes the bills Momma has given us and exchanges them for nickels that pour from a metal dispenser into a marble tray. In slots next to the small window compartments we deposit those nickels. Soon I have baked macaroni with a golden crust in a green oval dish and baked beans with bits of bacon in a small brown pot and yes, cherry pie, with the cherries so tart, and iced tea in which the sugar settles to the bottom no matter how much you stir. Oh, it is something to be with Momma, who gives and gives without stopping, at those brown tables with the revolving trays with olive oil and vinegar and jars of mustard.

When we finish with the normal food that the Horn and Hardart Automat has to offer, we step into the dark and go down, down into Pennsylvania Station. And no, Momma doesn't fall. I walk in front of her, always one step ahead, as a barrier from all harm and through the arcade to the Seventh Avenue subway that will take us home, and as we walk my hand is now in Momma's white-gloved hand.

When we say to Momma, "Where is Auntie Eve that she is not at our tabernacle? And where is Father, that he is not here as well?" Momma says, "You must listen so my words mean more than the winds that come and go. The tabernacle has not done right by your aunt. She has the greatness of America itself, but the tabernacle has vilified and then crucified her on the cross of its own willful misunderstanding. Your aunt had a vision of what life could be. Truth has an eternal nature, and when your aunt saw the godless of Manhattan availing themselves of the fleshpots of iniquity, she also saw the eternal damnation that such sinfulness invited. And she saw the buildings of New York City, how they rose tall upon the earth, not in pursuit of the heavenly father but as a way of flaunting the achievement of man. Your aunt saw what it could mean to have such a building in the service of the Lord, and so, using the mind and talents that God had blessed her with, she attached herself to one property, on Riverside Drive, and enlisted the aid of the tabernacle congregation so they could help to make it hers in the Lord. She saw the property as a way station for missionaries weary in their bones but with a fire burning in their souls: bearded angels from the plains of Kansas and clean-shaven saviors from the South, men who could embrace their own company because of the spirit so alive and brimming within. Auntie Eve saw herself giving them the rest they needed for the further battles to come.

"Your aunt produced a brochure of what the building should be, with the men and women of God asleep in every room. The congregation fell in behind her, and Auntie Eve took possession of the property. Then men and women who did not walk in holiness but drank from the cup of envy, allowing judgment to cloud their eye, began to whisper that Auntie Eve was doing herself right in doing them wrong, that money was being spent to adorn herself rather than secure the premises as a sanctuary for brethren and sisters of the flock, some saying that Auntie Eve was buying fine furs and precious antiques with their money."

"Did she do these things?" I ask.

"Can a cow give birth to a horse? No more could your aunt give birth to sin. And yet did the congregation pursue her, asking the district attorney of Manhattan to launch an investigation. Can you imagine anything more painful than to see your aunt vilified in the daily newspapers? 'She may look like someone's picture of saintliness, but she is a crook all the same.' So this vilifying district attorney said."

"What is vilifying, Momma?" Vera asks.

"It is a man pulling down someone above him with lies and more lies because he cannot stand the purity of her vision and sees it as a reproach to his own self-seeking ways."

"But what happened, Momma?" I ask.

"Even in a court of law, with justice at his disposal to shape as he saw fit, this district attorney could not get an indictment against Auntie Eve. The grand jurors saw her magnificence. They saw her shining light. And so they did not give the district attorney what he was seeking. A torrent of curses flew from his mouth on hearing their decision but Auntie Eve stood strong through all his vileness and even rained her laughter down upon him."

Momma doesn't have to explain Auntie Eve's laughing thing. We have all seen that the angrier someone grows at Auntie Eve, the more she laughs till she is doubled over.

"So Auntie Eve doesn't go to the tabernacle anymore because there were many like Judas Iscariot in the congregation and they betrayed her," I say.

"I would not call them Judas Iscariots, my son. I would stay within the bounds of reason and call them misguided."

"But Momma, were Pastor Odachenko and his mother all in white among Auntie Eve's persecutors?" I ask.

"Yes, they were among the stone throwers, it makes me sad to say. And so she has gone where she needs to be, to a church of her liking on the East Side," Momma says.

"And what about Daddy? Why isn't he with us at the tabernacle?" Vera asks.

"Your father must be where no roof can contain him. Your father has powerful currents that must be given expression," Momma says.

"Momma, what does that *mean*?" I ask.

"You saw Pastor Odachenko and the words he spoke this afternoon, my son. By your father's reasoning, it is not fair that any one messenger have a monopoly on the word of God. And so your father must go where no muzzle will be placed on his communicating nature if an explosion is not to be heard throughout all the world. Your father has a calling in the other world, but before he goes he must attest to God's kingdom is this one."

"But if Auntie Eve doesn't go to the tabernacle, and Daddy doesn't go, why do we go?" Luke asks.

"Only know that we serve to remind the congregation that we continue to bear witness to the crucifixion, not at Calvary but here in Manhattan. It is not for nothing that we are looking down at Pastor Odachenko," Momma says.

In this way does Momma speak to us on that night.

Sometimes in school when I learn something, I want to do it all the time. It is that way when long division and subtraction come to me. I solve the problems in my own arithmetic book and then take the books of my classmates and solve their problems, too.

And when I learn to read, I say, I am reading. A book with a color illustration of an organ grinder and his monkey. A red brick wall and a tree are nearby. But the chair I sit in does not feel comfortable. The cushion is not clean. The living room is not in order. I put the book down. I run out into the street.

It is Sunday morning, and Momma's red leather bag is on her bed. The bag calls to me, and because Momma is busy in the kitchen making lunch and my father is in the dining room, I go to it and open the gold clasp. The bag is stuffed with papers, but also contains an envelope with twenty- and ten- and five-dollar bills. There is change in the envelope too, and so I take a quarter.

Momma is coming toward me as I leave the room. I can feel her using her mind to see into the workings of my own.

"Are you holding something in your hand, my son?" she asks, in a voice lowered so only I can hear.

"No," I say.

"Why is your hand not open?" Momma is looking at me, not the fist I have made.

"I don't know," I say.

Momma leads me into the bathroom, where she closes the door and sits on the rim of the tub. Momma can hold my wrist but not my heart right then.

"Have you been in my bag? Is that it, my son?"

I shake my head.

"Why do you want to hurt me in this way, my son? Do I not have enough cares that I should have to worry that you are being led astray?" There is sorrow beyond description in Momma's voice. My hand opens though I don't want it to. "You must never do such a thing again." Momma says, as she takes the quarter. Momma is trying to take my mind and make it hers. But I see fear in Momma's eyes that my mind is not her mind. I feel something brighten in me, like now I am that train roaring out of the tunnel and going on its way.

Momma has a key for every lock in the building so she can go where she needs to go. She has a key for Addie Ault in room 6A1 and Joy Willard in 11C9 and Raj Singh in 8D3. For everyone.

Auntie Eve's apartment is a place of peace and stillness. It has the smell of baking and upholstered chairs and a sofa you want to sit on. Someday I too will live alone, without the clamor of sisters and the fear of my father. Someday I will go to Sweden too, and stand where Momma and Auntie Eve have stood on a cold night under lamplight. I can see it in my mind.

Auntie Eve's apartment gives me a hunger for my own life. Momma has made her lantern-jawed sister big in my mind as an example I must follow.

There is a lock on Auntie Eve's front door and a lock on Auntie Eve's closet door inside the apartment, too. Again, Momma proves that there is nowhere on earth that she cannot go. From envelopes does Momma take green bills and places them in her pocket.

"Momma, is that money to make us rich?" I ask.

"Ushtah, my son. There are no riches on this earth except for the Lord. This is money for us to live." Momma says no more.

With Eduardo Perez, from room 7C3, I play handball against the side of the building. He and his family have fled Cuba and Fidel Castro and his band of rebels. When the spaldeen bounces away, Eduardo says, "I get the ball for the ball go the street." But Eduardo's older brother, Raul, has seen Eduardo run into the street, and grabs Eduardo by the hair and bangs his head against the side of the building. I shiver hearing the hollow sound it makes on impact with the wall.

"Now will you go for the ball in the street? stupid boy," Raul shouts at Eduardo, who has crumpled to the sidewalk.

Eduardo is two weeks mending from his swollen head.

"I need you for something," I say, when Eddie can walk and talk.

"How am I to understand?" Eddie asks. His hair is black. His eyes are dark.

"I want you to be a lookout while I go into my aunt's apartment."

"What for I stand your guard? Do you want for my head to be broken in two?"

That night I lie down with my shame, that Eddie should thwart me in the way that he has.

The lobby has a Sunday morning stillness, broken only by the sound of church bells ringing on the next block. Auntie Eve has left her ground-floor apartment wearing a fox fur around her neck and slowly walks the few blocks to the subway station at One Hundred Tenth Street. Into the kiosk and down the steps I watch her go. In my pocket are two keys I have taken off Momma's ring and can only hope she won't miss while she busies herself in the kitchen.

The lobby is still empty when I return. I pause outside Auntie Eve's door and listen for Momma's footsteps. When I do not hear them, I turn the lock with the key. With the second key, I turn the closet lock. The thrill the sight of the green bills brings is like nothing I have experienced before.

An hour later, long after I have placed the keys back on her key-ring, she does not enter my mind but only says, "Have some chicken, my son. Have some chicken." If I have done wrong, I do not know. I have gone apart from Momma and yet I am with her still.

Once a year Macy's has a contest. Everything you can carry out of the store within an hour is yours. But there are so many things to grab—Lionel trains and games and baseball bats and gloves—and you must beat the clock before it beats you. That clock is ticking all the time. You want it to stop because it is causing so much pain as you try to make the whole world yours in the time you have been given. You want to drop everything and just run out of the store empty-handed if that is what it takes to stop the terror that the clock will beat you. All this has come to my understanding.

Doberman pinschers roam the aisles of the darkened store after closing, if you don't get out in time. Those dogs bite at you until you bleed to death and then they eat the portions of your body that they want to.

But now I do not have to enter a contest at Macy's with the clock tick-tocking in my brain in a contest I can only be tormented by because there isn't enough time. I can take my brother and sister to the world's biggest department store down on Herald Square and buy Luke a six-shooter and Vera a raggedy Ann doll.

"You are a very industrious man and will go far," the store clerk says, as I pay for the pistol and the doll by placing on the counter an orange roll of quarters and two green rolls of dimes.

"Where did you get the money?" Luke asks, in holy innocence. There is worry in his face and in his voice. Luke cannot go where my hands have been. It is not his way to be a thief in the night or in daylight hours either. It is for me to note this difference between us.

"I just did," I say, as if to say that I have access to mysterious sources of wealth that neither Luke nor Vera nor anyone else can possibly have. A smile comes to my face at this statement of my power.

But Vera's eyes speak their doubt, too.

"What's the matter?" I say.

"Does Mommy know?" She holds the bag with the doll against her chest with both arms, rocking it.

"Momma knows everything," I say.

Luke opens the box on the street and straps on the holster. "Bang. You're dead. Do you hear me? You're dead," he says, firing the pistol at my chest.

Good 'n Plenty, Necco Wafers, Mars Bars, Milky Ways, Tootsie Rolls, Mason Dots, Sugar Daddies, Chuckles, Goldberg's Peanut Chews in the red and brown wrapper. At the luncheonette around the corner on Broadway I buy these and other candies for Luke and Vera and Frenchie the Algerian, and all the neighborhood kids. I am Jesus producing the loaves and fishes. I am the sun. I am America.

Mr. Dolphus takes the bill from me. I have come to the counter with a box containing the plastic parts and the glue to make a model Soviet tank. The picture on the box of the dark green tank with a red star on the turret has won me. How sleek and low-slung the tank is. I wait for Mr. Dolphus to give me the change, but he just stares down at me, holding the bill in his hand. He is tall, with white hair piled high and a pockmarked face and bulging cheeks. He puts the bill in his shirt pocket, comes around the counter, grabs hold of the neck of my shirt, and walks me out of the store. After locking the front door, he frog-marches me up Broadway, prodding with a knee to my backside, one block after another.

"What are you doing?" I say, unable to fully turn. His knee bumps have begun to hurt and the shop owners and passersby seeing me being led away is like being naked in public. I had thought of Mr. Dolphus as a warm and kind man, like his store, but now I imagine his face full of stupid righteousness.

Into the lobby he leads me, where he turns me over to Momma, who stands at the far end, near the renting office.

"Your son came into my store and tried to pay for a toy with this," Mr. Dolphus says, handing Momma the bill.

"I see," Momma says. Momma thanks Mr. Dolphus. She says nothing to me in front of him. But I hear and feel the weight of her. I feel it everywhere.

Momma says this day is just for us as she takes me to the subway station. On the way we pass Mr. Dolphus, who is standing outside his store. Momma nods to him and he nods back, as if their understanding is intact.

In Pennsylvania Station I run far ahead in the arcade only to return to her side as she maintains the deliberateness of her pace.

"Momma, do you see the lobsters?" I say, pointing to the tank in the food store window, but Momma cannot be distracted from the quiet she has found. I am hearing and feeling Momma's mood. Her seriousness is reaching every part of me.

The tabernacle block has none of its Sunday quiet. Big trucks enter and leave the post office loading bays, and many of the buildings that look so lonely on our church day have people going in and out, as if the world has risen up and decided to make itself known.

"Momma, is the whole world going to hell and we're not because we go to the tabernacle and they don't? Is that so, Momma?"

"Be still, my son." Momma said.

But I can't be still. "Momma, is Duke Snider going to hell? Is Mickey Mantle going to hell? Is Willie Mays going to hell? Are all the mailmen in their gray uniforms going to hell?" I ask, for by now I know something of the world and the baseball players who are in it, and of what they do on green grass enclosed within giant stadiums on Sunday afternoons while Momma and Luke and Vera and I are listening to the disappearing words of Pastor Odachenko.

"The world is the world and the way is the way. Now hush," Momma says, taking my hand as we pass through the gate and come to the tabernacle door. The world is open for business, but the tabernacle is not, as the door is locked, but Momma persists by ringing the bell. And here Pastor Odachenko comes, wearing neither jacket nor tie, though his face and hair remain the same. But his mystery mother is not there, she who dresses in white down to her stockings and her shoes.

"Hello, Sister Manootdjian." I hear our name break apart as it comes from Pastor Odachenko's mouth.

The chairs have all been folded and placed against the walls in the room where we meet for Friday Bible Study and Sunday school. Several women stand on the lumpy carpet: Sister Henry, my Sunday school teacher, so much in the image of Momma, and Sister Hanasian, with her birthmark a purplish red stain over half her face, and Sister Floson, with her bad teeth, and Sister Carolyn Cummings, brimming with a love for the Lord that her flushed and sweaty face cannot contain. With Pastor Odachenko in the lead, they form a holiness circle around me. Momma is among them as they reach in and place their hands on my head. "We beseech you, Jesus. We beseech you, oh Lord God Almighty, that the light of Your mercy may drive the darkness of Satan from this young life. In the name of the Father, the Son, and the Holy Ghost, we command you, Satan, to leave. We say, 'Out now, Satan. Out." In this manner does Pastor Odachenko pray. Their hands are now heavy on my head.

But what is this thing within me that laughs and laughs and knows nothing of the conviction that grips them so?

On the third shuddering "Out" from Pastor Odachenko, I slip through their ring and bolt out of the tabernacle. Momma soon emerges, walking with the weight of sorrow upon her, as if the world has used her up and now there is nothing more to do but to die.

"You have caused me pain where none should be. What is it that I should be afflicted with such willful children that they cannot abide in the realm of decency and instead treat me like dirt beneath their shoes?" Momma cries. Weeping is Momma so that I should have to run into the street to be hit by the biggest truck to stop my pain. But instead Momma's tears drive me flat onto the pavement.

"Momma, now am I your piece of dirt that you can put *your* shoe on," I scream.

"Are you crazy, my son? Are you crazy?"

"Are you crazy that you would murder your begotten son? Are you crazy?' I shout right back at her. No one should make his momma die but no momma should make me die either.

"Behave, my son. Behave. Get up now. I will take you for normal food at the Automat."

I have failed Momma. This I know. My victory has been her defeat. "I do not know what to do," I scream, inside the Horn and Hardart, a piece of cherry pie and a glass of iced tea before me. Now I am crying. I cry and cry that Momma should look so old and abandoned in the light of our Automat day. I cry that my heart has to be so broken along with hers. I cry outside the softness of her that would enfold me. I just cry until I can cry no more.

The vessels of the Lord are lined up for filling. Assigned to goodness, they wait their turn in gowns of white to be received by Pastor Odachenko, who stands in the middle of the baptismal font with his pants legs rolled up beyond the water's height. Eagerly do the children entrust themselves to his care, allowing him to immerse them so their gowns and bodies are soaked with the holy water of the Lord. "You are now of the Christ and the Christ is of you. Forever are you in the paradise of his vision. Praise God, praise Jesus.

Oh, Jesus, Jesus, Jesus." Stinky Maldonado, Eddie Goyco, Reuben Alvado, Willie Peterson, Peanuts Kozinski, the Jones brothers, both Kenny and John—one by one they come for their dip. And among them are Luke and Vera. There Luke is, approaching the font and Pastor Odachenko eager to dunk him. "Don't let him do it. Don't let him," I stand up and call out, from the balcony pew I share with Momma. "Do not let him take from you what is yours and give you what isn't. Do not let him change you so you will be no more what once you were." This too I say with urgency.

"Ushtah, my son. Ushtah. This is the devil himself speaking. Sit down and stop your foolishness."

Now are the men of order coming toward me in their suits, the men who have custody of the velvet-lined collection baskets and who do right by the tabernacle by removing the denouncing ones who attack Pastor Odachenko. They have determination on their scrubbed faces, but Momma counsels with them. "He gets upset but I will see that he behaves," Momma whispers. Brother Frudash, one of those men, puts his fingers to his thin lips in looking at me before going away.

"You are going to hell," Stinky Maldonado says, after the service.

"Fuck you, Stinky."

"Ooh, you cursed," Stinky squeals, bringing his hands to his grinning face.

"What was that I heard you say?" Brother Frudash places his hand on my shoulder. His lips are very thin.

"I didn't say anything."

"No, I heard you," Brother Frudash says. "Did he say something, Stinky?"

"He cursed at me," Stinky says.

"Yes, I thought so," Brother Frudash says.

Momma comes by. "Is there a problem?"

"Your son has cursed Stinky Maldonado. Some cleansing action may be called for."

Momma takes me to her softness, putting her arm about me. "No, I do not think so. We will be going for some normal food now. Good evening, Brother Frudash."

"If I can be of any assistance, Sister Manootdjian."

"Thank you, Brother Frudash." Brother Frudash has a big car. He has two sons with big teeth. I see him take his sons away in that car. I see it all the time.

That night, in our room, I stare at my sister Vera, as she lies in her cot with her leelah pressed to her nose. "What?" she says.

Then I go and stare at my brother in the bottom bunk of our bed.

"What's the matter?" Luke asks.

"Nothing," I say, and climb up to my bunk.

Momma comes in for our nightly prayer.

"Johan is not good. Johan is bad," Vera says.

"Hush, Vera. We will all someday be with the Lord," Momma says, before turning out the light.

The Reverend Mother is the mother of all the nuns without being their mother. Her spotless white headdress stands out from the blackness of the rest of her garb. Her round, unsmiling face is dotted with those liver spots I do not see on Momma's face.

"You are a wild child. You believe you can live outside of rules and conventions. You cannot possibly know what I mean, but someday you will. We are an Episcopal school with our foundations in England. We do not subscribe to a mentality that incites other children to break out of an orderly double file formation and to run helter-skelter through the streets. Are you listening to me?"

"Yes," I say. Because I am. I am all ears for her severe sound while wondering how she might appear without that headdress.

"Can you tell me why you caused the other children to run as they did?"

"I don't know."

"Do you know that you and the other children could have been killed running into the street like that?"

"Yes," I say. She is talking about the cars and trucks and buses that control the streets of New York City. She is asking me to be more afraid than I want to be.

"Punishment is the only answer for someone with your pandemonium nature. You must leave the school for the day, and you must leave immediately," she says, making herself the wall of judgment into which I have crashed.

Miss Larkin, my teacher, is waiting outside the Reverend Mother's office with a piece of coconut cake. "Here, Johan, you must have this to take away with you. You are a part of us. Do you understand?" she says, folding the foil around the cake, for the Reverend Mother has been in touch with her about the course of action that is needed to quell my pandemonium. Miss Larkin does not wear the garments of darkness of Sister Mary Christabel and the rest of the flock but comes adorned in the raiment of the world, a skirt that shows her pretty legs beneath her knees and a blouse that show her thin arms. Her words send me into new spaces. I want to go with her wherever she would lead.

A boy passes by me as I sit on a stoop up the hill from the school and across the street. As I watch him enter the Negro hotel, a feeling of happiness more like crazy excitement comes over me.

Under the tattered awning of the hotel, I stare into the lobby. A cigarette vending machine stands opposite the front desk. Three willowy young Negro men emerge, their clinging, flowery shirts unbuttoned halfway down their chests and their thin legs wrapped in tight, shiny pants. Around their pomaded hair they wear dazzling head scarves. Their whole look and the coordinated ditty bop shuffle they have adopted— one arm hanging straight and stiffly down, a hand balled into a fist riding on their butt, and one foot dragging, all of it saying "I don't play. I don't play at all"—is riveting. They head, the three of them abreast on the narrow sidewalk, toward Broadway, compelling others out of their path and mocking time and any other thing life could throw at them as well. I don't know if they are the end of the world or its beginning. All I know is that they fill my mind.

Some minutes later, the boy comes back out of the hotel.

"Did you want something?" the boy says.

"Did I say I wanted something?" I say.

"Why are you sitting here?"

"Why are you standing here?"

"I'm just standing here. That's all."

"Do you want some cake?" I say.

"What kind of cake? I don't eat just any cake," the boy says.

"Coconut cake," I say, and hand him the remainder, which he holds up for inspection before taking a bite and then another bite until he has munched it all away.

Across the street Johnny Lacy and Edward Macy have left the school and are climbing the hill. There are others, including Alison Pauley, the girl I had kissed.

"Do you want to go to the park?" I say.

"Sure. Let's go to the park."

I go home first to change out of my uniform and into my jeans and Keds and polo shirt. My new friend comes with me into the building and the apartment and he doesn't defeat me by calling where we live a pigsty because he cannot, not when he lives in the welfare hotel for the Negroes. The welfare hotel is not a house of order. It is a building you enter in danger of never coming out.

We go that afternoon into the lower level of the park and then down by the highway. The cars are racing past, violent the way they always are and full of their own importance. Set in a wall of orange and gray stone is a black door half-opened.

We enter and close the door behind us. Ahead we come to a door-less frame in a gray wall, and through that we also pass. A short drop brings us level with four sets of tracks. Above are the spaced vents in the grass through which I have looked down many times, drawn by the rumble of the passing trains. Some distance to the north we can see the gray light of the tunnel give way to the bright light of the outdoors, where Tall Tommy and Luke and I had been that night.

"Let's wait. A train has to come," I whisper. Sounds travel far in the tunnel, and someone who means us no good could be nearby.

Far down the long straightway begins to curve and a strong light is cast on the bend and a light is lit in us as well. A train is making its powerful way and we will be its witness. We reach down for bits of rock ballast, and retreat through the rectangular space in the wall, behind which we hide, trembling. We hear the throb and feel the vibration of the engine as it approaches, and peek at the gray and white twin engine as it powers past, an engineer high up in the cab, before jumping down once again through the space in the wall to the tracks. It is not like it had been with Tall Tommy. This time there is something to say to this train. We boom the rock ballast off the boxcars of the Wabash Line. We boom it off the boxcars of the Erie Lackawanna, and the Southern Line gets no mercy for painting its boxcars green and hah, the burgundy boxcars of the Canadian Pacific receive a bashing, too, but nothing like the fusillade of joyous fury that greets the heartbreaking red and silver and yellow colors of the Atchinson, Topeka, and Santa Fe. When the train has vanished, leaving only warm rails in its wake, we can hardly stand from all it has put us through.

His name is Jerry Jones and he is my life. He lives in the Negro hotel with his Negro stepfather and Estonian mother. Estonia. The word sounds like a place built with cold stones, where no one can be warm and the smell of fish oil is everywhere. She has a wide gash for a mouth and wears tight blouses over her enormous breasts. She stares in store windows on Broadway, as if she has never before seen such abundance.

"Manootdjian. What kind of name is that?" Jerry Jones asks, when we have known each other a few days.

"It's Armenian," I say.

"What's that?" Jerry asks.

"It's some kind of country where the dead live," I say.

"There ain't no such country."

"Oh, yes there is."

"Then how come your father's not dead."

"That's because he got out before he could be dead," I say.

"My real father was Estonian, like my mother. Do you know what I'm saying?" Jerry asks.

"Sure. I know," I say.

Jerry has the woolly hair of a Negro and the broad nose some Negroes have, but his skin is the color of copper.

"The doctors did me wrong. I had an allergic reaction to penicillin. That's why my skin is all messed up. Do you know what I mean?" Jerry asks.

"Sure I do." Later I will learn that his sister Leah's skin is coppery too, and yet Leah's skin is beautiful while Jerry's skin is marred by angry pink blotches on his hands and arms and neck.

"My real father got runned over by a Soviet tank defending Estonia from the Communists. My real father's name was Nobleonian, so from now on I don't want you calling me Jerry Jones. I want you to be calling me Jerry Jones Nobleonian. OK?"

"Sure," I say.

Now when we go to the railroad after school, Jerry and I take out our things and rub up against the wall of the tunnel. Someday I will bring Alison Pauley with me and we will lie down together and cuddle in a little hideaway so the train can't see us but we can see it as it powers past. And Johnny Lacy and Edward Macy will be nowhere in sight.

In the fall we light small fires in the park, burning twigs and dead leaves. In winter we throw snowballs at the heads of the lamps along the park's pathways, cracking the bulbs, until something tells us to stop. In the spring and summer we collect empty soda bottles from the basement of buildings and take them back to the stores for deposit money. We gather together old newspapers in the yard outside the basement of my building and set them on fire, watching as the paper crinkles and turns to black ash. We light the fires with matches my father brought home from Jack Dempsey's Restaurant, where he now works. The matchbooks shows Jack Dempsey's battered face on the cover. They are all over the apartment. The fire consumes us. Everywhere there is filth—dog doo and broken bottles and garbage. And now there is the fire to help make things right.

The alleyways call to us. We scale fences and walls and gates. Dogs that bark and dogs that run silent menace us—mangy dogs of no pedigree belonging to the supers whose territory we are invading. Whole blocks we cover through these back alleys, our faces black as pitch. We are *exploring*.

And there is Boo, a very dark Negro girl with pigtails like wire from the hotel of the Negroes, who says to us, "Do you want to do it to me? Would you like that? Because you can." Words that make me go all funny inside. Into the bushes of Dead Man's Hill in Riverside Park we take her, where she pulls down her white underpants and we press against her and make her promise not to tell.

On Halloween we go to those houses of order where we can sneak past the doormen. Rubber masks conceal our faces. Grown-ups interrupt their lives to come to the door, the smell of cooking spreading to the hallway. Their lips are shiny from the food they have eaten. In our masks they don't know who we are or where we have come from. We have our hand out to the world and it is answering with corn candy and dollar bills and coins.

The subway calls to us. We duck under the smooth wooden turnstiles, hearing the shouts of the token booth clerks whose laws of order we have defied, but the train comes before they do. Down, down, to Forty-second Street we ride. Lost in the white lights, we buy a potion with the sulfurous smell of rotten eggs and apply drops of it to empty subway seats so those who get on board and sit in the vicinity will be seen as guilty in the eyes of one and all for the odor that has spread.

And there is the roof of our building, with the cedar-shingled water tower and its beanie top, and the parapet of death from which we drop spit down onto the human specks walking along Broadway. Onto the tarred roof of a smaller building to the south I toss my empty bottle of Mission grape soda, causing a man on that roof to shake his fist. I have come from church. The collar of my new yellow shirt chafes, turning my neck an angry red, and so I go to the apartment and change into a polo shirt. By this time Jerry has gone home. When I pass through the lobby, a small, wiry man with inflamed eyes grabs my arm.

"Ees you?"

"Is me what?" I say.

"Ees you the boy throw bottle to kill me?"

"I don't throw anything," I say.

"Where ees boy in yellow shirt. I keel him."

"I don't know any boy in a yellow shirt," I say.

"Ees you. Ees you. Next time I keel you."

Hah to the parties of Johnny Lacy and Edward Macy. They are my school but Jerry Jones is my life and we have escalator handrails to slide down and new routes to the subway to explore. At One Hundred Twenty-fifth Street the covered escalator to the subway station cannot contain me. A window in the enclosed entranceway offers a new route to freedom. I can climb through and raise myself up between the ties of the tracks and lift myself onto the platform before the train can ever touch me with the steel of its savagely oncoming wheels. This I can do with the quickness that is mine.

Momma asks Jerry if he is a Christian and whether he has taken the Christ Jesus as his personal savior. Jerry says he is something called a Lutheran. "They're Christians, too," Jerry says, "and very respectable."

What words Jerry's mother speaks come out as a shriek. To be an Estonian is to be from a country where drizzle and the smell of fish afflict you all the livelong day. People brush their teeth with whale oil and sleep in the remnants of castles built in bygone days. Always she is alone on the street and there is no need to go near her, for like my father she has been cut loose to live in the solitude that is the fate of the shunned. That is what happens when people come from Estonia and Armenia. That is what happens when they are not Americans. Alone, alone with hairs all over their bodies, and skin the sun cannot be bothered to kiss.

Jerry's father is a Negro of the American earth. He is lean, and when he cares to smile, he has the power to devour you. Jerry's father has rhythms and features that come out of the cigarettes he smokes and the cabs of New York City that he drives, leaving him fully exposed to the streets and apart from his talents. When I see him I want to fall down in love for the warmth that I am feeling but which he will not allow me to express. Because Jerry's father has Negro wisdom on his face. He knows who he is and he knows who you are, too.

When Momma gets out the rolling pin and the cookie tins and prepares the gingerbread dough so the sweet-scented smell fills the whole apartment, I stand in the door-less frame to the kitchen and use outstretched hands and legs to raise myself to the top, begging her to see me in the glory I have achieved so I do not have to be invisible.

There is no laughter from Luigi when I mention Jerry Jones-Nobleonian, who has become my very own and from whom I must never be apart, not even for Coney Island and the endless summer sands. Luigi's face shows only distress. It says that Jerry is the Negro hotel with its endless commotion, and more.

"Whats-a matter with-a him? He-a sick? Why his skin have to be-a like that?" Luigi says, on the Saturday morning we are to go to the beach.

"Please, Luigi. Please."

On the beach no one applies the word *underweight* to Jerry Jones-Nobleonian. Other things they say, not with their tongues but with their eyes. Not only Luigi, but the kids who nudge each other and direct their friends' eyes with a toss of their heads. Because the blotches aren't only on Jerry's face and neck and hands. They are everywhere, like someone has burned him with acid or lye. If Jerry sees those looks, he doesn't say. He just goes about on the feet God gave him.

In the afternoon Luigi takes us into a movie theater on Surf Avenue. On a big screen killer ants float downstream on fallen leaves. What would Momma say if she knew we were watching these moving images? Men sleeping in the jungle wake up screaming as the ants eat them alive. Oh, the world, and what it can do.

Momma does not go to the beach, not with her varicose veins so frighteningly blue on her thick legs. The building is not hers to leave on all occasions. She must be there with Auntie Eve for the dangers that can arise and with Tall Tommy and Little Tommy and the other handymen who live in the single rooms to assist.

And there is Pelham Bay Park, in the Bronx, because Luigi can go one way and then another in finding places other than Manhattan. But there are no rides or crowds or sandy beaches. There is only the bay surrounded by woodland and the rowboat Luigi rents so we can be out on the stillness of the water. In the distance stands a bridge I have no name for—not Manhattan, not Brooklyn, not George Washington—so big and frightening. We are in the deep water now, in the middle of the bay. Luigi has pulled in the oars and he and Luke are causing a rocking motion that will surely capsize us. My fear has come to Luigi's attention, bringing a smile to his face. "It is time for your little dickie to get wet," he says, and tosses me into the cold water. Down and down I go before surfacing, the boat a blur drifting farther and farther away and eels nipping at my feet. But Luigi and Luke have turned their backs to me as I doggie-paddle to stay afloat, my arms growing tired. How much easier to give up than go on. Suddenly something has come between my legs. On Luigi's broad back am I lifted almost clear out of the water. Shivering and covered with goose bumps am I delivered into the boat. "How's your little dickie now?" Luigi howls with laughter. And Luke says, "Now you've been baptized too, little brother."

"Someday soon I'm going to give that sister Hannah of yours a ride, and I'm going to ride her for a long time," Tall Tommy says. He has a plan to go to my sister's room, he says, a room no one but she must enter and where she keeps her privacy intact. Tall Tommy flashes a smile that shows his missing teeth.

Hannah says a thief tried to come in the night. And no, it was not Jesus, she insists. The thief placed a big ladder up against the wall of the building and tried to climb into her room from the alleyway. Then someone stuck a finger in the light fixture and a blue bolt of electricity flashed there in the dark that gave this person a terrible shock. That was the story I heard. A commotion going on in the world at large. Things big and surrounded by mystery. Things no one could ever explain even after they had been explained.

Things happen in the night but also in the light of day. "Signs and wonders are before our very eyes," Momma says. "We must be open to them wherever they occur."

Down the block from our building a car brakes to a sudden stop and a white man with a towering blond pompadour like a cresting Coney Island wave emerges. A sleeveless white T-shirt highlights his muscular menace as he walks slowly back up that street with no attention paid to the sidewalks of New York City, saying he is stronger than any car, and the road is in full obedience to his will. Toward him from the direction of Broadway comes a Negro boy-man with a slighter build, sprinting more than walking, as if some frenzy in his blood cannot endure a patient stroll. He too claims the middle of the narrow street, paying no mind to the marauding vehicles of New York City. An open barber's razor he holds in his right hand, Saturday morning sunlight glinting off the metal as he strops the blade against his thigh. Thoughts of slicing, dicing, criss-crossing the flesh of Mr. Pompadour white man with the razor brings a toothy smile to his face. But white man takes the Negro's weight and lifts him up, not to heaven's gate but only to throw him down through the canvas top of the convertible parked at the curb, then follows after, pressing on the Negro with all his white man weight. And oh does the Negro struggle to free his razor hand from the grip of the white man and unleash his blade upon such whiteness and make it redder than red. And oh is it only a matter of time before such a thing should come to be, that the blade can slash the white man's eyes and cheeks and nose and throat and every abdominal feature that it seeks, the man of Negro rage slicing him into an oblivion that has no end before running a crazy pattern through the streets to his temporary freedom.

What does it mean that a white man is dead in the blood-soaked convertible? And what is the jubilation that drives some of the Negroes from the Negro hotel to dance in the streets? And what is it to be a white boy with fear of the waves of violence still to come after seeing what he has seen?

"Momma," I say, "a white man was made to get up and a Negro man was made to get up and now one of them is dead."

"We cannot have this." Momma says, of the anarchy in our midst. A call has gone out to all the corners of the world for dashiki-wearing Ethiopians and Nigerians and for those in the deepest reaches of the Belgian Congo and for Koreans and Chinese with mathematically gifted minds and bearded, turbaned Sikhs and Indians who shed their dhotis to wear the garb of America, all of them streaking for the universities of New York City to obtain the educations they are hungering for. Momma says she can house those whose cooking fills the halls with the smell of exotic spices but not those who have violence in their bones and their blood unless we wish to become like the hotel for the Negroes, where only the other week a decomposing body stashed behind the refrigerator in the communal kitchen caused an unbearable stench throughout the block.

The cars of New York City are violent and the men are violent and some of the women (are you listening, my sisters?) are violent and even the buildings will fall down on you if you are not careful.

At One Hundred Twenty-second Street and Broadway the train clears the tunnel and climbs a grade onto a fragile, corroding el high over Broadway. When the train relinquishes its darkness for the bright light of day, it does so under the watchful eye of the Juilliard School of Music and the Jewish Theological Seminary.

Barnard College has a fence of forest green to hide it from the cars and the people out on Broadway who want to look and look. It has rich soil Jerry and I can sink our hands into for earthworms and an archery range with a bull's eye target and women of excellence going about in the heaven of their own minds. Barnard College has a friendly manner, but One Hundred Twenty-second Street, just beyond its confines, does not play that way. Cars tear up the hilly cobblestone street where two Negro boys are lying face down in their own blood, having been shot in the back, and only the arrival of the police can compel the cars to cease their rampage and detour at a reasonable speed, the cars expressing their frustration with savage bursts of acceleration once beyond the detour point.

The Negro boys are not yet in death, but lie still with their eyes open, like the fish down on the pier at Coney Island, flounder and fluke hoisted from the sea on the lines of the fishermen and laid out on the wooden slats to expire where everyone can see them.

A burly white-haired man, in jacket and tie, stands with his back to the boys. Two police officers with open pads and pens are speaking with him. Sparks of justification fly from the man's mouth that boys their age should try to surmount his authority by relieving him of his wallet. "In broad daylight they attack, me lads. Do I have to tell you what that means? Thirty years on the force and I've never seen anything like it." So the white man says, that yes, they with smiling impudence should try to topple his regime, making it only a sample of the full-fledged anarchy they would soon be delivering if not held down with the iron fist of those who can be made to get up.

"That ain't right," Jerry Jones-Nobleonian says.

"What isn't right?"

"Shooting those boys like that. That's what ain't right."

We climb on the gray slabs of stone of Grant's Tomb before going inside to the rotunda, where tattered Civil War flags are on display. Down below are two giant coffins. Then we hang out in nearby Cherry Park, next to the International House, in a part of Riverside Drive no one must ever take away because of its smell of the north and the hope and the ache it brings on in summoning us back into American history.

That night I say, "Momma, the white man with a gun shot the Negro boys who had no guns, just as the Negro man with a razor slashed and slashed the white man who had no razor until the white man was no more for this earth. What is happening, Momma? Who are these people who are being made to get up, and why?"

"The world is full of guns, my son, and full too of mayhem men of violence who summon their fury as if it is the answer to their every need. But we are preparing to leave this earth for our heavenly home. Now have some chicken, my son. Have some chicken and Bird's Eye peas and a baked Idaho potato. I made it just for you."

That the potatoes should come from Idaho and that I should saturate mine with salted butter to make it even more delicious.

Something has gone wrong in the House of Order. Not with Langley Farmer but with my classmate Francis Cartwright, who lives with his father and has no mother in sight, just as Langley Farmer has no father conspicuous to our eye. Sister Mary Christabel has sounded an alarm. The theft of Amanda Crichton's stamp collection needs our full attention and she has set a date for its return, lest the punishment be severe. Within days Francis Cartwright has been squeezed from the code of stealth he operates by and comes forward with the missing collection into the light of day, with his father at his side, who is there to ensure that his future is intact. It is clear from the physical closeness of the one to the other that his father has taken a strong hand with his son and guided him back to the path of righteousness while reserving the right to keep his free hand in his pocket, where it needs to be.

Francis has a permanent wound on his face. Though it is not a thing that bleeds, it keeps his face from smiling and in a state of tension that the eye can see.

But Francis Cartwright has special skills that surpass his thievery and his wound. He is quick with the numbers that Sister Mary

Christabel assigns us. He dives into long division and scales the heights of the most staggering sums, making quick work of every problem with a Scripto mechanical pencil that needs no eraser. The marks he makes on his test papers are light and stylish.

Now my face has a wound that it cannot surmount. The school has recognized the excellence of Francis Cartwright, skipping him to the next grade, and in doing so has caused me to feel like thin paper in a strong wind. There is no way to look Francis Cartwright in the eye ever again. He has won and I have lost, lost, lost, and now he must be driven down into the ground of nonexistence.

For all time has the House of Order proved that it is on the winning side. For all time.

Danny Hurwitz lives down the block in a building with a portico, right before the hill where stands the hotel of the Negroes. Danny wears glasses and reads comic books with an intensity that shows in his fevered face. When he rides past me on his bicycle in front of bulldog Harry Frug's radio store, I kick the wheel so he and the bike fall over. Danny just lies there on the pavement. His glasses have fallen off.

"Why did you have to do that?"

"Do what?" I say.

"Kick me?"

"Did I kick you? Did I?"

"You kicked my bike."

"You didn't say that. You said I kicked you."

"No," Danny cries, and hurries off with his glasses and his bike, leaving me in shock at the harm I have done him.

My brother Luke is not negligible. When the hurricanes visit us, with all the late-summer ferocity they can summon, making our island captive to their strength, he roots from the Broadway window of our room for the winds to topple Harry Frug's radio shop sign from the support bar so it will crash to the avenue, never to rise again, and the forces of nature can be triumphant. And there it is, the green sign swinging wildly on the bar, to and fro, and Luke smiling as if nature's power is his own and magnifying him with the strength that it is showing.

The sign lies there on the sidewalk, sad and broken, with no one to hold it, no one to love it. The names Philco and Zenith and RCA and Magnavox, once a neon glow for all of Broadway to see in the night, are now but bits of glass and escaped gas, the whole thing a piece of refuse for the world to regard with the disdain it can muster, the wind-blown rain lashing the sign good, so very good, out of sight of the sun. The raindrops big, like those gray sinkers the fishermen attach to their lines and cast into the polluted waters of the Hudson in warmer weather.

Luke pins me against the wall with his hand against my chest, his eyes ablaze with smiling malice, before he lets me go. From my bunk I watch as he presses his nose into his forearm, as if he cannot get close enough to skin and blood and bone. The room is all his with the silence he has created, as if he can make time itself stand still. In the full-length mirror on the back of the door he later inspects himself, his teeth making a dull sound as he chomps them together. Turning to me, he says, "Your blood *stinks*. It's thin as water. Dr. Pfeffer says so."

Sometimes my brother just wants me to go away, as when he drops a shopping bag full of incinerator soot from the roof of our building that lands with a loud pop in the alleyway a foot from where I stand. No binoculars are needed to determine the smile on his face as he looks down at me from far above.

But I have my own violence to offer. In retaliation for my brother striking me with a rock in the back in that same alleyway, I toss a

Borden's milk bottle that flies in an arc and strikes him on his head as he flees.

When Luke runs to Momma with blood pouring from his scalp, Momma says, "What is the meaning of this? Are you crazy, my son?"

"Momma, he hit me with the rock of ages," I shout, but Momma has not the least regard for what I have to say as she hurries Luke off to the hospital.

A fin-tailed Cadillac has parked below our Broadway window. A small man in the finery of the earth, a full-length leather jacket and shiny black shoes, steps out from behind the wheel.

"It's Oil Can Harry," Luke says. The man wears no top hat or coat with tails, and his mustache is not the length of the cartoon character's, but it is for sure that he has tied Auntie Eve and Momma to the railroad tracks many times. Simon Weill is the owner of our building, and his arrival summons dread. Momma says he has the power to place us and our possessions in the cold and pelting rain, with no place to sleep but between the parked cars.

"Mrs. Manootdjian, how are you?" Simon Weill says to Momma. He does not live on the plane of the familiar with her.

"Very well, thank, you, Mr. Weill," Momma says, coming back strong and correct in her response as well.

"Is Miss Hedberg here?" Simon Weill asks. He is bold about showing his face to the world with his black hair slicked back. In a quiet, weary voice he speaks, but his words travel far.

"My sister is expecting you," Momma said. "Let us go inside."

Expecting.

Spice cake is set out on the marble-top table, and the strong smell of brewing coffee has spread through the apartment. Momma makes the same cake, pouring the batter into a round-shaped baking tin. Momma also makes a delicious apple pie, which she sprinkles with cinnamon. The pie tastes great when warm and even better cold from the refrigerator.

"Come, look, Mr. Weill. Have you seen my new painting?" Auntie Eve points to the portrait of Jesus in a robe with a mane of brown hair and a beard against the backdrop of a powder blue sky with puffs of clouds over the doorway to her kitchen.

"What did you pay for that thing, Miss Hedberg?" Simon Weill has placed an amused eye on Jesus in the sky, and has said with that one look everything he believes and doesn't believe.

"Pay? I would have to see," Auntie Eve says.

From the inside pocket of his jacket Simon Weill slowly takes some papers that do not challenge love but simply ignore it. "I have here an agreement for the new washing machine you requested. This is a contract for delivery, installation, and maintenance of the equipment, with terms of payment specified," Simon Weill says.

"A washing machine? What is that you say?"

"A washing machine, Miss Hedberg. As you may remember, you were calling me several times a day about the need for one." A tone of weariness has come into Simon Weill's voice.

Auntie Eve begins speaking with Momma in Swedish, but Momma does not let her fly away on a foreign tongue. She guides Auntie Eve to the paper that Simon Weill has laid out on the table and places a pen in her hand for her signature, while Simon Weill looks on.

"Just remember now, ladies. We are one, one," Simon Weill says, pocketing the signed document and bringing his two index fingers together.

Momma speaks to us that night, saying this: "Simon Weill has a nose for the possessions of the earth. He comes to us with a duplicity born of his own greed and would lay Auntie Eve in her grave like the men who have come before with account books and forms and regulations that those bound to the earth must rigidly rely upon. They hit Auntie Eve with the word *receivership* and said she must not spend one penny, not one single penny, without submitting endless forms. Big were the boils that grew on her flesh, but great was the humility with which she bore them. Because the men of the earth who had their ledger books and their numbers saw the purity of heart of Auntie Eve, they had difficulty abiding her presence."

"Tell us again how Simon Weill came to the building," Luke says, for Momma has spoken of him before.

"Simon Weill offered Auntie Eve a long-term lease but now he goes where he does not belong, taking store rents that are not his to take. The TV store. The hosiery store. The Drago shoe repair store. The luncheonette. The clothier. All of them."

"But why did she let them do that?" Luke persists.

"The store owners would revile your aunt when she came to them. They would dismiss her as if she were nothing more than a hanging string."

"What is a hanging string, Momma?" Vera asks.

"A hanging string is something negligible in the air. If you should see it drifting about, then you would simply say, 'Hah, that is just a hanging string and I will pay it no mind or I will snatch it and dispose of it as I please."

"But why did they say Auntie Eve was a hanging string?" Vera continues.

"It is not for the world to embrace goodness but to shun it. For our reward we must wait for the next world, I am afraid," Momma said.

"So what happened with the store rents?" Luke asks.

"Would you say of Simon Weill that he is a hanging string? Could it be in the mind of any storeowner to think such a thing? Simon Weill does not even ask for the store rent. It is waiting for him when he arrives. As I have said, the world has sworn its allegiance to the tribunes of darkness while forswearing the angels of light."

Momma is saying Simon Weill is not Tall Tommy and he is not Luigi. He does not play the harmonica and sing "Home on the

Range." He does not dispatch me to the store for the sausages that sizzle on the grill and that send you right to heaven when eaten on a roll with a slathering of mustard. Simon Weill just stands there in his power that no amount of scripture can ever touch, unable to take him down or raise him up. At all times does Simon Weill stay level on his own ground and bring the world to heel with the authority of his soft and weary voice.

Momma is saying Simon Weill is our real father. Momma is saying his darkness has dominion.

Frankie Dugan has red hair and freckles and smells like a Catholic and wears wrinkled shirts. He is chubby in his body and in his face but his bat tells a different story, making the softball sail in an arc far beyond the distances anyone else can deliver it to on the grassy fields of Riverside Park. And I can catch or try to catch the balls he hits with my genuine cowhide glove with the red Rawlings label that glows for all the world to see, a glove I can preserve forever with linseed oil. Because his power is not to be seen in his easy swing, it can only mean that he holds a magic wand, and so he has the status of a sudden god by this one feature where his excellence is found.

Frankie Dugan does not live on Riverside Drive or in the House of Order, but far to the east on a street of turmoil in an area he calls Yorkville, where tenements abound and laundry on clotheslines snap in the strong wind and tenants sleep on fire escapes when the heat of summer comes. I am shocked; my heart flies apart at the anarchy I am seeing— a street with no sanctuary from itself, where the sidewalks and the apartments of those who occupy them are virtually one. It is a Catholic street full of the pummeling fists and loud noises of passion children and the saloon features of red-faced grownups. It is a street of the cucarachas, Frankie Dugan says, with a laugh that lifts him high above everything he sees, like the softballs he sends into orbit with his Adirondack Slugger thirty-four ounce wand.

But Frankie Dugan and his family are free to move, and soon do, miles and miles and three different subway trains from the Episcopal school. Momma does not hold me back from visiting him at his new home. I board the familiar IRT West Side local to Ninety-sixth Street, then the downtown express train two stops to Forty-second Street, the same trains I take with Momma to the tabernacle, before setting out in a new direction to Queens, the train breaking free of the tunnel to find the open spaces of the el, along which it speeds as proof it has no need of darkness to keep itself going. The stations have names that shout their unfriendliness. Suddenly I am on a voyage out to sea without the guarantee of a return, even though I tell myself those rails I watch from the window at the front of the first car next to the motorman's cab are not water going where it will but a tidy course committed to a destination.

Frankie Dugan now lives in the top floor of a two-family house on a street with trees. "No cucarachas," Frankie Dugan says, and follows with much laughter, as it is his way to laugh and laugh. Rooms lead to bigger rooms and everywhere the grownups hold drinks with ice cubes that rattle in the tall glasses they clutch.

We go off to a lot down the street where Frankie hits his long fly balls and I hit shorter ones to him. I shag flies, making basket catches a la Willie Mays and over-the-shoulder catches, too.

I worry for Frankie Dugan, that he should be far away in Queens, as I return to Manhattan, but it cheers me to see the stations with the strange names in reverse—Junction Boulevard and Eighty-second Street-Jackson Heights, and Seventy-fourth Street-Broadway, knowing it is not the Broadway of my own but some utterly lonely imitation far from the familiar on which I depend for the warmth of love—and to soon follow the descent of the train on the tortured metal curve of the el past the Silvercup factory, leaving behind the light for the darkness of the tunnel, with all its possibilities for hiding, and imagining the power of the train itself revealing itself while I press witnessing against the tunnel wall a fractional distance from its torrid path. Momma, of course, waiting for me, back in the building where she can always be found.

In the Times Square station a man comes for me on a hurried slant. "I need you for something. I'll give you a quarter," he says, shepherding me along with a damp hand on my back and making his urgency my own. Into a phone booth he leads and closes the folding door. His hair is wiry and beads of sweat have gathered on his face and neck. He unzips his fly while holding the receiver to his ear, then says I am to touch his thing, which protrudes big and stiff and veined. "Don't make me hurt you." Outside the cramped booth people rush by, and though they are near, they seem far away, and I have no voice with which to cry out. His threat controls me. His thing feels firm, like hard rubber, when I place my hand lightly on it. "Harder. Faster. Back and forth," the man commands. Goo soon splatters the black telephone box and drips onto the floor.

The man reaches into his pocket for the quarter he had promised, pressing it into the palm of my hand. "Stay here. I'll be watching to see that you do."

I stare at the black box, soiled with the milky substance, before fleeing down the stairs to the uptown express among the blur of men and women. There is no use calling out. No one could possibly provide protection from this man.

I do not go near Momma with what has happened, and there is no consideration that my father should have a part in such a thing, but I do pick up the phone and speak with Frankie Dugan. I give him the truth as I can, wanting him to see that I was not an agent in my own demise but had simply been tricked.

"It was come. The creep made you jerk him off," Frankie Dugan says, establishing himself in that moment as being in the world in a way that I am not, and angering me at the same time that I should be so trespassed upon with laughter for a thing I did not know, this word for the milk that came from the man's body.

"No, no, it was milk," I insist. *The man had given white milk, which meant that a Negro man would give black milk.*

Abednego Suarez has come to the school premises. He is enormous, twice the size of the other boys. Excitement is in every word he speaks in Spanish-accented English. "I will tell you something, and this you must hear," Abednego says, flapping his hands back and forth while his forearms remain positioned on the vertical. There are whispers and giggles about Abednego. There is shunning of Abednego when he so much as comes near with his hands of a *queer*, refusing with an "Ooh" the Hi-C orange and grape juice in paper cups and the Graham crackers it is his turn to serve at the mid-morning snack break. In tears does Abednego rush from the room, tormenting laughter following after him.

We do not see Abednego Suarez at school the next day or the day after. A whole week and then another passes without him. He has just disappeared. Then, one day, as I ride the West Side subway downtown, there he is, towering over everyone. Though I want to slip away, I can't, not when he sees me.

"Where have you been?" I ask.

"I goes away. It is a school I so much detested. So many of the stupids. I am now at the school where I belongs. So much better."

I have not been entirely innocent, and so I receive his words as if they were as much for me as for the others.

"I make goodbyes to you here," Abednego Suarez says, some stops later, and gets off without looking back.

There is a store sign that no hurricane has ever blown down. The sign belongs to the drugstore on the corner of Broadway opposite the building where I live. That's right. It belongs to the House of

Order. The sign does not swing freely in the wind on a metal arm, inviting its own demise, but is bolted flat to the side of the building. It reads "Prescriptions" and glows neon red in the night. I spell the word out loud and from memory, with Jerry-Jones as my witness, and a door opens.

Johnny Lacy is from the South. He was born under a magnolia tree. He runs with his upper body twisting away from his legs, as if the two are of separate minds, but does not let his condition keep him from the athletic field.

All of Riverside Drive, where Johnny Lacy lives, is one long House of Order. The corner building that shelters him is of brown and white brick and has the capacity to endure the winds off the river and the depression of gray wintry days.

Every inch of Johnny Lacy's apartment has a design I cannot explain, from the window treatments to the carpeting and the furnishings. Where does such quality come from?

If I say that Johnny Lacy is only with Edward Macy and those they have claimed for their own, then I also have to tell you that now and then Johnny Lacy has tried to be with me. But Johnny Lacy's ways are not my ways, his mother and father are not my mother and father, his house is not my house. And if Johnny Lacy does not know this, he knows it soon. Or maybe he has always known.

"Don't fire that BB rifle," Johnny Lacy says.

He has seen me reach for the rifle, which had been resting against a wall in his room. I don't go and shoot him in the face with it, ping his eyes for calling my apartment a pigsty. I am not ruled by hatred of that kind. I just do not care. His house is not my house. His world is not my world. I have no thought for what it might do to pull the trigger but only the urge to do it. And so I ping his ceiling twice before he can grab hold of me and, because he is stronger, throw me out the front door of his apartment. It is all right. The buildings—some of them—have barriers, but the streets have no barriers. Anybody can be on the street. *Anybody.*

Another has come for me, not as Mr. Urgent did, this one as I am leafing through old copies of *Sport* in a used books and magazines store in the Times Square subway station. In the doorway he is, his dark eyes only for me. They are eyes that *know*, that say I am the one. His smile says the same. In spite of all that my stranger has aroused, I cannot go to him, instead placing my eyes back on the blur of pages before me. And when I put down that magazine, he is gone, I know not where, lost to me in the underground mazes that have drawn him away.

Now at the tabernacle when Momma has her urge to stand up and speak her unintelligible words, I too have an urge that tears me from our pew in the balcony and down the spiral stairs. Within minutes I have sped through the Penn Station arcade onto the IRT one stop to Times Square. If Momma has a world, I have my own, and it here, in the subway store, where I stand with a used issue of *Sport* magazine in hand. But he does not come. He does not stand in the doorway. There are men, yes, but they are not my man, none of them placing their eyes on me for one second, or if they do, only to move those same eyes somewhere else, as if to say I am not important in their sight. And so I return to the tabernacle, and climb those creaky stairs to the balcony, where Momma still sits. Empty I am, empty, even as Momma has been filled up.

But he lives in my mind, and one day he is there again, in his black overcoat, standing on a crowded bus on traffic-clogged Fifth

Avenue. Once again his eyes are only for me. Once again I cannot go to him, my fear having rooted me to the spot.

Momma has sent me to our dentist, who has an office in the Atlas Building, there in Rockefeller Center. My stomach drops as the wood-paneled elevator quickly rises high above Manhattan. Behind a frosted glass door with his name on it does Dr. Milllsley do his work. Normally I would be in dread of Dr. Millsley's slow drill and the shocking pain when the bit strikes a nerve, but now I am the prisoner of a fantasy so intense I can't be sure it isn't written on my face as I leaf through a copy of *National Geographic*. I am in a bathtub, not with Luke and Vera, as so often I had been when I was smaller and Momma found it convenient to bathe the three of us together. I am alone in the tub, and it is not Momma who is bathing me but the man on the bus. Every part of me he touches, causing an agony of pleasure I want never to end. Dr. Millsley's patter goes right by me as he selects from an assortment of stainless steel utensils on the enamel tray and begins his aggressive probe.

Hannah is not always happy in her life. She is sad that her life has gone away from her before it had really begun.

"You must have compassion and you must have love. The trials and tribulations of life are many," Momma says, when I am vile with my tongue that Hannah is still among us with her black moods and billowing rages.

"Momma, I did not say I do not have love for Hannah. But she walks with her forearms up and her hands hanging down so she can be fast with her smacks. Momma, she lives for smacking and smacking with her tongue clamped between her thick lips."

But Momma has her distant ways. She is like Jesus looking down from the sky. She has forgotten what it is to be on the ground looking up. "Oh, go on with your foolishness," Momma just says.

There are Sunday evenings, like this one, when my father stops his disappearing ways and holds fast to connection. He and Momma will be stepping out to the Swedish church. When Momma and my father go out together, it is not to see people but to see the Lord. Momma has brought my father to Him so he can be tethered to something more than the wind and a past that does not speak its truth coherently in his mind.

The Swedish church has the order of its East Side location, the safe and quiet streets that speak of wealth as a barrier to tumult, including a toy store that features Lionel trains. Yes, the Swedish church has the chronic order of the Swedish nation, which demands cleanliness in its house of worship and pews of varnished wood.

"You just leave these brats with me. I'll get them in line," Hannah says.

"Ushtah, Hannah, must you speak in this way?"

"Do you want me to mind them or not?"

"Yes, of course, Hannah. I am very appreciative."

Momma can only hope to douse Hannah's anger with continuing kindness and understanding. She is held hostage to Hannah's fire.

The house phone rings shortly after Momma and my father have left. Hannah drags herself across the room. In one hand she holds the receiver, and in the other a carton of ice cream. "Yeah, what is it?...You want what? A new fridge? This is the Sabbath. Do you have a Sabbath wherever you come from, mister?...Be grateful we let you in this building, let alone this country...I'm not in my right mind? Look who's talking...Don't you talk to me that way. I know where you live..."

King Kong is playing on *Million Dollar Movie* in the darkened living room.

"Hannah, why can we watch a movie on TV but not in a movie theater?" I say to her, when she has gotten off the phone.

"Be quiet," Hannah says.

Momma has her ways, and stays rigid within the confines of them, allowing herself, with my father, to only watch Oral Roberts and his faith-healing ministry, live from Tulsa, Oklahoma, on Channel 9 on Sunday mornings. With his suit jacket removed and the sleeves of his white shirt rolled up and his hair falling into his face, Oral Roberts lays his hands on a woman in a wheelchair and shouts "Heal" and the woman rises from her wheelchair and walks about and cries out "Praise Jesus." As Pastor Odachenko says, "The majesty of His miracles must not and will not go unspoken."

"Hey, Hannah, what kind of ice cream is that you are eating?" Luke asks. He and Vera and I are sitting on the sofa, which is really a bed covered with a spread. The sofa has no backing, and so our heads rest against the bare wall and cause these dark spots that soap and water can't take away.

"Mind your own business," Hannah says. Hannah eats her ice cream right out of the carton. Soon she is scraping the sides of the carton with her tablespoon.

"I was just asking," Luke says.

"Didn't I just tell you to mind your own business?"

"He just wanted to know," I say.

"Listen, you brats. I'm trying to watch a movie."

"You're a brat," I say.

Hannah slaps my face. "Now will you shut up?"

"You shut up."

And so Hannah slaps me again, this time harder. "Have you had enough? Do you need more?"

"You need more," I say.

And so she slaps and slaps and slaps some more, and each time she slaps she has her thick tongue clamped between her thick lips, as if nothing gives her greater satisfaction than to have her hand meet flesh.

When Momma comes home, and I can have her alone, I say, "Momma, my face was on fire from what Hannah has done."

"The little brat got fresh with me," Hannah says, being within earshot and once again holding her hands high and dangling.

"Ushtah, Hannah. He is a child. Have you no sense?"

"Spoil him. Go ahead. See if I care," Hannah says.

"Hannah, I beg of you. I beg of the both of you. Let us be reasonable. Do you wish for me that my night be sleepless? Is that what you wish for?"

Momma is saying something now. Momma is saying she might have to fall down dying if we don't hold her together.

Now on those Sunday nights when Momma is out with my father Hannah sends us to bed before she begins to watch *Million Dollar Movie* and eat her quart of ice cream.

"I don't want any trouble tonight, and I mean business," she says.

When Hannah turns off the light and leaves, Luke says, "Let's pay the Load a visit. We'll put a blanket over our heads. That will really scare her. What do you say?"

The Load. It is what Luke calls her when he isn't calling her Mount Hannah.

Momma has taken her love light with her and left us in the dark. Luke leads the way, I am in the middle, and Vera is last. We are depending on Luke to guide us. Crazy noise we make when we arrive, causing Hannah to erupt from her chair, the only light from the glow of the TV screen. Sparks, flames, everywhere the smoke of her fury. "I'll kill you goddamn brats." Now has she something even better than *Million Dollar Movie* and the quart of ice cream with a tablespoon stuck in it.

Run from irate Hannah. Run from the rage that is hers alone. Run to your beds for safety. But Hannah storms into our room with locomotive power. See her take Luke unto herself in the way she must. See her administer to his flesh. See her as she places her tongue between her thick lips and whap whap whaps the blanket under which he cowers. See as she seals it into my memory for all time what she can do.

Vera now has a puppy she calls her own, a mutt with a white coat and brown spots. Vera calls the puppy Sadness. I say that is no name for a dog.

"Sadness is in her eyes, so Sadness she has to be," she replies.

When night comes, Luke and I take Sadness into the park on our walk. On the way to the park, we pass the hotel for Negroes and, at the bottom of the hill, the corner building on Riverside Drive. The district attorney for all of Manhattan, the one who spoke poorly of Auntie Eve in bringing an indictment against her, has an apartment in this building, Momma says. It has an ironwork awning and a doorman to keep out those who do not belong. Oh, what a house of order, surpassing many of the houses of order I have already made a note of in my mind.

We head south on the top drive of the park, along the bridle path. A low retaining wall runs alongside the path. Beyond the wall is the lower level of the park.

"Someday I'm going to move out. It will be nice. You'll see. And you can come live with me. I'll be able to get working papers and find a job. I'm sick of Hannah. I'm sick of all of them."

There is a new building of tan brick. Maybe we could live there. And a light burns in an apartment at the top of a taller building a few blocks south. Maybe that apartment will be ours. Or maybe the apartments will all be gone before we are old enough to have them.

"Do you believe in God?" I say to Luke.

"When I'm walking like this, I believe in God," Luke says.

The more we talk about God, the more excited I grow and the more my love for Luke grows. The darkness is a blessing in which this fragile love can be felt, a love that would only embarrass or even destroy me if made visible in the light of day. Even so, I fear I have exceeded the bounds of closeness. In the morning I must recoil from this night time excess.

In spite of all I have said, there are those times when Edward Macy is with me and not with Johnny Lacy, this in spite of all the claiming of each other and of others that they have done. Unlike Johnny Lacy, Edward Macy does not live on Riverside Drive. He lives up the hill, toward Broadway, in the building next to the Presbyterian church, whose bell in the tower tolls every hour. Though it is not on Riverside Drive, the building has a high degree of order—an intercom and a clean lobby and landings and apartments that house families with children; it is not the kind where the men and women of the single rooms, such as Tall Tommy, would find a home. And yes, he has an apartment he doesn't have to keep other kids out of, for fear of what they would think and say and, as I have noted, a father who has the power and authority to walk with one hand in his front pocket, as Edward himself has been taught to do.

When I say to Edward Macy, "Let's go down to the railroads and bash some trains," he pauses and scrunches his lips to one side of his face, as others do, before saying, as others do, "Let's not, and say we did."

Edward Macy's mother has a permanent tan and permanent beauty. She has a fire, too, that her fine clothes and fine features cannot contain. It burns in her big dark eyes, like oil set ablaze, and causes her to revile the head of Edward Macy with a broomstick. His head swathed in bandages, he emerges from a hospital the next day. What has caused his mother's wrath? Was it his thick lips and the way he has of scrunching them? Or was the trigger all that wire that makes his mouth a metallic mess?

But Edward Macy regains his power. Once again he can be seen walking with one hand in his front pocket and wearing that smirk and with Johnny Lacy at his side. "Manootdj, let me borrow your baseball glove. I promise to give it back tomorrow." The glove is a Carl Furillo model, with a large webbing and with the red Rawlings label over the hand strap. To break the glove in, I have applied neatsfoot oil to the genuine cowhide leather and placed it under my mattress with a softball in the pocket.

Though I do not want to give it to Edward Macy, the power of them together is too much for me. The pigsty knowledge they have of me is in their smiles that reduce me in my own mind.

"Gee, thanks, Manootdj. Isn't Manootdj great, Johnny?"

"Sure. Manootdj is great," Johnny Lacy says.

For all the rest of the day I think about my glove and the angry things I will say and do if Edward Macy is not careful with it. But the next day comes and Edward Macy says nothing about the glove. He just walks on by in the close company of Johnny Lacy and Alison Pauley as if I were not there. All day does he seem to have them as an escort. And so I think to wait after school outside his building on the next block, where I might have him alone for a minute, as now my glove is so big in my mind that nothing else can be there.

But once again it does not happen that I can have Edward Macy all to myself. There Edward Macy is, turning the corner of Broadway, but still in the company of Johnny Lacy and Alison Pauley, as if even in their dreams they cannot be apart. And the three, from afar as they turn that corner, would seem to have eyes only for me. And yes, both Edward Macy and Johnny Lacy have one hand in their front pockets. So now it is for me to stand there and await them given the prison of self-consciousness their attention has placed me in, as Cowardice and Strangeness would have been the new names they applied to me for all the school to hear should I run from their approaching presence.

"Were you looking for something?" Edward Macy says, standing within a foot of me and flashing the metal in his expensive mouth.

"Do you have my glove?" The butterflies in my stomach make it hard for me to speak.

"Gee, Manootdj, I'm sorry. I must have forgotten it in the park yesterday."

"You forgot my glove?"

"That's what I just said."

He says his words like a blunt rebuff, as if asking how much more time does he have to devote to this matter and with just a hint that he is running out of patience. That is how I hear his words, while having no regard for my own. Because my own words are not there anymore. They have been taken away. Edward Macy has taken them away, and Johnny Lacy and Alison Pauley. They have shriveled me, making it as impossible to speak to Edward Macy words of anger as it would be to hurl a boulder.

And so I say nothing and give to Edward Macy a smile that says the glove is not a matter of importance. Because the understanding has come to me that I would only be shaming myself in their eyes if I made it important. In that moment I see that I have to hide myself away in the presence of Johnny Lacy and Edward Macy and Alison Pauley and be defeated from the earth.

There is a giant rock on the opposite side of the street from where Edward Macy lives. The rock stands between two small buildings. Like a remnant from the earth beneath our feet it is, some reminder that nature, not concrete, once had its way on this paved-over island. Sometimes Jerry Jones-Nobleonian and I climb up on that rock and stare down at the alleyway below, and from that height we can also see the back of the house of order, as we are looking south, to the block on which we live.

On the ground floor of the house of order is a bay window filled with plants. So pleasing to the eye is this rear window, secluded from the street, that I will stare at it for minutes at a time, as at a vision of the harmony that my life to come will have. The plants belong to Florence Wilkerson, an older woman whose stomach rumbles during the piano lessons she gives me. The black keys, the white keys, the quarter and half notes—I have no fever for the world Momma affords me, neither a musical ear nor musical tongue. I neither play nor sing "Hard-Hearted Hannah," as Rachel and Naomi once did. It is a language apart from my own.

She has a solitary way, Miss Wilkerson does, living alone in that ground-floor apartment right off the marble lobby, with the uniformed doormen and the soft sofa and chairs, and the atmosphere of peace and warmth beyond anyone's understanding. Then one day it comes to me that Miss Wilkerson, with her light skin, not quite white, is a Negro, as it comes to me that Herbert Hall, who owns Hall's Clothiers on the southeast corner of Broadway and One Hundred Thirteenth Street, and who has that same skin tone, is also a Negro. It comes to me that neither she nor he is hiding who they are, but they are not proclaiming it either. They are simply saying, if you see it, you see it, and if you don't, then you don't, but once you do, you will not see us the same way ever again. You will understand something, even if you don't really understand. Wherever your understanding is, you will keep it to yourself and go on about your day.

Something else I see while standing on that rock is a man decidedly Negro, with the rich black hue of those Negroes who come to our building from the continent of Africa. The man is naked and standing over a sink as he strokes his thing. I cannot take my eyes from him, waiting, waiting, with fear as my god, for the gobs that spurt into the air before falling into the basin. All this I see from the rock where Jerry Jones-Nobleonian and I stand. Once more I am seeing that men in private have capacities beyond those they show on the street.

There is more life on that block too, proving to me with a certainty that, while Edward Macy is big in my mind, others have their place, like Johnny Donatelli, the second son of the superintendent of the building where Edward Macy lives, who says "you'se guys" and not "you guys." And there is Ingrid, blond and my age, who causes the light of love to turn on in me so that I can hardly speak my name and from her have to run, so much fear and shyness has her smiling presence on the sidewalk summoned that I must stay away lest I lose her love should she see me as I am.

And there is the rhyme we chant outside the building across from where Edward Macy and Johnny Donatelli live: "Ching chong Chinaman sitting on a fence/Trying to make a dollar out of fifteen cents." Saying it once, twice, as many times as it takes for the bent old man with the long braided hair and goatee to emerge in his quilted jacket from the basement and chase us up the block toward Broadway, the time coming when I look back over my shoulder to see if he is gaining and run straight into a pole, the impact dropping me to the sidewalk, where, as I lie dazed, he stands over me and drops a mouthful of spit on my face.

And there is the game we play call Loadsies. We scoop out the cork in soda bottle caps and add melted crayon so the caps will have weight. Small boxes spaced five feet apart and numbered one to eight are drawn in chalk on the street to form an open square. The goal is to flick the cap with our index finger into each box, and whoever gets into all eight boxes first is the winner. If we can, we blast each other's caps out of the way in the process. There we are, Johnny Donatelli and Jerry Jones-Nobleonian and I, playing Loadsies in the middle of the street as Johnny Lacy and Edward Macy walk on by, and we don't go to the sidewalk for them and they don't come to the street for us.

The thunderstorm has come and gone, and now the breeze coming in through the open chicken-wire window in the lobby carries with it the smell of dust. The sun is once again burning up the street and the Nemo Theater down on One Hundred Tenth Street and Broadway is calling in a way I cannot resist. On the marquee, as I approach, I see the name *Rififi*. What is that, Rififi? There is no one in America named Rififi. A woman enclosed in a narrow booth tears an orange ticket from a roll and hands it to me after I give her my money. Inside, an usher stands on the sloping carpeted floor and takes my ticket. I have left behind the scorching street, and now air-conditioned darkness and the smell of buttered popcorn greet me. I fumble my way to a seat on the aisle. On the big screen are actors speaking in French, with English subtitles. A rectangle of black obscures the bare breasts of one of the women. I am not there five minutes when a hand clamps tight on my shoulder and I am dragged from my cushioned seat up the aisle. Now I am back out on Broadway and Hannah is holding me by the shirt collar so I do not run away. But how has she found me?

Into the lobby she hauls me. "Do you know what the little brat was doing just now? He was sitting in the Nemo Theater watching a grown-up movie. That's where he was."

Momma saying, "Hannah, please," because Hannah cannot contain herself.

"Don't *please* me. This is the thanks I get?"

"But Hannah. We are in the lobby. There are people…"

Momma saying to me later, when she could be free of the affliction of Hannah, "Be enveloped in the Lord, my son. Enveloped. Do you understand what I am saying?"

"I understand, Momma. I understand," I say.

Little Tommy has come from West Virginia to be with us and has muscles that bulge and a girlfriend he beats, causing her to go and live elsewhere. Little Tommy paints the rooms in the building, applying coats of Hedberg green, a light green that Auntie Eve favors and which he has named for her. He smokes Chesterfield cigarettes and goes to the racetrack to bet the ponies and stands outside the luncheonette every night waiting for the *Daily News* truck.

One day painters come to the building and go where Little Tommy has never gone. From Broadway they can be seen standing on a scaffold lowered from the roof. Quickly the big blank wall gets two coatings of cream-colored paint. Then, more slowly, words painted in a bright red begin to appear. When their work is done, several light fixtures, with powerful bulbs, illuminate the hand-painted sign so it can be seen by those on the Upper West Side both day and night.

> For the wages of sin is death; but the gift of God
> is eternal life through Jesus Christ our Lord.
>
> Romans 6:23

"Momma, what has Auntie Eve gone and done?" I ask. "Now everyone will know our name and we will have nowhere to hide from what they will call us."

"Auntie Eve is witnessing for the Lord. It is something we all must do now that we are living in the last days. Do you not understand?"

"Momma, you are saying it, but I am not saying it. You have had your life. Can you not let me have my own?"

The school is in two buildings and has only the nuns to maintain it. In the basement is the cafeteria, which we crowd into for lunch. On the floors above are the classrooms, and at the very top are the rooms where the nuns are allowed to live. Sister Mary Christabel notes on my report card that I do not obey group rules promptly. She tells Momma that I show a contrary spirit and that a demerit will be issued for each wrongful act. Three demerits mean that the school can have me on its premises all day Saturday .

It is a laughing matter to me when the demerits are issued, as they bring me attention. But the nuns have serious work they want me to perform. I am to scrub the walls clean of dirt and wash the floors. And then the floors are to be waxed. "More elbow grease,"

Sister Mary Christabel says, as I apply polish with the rag. Her face has been bleached of life, leaving only a cold severity.

Luke has a fishing rod and a Halicrafters shortwave radio and a drum pad and a drum set so he can work on the beats that are in his bones. He can do a feathery tease on the snare drum and demand a deep boom from the bass drum. A teacher named Lenny Malderon is within range to give him the instruction that he needs.

Luke has the mental and material substance of a boy in his mind and body, including the private parts that will take him a long way. He can bicycle far on his Schwinn, causing the whitewall tires to plead for mercy, and he can swim the waters of the Hudson, diving off the pier and bringing a look of amazement to the impassive faces of the Negro fishermen who catch the shad that feed on doo. And he has learned from Luigi to capture the eels in the polluted waters of New York City in his bare hands, and now deposits their slimy substance in the kitchen sink, the whole pale dead mass of them, their obscene off-whiteness enough to cause a shuddering revulsion. Momma is pinned to the ceiling by the horror of what she is witnessing, while Luke luxuriates in laughter at the hysteria he has wrought.

Luke is not repelled by dust on the window sill or the shabbiness of our room in a certain light. His substance has him going on, regardless of the weather. And when he can't, he can bore his nose into his arm for recharging.

Luke knows things it is beyond my mind's ability to possess. He can create a model train layout that takes up half the room. We have a tunnel of papier-mâché where our Texas Special A and B unit diesel can hide before it comes out and a trestle it can cross and a signal bridge and a station where the train can get some rest, and a siding for extra rolling stock. And Luke can hook up the Lionel transformer so power flows when he turns the lever. Luke and I bought the Texas Special train set on sale in the toy department on the fifth floor of Macy's. And we have a gantry car to make sure the workers get to where the work is going on so the tracks can be secure.

But my mind is not quiet. The Texas Special is not good enough. The red and white colors of the A and B engines do not please. And what is a second engine, a B engine, without a cab? And the narrow gauge "O27" track the Texas Special runs on will not accommodate the nicer-looking trains that run on "O" gauge track. We have been denied the twin A unit diesels of the New York Central, the Southern Line, the Santa Fe. No, the elements are not right, and my mind is a torment that this should be.

Like Johnny Lacy, Winston Trowbridge has a Riverside Drive apartment. It too defies description as to its beauty. The building has two entrances, one on the side street and one right on the drive. At both entrances are doormen who stand ready should you not be right for the premises.

In his room gap-toothed Winston Trowbridge has built a model train layout. He stands at the big black transformer wearing a denim engineer's cap. Over the plywood board is stapled a cover of green grass, on which are laid out magna-traction "O" gauge train tracks. There is a main line around the perimeter of the board and inland routes and sidings and tunnels through mountains made of papier-mâché. A Santa Fe twin engine passenger train with Pullman cars and an observation car and a baggage car speed along the tracks, while on another route runs a red and black Seaboard Coast Line switcher engine. Without thinking I throw a switch and derail the Seaboard engine and the several freight cars it is pulling.

Winston Trowbridge is big for his age, and now there is fire in his small eyes set deep in his pale, pimply face. Like Johnny Lacy, he takes me by the collar and rushes me out the front door.

"You didn't have to do that," Luke says, as we climb the hill to Broadway.

But I did, I do not say.

My father has bought Luke a shoeshine kit, with black and brown and oxblood polishes, buffing rags, and an assortment of brushes. "It is time for you to earn some money. Don't be a burden to your mother. Shine some shoes," my father says.

"Where?" Luke says.

"Where? On the street."

"I don't want to shine shoes on the street," Luke says.

"You don't want, you say? Do you want for me to become aggravated? Is that what you want?"

"No," Luke says.

"Then do as I say. I am your father."

Papandreou's florist shop is right next to the Whelan's Drug Store on One Hundred Tenth Street and Broadway. Mr. Papandreou's hair is as gray as the smock he wears over his shirt and tie. "Work, work. Run, run. You'll be rich someday," he says. It is Christmas break and he sends me throughout the neighborhood with bouquets and potted plants, and a song of joy begins in me as I make my way through snow-filled streets, imagining Momma so proud of me. The buses of New York City have chains on their wheels that go *click click, click click*. The boys of Broadway stand on snowbanks and punish the buses with snowballs thudding loudly against their closed windows and startling the passengers but I am too busy for that now—I am working.

Soon my pockets are bulging with coins and dollar bills given to me as tips. I go down with Luke to Macy's to pick out a gift for Momma. A set of marked down plastic dinnerware catches our eye. The dinner plates and smaller plates and bowls are bright red, and others are bright orange or dark blue. And there are cups with saucers in the same vivid colors. Now we can get rid of the cracked and chipped and mismatched dinnerware and have the beginnings of a house of order. It is for me to imagine the happiness on Momma's face when she tears off the gift wrapping and opens the big box.

The colored lights on the tree in our living room offer a warm electrical glow—orange and blue and red and green and all the colors that can make your heart fill with longing for things it cannot even express. But the lights must be off when we sleep so fire does not snatch us from our lives.

In this season of joy has Luke entered the darkness. No sooner do we set the box under the tree than he wheels and socks me in the stomach. Onto my knees I drop, unable to draw a breath. Only a malevolent smile meets my upturned face as a reminder of who he can be driven to be.

Not a day goes by that Momma doesn't think of Rachel. "She has such a fine mind," Momma says. "All my children have fine minds," Momma adds, saying what may not be true. And now, because it is Christmas, Rachel will be riding the train down from the north where she has been at college. Just because she has gone away does not mean she cannot come back. And just because the front door is closed doesn't mean she can't walk through it. And just because Momma comes toward her with a cry of delight does not mean Rachel cannot push her backward into the Christmas tree, toppling Momma, toppling the tree, causing gifts to be crushed and bulbs to be broken because of the rebuffing stance that Rachel now is showing.

Momma sits with full understanding of what a daughter can and will be with the collapsed tree on top of her till Luke and Hannah and I can come to her rescue. Because it is not for Rachel to give a helping hand to one she has disposed of in this way, not when the fever is still upon her. Father has received word of the insurrection and now roars into the living room like a locomotive at full throttle, his smacking hand positioned high above his head so maximum power can be brought to bear. He is not in his robe but wears only an undershirt so his hairiness can be exposed, tufts on his shoulders and his back. Father discharges no words from his mouth. He does not say, "Have you made me to get up?" He does not say, "Have you assigned me your death?" No. But even so does Rachel sense his oncoming wrath and flees for her very life out the front door through which she came.

The absence of serious annihilation brings only small relief, for now there is the matter of Rachel's monstrousness, that she would so embrace the realm of cruelty in the ingratitude to Momma that she has shown. It is for me to cry and cry and to regard time as the enemy of my life in the demands it makes upon me to rectify immediately and in all ways the delinquency of these older sisters. Momma, I am here and I am sound and I am on the earth to do your will with the straight line I now must walk, I declare. Now must I live even more fully in the embrace of her goodness. Now must I see even more the whiteness of her light. Now must I assume the full burden of making things right. No one exists but Momma. No one has ever existed but Momma. No one ever can.

Sister Henry is bathed in the love of God at the Friday Bible school and would take us to her warmth. Pastor Odachenko and his mother in white are not to be seen. His disappearing words will not be with us again until Sunday. Luke and Vera and I have come from the Episcopal School and the nuns of severity to be with Sister Henry. She tells us of the rocks of old, and the men in robes who walked upon those rocks and knelt down to God before Jesus was so much as on the earth.

There are doors that Sister Henry comes out of but which we ourselves must not go through.

Something is happening. The trains are nearby, in Pennsylvania Station. And the trucks of the post office are just outside. I can hear the rumble of both. And the pages of my gilt-edged pocket Bible are stuck together. And the words "verily, verily" float through its leather cover and dance giddily around the room.

Hannah is waiting outside the gated entrance. Though darkness has come, the sun is in her face. Gone are the scowl and the slapping position of her hands. With Hannah is her friend Hazel. They have come from somewhere in the world to be with us.

Hazel is plump, like Hannah, and her volume is turned to loud, also like Hannah. Clouds of cigarette smoke she exhales. Makeup layers her face and mascara lies heavily on her lashes. She is hearing wedding bells, she says. A man named Charlie. That my sister should have a friend. That she should come to us beyond the apartment and leave her fury behind.

IRT. It stands for Interborough Rapid Transit and is like no other subway in the system, running on a narrower gauge track. And it does not only love Manhattan, but will shine its light on other boroughs as well. Now the subway is Brooklyn-bound through a long stretch of tunnel during which there are no stations to stop its progress. Ocean water is all around us, waiting to get in. The train has no time to fool around once it leaves Wall Street. No shilly-shallying, no dawdle-dancing, as it streaks for Clark Street. For every ten yards on the straightaway, there are ten yards more.

The St. George Hotel comes down from the street to meet the Clark Street station. An elevator. An arcade lined with shops. The world's largest indoor swimming pool, a sign says.

Luke cannonballs off the high diving board, arms around his bent knees, parting the water violently. He does backflips and twists, cleaving the water cleanly.

I stay in the chlorinated pool until goose bumps cover my flesh and my lips are turning blue and my teeth are chattering. There is a steam room where old men with breasts and big bellies and skinny legs stand in the mist. I feel safe and warm sitting on a bench in the mist of hissing steam. No more cold water. Not now. Not ever. No cold must ever touch me again. In their presence, my blood stirs. But the goosebumps have gone. Now my skin is wrinkly and itches, and so I flee. Even with a towel around my shoulders, I am cold. Luke and Vera have remained in the crowded pool, but I am far away. My body is disappearing before my eyes. My feet are all bones. My legs are bones. The screams echoing off the tiles, the reckless dives from the high board, the sound of bodies impacting with the cold water are too much. I find a shower stall and give myself to the warm stream from the nozzle. But here is Luke, looking in, his wet black hair plastered to his head. He stares down at my naked body. "Mine is twice as big as yours," he declares. A jack o' lantern grin lights up his face. He has been waiting forever to say these words, to drive me deep within myself so that I can never come out.

Hannah has a private part, too. She wears a robe that hangs open. There is a dark patch below her waist that can only be one thing. I am seeing what I am not supposed to see. Some jolt of electricity sends me flying backward beyond the apartment and into space. Deeper and deeper into the universe am I driven, and yet I am still not safe from what has been revealed.

Hannah has her own worldliness, a course she must chart for her own survival, though she does not sing about hard-hearted Hannah, the vamp of Savannah. My father gave her the name Armenouhi so she would be his Armenian daughter forever, but the call of America was too strong. She threw the fifty-pound name in a ditch so she could be free, and now it sits there, sad and neglected in all weather.

Broadway is not a straight line. If it is allowed to go far to the north it will break free of the clamor of buildings and houses into the trees and reclaim the purity of another time. To the south it winds so you cannot see from one end to the other, not even on a clear day. Stanley's Cafeteria is around a bend, and has more space than it knows what to do with. If you enter you must remember to take a ticket from the dispenser machine. The men and women behind the counter, where the hot dishes and sandwiches and soups and desserts are served, punch your ticket. The more you buy the more they punch. It is a place that you worry things could be out of control even as you eat your lemon meringue pie, but the bright lights and hubbub are important in reminding you there is a world that comes alive at night and you are not yet a part of it.

Momma says that even though the war has used Tall Tommy for its own purposes, he must hold his own in the single room she has given him. "He is a grown man. He must not be a lazybones and lie down and die," Momma says, and so she calls to him, saying the building has urgent need of his services.

It is for Tall Tommy to shovel ashes and burnt cans and glass bottles that have burst in the heat from the basement incinerator. Into the metal garbage cans he deposits them and hauls the cans up the ramp on a hand truck. And in daylight hours it is for him to work closely with Auntie Eve on her mattress strategy for the building. From one floor to another does Tall Tommy lug single mattresses and double mattresses, those that are stained and those without blemish. The bigger ones he carries on their side. The smaller ones he makes light of by transporting on the top of his balding head.

"Now we must move them once again," Auntie Eve says, after Tall Tommy has dragged or carried four mattresses from their rooms to other rooms. But Tall Tommy is tired. There is sweat on his brow and he is breathing heavily. When he shows some crossness, going against her with words in challenging her mattress strategy, Auntie Eve places her laughing thing upon him. It is laughter that comes so strong as to leave her weak and helpless, laughter that slides her down the wall and to the floor, where she laughs and laughs, her laughter speaking for her now that such foolishness as Tall Tommy is displaying should be here upon the earth.

Momma has made a decision. Her wisdom has called her to it. She will keep my father away from me so he can focus entirely on the Christ Jesus, because his condition gets too great if he has responsibility for my life. He can only do what he can do, according to Momma. And, of course, it is a conclusion I too have come to, based on all the facts that I have gathered.

And yet it grieves my father's heart that he cannot be a part of his children as Momma is a part of us. And so he says to Momma, "Maya, I must go with my sons and Vera to Coney Island. I cannot have it be that the men of the building are with them and I am not. It is not as a man should be to walk the streets of Manhattan alone without his children, to be sitting in the Horn & Hardart Automat alone without his children, to be preaching the word of God without his children. Where are my children, Maya? Where are they, that they are vanished from my sight and go where I do not?"

My father runs toward silence. But on the Saturday that we are entrusted by Momma to my father's care, that is not so with Luke, who must be boisterous in his reckoning with the out-of-doors, casting down his top on the pavement with the hope that it will spin forever. My father sees the anarchy of Luke's way calling attention to itself, and so he lashes out, right there in front of Harry Frug's radio shop, where Harry Frug himself stands in his chunky stature, stubble dotting his double chin and a smile of craftiness filling his face. His eyes assess us behind the thick glasses, with Zenith and

Magnavox and RCA and Philco there in the store windows and the sweet smell of vinyl records in his hairy nostrils.

"Ow," Luke cries out.

"Do you want more, my son? Do you want more of my hand?" my father says, redness showing on my brother's face where he has been struck.

Harry Frug sees all this, the facets of my father's condition that the ministry and the literature of A. A. Allen cannot erase. He sees my father out on the street without a shop of his own, for what shop would have him with the temperament he is showing?

And so I say to Luke, in a voice that is mine and mine alone to hear, Oh, willful one, you who would seek to find what is not there to be had in the way of an embrace and so take the slap to the face instead as the sign of Daddy love that you are seeking, why must you be bonded to your own blindness, rather than run off into the green pastures of aloneness and there find your freedom? Can you not wed yourself to something more than our father's hand?"

Is it wrong to say my mortification is fatal that Harry Frug should see this soreness of my father reigning in the morning light right here on Broadway? What can be the significance of the event but that it again withdraws me forever from the jurisdiction of my father, and for a reason that shouts its simple essence every second that I breathe—it is simply too painful. Time would have to cease for me to bear the agonizing fear of his aggravation rising so he is made to get up. For while Luke can endure my father's blows, for me they offer only annihilation.

All of the shop owners are now standing in front of their establishments for the procession of shame we have undertaken, but my father is elsewhere with his mind. My father does not put the regard of others upon himself. He has his own drum, and its beat is a sound only he can truly hear.

We know better than to ask my father for pennies for the salted peanuts or small boxes of Chiclets gum in the vending machines attached to the station columns as we stand on the subway platform. No train is sleeping on the middle track as we arrive. There are only trains in active pursuit of their destinations. My father has prevention in mind in pinning us severely to the wall with his arms extended as the local roars in so no sly accident resulting in death can occur.

Because he has a handkerchief that he wets with his saliva, he can administer to Luke's injured face, dabbing at Luke's cheeks and brow in a restoration effort. Nothing good can come from him touching my face with that same rag, though as he does I commit myself to not dying from what he has put upon me, the smell of him so acutely strong in his saliva.

My father has skinny legs and arms, causing me to see where my own have come from, and his exposed flesh cannot be proud in the open air, given its whiteness and the predominance of hair, where American skin, so tanned, so hairless, sings of the sun that has been kissing it. My father's flesh speaks of its own fatigue, while his bones are protruding where visibility should not be.

Luke is adamant in his enterprise of making the water his own. He does not stand on politeness or timidity in wading forward in a straight line. No twisting as the first wave breaks against him. He dives right into its momentum, its cresting strength like the pompadour the doo-wop boys are affecting everywhere we go, with street corner harmonies the essence of their sound. And even if the wave does with him as it will, bringing his progress to a halt, the ocean can only check him temporarily, for there he is raising and lowering first one arm and then the other while holding his face steady below the surface in a statement of his intimacy with the depths he is seeking. He is simply powerful in his assertion of where he must go. I have no vision by which to see but through the lens of fear as to where his action is leading as he moves out beyond the breakers.

Momma says Luke has the substance to go far, that he is her little man of strength, but I wish he would be more than a speck upon the water so once again I could breathe. Where his ability has come from I cannot say, anymore than I can know why he has flesh I do not possess.

Behind me the Ferris wheel rotates slowly, high above the boardwalk, its passengers sitting in those little boxes. On the beach itself are sunbathers gathered under large umbrellas with their coolers and radios. Among them are two Negroes, young and male, of New York City. They have come to where the water meets the shore, and put down towels far back on sand that stands little chance of getting wet. But the men of the pompadours won't let them be. They have an aggression pact with their own minds. Nothing could ever be as satisfying to them as the deaths they now are seeking with fists incited to the striking point, for they fear the presence of the Negroes positioned on the beach, how they have it in their plan to multiply and multiply and make the white man nothing but a small and insignificant part of the world of darkest blackness still to come.

I see the Negroes rise from off their towels. I hear them speak in the outraged tones they summon. I hear the rush of fury in their words and the high alert their systems now are on in meeting the eradicating impulse of the whiteness delegation head on. But they are two and the whites are many. When the war comes where peace had been, when I hear the thwack thwack of fists on flesh and see the Negroes returned to the hot sands by the blows that they receive and the whites raise metal garbage cans to wreak devastation upon their fallen victims' skulls, I must retreat to the water's edge that the flames of violence not burn my flesh a thousand times more than the sun is doing. The violence is in me and around me. It is in the sands now speaking and the molecules of air that maintain their unseen power. It is in Luke who has vanished over the horizon and in my father, now the peacemaker, lurching in protest toward all that he is witnessing. My father tries. He so very much tries to halt the merciless men, for his own sense of justice has been aroused.

The white men of the pompadours do not take the pleasure they derive from their fists to my father's face. They do not break his nose or split his skull. Nor do they hear him as he screams that they must be arrested for such a crime and as he calls out for an ambulance to be on its way so that the pummeled and bludgeoned and prone Negroes can be rescued from the course of perishing that they are on. The white men of aggression flee into the crowd that has made them their own. They are the vanguard of freedom, the crowd shouts. They are patriots of the old and current order that now is threatened. They are fists upon the flesh of the anarchy they fear is coming to throw garbage on the streets, to break the windows of their orderly homes, to steal their wives and rape their children and molest the very air they breathe with the maddening dedication of these Negroes to the moments that they breathe.

I see, under the scorching sun, the two Negroes of New York City bleeding into the indifferent sand. I see no one to comfort them but my father. I hear the ambulance of mercy screaming in the distance, but all I really see and hear is the fury of America set on perpetrating annihilation as Vera and I tremble at the water's edge waiting for Luke to make himself bigger than the speck he presently is.

Momma says it filled my father's heart with such joy and love to be with us that he would again like to take us to Coney Island.

"I can't," I say to Momma.

"You can't? Why can't you?"

"Because Momma, I can't."

"Your father will be very hurt."

"Momma, the day is waiting for me. It has open spaces. There is light in every corner of the street. Do you want me not to breathe?"

"Do what you must, my son."

There is a stoop next door with a wall I can peer over as I wait for my father to emerge with Luke and Vera. I can be near my father but away from him, as I can be near the trains but far from them as they move through the tunnel under the park. The building is of brownstone and full of mystery. It has apartments I have not seen, where people lie in their beds in seclusion from Broadway. It has a fat man who rides a white motorcycle and who bellows arias in the night. And it has an old Negro superintendent, Otis, who smokes a cigar and says to me, in his slow-talking way, "Johan, make your joyful noise." It's what Otis always says. Otis has come up from the basement, where he lives, with his scary German shepherd that looks like a wolf. "Say," Otis says, "Is that your father and your brother and sister coming out of your building?"

"Yes," I say.

"They look like they going someplace and you look like you going no place."

The coal truck has arrived, and soon a load of coal makes a racket sliding down the chute into the basement. And there is the old Jew with his hand cart calling up to the tenants on the block, "I buy old gold."

The playground in the park has jungle Jim bars and swings, a slide, and a seesaw. Metallic hardness is everywhere. Outside the fence sits a man. A smile shows on his pale face. "How's your dickie today?" His words send me flying away. But those same words own me. As far as I have run, I am pulled back, back toward Dickie Man. Dickie Man will take me into the railroad tunnel. Dickie Man will take me into the bushes. But Dickie Man has gone. Bad, Johan, bad, that you ran from Dickie Man when you could have stayed.

Momma says we must go where the fresh air can be found. She says the country awaits us in all its green glory so our days can be normal. A man named Phil sweeps Vera Severa and me into his waiting car. He drives us on highways I have never seen with the window rolled down and his arm upright in the frame. From daylight into darkness does he drive, and now the stars are high above. In front of a house does he deposit us. A woman who says her name is Helen stands with her two daughters, one chunky and the other with the word "beauty" stamped on her forehead. We are led to a room upstairs with a skylight that allows the stars to keep an eye on us.

When I wake in the morning the bed is wet. I flee from her anger down the carpeted stairs. A fruit bowl with apples is on the table and beyond the door stands a bicycle without fenders. Its orange frame and balloon tires beckon. Around and around the circular dirt road I go.

When nightfall comes Phil and Helen play poker with some guests. They see each other and raise each other and ante up as chips of different colors fly. One player is holding his cards close to his vest and showing a poker face, someone says. Wine and cigarette smoke and loud laughter are everywhere.

Helen has outfitted my bed with a rubber sheet. "Try to hold it in," she says. The girls lie to either side of my bed, and Vera Severa farther away. Downstairs the noise continues long into the night. The grownups have intensified their pleasure in the worldliness they have found far from the tabernacle of wrath. I cannot contemplate a fire everlasting when I am in their midst. I must have other places to go with my mind.

Betty, the older daughter, asks me if I would like to hear a story. I am flat on my back and close to the girl smell of her freshly washed hair.

"Tell me about the trains. Do you have any? Do they come near? How far must I go to get to them?" The laughter from below tears through the floor and ceiling and into the sky.

"Paula and I were walking by the railroad tracks…"

'Wait, wait. Walking where?'

"Near here. Now let me go on. We were down there by the tracks when the train came along."

"Was it a freight train or a passenger train."

"It was a very long freight train and made a lot of noise. The train finally passes us, and then it stops all of a sudden and these men from the train, they grab us and take us into the caboose."

"What?"

"What do you mean, 'What? That's just what they do."

I sit up. "But what happens? What happens?" If Betty sees that I am desperate for an answer, she still says it is for another night to know, and Paula— what kind of cold, cold name is that?—says, "I want to go to sleep. I'm tired." What reason can they have for not being alert to the injustice that has taken place? Does no one see the danger they are in, with every passing second the motion of the train taking them farther from their family? Who can find them now that they have gone so far away and farther and farther still with every passing second? Who will bring them back to the love that they have now lost?

Phil and Helen remain alive. There has been as yet no fire as punishment for their worldly ways. Phil takes the wheel so we can go to a state park and watch the fireworks shower the sky on the Fourth of July. Phil drives with his sleeves rolled up on his biceps and his left arm in the open window. "Women drivers," Phil says. There is scorn and dismissal in his voice. He is standing on a statement that requires you to fall in line behind him.

Massachusetts is a space that has not been filled. There are no tall buildings abounding. There are just people standing in a big field watching the sky light up with giant roman candles and showers of blessings and streaking meteors with their own explosive patterns. The fireworks come singly and as a bombardment of falling colors in the sky. They open with a thud in the air and the people go "ooh" in gasps of appreciation. The Fourth of July is red, white, and blue. It is people in the park in the dark.

Phil backs the car out, then goes into forward motion on all the roads he is privileged to drive. I am lost but Phil is found. He has contacted a doughnut shop to stay open for us. It hangs there in the night, with nothing else around, and operates in a silver light.

A chocolate doughnut is delivered. Never has there been a doughnut such as this, glazed and golden and topped with a thin layer of chocolate. Oh, to surrender to such a doughnut in a car full of people in the dark of Massachusetts, to devour it to the point it cannot be seen, and to then be told there is no more, my mind committing to memory this aborting of my joy.

All that summer are Betty and Paula unrelenting in the nighttime tale of what their railroad abduction has come to mean, that they should be the captives of the men of the caboose and taken far from those they love. The ache I feel for their removal follows me into sleep. In the morning, when the sun kisses the earth, the fender-less bike ensures my happiness. Every day now a gray-haired woman with a long face strolls out of the bushes to offer me iced coffee, a treat I take to, that I should have for my mouth something other than soda and water.

A dump truck laden with steaming asphalt idles at an intersection. The smell causes delirium. The work crew are out there in jeans and boots. When cars come, they listen to the traffic cones and go around them. A steamroller ensures that everything is on the level. The men are on the ground. Light and strength are everywhere. America is taking care of its business, wherever America is to be found.

Later there is a farm. Chickens everywhere, busy with their erratic struts. The smell of chicken doo is also everywhere. A man holding an ax rushes out of a rundown house and grabs a bird by the neck and places it on the chopping block. The headless chicken does a crazy walk before keeling over into oblivion. A tractor takes off into a plowed field to show that life goes on. Tomatoes growing fat on a vine and furrowed fields. Elsewhere cornstalks have grown to a height providing green cover for my disappearing self.

Whoever made this bike had my heart in mind that it should be so substantial. With wheels in motion I defy the earth to pull me to it. I shout that I can stay erect in all kinds of weather, and after nailing my fear to the nearest tree ride without hands around the sharp curve. When I see the car approaching it is too late to move my hands to the grips so another direction can be taken. Into the ditch that awaits me I fly.

The car that drove me from my path has the recognizable feature of Phil with his left arm out the window. In the front seat beside him my sister Hannah has shown her face and now she climbs from the car to show her totality, standing over me with Phil as I lie in the ditch.

"He was showing off," Hannah says. "That's all he ever does, the little brat, is try to show off. And now look at him. Hah hah hah."

The lake of shame is wide and deep and lacks any shore to stand on. Show off. Those two words obliterate my function on this earth, paralyze me in my resolve to be number 1 for Momma and for all time in her eye. I am stripped naked. I am reduced.

When I enter the house, Hannah meets me with a smile of pleasure at my disgrace. It is a smile wickedly triumphant and just for me. I receive it as the barrier she has meant to erect, blocking me from all good feeling, and tell her to go to hell though she hasn't spoken.

"What did you say?" Though her voice is full of rage, I can only go where I have been in saying the same thing again so I can live in the opposition that is required. Hannah smacks with her fat tongue clamped between thick lips. Even as I try to cover up, her hand finds my face and so I curse her again as if to assert I will never die. Hannah has a hand that is born to hit flesh. "You're not home now. You don't have your mother to protect you," she screams.

From the bowl on the table I grab an apple and throw it hard at her head. Then I throw another one and another one. I will kill her into death. I will drive her down where only the dead can go.

"You," Phil says, grabbing me hard by the shirt collar. He has the face of a man, hard and betraying in all its features. "You throw another thing in this house and you'll really catch it. Do you hear me?" He has a finger in my face to show his striking force. "I said, do you hear me?" But I am stuck on my silence that they should do what they want with me and so I lie down on the floor where I can find my resting place.

There is a car ride around the bend where the bicycle used to go. Betty by now has confessed that the men of the railroad did not abduct her or her sister. I am astonished at the world she has taken away with her admission, and how she could so easily discard it when it meant life itself to me. A bumblebee flies in the window and stings me on the finger. Its relationship to me is so personal that it forsakes its very own life. There it lies on the floor, black and yellow and no more.

Naomi has grown big in her belly and Chuck's voice is a constant quarrel. People in his very department at Columbia University do not see fit to confer on him the respect he deserves. Instead they show envy and jealousy and maliciousness with their every word in their purpose of bringing down his greatness. Chuck's eyes are cunning with their own willfulness and his selfishness is insatiable, Momma says. And yet does he show his face to the world with his wound gaping so all can bow down to him in his time of trial and tribulation.

When the baby comes, I stare down at her, laid out on her back on the living room sofa. Her beaming face. Her chubby legs.

"Aren't you happy to see your little niece, Jeanne, and to be an uncle?" Naomi says. Her big belly is gone now.

"Yes," I say.

"My husband is a real man. Real men give their wives the gift of motherhood. Are you going to be a real man, Johan?"

"Sure," I say.

"You're going to be a he-man, like my husband, Chuck?"

"Sure. Sure I will."

"You're a funny little Svenska pojka, Svenska pojka," my sister says.

I don't want to stay with the baby. I don't want her here and I don't want her in room 9C3 with Chuck and Naomi. I don't want her anywhere here on this earth where there is not order.

Luigi has not gone away. He has not been rescued from my life. When Luke and I go to him, he says, "No mess around with-a that-a chair, you sum-ona-bitcha bums," pointing to an armchair that he has newly upholstered with a white fabric. I sit in the armchair anyway, as if Luigi's words mean nothing, causing him to chase me out of his workshop. In his hand he holds a frying pan. He brings it down hard on my head, driving me to the cement floor.

"Sum-ona-bitch, I tell-a you no sit-a in the chair. Wassa matta? You-a sick in the head-a?"

If I lie still Luigi may not hit me anymore. And now the elevator door has opened, and I hear my sister Naomi's voice far above. "What is going on here? What have you done to my little brother?"

"What he do to me, lady? Thass-a the question."

"Don't you ever raise a hand to him again. Do you hear me?"

My sister Naomi having words with Luigi on my behalf. I do not understand. I do not. My heart doesn't know where to go with her.

The little park has a bronze water trough used by horses before the cars came and had their way, and benches where old people sit and toss bread crumbs to the cooing pigeons. It is a summer evening and I am sitting alone when I see my father in a suit and tie pass by under a stand of plane trees. A smile of deep contentment has come over his face. He moves along as if in a dream that sets him apart from his surroundings. Many times has Momma told me that my father is a walking man and that it is nothing for him to return home on foot from the midtown restaurant where he works. Though he is my father, it could have consequences if he turned and saw me as well. The sight of him outside the apartment is enough to startle. What does so even more is the long, thick cigar he puts to his mouth. I feel I am seeing what I am not supposed to see, and having seen it, I am in turmoil.

Mr. Worrell has come to us from the cold of Canada. He is big and powerful and silent, and sees the world through thick glasses. He sleeps in his overcoat and causes his roommate to flee for his life on the threat of death. Week after week the fire alarm sounds, causing the building to vibrate with terror. Tenants flee a compartment that has filled with black smoke and mill on the landing as the wail of fire trucks draws near. Soon firemen enter the smoke-filled compartment with their axes and hooks to confront the insatiable flames that would, unchecked, lick and incinerate and purify without end. Fires on seven, eleven, nine, and now room 6B3 has been hit, a pile of rags ignited against the door of Miss Helen Houlihan, her surname heavy with her Irish heritage. She it is, plump Miss Houlihan, whom the hook and ladder men coax from the ledge down their metal steps of mercy. A rumor spreads. The fire is Mr. Worrell's fury, his remorseless revenge, for Miss Houlihan saying no to his love fire.

Where are you, Mr. Worrell? Why do you not tell me what it is to be indifferent to this structure you would burn so casually? How is it I cannot breathe owing to the excitement you have brought? What is it that you inhabit my dreams, standing on the parapet on the darkest of nights as we stare up at you from Broadway below?

Momma has me descend into the basement. "You, on your long legs, run and turn on the boiler, so we will not have this cold in our bones." So Momma says. I mustn't tell Momma that the errand terrifies me, as she will only tell me to go on. The elevator takes me down and down again. Because it is Sunday the laundry machines are at rest and Luigi has locked his shop. Only the commotion of the circuit breakers in the elevator room can be heard and in passing I jump at the sudden flash of electrical blue. There is violence in that complicated room and any moment a rat will appear and freeze me in place. Lurking too is Mr. Worrell. Any second he will also materialize now that the switch has been thrown and the boiler has roared to life. I sit on the steps leading down to the massive cylinder and wait for him.

"I am here for you, Mr. Worrell. I am here to see your face of evil. Show it to me, and show it to me now," I say. And then I say it and say it and say it again. Louder and louder do I say it to bring the confrontation to life. My nerves are not of steel. The sound of the boiler is the sound of a fiery ocean. It is a roaring and a rushing in my ears. My words become a kind of chant.

A small semicircular door is only ten feet away. I have only to open the latch and I am in the alleyway and available for my own freedom. But it may go harder on me if I try to escape. Such action will reveal my true intention of abandoning Mr. Worrell, who has enough fire in him to melt all the snow in Canada.

A hand is now on my shoulder. It is only Luke. Momma has sent him to fetch me.Even as we return does the fire alarm sound. Momma, it is too late. Turn back the wailing fire trucks. Turn them back now. Do not allow false hope to have its day.The flames of iniquity have arrived, and here we must abide, on the street with ashes all around, I shout, but neither she nor anyone can hear.

When the firemen arrive once again in their giant hats and fire-retardant coats, I call them the men of strength that they are. They smash down doors, they break the window glass so it can never stand again, they disappear the smoke. I tell them I was afraid they would be too late, and am afraid now that they are leaving at all that can happen again, so monstrous and insistent are the ways of Mr. Worrell. "Fire is his truth. He will allow nothing to stand in its way," I say, before Momma shushes me. The firemen possess the camaraderie of men. I stare and stare from behind where Momma stands.

Mr. Worrell's glasses need cleaning, his face is unshaven, and his hair has been whipped by a wild wind. He alters his gait for no one; his studied slowness is a song of praise for methodical endeavor. The firemen and fire marshals assembled do not cow him.

"Mr. Worrell, I will follow you to the ends of the earth. To the very ends," I vow silently. He turns and stares, seeing right through Momma to me. And when he has annihilated—yes, annihilated—every living thing with the power of his mind, he walks on by, with no regard for the manmade prison of gossip, speculation, and outright backstabbing that the tongue needs only the prompting of a malicious or misguided heart to perform.

Oh are the fire alarms made to sound. Oh are tenants fled from their lonely rooms in unspoken gratitude for the sense of community his ongoing menace brings. And oh are the forces of goodness brought to bear in trying to halt his demon ways. I kiss Mr. Worrell. I hug him. I sing his numbing terror in the heart of me.

A fire in 11D2. A scorching blaze in 3C3. Smoke to obscure the heavens pouring from 5A3. How much can any one take before the driven man is led away?

Momma doesn't tell me how Mr. Worrell was made to disappear so the wounds to the building could heal. She does not tell me if he vanished in the darkness of the night or in the bright light of day. But this she will say, with conviction in her sound: "This is but one tree. There will come a time when the entire forest is ablaze, forever and ever."

The night calls to me. I hear its distinctive voice, saying there is life I must have beyond the walls of the untidy apartment. It directs me to the subway. Go to it now, it says, and find a men's room where, at a urinal, I can stand with my sneakered feet on the wet cement floor stinking of pee and disinfectant among the men who likewise position themselves. Go with your longing and be with these men who dawdle endlessly, stroking their big hard things, the voice says, making urgency my master.

Columbus Circle. Times Square. Fourteenth Street. I look for my love where I am led.

Oh, adventure. Oh, life. Is it the same voice that compels me to plead with Momma for money for a grandstand ticket at Yankee Stadium? The vision of green grass and the dirt infield turned a rich brown by the hosing of the groundskeepers and of men in pinstriped uniforms is too much to resist. A life beyond my own is calling me, and Momma says yes to my pleading, and so I bound for the subway to Ninety-sixth Street, where I catch an uptown train through Harlem to One Hundred Forty-ninth Street, and soon I am on a third train that sheds its hiding place for the elevated tracks that bring us in view of the cream-colored walls of the stadium and a patch of outfield grass, and now I am in another world. I am in life, the life beyond the tabernacle walls.

But now I am not alone. I am once more with my father walking through the Times Square station to catch the train to Astoria, Queens. He holds my hand in his as we push through the rush hour throng. He has left Jack Dempsey's restaurant to be with me and I with him in a connection that Momma has arranged. Because Momma has spoken. "You must not deny your father anymore and break his heart. It would mean the world to him if you would go and hear him preach," Momma says, asking me to cancel the freedom of my own life.

The Mad Bomber has been here. He lives in the hearts of millions. He places ticky ticky boom boom where people are known to go, so their legs can be blown from their bodies and they can grieve for what was never theirs forever in the first place, the crazy man says. There are juvenile delinquents wandering about, offering oily hair and stiletto knives and menacing tongues. They are dark jewels in the underground labyrinth.

My father lets me talk within the confines of my own mind. He does not impose internal silence upon me. My father is the Mad Bomber. He is explosive wherever he may go, and I am the only containment policy he will ever know.

Astoria has blocks that go on without end and rows of small buildings. Astoria lets you see the sky. The air is soft and hungry for life. Possibilities for pleasure are intact in each blade of grass. It is spring. The monotony of concrete is not a lifelong threat but a peculiar adventure in the weakening light of day. Happiness and surpassing joy live in the coffee shops of this section of town.

We come to a private home, where my father takes me into a garage cleared of cars so folding chairs can be set out in the vacated space. Women bring coffee and water from the house next door so the men who have gathered may drink. A podium is wheeled in on a dolly and a picture of the Christ Jesus is tacked to the wall.

Though my father has a voice, it is muted so only the frantic movement of his arms can truly speak. Mortification pours in upon me from the ends of the earth that my father should be so afflicted among the brethren, the men of substance with thick necks. My shame is that they are enduring my father, that he is not part of them. He stands alone before them and he is weeping. He cannot stop himself. I hear the words "My dear wife" and "who has been so good to me."

From the back of the room I stand and sing the Robert Hall clothing store jingle loud and clear and true, as if my voice is carrying American candy to the deprived of the earth. I sing of values going up, up, up and prices going down, down, down. I sing so my father will be seen more fully in the glory of his Robert Hall suit that covers so many of his Armenian bones and allows him to feel spectacular on the earth. I sing standing on a chair so it will be known that I am the Almighty.

There is pandemonium in the courthouse that the garage has now become. The men roll up their sleeves and lay their hands upon my head that the power of the Christ Jesus may flow through them and elevate me to a place I have never been. How they shudder. How they beseech.

I run through the streets of Astoria, Queens, past the Greeks staring out from their quiet coffee shops and into the subway station and mock the turnstile and its impediment purpose with a single leap. I mock the token booth operator in his stationary vigil. I mock the trains that think they are truly a part of the tunnel when they are only passing through so darkness can return. I mock my father that he should think he can place a hand on me where I have fled.

But now I am mocking no more, for I am in my bed and the fate of my nation is in the balance as my father is poised to strike. He has massed all his troops on my border and a riot of angry sound is coming from his council of war. But Momma is there to block his path with her words of reason. "Hayk, the boy is ailing. He says things he doesn't mean. I will speak with him so this doesn't happen again. You must not punish an afflicted mind." Momma talks with sweetness on her breath and softness in her soul so she can begin to effect the calming of his rage. And yet, how the walls do tremble while even the sheets on my bed petition for the right to vacate the premises rather than abide in such a potential theater of conflict.

None of this has happened. I love my father to death. To death.

"Johan, you with your long legs. Run for me to the pharmacy to fill this prescription so my night will not be sleepless," Momma says. No one wants for Momma to be sleepless. We have seen her up late at the dining table reading her Bible. We know the toll it takes on her the next day, that she should be deprived of her normal self.

On my way to the pharmacy I stop halfway there to stare into the window of the only store on the long block. Used books on shelves sleep in the dust motes of afternoon light and into the night in this store that is never open and whose name, "Harwyn Books," appears in raised gold letters against a black background on a sign for all who pass by on this residential street to see. The store stands out as a place of neglected quality where there can be rest from the noises of the world, but when I ask if I can come and sleep there too with the books so old, I hear it said my time has not yet come for living in the shadows where at that moment I long to be.

That a store like this should stand alone and make such inroads on my mind. That it should go back to another time and clearly have its life threatened by the changes that are coming. I want…I want eternity to be the golden glow that lights my life to everything around me.

On the same south side of the street, just before the squat and dark water station on the corner of Amsterdam Avenue, stands a small, narrow fire station, with firemen of strength and a triumphant red fire engine and a fire pole and a Dalmatian. And on the opposite corner stands an apartment building where the party of life is being held. It has modernity and lightness in its golden bricks and casement windows. It is a building that says the sun is shining in all weather.

Under this building stands Ridge's Pharmacy in its own solitary importance. Amsterdam Avenue runs parallel to Broadway and must not be taken lightly. Right across the street is St. Luke's Hospital and a block south is the brooding presence of St. John the Divine Cathedral. Understand where you are when you speak of this avenue.

I hand the prescription to solemn-faced Mr. Dollops, as gray as the smock he wears over his shirt and tie.

"It will be about ten minutes. Have a seat," Mr. Dollops says, looking down at me sternly through his bifocals.

Have you ever seen a Parker T-ball jotter or an Esterbrook or Sheaffer fountain pen, or smelled blue-black ink in a bottle and wanted to make it your final resting place? Have you ever wanted to bring order into your life with good penmanship? Have you ever needed accumulation before your starting point could be reached?

Behind the two chairs is a cabinet with sliding glass doors containing these pens. Mr. Dollops being alone in the store, I reach behind me as I sit and begin to inch the glass door open. In the rear I hear Mr. Dollops pecking at the keys of his typewriter in preparing the label for the prescription bottle. My hand is reaching inside the cabinet when I feel a hand grab me by the back of my shirt. Mr. Dollops has come out from behind the counter. He drags me toward the front door and tosses me out onto the sidewalk.

'Don't come back here again," I hear him say, as he tosses the crumpled prescription at me.

I walk slowly back toward Broadway. The shame is strong. I had heard a voice saying no, no, don't touch that glass door, but it was not a voice I could listen to enough to obey. And now I have given Mr. Dollops the opportunity to throw me to the sidewalk, as if I was dirt, as Momma would say, and as if he could tell, from the moment I entered his store, that I would need watching.

At the Whelan's Drugstore at One Hundred Tenth Street, there is nothing I must steal, only what I must get for Momma in this environment of bright, shadowless light. Like Mr. Dollops, Mr. Delfonico takes the prescription, and after filling the amber bottle, pecks at the typewriter keys, applying the pressure needed to bring Momma's name to life on the label.

The apartment is dark, and so I turn on the light to dispel all peril. Momma is there in the sudden brightness. "Did you think I would go away, my foolish son, when my night has to remain sleepless until you arrive?"

"No, Momma, I am here. Do not speak such words. I forbid you."

Momma snatches the bottle and from it takes a pill and swallows it with the glass of water she has poured. Momma is in her robe of white. Momma is with her hair hanging down. Momma is with her bare legs exposed in a shock once again to my senses that such affliction can be upon the flesh and turn its whiteness veiny blue and red. I have let Momma down and now she must die and I must die. But Momma doesn't die. Momma survives to emerge into the place of her own returning sweetness. In a soft voice does Momma sing. She sings a church song not of lamentation or of grief. She sings of how he walks with her and talks with her and calls her his very own. This is what Momma sings.

I would tell you that Momma rocks me into my own place of peace. I would tell you that the peace of sleep descends on me right then and there, but the apartment exists outside the bounds of order so my mind cannot be rocked to rest. I take a broom to the disorder I see all around me, as I see my father often do, so dust and dirt and garbage cannot be on the floor.

"My Svenska pojka," Momma says, when she is beyond her anger and her singing and all is sweetness once again.

But Momma is not always Momma as I would have her be, and you shouldn't think she is. Tonight she violated my sovereignty by calling me names that are not mine. "Luke, I mean Hannah, I mean Naomi, I mean Rachel, I mean…," she says, standing with spatula in hand, as the hamburger spits in the frying pan and the Birds-Eye peas and carrots boil in a pot of water. Momma must never be given the right to lose me, to make of me an interchangeable thing. "No, no, no," I say, but still do the names spill from her mouth as if I have nothing to identify me. Momma has showered me with her forgetfulness, and for this I must see the color red and withdraw to my room.

For the longest time does Momma not come knocking, a precious time in which my anger can rejoice even as my ears strain for her very sound. Oh that I can be so very wronged. Oh that I can feed the wound so my anger sings. Oh that a nation can harm itself by the starvation principle on which it rests.

Now I hear her footsteps in the hallway approaching as a neglected dog hears its master. The sound of Momma is a sound made only for me. I am sitting in the bottom bunk when she knocks upon the door. But victory is not mine should I go ahead and answer, only weakness and death.

Momma does not knock twice. She is Momma. She opens the door so her visit can begin.

"Why are you not at the table, my good son?"

Momma's fatigue is no impediment to her good cheer. But it is for me to bring her into line with the gravity of the situation by making no response.

"Do you not answer me, my son?"

A word will pull the plug on all the power I have stored. I must send Momma away with the awareness of what she has done so she will return and return and return once again and I will not have to die in the cold place she has left me.

'Why do you treat me this way, my son? What is it that ails you?"

Is there good cheer in her voice now? Are you hearing any such thing? Or are you hearing what punishment can wreak when it is properly applied? Momma must now receive the crushing defeat she deserves so her full attention can be returned to where it properly belongs.

"Leave me alone." I say those words. I can afford to say them now from the power I have developed.

Momma goes away. Do I hear her chuckle now at all the torment she has wrought? Do I?

But it is not a small thing to hurt Momma, not when I know it can be fatal. Now I am still angry but also frightened. Now can I only wait for her return. Now is it only Momma time, the time of pain before I hear her footsteps once again. Now does she come without knocking with a hamburger on Wonder bread on a plate with steaming carrots and peas. To this I must say no until Momma stands there with plate in hand and cries and cries. I have made her feel like dirt beneath my shoes the way that all her children make her feel. Now must I be made to understand what it is to be Momma with the sorrow and the grief she carries. Now must I throw away my anger and my resistance. Now must I cry too that Momma carries such a burden and, when my tears have dried, eat the food that she has brought for me in the room where for now I exist alone, living once again in sweet harmony with she who brought me here.

Luke has found a girl to be with in a building with an intercom and the shine of cleanliness on One Hundred Fourteenth Street, the same building where Edward Macy lives, but neither he nor Johnny Lacy has claimed her for their own. Her name is Kimberly, the syllables tumbling forward, and she lives on the strength of her blond hair. Her younger sister, Madge, is present in a glow of pink pajamas and I am dizzy with the thought of what she means. All I know is that their mother is also present and says they are from the South. When we leave, Momma is on the corner. There on Broadway does Momma weep over the affliction to her that we are that we are out so dangerously late and even as I am pulled into the thought of her perishing does Luke dance on the moon with the happiness he is feeling.

When I go back to the building with the intercom, it is not for Kimberly or her sister, but for Johnny Donatelli, the super's son. The apartment has a nipping Doberman and drooling boxer that come too close and a human as well as animal stench. Mr. Donatelli has takeout power in both fists and Mrs. Donatelli is hugely fat and both sit shelling and devouring a bowl of pistachios.

Johnny Donatelli wears his shirts buttoned at the top and has the proportions of a god to go with the recklessness of his life. He is wiry strong and throws me to the ground to show it. Headlocks and half-nelsons are his calling card, and satisfaction is all his to pin me. Johnny Donatelli goes to the school of the Catholics, where they hit and hit, and has a father who can hit and hit, but now he flies about in his own exuberance on the streets of New York City, calling out, "Come on, youse guys," to Jerry Jones-Nobleonian and me, and flings the dog shit of New York City upon us with the stick that he has found and laughs and laughs that he should be so fiercely free.

Arnold is also on One Hundred Fourteenth Street. It is a block that has its own hotel for Negroes. He is a boy with a face of smiling anger, his black skin pulled taut over his hard skull, and walks upon the earth with his white teeth showing in a mouth not shaped for kindness. Arnold smiles that he has no breakfast. He smiles that toothpaste is a rarity and sisters are an abundance and that space is not to be found in the single room the family has come to occupy. When he walks it is upon the particulars of his own Negro-ness in an attitude of mocking apartness, as if he is but a shadow upon a world he has no investment in. He has no play in him, as when he says, "Don't be playing with me," and shows indifference to the wind and all the elements that would seek to nourish or afflict him.

No one knows why Arnold should have the power to command Johnny Donatelli to stand to his attention with his back to him or why Johnny Donatelli would allow Arnold to jab his knuckles into his spine over and over so Johnny Donatelli has to fall slowly to the ground with no ability to get back up. No one knows why the smile of hatred should only grow in the process Arnold has initiated. All you should know is that it is there and ready for you, too, in the fear of inevitability that he spreads from his position of being a Negro person on the streets of New York City. Because Arnold has no never mind in regard to the minority that he is. He knows only the power he is so adamantly imposing.

Now when word comes to Raymond Donatelli, the older brother of Johnny Donatelli, of his fallen sibling, Raymond Donatelli has no choice but to go down the hill to the building of the Negroes and call out to them in his cold rage, and they call back to him, and the noise of war is heard all around, the street weaponry of baseball bats and flashing knives and broken bottles brought to bear by the Negroes on Raymond Donatelli that he should no more be on this earth. But Raymond Donatelli breaks the faces of the Negroes as they come and they break his and over and over is this act repeated. To the windows overlooking the street are apartment dwellers drawn to bear witness, with white people afraid for their very lives while the Negroes exult in the paradise of revenge they are seeking, as the wail of police cars is heard in the distance.

And so it is for me to know dread, a dread that enters my bones to stay for easy recall, at what it is that people can do and the physical affliction that they can cause, and fall in love with Raymond and Johnny Donatelli and all aspects of their Italian nation, while shunning the smiling face of Arnold even as it seeps into my own.

In the wilting heat of summer, the Negro boys of Harlem arrive in bicycle caravans, riding without hands and facing backward on their seats or standing on their heads on those very same seats. They come in the full measure of their furious need for expression, leaving me to acknowledge a power that is not my own that they should make merry in each moment they are living, and be spellbound by the arsenal of combative freedom that they express in reuniting with their kin in the two buildings primarily for the Negroes that have been established on my block.

Luke has put Wildroot on his hair to command how it stands on his head and walks cocky but innocent with a garrison belt buckled on the side. Once a week he goes to Ziggy Brothers, down on Ninety-ninth Street and Broadway, where color-drenched window signs scream out the sale that never ends. He buys paisley shirts and striped shirts and flips the short sleeves up to bare his biceps. Luke is my brother, bigger in his dimensions and in forward motion with the things that he must get.

"His foolishness never ends," Momma says, that Luke should not listen to her but go his own way into the world he wants. "You are my good son," Momma says to me. "You are not afraid of a little dirt. You are not afraid to wear hand-me-downs," meaning the shirts that Luke discards. Momma pulls me close to her.

Winter makes the Negro boys of New York City fewer but not none on the street where I live. When we pass two as we are turning onto Broadway, and they turn around and follow us, I cannot move, I cannot speak, in the face of the lethal instruments headed back our way. Butch and Leroy are strong in their bodies and their minds, needing no food to give them muscle nor toothpaste for their teeth to shine so white.

"Why you be calling me a nigger just now?" LeRoy says. He addresses himself solely to Luke, who does not know to move cautiously within the lines of their investigation, and answers instead with the freedom the earth has given him.

"I didn't call you anything," Luke says, sounding the aggrieved protest of the unjustly accused. Luke does not know about smallness. He does not know how to stay low to the ground when so many signals for death are waiting for him on the streets of New York City.

"You be calling my friend LeRoy a liar?" Butch says. "White boy be calling us liars?" His words have summoned anger to his face and now there is the punch and then the next, sending Luke down into the snow that turns so red from his bleeding nose. Do I do something? Do I transfix them with my stare? Do I impose a strength that is not there? Or do I live forever in the cowardice of my ways that does not allow me to come to the aid of my fallen brother? You know the answer, as my brother knows the answer. Not one finger do I raise. Not one single finger.

Nowhere is it written that a brother can keep his guilt to himself. When another Negro boy walks alone on the other side of the street, headed for the Negro hotel that will have him, do I just watch or do I make a snowball, a big soft round one, and lob it gently in his direction far enough ahead that it will surely miss and he will see the playfulness of my intention so that anger will not have to be a part of who he is with me? He picks up a thin piece of board, and with it does he come slowly, methodically, toward me, so that I can only wait to receive him, and when I would explain, does he smash me in the face with the board and send me down into the snow where Luke had been, and then does he toss the board on top of me, as if the word *play* is not a part of his speech, except to say, "Don't be playing with me. I'm not playing, not playing, not playing." And it is not then for me to ask "Why is it you are not playing?" It is not a question to ask the likes of him, whose anger is a totality bred into his very bones.

The pain is there, but it does not have the staying power of the image of him focused on his own intention with the board held at his side and the patience that he showed as if the board and my face had been ordained to meet and so haste had no necessity of being in the picture.

You might think we were destined to be in each other's life forever, and that we would meet and meet on the streets of New York City, and that finally, and in full proof of love's call, that he would cross from his side to mine or vice versa and we would declare a bond, as would Luke and his assailants, but territorial enclaves get established, parts of the city get sectioned off by the will of those who occupy them. There are those whose anger is born of their deprivation on seeing the hegemony of white faces in the land of plenty when they have none so that, even when they are on the grounds of whiteness, they seek to establish their own canceling hegemony in an act of will and courage and flaming rage in defiance of their numbers, knowing what it is to be held down and who the culprit truly is affirming their lack of worth. All this is part of what it means to live in New York City, and don't be here if you don't understand or stay until you do.

Boris Kirilov sings "Love Me Tender," as if he was Elvis with blond hair. He lives in a spacious apartment in a building that overlooks Morningside Park and close to Harlem. A women's hospital stands nearby and the Cathedral of St. John the Divine as well. Down on the street the Number 4 bus heads east along One Hundred Tenth Street past Boris's building, before turning down Fifth Avenue.

The elevator has an operator. Old and weary, he pushes the gate closed, then sits on a stool and pulls a lever. The elevator begins to rise. Floor after floor it passes to the very top, where Boris and his gray-haired father await us. Boris's father left everything behind in the Soviet Union. Now he has to stand alone in the apartment without a wife, as Boris has to stand alone without a mother. Boris's father is an artist, with only his canvases as a shield, while Boris wears his hair very long and out of keeping with crewcut America. The apartment has a Russian coldness to it. I am standing where I have never stood before.

Luke is tight with Boris and his other classmates. He can open himself to the life of the school. There is Robert Montaverdi, with the skinny neck and bulging eyes. There is Barney Blair, whose face holds its own in any circle because of England from which he came. There are so many who place Luke in their embrace that he must go back and be with them while maintaining indifference to his failing grades. And the girls. They send him through space with the affection they are showing.

Boris has a need to define himself. It is America and he knows not to be a sitting duck. Whitey. The name he gives himself goes with his white chinos and T-shirt; only his garrison belt and high-top Kids are reserved for blackness. Now, with his pompadour in place and Elvis in his head, he can take the stance his mind is calling for. "If you're looking for trouble..." he sings within earshot of a cluster of Negro boys of New York City, who have no kind regard for the whiteness of Whitey or his Elvis Presley hair or the deterrence he would create with his garrison belt buckled on the side. Like hornets do they swarm and attack, and soon his whiteness is saturated with red. Summer has become their season of vengeful wrath. They drag us from the shops where we cower and the beds where we hide. They are in all the secret passageways and the molecules of air. One must feel deeply the power that they bring and never set foot on their third rail again.

To the north there is paradise on a street called LaSalle, where Claremont Avenue meets its end past the high walls of Cherry Park. The names Serge and Bosco and Terry attach to faces with a legendary toughness far in advance of anything my block knows, except for Frenchie the Algerian. I hear street corner harmonizing, I see them smoke and spit and hear them call up for Carol to come on down to the stoop where they sit. I hear the words *Freight Kings* and of the boxcar they broke into and of merchandise they stole and how someone snitched so a baseball bat was summoned to his head as a lesson to never rat out anyone again. Increasingly I hear the fear that is now upon me that this is a block that shouts its pain and lives upon its fire escapes and washes its cobblestone streets with blood and that Luke and I have strayed too far.

Elvis Presley is not white or Negro with his pursed lips and shaking legs and mountain of black hair. Elvis Presley belongs to his own nation, existing outside of school and every structure but his own. Elvis Presley sings "Be Bop a Loola" and the word has vibrational power out of the echo chamber from which it comes, sending shivers of longing and excitement through every part of who you are. Elvis Presley sings "Love Me Tender" and you have to go down into the valley where he has plunged you in bondage to his song.

Now when Luke walks the street his hair is held in place by Wildroot. The white cream has a smell all its own and affirms his Elvis Presley worth.

When I have not been to the barber for too long, Momma says again that I have hair that belongs on a girl. "My Svenska pojka," she says with a laugh in her voice that means I am not Luke, who is strong in all his features. Momma says I am to maintain the appearance of American-ness and that curly hair on a boy is a violation of what America stands for and must be straightened now.

The bathroom has a door that locks and sour-smelling towels and a bottle of Wildroot that promises victory over kinks. I apply a gob to my hair and work it in with my fingers so I can have the even application of its power. If a little is good, more is better. Soon my head is gooey and glistening, but I am not Luke with his wavy pompadour. My head is an oil slick with streaks of whiteness.

Luke laughs in triumph that I try and fail to be like him, but Momma comes to my aid and claims me for her own. "You leave my little Svenska pojka alone. He is my very own," Momma says.

Sammy Rawson's handsome face and straight brown hair parted neatly on the side and his American name qualify him for Johnny Lacy and Edward Macy, but instead he has come to me in the fifth grade with his lonely boy look. Sammy Rawson has heard from Johnny Lacy and Edward Macy that I try to steal pens from the neighborhood stores and says he wants to do some stealing, too.

The Columbia University bookstore is on One Hundred Fifteenth Street and Broadway, just south of the mall. There are pens in glass cases, shelves stacked with stationery and notebooks, and book covers for all the Ivy League colleges. And there is another such bookstore belonging to Teacher's College at One Hundred Twentieth Street and Amsterdam Avenue. But there are too many watchful eyes to steal anything from either store, and so Tommy takes me to his home, a suite of rooms in Butler Hall, a university-owned residence near Morningside Park. He has a silver-haired grandmother who sits in an upholstered chair sipping tea and parents who are not to be found. He has been living with her for a year, he says. Some kind of sadness sits in the room with us that Sammy should be alone with his grandmother like this. Sammy says as much with his eyes before I leave.

Because it is another summer, Momma says enough is enough. Luke and I must not abide the heat and bad air of New York City for another moment but ride north into the country where the air can have a chance to be normal. Momma packs old suitcases with our clothes and hails a taxi and makes it her own, as there is no time for the subways of New York City on this day. Momma tells the driver there must be no foolishness and to hurry us to Grand Central Station. The driver is happy to do what he can for Momma.

Momma accompanies us onto the train but steps off before it goes into motion. We leave her nothing but the train's vanishing red lights as she stands on the platform watching it slide into the darkness of the tunnel, because a train is not for staying still for-ever. And it is not for staying in a tunnel forever either. When we break free of darkness and light is on the day, America is not so suddenly and so very loudly singing. In row after row of dilapidated buildings, men and women fix our metal caravan with unsmiling stares while remaining faithful to the motionlessness of their own existence, prisoners of heat and dirt and unruly streets. Saying to us, go on your railroad trains to where the trees and babbling brooks await you, but you have seen us and we have seen you and payback is coming. The streets of dirt and commotion fall away and green growth in increasingly seen and houses privately owned are soon featured in the landscape to the rhythm of the steel wheels, with Momma's face on everything.

A ramp leads us to a big room with a Ping Pong table, natural light coming in through its one window. Beyond this big room is a small room in which we are allowed to stay in an endless narrow corridor.

The morning starts with dew on the grass and on the windshields and bodies of the cars. From somewhere come the piercing bugle blasts of reveille. The flag is raised and the pledge of allegiance is said. We are in New York State, but I don't know where. Something called Pine Acres, and without a railroad track in sight.

A room looks down from the main house to the curving drive-way. The room has a screened window. Stan Musial has hit a home run over the right field wall at Ebbets Field. Someone says it was on the TV. A light of life comes into me, and with it a terrible ache. I am not in Brooklyn. I am not in the room. I am under the sun in an afternoon without end. Someday I will get to that room where Brooklyn and the world are being seen.

Somewhere there is a paved road. A car drives along it. Someone shouts out "Buick." "Chrysler," another one says, as the cars pass. But there is no violence, none whatsoever. The road has a shoulder we can walk along. No cars need to hit us where we are. The Buick and the Chrysler are far away even when they are near. The crunch of gravel is deafening. That gravel is ours for taking, should we wish to.

In a big meadow are we told to play badminton. The birdie sings when we hit it with our rackets.

A boy named Derwood has arrived. He is chunky in his body and has big teeth. He is neither black nor white but something in between, like Jerry Jones-Nobleonian without the spots. A girl named Delray plays with Derwood all day long. "I'm going to make a man of him," she says. They too are in the corridor, in a room I do not visit.

Joe is a part of the camp and in his teenage years. He is big in his body and says he has the features of the Lord Jesus. He is a counselor for those with rooms in the corridor. From somewhere his two much younger brothers have appeared. I don't know anything but to stay away from them, as there is a barrier of painful coldness between us. And yet Joe takes me into his warmth, putting his arm around my shoulders by the Ping Pong table and walking with me into the corridor.

"You don't like my brothers, do you?"

"No," I say, and now his brothers step like wolves from behind the door, free to do the violence to my person that Joe's Judas move has invited. They knock me to the ground. They beat and kick me for the crime I have committed and run away laughing at their victory.

Then Joe wedges a chair between our door and the opposite wall in the corridor so we cannot leave our room. And the heavy screen over our window keeps us sealed in.

When it comes that we can loosen the position of the chair against our door and secure our freedom, then do we go forth and hit and hit Joe and his brothers and bring them down.

This is a lie. Completely. We hit no one but each other. It is Luke's mouth. In opening and closing it he makes a sound that is wet to my ears and seeks to annoy me. And so I hit and hit and hit until he pins me to floor.

Oh Momma, why do you send us where you are not?

Johnny Andrews is waiting for us outside his building, next door to Langley Farmer's house of order. He lives on the second floor in an apartment above a portico and has trains we have not seen. They run all over his spacious room on the Lionel O gauge track we cannot summon to our life. He has the Santa Fe and New York Central and the Illinois Central and the Wabash Line. He has the Rock Island Line and the very green Southern and his heart is broken open by the pantograph behemoth of the Pennsylvania Railroad.

Johnny Andrews is Negro and wears the khaki slacks and Oxford shirts and penny loafers I see on Johnny Lacy and Edward Macy. When we ride with Johnny Andrews, we ride and ride and then ride and ride some more through a tunnel that allows for shafts of holy afternoon light. We ride in the reckless rampaging way a subway should, on straightaways and curves that bring on the screeching of its wheels, the train now in the groove with its own commotion, extending us beyond Pennsylvania Station and the tabernacle for Christ Jesus. Johnny Andrews saying, Depth? I will show you depth. I will show you the distance you need to go should you ever wish to be with me.

Ebbets Field has a curving face full of windows and Negro boys showing no fear of heights as they scale a wire fence. Anarchy is afoot that Brooklyn minds have conjured. Where the tickets lead is to an outfield view that brings no sense to where we are. A fly ball is hit and yet the catcher runs under it in an erratic circle with his mask far-flung. Roy Campanella applies his squat power to a pitch and breaks the seat right next to me with his home run swing. Paper blows in the wind and the bases are tilted on a field that is not level with the earth. The New York Giants have come to Brooklyn and mean business with the squad they have; that Foster Castleman should have such a name and show such harmony with the ground balls that come to his glove.

Don Newcombe's uniform is a pure white with powder blue and a burning number 27 on his broad back. Newk throws hard. He throws fast. He throws from over the top and has a windup all his own. In a snap the ball is featured in the catcher's mitt. Gil Hodges crouches on the rich brown dirt so he can be ready with his first baseman's glove and Jackie Robinson is on fire. The National League means something old but new and apart from anything the American League can be. Yankee Stadium is Ballantine ale and Mel Allen and white men with hot dogs in their mouths. The National League is old newspapers blowing across the outfield grass and billboards that catch the eye. It is a ballpark with the forlornness of a city at desolation twilight coming alive in the electric combination of grass and steel. I only know that we are high up and Brooklyn is all around.

Johnny Andrews has raccoon eyes. There are circles of darkness around their brilliant whiteness. He is not a tormented Negro. He does not live in the unending anger of those in the hotel down the block and claims no allegiance to the warrior kingdom they represent on the streets they walk: no fist-balled ditty bop shuffle, no conk over pomaded hair or death-defying colored shirts or pants with toreador tightness. He has not taken to their sound or their in-the-moment mode. Johnny Andrews and Luke display their mechanical minds upon the Hallicrafters shortwave radio. I can only admire the radio, a gray metal box with a glass window that houses an active brain.

If Johnny Andrews has sorrow in his life, it is not because of his mother, who offers him acclaim, or his grandfather, who walks with the age that he has come to.

The three live together in an apartment to which we are not invited. About his father there is nothing to report. He does not broadcast from Hamburg, Germany, or any other outpost on the shortwave radio, and shouts no hellos in the subway tunnels through which we ride. We only know that he is not here upon the ground that Johnny Andrews walks.

Claremont Avenue runs parallel with Broadway and has quality upon the complicated faces of the buildings that run along its west side. The buildings of Barnard College stand on the east side of the avenue from its southern tip to One Hundred Twenty-second Street, where the gothic buildings of the Union Theological Seminary rise. Chock Full O' Nuts on One Hundred Sixteenth Street and Broadway stands as a cheerful gateway to this avenue of Ivy League success.

White boys with genius faces emerge from the well-maintained buildings of Claremont Avenue in khaki pants and Oxford shirts and penny loafers worn without a hint of socks to greet Johnny Andrews while the wood-paneled station wagons of their fathers stand at rest in their parking spaces. Against the wall of a Barnard building with wire screens on the windows of its cafeteria they play handball. A Spaldeen is a thing of magic in the hand of Johnny Andrews. Time and again he cuts it low and close to the line in retaliation for the nerve they show in sending it his way.

How Johnny Andrews knows such boys, who have order at their core, is not a mystery, as he has excellence to match or surpass their own in the quality of his mind and his handsome face and athletic body. Now is he, so rich in blackness, yet part of the landscape of their white boy minds, a fact for them to marvel on.

The school is good to me. It lets me read out loud First Corinthians, Chapter 13, *When I was a child I spake as a child,* in the small chapel during the morning service. In my ears are Momma's strong if whispered words: "Do not let them take you away from Jesus. Do not let them obscure the great fact that he is the way, the truth, and the light and in so doing plunge you into worldliness." Momma saying I must persevere with her faith, that the power of their God is but a pale approximation of what He can do in the omnipotence of His unbounded ways.

In spring the silver and green Campus Coach line buses roll up in front of the school for our picnic day in Tibbetts Brook Park, in faraway Yonkers. There are forays into the hills, and franks and marshmallows speared on sticks for roasting on the open fires. Nuns in black are seen among the tall trees and in the meadow. My senses report the smell of waxed paper, the victor of the one-legged race, and the thud of the bat as it connects with a softball lob. The air is everywhere and I am in it.

Deborah Baird has beauty different from the sunlight of Alison Pauley's blond hair. Her hair is brown and refuses to exceed the length of her neckline. Internal currents are alive and visible in her serious face. Her mind accompanies her wherever she goes, and always she is alone, as if she has need of privacy for her thoughts. Johnny Lacy and Edward Macy have found no way to claim her for their own; she exists as a solitary star in her own universe. And yet her beauty is undeniable, a magnet for all who would occupy her space. Even the freckles on her nose summon delirium.

But Deborah will not retreat if you approach her. In Riverside Park, where she has gone to walk her dog, I say to her, "Is your dog a he or a she?" She lifts her terrier by its forelegs. "You tell me," she replies, the dog's penis on full display. And so does she defeat me, transforming my question and the connection motive behind it into a hellish bomb of shame that shuts me down completely, making anything more than a weak smile and quick departure impossible.

Alan Banner is new to the class. He has hair that stands at attention and some notion that Deborah Baird has a liking for him. He says we should go calling on her at her home so he can feel her up. *Feel her up.* Those words sound wrong in my ears. Deborah Baird lives in the same building as Edward Macy, but is no more part of his world than she is in the domain of Johnny Donatelli, the super's son, so when Alan Banner and I come calling, she is there to receive us on her own and with no flock of friends in sight. Deborah Baird, having forthrightness in her bones, opens the door wide and allows us in, saying with her action that she may be private but that does not mean she has anything to hide if we come knocking. She has showed me her dog's penis and now she shows us her apartment. Her mother is out working, she says to Alan Banner when he asks, and no, her father does not live with her. When it happens I cannot say, because it is all delirium in my mind, but Alan Banner does just what he said he would, causing her to scream in anger. In a hurry is Alan Banner out the door and gone the next week, disposed of by the Reverend Mother.

The books are my own. The school says that this is so. But they are a burden on my sight, a reminder of everything I failed to do. They must not sit in my summer of freedom. They must be removed from sight so they may never again be seen and I can have my new beginning in the air of summer.

The mimeographed reading list contains in blue ink the books a child should read to end the idleness of his mind and spark his wonder about worlds unseen. So Sister Mary Christabel says. They are books with titles like *The Count of Monte Cristo* and *Treasure Island,* full of harbor lights and island mysteries and men in iron masks with strong intentions. They are designed to forge in you a connection with foreign lands and centuries not your own. They are places for children to go when they cannot be with themselves, when the agitation of their own feet, the climbing, the alleyway exploring, the dogs in full-throated barking are not enough. But that time has not come. I do not need their weight upon me when I have green grass of the park to lie in and alleyways to explore and the trains are running all the time and wild scallions can be pulled from the soil in the carefreeness of summer.

An older sister is upon the earth to go here and then go there. Naomi, like Hannah, is mostly in the vicinity of the building, where she can be sustained by those who are supposed to love her. And yet the single room she shares with Chuck and Jeanne, their little girl, has no air she can breathe that does not smell as stale as her life. She reaches for her happy pills while Chuck drinks endless amounts of wine. Day and night are his sliver lips around the mouth of green pint bottles in seeking what peace he can find. Every day is Naomi taking money from Momma so she and Chuck can go to the New Moon Palace for Chinese food, for they do not cook, although they have a stove and a small refrigerator in their room. And as for Jeanne, she is more and more in the care of Momma when it comes to feeding.

"They mean Naomi no good, " Momma says.

"Who are they?" I say.

"Those who dispense these pills to the troubled and the afflicted without an ounce of love or caring, as if a pill can treat the condition that afflicts her."

"I wish they would leave. I wish they would just go away. And Hannah, too," I say.

"Have I not told you before what it is to have children that you must care for and worry about night and day? Have I not told you this, my son? And have I not told you what it is to have a condition?"

Momma and her talk, professing not to be troubled that Naomi should be so near while she herself has come so far, plunging into frigid waters and swimming the Atlantic with only the fishes of the deep singing sweet songs for company to the shores of America. But though Momma does not listen to those who find fault that her daughters are in dry dock and not upon the high seas with their own lives, yet can she be heard to cry at night that children of hers should be so failure-bound. And when I hear those cries I know I must assume the mantle of obedience and walk a straight line for her whose heart is broken daily.

"My prayer is that we will all be in heaven together. That is my prayer," Momma says, once again, and when she speaks in such a way, with only darkness around her, then I must be silent for the moment amid the anxieties of my own mind.

Harry Frug is outside his radio shop among a throng from the neighborhood clogging the sidewalk, their heads skyward in the direction of the ninth floor of our building, where Naomi stands on a narrow ledge in a yellow robe.

Have you seen the concrete of New York City? Have you seen its hellish firmness or witnessed its patience? Do you imagine steel and metal and all matter of our street to cushion the falling flesh of those we only want to love?

The firemen of New York City have come in their shiny red trucks and even a hook-and-ladder and the police have shown themselves as well in their black and white patrol cars with sirens wailing. Though I want to run, fear that if I move Naomi will too roots me to the spot. Her life depends on my remaining perfectly still. Now one of the police officers has appeared in the window. He is leaning out, talking with Naomi, trying to coax her inside. His hand he gently offers and she takes it. I drift away and find a stoop to sit on and hold my head tight and tighter between my hands. An ambulance has now arrived with some wailing of its own.

"It is some modern-day phenomenon, the way these doctors routinely dispense pills. I don't know how many times I have suggested to your sister that she drink a little when she is blue instead of relying on these medications, which do nothing but undermine the stability of our home life," Chuck says, drawing on his Pall Mall and flicking the ash into an empty cardboard coffee cup on the table by the armchair where he sits in the lobby. "Of course there are those who will see some kind of histrionics behind public displays of this kind and say she is committed to neither life nor dying, thus reducing this averted tragedy to a high-wire act, a stunt. They will say further that one way or another she is desperate to be seen. If she can't wow people with 'The Man Who Got Away,' then she will stand on a window ledge poised to swan dive into the pavement below. But with their little minds they will not understand her passion. Your sister is a woman who wants more than life can give her."

Momma says Naomi is being kept for observation in a psychiatric unit of St. Luke's Hospital. "The doctors will give her more of those pills. They are in love with their own minds and put ideas into her head. They tell her she is sick when she isn't. They would drive her to her death if they could," Momma says.

"Chuck says the same thing," I say.

"He is a very selfish man. The drink makes a man selfish. It infects him with foolishness and lies and leads him into darkness and death. We must grasp the life of the spirit. It is only that which turns us to the light. Are you listening, my son?"

"I'm listening, Momma," I say.

"Because you must have ears to hear if you are to be saved."

"Yes, Momma."

"Salvation is our only goal. Our *only* goal," Momma says.

Luke's classmate Jason Justly is a physical presence with the power to make you fall down dead that such beauty should stand before you. Beyond that is he athletically gifted with the ability to swing a smoking bat and sky for deadly jump shots from all spots on the court. Yet does he hold himself in an unassuming way even as the heads of the girls turn and turn.

Luke says a social connection must be made and it is not enough to stand in classrooms or on street corners with Jason Justly. We must bring him into our apartment. All the alarm bells are ringing in my head even as my brother speaks. Has he lost his mind? It is true that we have painted our room and covered the wretched wood floor with linoleum so that it has a semblance of order, but does he not see that the rest of the apartment is a project beyond our ability to complete?

Action is Luke's instruction for the day. We are to create order where none has been. In the hallway outside our room, we sort through piles of paper on a bookshelf, tossing most of them, and stand what books there are on the vertical. With soap and water do we attack the dirt stains on the living room wall where our heads have been as we sit on the sofa bed and scour the oilskin cloth that covers the dining room table. A day we put aside for this effort.

Still is it like nothing the world has ever seen to have Jason Justly at our apartment for a sleep-over. It is not for me to close my eyes all night. My father feeds him the bones of deceased Armenians. Momma reads to him from the Book of Revelation, warning him of the beast who is soon to walk the earth. The predatory intentions of my older sisters are madly manifest when they arrive with knives and forks to devour him, vengeance being all theirs when he does not kiss the big feet they place before him.

And yet does Jason Justly live to see our apartment in the light of day. Yet does he rise from the cot he has been given to use our squalid bathroom and to see my father in his tattered robe. Where are you from, Luke, that you have acquired such blinders and cannot see what you have done? Do you not fathom the dimensions of the shame that spreads from me to everything I touch that has our name upon it? Do you not see the lowly position where we have been placed that no cleaning can disguise? Do you not see that Jason Justly has no blemishes upon his body or upon his mind and is from a world we cannot acquire? Do you not see that it is death to have him present in our hovel home?

If Jason Justly has a father, he is not on the premises of the East Side apartment where Jason lives with his mother. Nowhere is there evidence of him in the clean, uncluttered spaces of these rooms where only the stamp of normalcy can be seen. You do not ask someone such as Jason Justly where his father has gone. It is not a question you insert into his mind, not when he has the quality of the birth he has been given. Because Jason Justly walks on the high ground of his own self-respect. He has the energy of his own endowment to see him through.

A summer league is in session for those who would elevate above the humdrum street by wearing uniforms on the baseball diamonds of Manhattan. In Riverside Park and on Randall's Island and at Baker's Field at the far end of Manhattan are boys set in motion on the base paths and in the outfield and on the mound. Danny Cott Logan comes over the top and from the side, raising and rocking and firing his express, the ball thudding into the catcher's mitt. From Harlem and all over the West Side do we come in the summer heat to have a futile whack at Danny Cott Logan's hardball stuff.

It is one thing to have strength. It is one thing to have power. It is another to be an upright twig upon the earth and to hold a bat that is thicker than your arm. Danny Cott Logan's fastball rises and it dips. It snaps and it snarls. It hisses in a backward motion like a cat with arcing back before darting forward over the black outline of the plate. It is for Danny Cott Logan to dispatch me with a weak groundout to the box.

And it is for Jason Justly in his sleeveless T-shirt to swing a weighted bat in the on-deck circle and then to tap the iron doughnut free and stand waiting in his own cool breeze. And it is for Jason Justly to make the scene come further alive with the cracking sound of bat on ball and for us to watch its elegant arc far over the left fielder's head. There is no one with the gracefulness Jason Justly shows with his elegant glide around all three bases and the lightness of his home plate touch.

Because Jason Justly can wear a yellow T-shirt and make it sing and do the same with the blue jeans he fills so well, it is for me to listen to this music that his body makes and, when he is out of sight, to replicate the garb that gives such credence to his look. But now, before the full-length mirror, I see the clothes that in my mind were making such a sound so bright are crying their despair at the poor imitation that has been achieved. It is for the mirror to tell me that Jason Justly cannot be approximated with the bones and flesh that I am made of. And Momma can do nothing to protect me from this truth by holding me to her and saying I am her Svenska pojka forever.

And yet truth has no staying power in my mind if my words are meant to stand for something. The words I speak in the presence of Jason Justly arrive without warning that I should hear myself say, "I have a superiority complex" and yet the words are all my own, emerging from the center of my being. Justin Justly cannot just walk on by. He cannot endure an affront of this magnitude to the reality he lives in, for Justin Justly walks humbly on this earth. Always must he ask, "Does this stand the test of truth?" No other question need apply. And because mine doesn't, he must bring me level with his reality, with matter of fact strength and nothing more saying, "You have nothing to feel superior about." For days if not centuries am I sent reeling by his righteous rebuke.

Now the boys who do not play, saying "I'm not playing with you" with deadness in their eyes, have appeared on the streets of New York City, where they do their diddy bop strut, one arm behind their back and hand curled into a fist. And so I won't misunderstand, one says "Don't make me motherfucking hurt you" as he holds an icepick against my belly. I give him what change I have, fearing it is not enough.

A week later some Puerto Rican kids kick over my bicycle as I ride by Grant's Tomb, and because they have no play in them either I do not resist when they ride off with it. There is shame that

I have done nothing to stop them, but I fear their hurting mentality and the sharp weapons in their pockets to do their hurting, their stabbing, whatever it is that they have been born to do. I know the word *coward*. I know it is meant for me. You don't have to tell me in your thoughts or with your mouths. You can keep it to yourselves, if you please.

Now in my dreams are there knives. Always must the violence come. Always must I awaken before it can happen so I can be apart from the blood and pain that must follow. It cannot, I say it cannot, be for me to witness such penetration.

The school has moved farther south, leaving the two buildings that face the Hotel of the Negroes for a Riverside Drive location six blocks away, where now the school will be housed in a former mansion with large formidable windows and an exterior of dull marble whiteness. The previous owners have fled into history so the nuns can more permanently stamp the word "serious" on our foreheads. Someone says the departed have taken to hiding under the floor, but wherever they have gone, they do not come out.

The fall has come, and with it brisker air encouraging us to drink from the cold but fortifying cup of knowledge, the nuns say. But there is also Columbus Day, when I can be away from the rigors of their mentality in Riverside Park with Jerry-Jones Nobleonian, where the itchy balls have been falling from the plane trees. If we start in the railroad tunnel, we do not linger there, heading north to its end and the full light of day. We follow the tracks to One Hundred Twenty-fifth Street, where strong men in blood-smeared aprons unload a refrigerated boxcar. All along the tracks are metal hooks on which sides of beef are hung. Farther on, we pause at a crumbling loading dock.

"This isn't good," I say to Jerry.

"What's not good?"

"Look at these sidings. The railroad tracks are rusty. It's like the railroad is slowly dying."

"That's right, man. It's over for the railroads. Trucks are what it's about now. And airplanes."

His words separate me from him. Unfriendly words they are, telling me that the gray and white engines of the New York Central will not forever be running on these tracks and through the deep woods to the north.

Fear enters in this no man's land where we now wander, fear of knives and more knives wielded by those who don't play. And so we drift south again out of the yards and onto the top level of Riverside Park. A motorcade of limousines, American flags fluttering on their hoods, approaches and stops in front of the boxy new building that stands on the corner of One Hundred Twentieth Street, opposite Riverside Church. And there is Dwight David Eisenhower seated in one such limousine and waving to the crowd. President Eisenhower it is, with his bald head and warm smile, though no one should be fooled or forget that he had the power to make the Germans fall down dying and now has the power to lead our country. Everywhere are policemen seen so no one can hurt the President, whose head is aglow, as if with some soft inner light.

Someone says he is there to dedicate the cornerstone of the new building. The cornerstone has a small stone jutting from it, we see, when the president and his motorcade have gone. Inscribed in the limestone are the words "This stone is from the Agora in Corinth, where many hearing Paul believed."

"President Eisenhower is the light of the world. God was working in him that he saved us from the Nazis," Momma says.

"The building will have many religious organizations. That is what they were saying, Momma."

"Yes, but do they have the one religion by which the building can live in the Lord, and without which it cannot? I am suspecting that it doesn't," Momma says.

"Why, Momma?"

"There are those who make professions of faith but who have not truly received the word," Momma says, putting her doubt upon the building.

The world is made up of *pi*, Sister Mary Elise tells the class. It is everywhere that a true mathematician casts his gaze. She speaks at a distance from my mind and makes the blackboard a threat with the numbers she places there with a loud, attacking piece of chalk. With one swipe of the eraser, the figures are all gone, and over the cloudy residue new ones appear.

Outside the Puerto Rican boys wait to hit us in the face with dead pigeons. They do not care about *pi*, but live solely in the delirium of ecstatic revenge that we do not see them better than we do. Those who can escape the tussle go to the corner pizza shop, but it is a place I know not to go, given the dangers a congregation of my schoolmates can pose when planning parties for their own while Phil and Don Everly are having their say, singing "Bye Bye Love" into young ears.

The next morning *pi* is still there, summoning me to a level of understanding I cannot rise to. And now there are formidable quantities of Latin and French and something called earth science, and textbooks that weigh ten pounds.

Cynthia Belton is a girl with a face that has bypassed youngness. She has *pi* in her pocket and a statement in need of immediate release.

"You took my pencil case. Now please give it back."

She seems strangely small for her age, but her father looms large with a topping of white hair to crown his intellect. He comes from England, where fairness is the rule.

"Have you taken my daughter's pencil case?" He wears glasses to fortify his face and a suit and tie, and the leather bag he carries bears the documents his mind has manufactured.

"No," I say. And in fact I haven't. Not a thing have I taken from Cynthia Belton that she should come at me with her accusation.

Luke may be a "Blue Moon" angel with his pompadour his most remarkable feat. He may establish himself in a booth at the pizzeria with the boys and girls of the eighth grade, but the school is a train pulling out of the station on which I stand. I don't understand *pi.* I don't understand my life there. And so chalk must be thrown and spitballs must fly. No one must pay attention to me except for the antics I perform, which lead to my now and then banishment from the class.

When I enter the boys' bathroom on the second floor, Johnny Lacy and Edward Macy are facing the door, as if they have been expecting me. Their appearance of unity is unsettling, as are the smiles on their faces that suggest they know something about me I would rather they didn't. The moment has presented a naked truth. They are better than me, stronger than me, smarter than me. In every department are they my superior. It is that which their smiles convey. Yes, they have fathers who walk with one hand in their pockets. Yes, they have homes that blaze with beauty. Yes, they have the superiority that their minds have conferred. And yes, they are in full expectation that I will disintegrate before their very eyes. They are in that moment the party I have not been invited to, the social monopoly that keeps me apart and requires me to flee to the streets. Their grins are a torment, claiming ownership of my very being.

A box containing toilet paper is nearby. I take several rolls and fling them one by one out the open window at the convoy of nuns on the sidewalk below as they are returning to the school. The power of surprise is mine. I have done what I need to do to break the bond of this unbearable intimacy with Johnny Lacy and Edward Macy. I am throwing the toilet paper to save my life. And yes, the nuns look up, as well they should, to have rolls of toilet paper bouncing off their black robes. And yes their pale faces register surprise that a convoy of the mighty should be attacked by a minion of their state. And so too do I register the changed expressions on the faces of Johnny

Lacy and Edward Macy. Now, though they are looking at me, it is I who is looking at them—at these faces that a minute before were the picture of mockery now expressing smiling astonishment at what a boy can do when his power is unleashed.

I am now alone in a room where the Reverend Mother has told me I must wait. In the hallway do I hear the noise of the children of innocence and their laughter. The window facing west looks out on the trees of Riverside Park and the Hudson River, and along the drive the cars and buses of New York City are going on about their day. Immediately below are the wide stairs of the school leading to the entrance.

Soon does Momma appear at the base of those stairs and begin to make her slow ascent with the weight of all her sorrow upon her. Momma does not lift her eyes to the window where I stand, and I do not open the window and call down to her so she will know where I have been positioned. Momma is being Momma, in keeping her focus on the step before her in the methodical nature of her ways, with the earth an affliction she must bear. These steps lack the steepness of the staircase from the subway to the church. There is no urgency to support her from behind should she fall.

Momma is somewhere in the school, but I do not know where. When the waiting goes on, I remove my jacket and make it a pillow for my head in the corner where I lie curled on the floor. Someday I too can be a floor, or a window, or a wall, and feel nothing of what I am feeling now.

When Momma comes, she comes alone. "Give me your hand. We must go," Momma says, reaching down for me.

"Momma, are they reviling me? Are they casting me out to the ends of the earth? Momma, have they been made to get up so I can be free?"

"What ails you, my son? What ails you?" Momma says, when she can finally speak. "Why do you cast yourself into the wind of turbulence where the peace of God should reign?"

Momma holds me by the wrists and searches my mind. But her eyes are not now an invading army of *knowingness*. I can tell her only what my thoughts have come to be, that the privileged have taken it upon themselves to remove me from my seat and drive me into the street, that they have assigned me to the alleyways and byways but not to the bastions where their faces preside. I tell her that their last names rely on vowels and that they show a smug and assuming superiority over the name that I can muster. I tell her that their fathers walk with one hand in their pockets and sit with the Reverend Mother on the throne of power. I tell her that I am not an American boy. I tell her that I am just a Negro of New York City.

"Ushtah, my son, ushtah," Momma says, but fear has replaced her repudiating strength. Momma escalates into the air, where she can hover with a face of stupefied wonder, as I interpret the world to her. She is waiting now on God for the next move she should make on an earth that cannot hold her feet.

There is no structure to be had at this new school. Its shape has gone all to pieces, if it ever existed. All day long people drift up and down the wide, winding marble staircase while holding onto the wrought-iron banister. Edwin Schwartz has food stuck in his braces. Melanie Gringold has glue in her brown hair. Johnny Kumarte walks about in his underwear and fat Alice Katz eats candy bars all morning long.

At the lunch hour some of us sleep on the floor. Others drift into Central Park and lie on the benches. I allow myself to be blown down Columbus Avenue, where hot dogs with sauerkraut can be bought at Seventy-second Street and you can eat standing while the cars and buses go rushing by.

Momma has told me I am special even if I can't do *pi*. She will not have me in the public schools, where violence is unafraid to go. She wants me safe in green pastures and still waters, and yet where people of quality can be found and aspiration lives so I can have the education that she lacked.

Mr. Cacciote says science is seeing. It is the air we breathe and the water we drink. Mr. Cacciote implores us to see science everywhere, even in the beds where we sleep. We listen to Mr. Cacciote with full stomachs and our heads on the desk.

Now that I am away from my Episcopal school, now that it has uttered the word *expelled,* I cannot be part of its garden. I cannot attach myself to the quality I was exposed to given the books that went unread. There is an ache for where I once was, and a shame at where I now am.

Momma tried to get me into good schools, but they measured my worth and told me to go away. They saw my flat head. They saw my small mind. They saw my failure with *pi* and my meager thighs. They saw my bad teeth. They told me I was worthless in America with my long last name. They told me there was a bar against my existence and that they had placed it there. They said this from behind the big desks that they commanded.

Today we are intent on denying access to Mr. Cacciote. Chairs, desks, shelves are piled against the door as an impediment to Mr. Cacciote's science. The man cannot get in and we cannot get out. We fall to the floor laughing. Outside a commotion can be heard. The principal himself has been called. Mr. Foley pounds with an insistence Mr. Cacciote cannot summon, and uses force when we show ourselves unwilling. Flushed and sweating does he enter the room. "You must not…you cannot…" Our hands clamp tighter on our ears.

When Mr. Cacciote is finally alone with us he says, "I saw some science today. I would like so much to tell you what it was I saw, but first, if we may, I would be more than interested to hear the science you yourselves have been privileged to see."

"I saw fire in the basement. It burned my mother and my father all to death. I walked on a string high in the air just so I could get here," Melanie Gringold says.

"That's some very imaginative science," Mr. Cacciote says. "The inexorable progression of combustion and the saving grace of balance. Excellent. Excellent. Now how about you, Edwin?"

"I saw a fat man on the subway platform and pushed him off for his own good. The train cut off both his legs. He thanked me from the bottom of his heart for helping him to lose weight." Edwin Schwartz sticks a finger in each wide nostril.

His hand supporting his chin, Mr. Cacciote studies Edwin for a moment. "Edwin, you have illustrated again a key point about good science. Creativity is behind all groundbreaking discoveries."

Mr. Cacciote turns his attention to Johnny Kumarte, who has his head on the desk. It is kind of creepy to see his head like that with his big eyes open. "Johnny? Oh Johnny?" Mr. Cacciote calls to Johnny Kumarte softly, from a wooing world of warmth. Johnny Kumarte raises his head ever so slowly. He then stands up and walks some paces toward the back of the room, the fingers of his right hand twitchy. Johnny Kumarte is clearly getting ready to sling some heavy lead. Johnny Kumarte is no amateur gunslinger. He draws fast, sweeping his left hand over the hammer to cock it and plugs Mr. Cacciote with a bull's-eye to the forehead. Mr. Cacciote does not fall down dead. He straightens his tie and tries to get his shirt collar to behave.

"Thank you, Johnny, thank you. That was a clear refutation of the idea that science is inherently tedious. You have brought it to life in a powerful way."

The window is open. Nobody jumps.

Trudy Powell has come to save us. It is spring in New York City and no time for the destruction of the innocents, she says, announcing that we are going to Yankee Stadium and that the prime minister of India may join us. But the prime minister is not among us on the night Jim Perry of the Cleveland Indians shuts down the Yankees in a no-nonsense way, throwing over the top with all the meanness he can muster.

The grass glows green, the lights shine bright, the infield turns a rich dark brown with the hosing that the groundskeepers administer, and everywhere on outfield billboards is the song of America being sung. I do not like for the Yankees to be cast down in this way. I am identified with their pinstripe worth. The nighttime air is chilly, and the score lacks warmth as well, that Mickey Mantle should have to fan and fan with futile swings from the left side of the plate.

Trudy Powell is not finished. "We must go where your father lives in daylight hours," Trudy Powell says to me, with school in session. By the hand she takes me and we ride the bus down Broadway to Jack Dempsey's restaurant. There my father is, beyond the colorful bottles at the big oval bar and standing at the gleaming silver cash register. Looking up from the bills he has been counting, my father turns and sees me with eyes that smolder. Slowly he approaches. There is pain. There is shame. He is a stranger. He is my father. He is…

"Who are you, please?" my father asks, unsmiling.

"Who am I? I am Trudy Powell," she says, as if her name could be enough.

"And do you know who I am?"

"I believe you are Johan's father. Johan told me that you work for a very famous restaurant, and so here we are. I'm so glad to meet you," Trudy Powell says, thrusting out her hand.

Just like that my father's face breaks apart into a smile, as if he is falling, falling, from the great height of his severity and can't stop the plunge. My father is helpless against Trudy Powell.

"You must not think a father is a sometime thing, a negligible figure in the proportions he brings to bear. They have a place in the world," says Trudy Powell, after my father has gone away. When the hamburgers arrive, we eat in the silence that has come over us.

In a large room the chatter of boys goes on uninterrupted. I hear the names Mickey Mantle and Whitey Ford and Elston Howard and Yogi Berra. I hear the disappearance of difference that would keep me silent. A door has opened and I can walk through it. Now I too am talking. Batting averages. Earned run averages. Mickey Mantle and Frank Robinson and Willie Mays and Duke Snider and hammering Hank Aaron and Stan Musial and Warren Spahn and Lew Burdette. And there are other names too, like Oscar Robertson and Jerry Lucas and Jerry West and NIT and NCAA and the St. John's Redmen and the Providence Friars and St. Bonaventure Bonnies and Wilt the Stilt and Bill Russell and Bob Cousy.

Though Marty Bauman is truly a boy, his face has more age on it than it should. His hair and his eyebrows are lighter than blond and his face is whiter than pale. His baseball words fly across spaces at a volume and an intensity he cannot control.

If I have been missing the quality and the structure of the Episcopal school, it is not for me to bring it back. Once I had Sister Mary Christabel, and now I have Mr. Cacciote, who tells us silence is also science in the classroom that features the hush that he has imposed.

Marty Bauman says I am not bound to the paths that I have been on, and that it is possible to sleep in a bed in another borough with the moon overhead and Broadway not in its midst. Marty Bauman wants to show me that a train can go up as well as down and that I can emerge from a station I have never seen onto a street I have never walked. Marty Bauman wants to show me what it is to live in a building of blond brick on the Grand Concourse in the Bronx and to stay in an apartment with a sunken living room.

Marty Bauman's father is a doctor. I sit with him and Marty and Marty's mother at the dinner table, a candelabra like antlers in the middle of it. Marty has invited me for the seder. Matzoh ball soup, gefilte fish, food foreign to my tongue, is served. The air is heavy with the silence that has been imposed. This is not a dinner but a funeral. Dr. Bauman is intensely unhappy with his son's big head, I am left to conclude, while I am invisible in his parents' eyes.

That summer Momma rewards me with a departure. I have been reading *Sport* and *The Sporting News*. In winter I am kept fully abreast of the latest rumors from the hot stove league and in summer, as now, I am up-to-date on the action on the field. I am eleven going on twelve and the city streets have their entertainment: loadsies and off-the-wall and stoop ball and high-top Keds to enable my exploratory urges. But now I have seen the great Mickey Mantle and what the number 7 can mean on his broad back and the patience at the plate of number 6, Stan Musial, in Cardinal red, and the fleet feet of Luis Aparicio of the ChiSox and the happy play of Minnie Minoso and the off-the-table curveball of Camilio Pascual and the sullen back and forth of the bat as Vic Power awaits the pitch and the baleful home run mastery of Eddie Mathews, who dares to have only one "t" in his last name and to make the number 41 come alive with his nonchalant left-handed power. I know what is a Comiskey Park and for the sun to burn away the wetness in Milwaukee County Stadium or for big George Crowe to go deep in Crosley Field and to fall down dead at the sight of all legs Frank Robinson in his Redlegs uniform. I know what it is to see the elegant high leg kick of a Warren Spahn and to have an able part of the pitching corps in Bob Buhl. I know what it means to have a number working for you in terms of your personal happiness: 18 and 3, .320 batting average, and to witness line drives to center and to right and down the left field line. I know the smell of hot dogs and what it is to eat them and what a patch of outfield green can mean when glimpsed from the subway el. I know what it is to see from afar men playing in stadiums built for remembering.

The bus has wheels that are not required to round the bases and cannot be defeated by a sudden downpour. They are only asked to stay in motion on the interstates of America. They are Greyhound wheels that say "Leave the driving to us." And when the bus pulls out of the terminal near Penn Station, it cannot travel on the rails or take the tabernacle of the worshipful with it. It must go out on its own with a clear vision of the America that is waiting, traveling with purpose over the roads it was made for and shunning those unfriendly to its width. Everywhere there is the smell of burning rubber and the twisted wreckage of the cars that have gone astray. Everywhere men, women, and children are suffering the pain of their own burnt flesh. The trains are not laughing in pleasure at the carnage. They have adopted the blinders of horses. They too know to adopt an impassive face in the conquistador's arena of triumph. Do you know the ecstatic heartbreak of a city like Pittsburgh, covered in its own soot and with a name like the Monongahela River to contend with? Or to visit a trolley track that holds off the asphalt standing by or to have the words torn out of you in acknowledgment of stupefying pain that Momma is not where the city is to be found or to experience tunnels so very long carved in the mountains that the bus takes it upon itself to explore? Where are the men who built these tunnels? Where are their jackhammer biceps and their helmets and their lunch buckets and their white T-shirts and their flannel shirts of many colors? Have they left their thermoses behind? Their newspapers? Show me the waxed paper in which their sandwiches were wrapped. Just show me, that I may have some vestige of the manliness in which they stood outside of books and fully in the actions that they took.

Fruit and vegetable stands along the road offer the produce of those living close to the earth, who sheathe their hands in soil in going where the worms are to be found; those who know the put-put-put of a tractor coming to life and how the smell of burning shucks of corn can root them to the land forever; those who live in ramshackle homes and have a very private understanding with their very own Jesus of what it means to wear their Sunday-go-to-meeting clothes and next day stand shoeless by their roadside stalls, their mouths crowded with bad teeth.

The signs along the way. The sky open and clear and endlessly blue. The sun, egg yolk yellow, pouring down on America.

Ben and Anna met.

Ben and Anna fought.

Ben-Anna split

Ohio and Indiana cannot stop us. The space between me and Momma now an ocean the land seeks to disguise.

A potbellied man in a St. Louis Cardinals uniform awaits me at the side of the road. Even in the darkness the white and the red of his uniform explodes. The camp is only a short ride away in his pickup truck, which rattles over a dirt road. The man leads me to a cabin and shines a small flashlight at a bunk bed and pats the top berth.

The pain has a life of its own. That I could have done such a thing to myself. That I could have left Momma so alone. Slowly the song of the crickets comes to my ears, a song with its own deep-throated rhythm. I take off my sneakers but sleep in my clothes.

In the morning I am woken not by crickets but by the sound of a bugle. Reveille is being sounded. Daylight leaves me no place to hide. There must be twenty other bunk beds in the room. Boys snap towels at each other's bottoms. I hear water spraying from the shower heads and the sound of their voices echoing off the tiles. No light should be so clear. No light should be so pitiless.

The day is the pledge of allegiance and frosted flakes for breakfast and men with tanned, weathered faces hitting fungoes and ground balls to kids of all ages on the several baseball diamonds. It is sitting alone when others sit together. It is a man with a scrubbed face telling me I need to wash behind my ears. Mostly it is Momma pulling me to her, saying it is no use, Momma is everything, the lighted ball field in the night and every thought my mind can make.

I have come upon a sea I cannot swim. I must turn back. I must.

"What is that you say? A collect call?"

Momma does not have a voice that fails to recognize me as her own. This is the voice of someone with clothes hanging from her gaunt frame. It is the voice of Auntie Eve. She does not know me, not in the way that Momma can.

"Yes. A collect call from Johan in Cuba, Missouri, for a Mrs. Manootdjian?"

"Missouri?"

"Ma'am, will you accept the call?"

"Maya is not here." Maya is Momma. Momma cannot hide behind any name but that.

"Ma'am, once again, will you accept this call?"

Under the bright lights of the ballpark a boy lashes a line drive over the centerfield scoreboard and runs the bases with powerful, long-legged authority.

In the morning a woman speaks to me. She has a birdlike gaze and severity.

"Someday you will have to stand tall and be a man. Your momma don't want you the way you are."

Her words burn like acid and follow me onto the bus.

To be a Momma in New York in summer is to suffer the peril of the heat and sorrow over a family that has not risen to her level. It is to be hopeful of the power of ancient texts to heal her afflicted offspring. The bright lights of the city are burning and the gnashing of teeth has not yet begun. An unfettered sparrow darts among the movie marquees on Forty-second Street but will be nailed to the cross soon enough, a voice is heard to say. Garbage is piled high; the rats are king.

Chuck sits slumped in the lobby in a posture of passivity, his legs spread, keeping the building safe with his science mind at rest. He has his standup hair and hawklike stare.

Momma is sitting alone in the dark as I enter. She sits in a chair I never see her in. It is after midnight.

"Are you here? Have you too come to give me trouble?"

"Momma, what is it you say?" Momma wears her robe of white. Her hair is down.

"I am in pain. That is what I say. I have come from the hospital." Momma is softly moaning.

"Momma, do you need to go back? What am I to do?"

"I have been to the hospital for an operation on my varicose veins. And now they want me to come back so they can do the other leg. But I will never go back. Go away now before I say more. Go, I say."

"But Momma…"

Momma turns on the lamp light and I gasp. Her bare legs, an angry purplish red, knock me back like a blow to the chest.

Sadness has toppled the garbage can in the kitchen. Coffee grounds and gnawed meat bones and banana peels and peach pits and a slimy butter stick wrapper have spilled out on the worn-through linoleum. No, I say, no, fetching broom and dustpan so order can have its beginning.

Momma remains in a state. "You will not defeat me with your willfulness," she says. The men who drive with one hand on the steering wheel lean up against their double-parked cars outside the tabernacle. They have come in the summer heat to take us away from Pennsylvania Station and Macy's and the General Post Office and the life we know on the streets of Manhattan. Stinky Maldonado is there and Eddie Goyco and Reuben Alvado and Willie Peterson and Peanuts Kozinski and Kenny and Johnny Jones and all the rest. Soon we are on the Henry Hudson Parkway, going north to the George Washington Bridge. Then we are on the Palisades Parkway. Then we are going and going to the Catskill Mountains, where Momma says we will have the fresh air of the country. The man who drives has rolled down his window and rests his left arm in the frame. Though he is in the front seat, he fills the whole car.

Hours later we come to a town called Phoenicia, with tall trees along the main street. Some miles later is a smaller town. Lanesville has a gas station and a general store and a post office and nothing more the eye can see.

At the turnoff our car rumbles across a small bridge spanning a creek and climbs a rutted dirt road. In a circular driveway we get out and face a white clapboard main house with a peaked roof. Then I am led down a flagstone path to a small cabin for boys. The screen door bangs closed each time it is opened.

My room is at the back of the cabin, with a window that looks out on a field, where heavyset women are taking down the wash from clotheslines and folding it in baskets. The room smells of mildew.

That evening, in the driveway, sits a lone car, a Lincoln Continental, with whitewall tires. The men of the tabernacle have all driven away. We gather in the main house, where at a long table we are given a meal of grains and thick slabs of meat. A worried-looking woman with her gray hair in a bun moves slowly among us, as if she is all alone except for her Jesus, on whom she calls to give her the warmth she needs in the cold of this world.

Pastor Lysenko stands at the head of the table and says grace. He is a stump of a man. Though it is mean to say, little pig eyes blaze in his pasty face, and on his head sits an orange toupee.

"We have suffered the little children to come unto us, dear Jesus, and we pray in your name that they will be grateful for the gift that we have given them." In this way does Pastor Lysenko pray, his words like hot grease spit from a frying pan.

The smell and the sight of the food leave me unable to eat. I am grateful for the bread and butter, and the two glasses of milk I drink. Some of the grains and meat I place on a napkin and hide between my feet under the table. As for the rest, I spread it as thin as possible on the plate.

"You are skin and bones," the sad-eyed woman says. "Underweight." She runs her finger up and down my ribcage. "Like a washing board," she says.

Shame takes away my ability to speak. *Underweight.*

Outside the main house two boys play a game of stretch, their legs moving farther and farther apart with each throw of the jackknife into the turf.

Facing the main house is a tiny shack with a window that opens on a counter, where Pastor Lysenko sets out boxes of candy: Goldberg's Peanut Chews in red and black wrappers; Milky Ways; Mars

Bars; Necco Wafers, Sugar Daddies with yellow wrappers brighter than the sun; Good n' Plenty; Tootsie Rolls.

"Single file, children, single file. And have your money ready to purchase these delicious candies," Pastor Lysenko says.

That evening we are called to the tabernacle, a wooden structure with aluminum siding. On a stage raised a foot off the dirt floor Pastor Lysenko loosens his tie. His words are now a five-alarm fire. Pastor Lysenko is ablaze in the cool mountain air, full of holy smoke. The adults are among us in the congregation, the thick-bodied women I saw in the field and the sad-eyed woman who served us dinner and the counselor for the boys, Bob Pellalugra, and his wife, June, for the girls. Bob Pellalugra looks mean, as if he wants to hit someone and can hardly wait. He wears his hair in a flat top, every strand standing at attention.

When Pastor Lysenko summons us to the prayer rail at the end of the evening, beseeching us to give ourselves to the Lord, Vera heeds his call, as do the other children. But I cannot go. Pastor Lysenko does not have my love. He does not have my heart.

An ache of longing is growing in me for Momma. I can't speak. I can't stand. I lie curled up on the bed. Momma must come for me. Her softness must be mine again to lose myself in. I must have her warm understanding so my life can be my own once more. Everything is the hardness of rocks at this camp. Momma is the sun coming through the window and warming my back and neck. But I must have her as herself, not as the sun. I must. Momma, I see you walking up the winding road past the main house and to my cabin to take me home. I am in a panic. If she does not come for me I must get home to her and end her suffering. I must care for her. I must make everything all right for Momma. She needs me and time is not my friend. She could be gone before I get there. No, no, no.

Reuben Alvado and Eddie Goyco call me Flathead and Square-head. I throw rocks at them as they run away laughing. "Are you crazy? Are you? You could kill them with those rocks." Pastor Lysenko says, I do not tell Pastor Lysenko what I know, that they are trying to slay me with the names that come from their laughing mouths.

In the evening the tabernacle is on fire again from the blazing words of Pastor Lysenko. Weeping and wailing and gnashing of teeth are happening at the prayer rail the children have been summoned to. Reuben Alvado and Eddie Goyco come to me, their eyes glistening with tears. "We did you wrong when we should have done you right," Eddie Goyco says. "We will never call you Flathead or Squarehead again," Reuben Alvado says. Their apology is a burden too great. I cannot be responsible for such fragile goodness. I smile and leave their words right there in the night air as I run away.

During the day we go down to the creek and wade gingerly in the shallow water. The rocky bottom can be hard to stand on. And there is a field nearby where we can run, but the yellow jackets get angry and sting us. And there is the plaster mold of Jesus with his disciples at the last supper, over which I pour brown paint. June Pellalugra says, "I've got your number," as if she has reached in and seen every bad thing about me. She looks older than her husband. It is those thick glasses she wears.

In the evening a chorus of crickets is heard in the dark. On into the night we hear their sound. And we have a sound of our own, our voices rising in song in the tabernacle when Pastor Lysenko is not ranting. A counselor named Dawn sings "Rescue the perishing, care for the dying/Snatch them in pity from sin and the grave/ Weep o'er the erring one, lift up the fallen/ Tell them of Jesus, the mighty to save/Rescue the perishing, care for the dying/Jesus is merciful, Jesus will save." She is young and pretty and sings with joy in her face and has no need of the hymnal and never have I loved anyone the way I love Dawn. Not Alison Pauley. Not anyone.

But the next day she is gone. She has fallen and is lost and cannot be with us anymore because someone says she has been with a man in the night. It is unbearable to think of her as perishing without any hope of rescue. I don't know how to live with such darkness.

Bob Pellalugra has called a meeting of the boys and girls and stands in the middle of the ring they have formed around him. He holds me by the neck of my shirt. His lightning bolt of righteousness has struck after an excavation of my dresser drawer, in which he unearthed a pack of Marlboro cigarettes and a book of matches.

"What are these?" he thunders, holding the red and white box in his hand.

"I don't know."

"You don't know? You don't know?"

"They're cigarettes."

"And what were they doing in your dresser?"

"I don't know."

"They just flew in through the window?"

Earlier the sun had been bright in the sky, but the clouds form fast in the mountains, and once they come, they do not leave for the rest of the day.

"I didn't smoke any cigarettes. The pack is unopened."

"But you brought them here to smoke them. Why else would you have brought them?"

"They were for a neighbor. I forgot to give them to him."

"You lie with every breath you take." Bob Pellalugra drags me up the cabin steps and tosses me in my room. "Stay here, Satan. Stay here. And if you don't, I'll beat the devil right out of you."

There are others who must stand in the circle of judgment as well, if not this day, then the next. Now Bob Pellalugra holds Peanuts Kozinski by the neck. "Do you think Jesus wants filth?" he says to us. "Or does Jesus want us cleaner than snow? Are these underpants cleaner than snow, children?" With his other hand Bob Pellalugra holds Peanuts Kozinski's underpants away from him by two fingers. The brown stains send a shiver of revulsion through me.

"Cleaner than snow," the children answer back.

"Filth, do you think the Lord wants me and my wife to spend whole days scrubbing the filth from your underwear on a washboard? Is that the Lord's work? Go to your room and pray to the Christ Jesus about your filth and don't come out until you've prayed real hard."

Peanuts is small. He's like a chipmunk. You have to listen closely to hear what he is saying, when he talks at all. His face is fixed in a permanent half-smile that may not be a smile at all. We can see that he is crying as he walks with his head down back to the cabin.

Now when the children and adults are at the prayer rail after the sermon, I go down to the basement of the main house and enter the dark kitchen through the screen door. With my flashlight on, I find the boxes of candy. Oh, Milky Way. Oh, Mars Bar. Oh, Tootsie Roll heaven. In the meadow I sit under the half moon eating my take, savoring each bite. Fireflies appear as glowing specks of light in the night air. A raccoon noisily seeks for food in the rusted oil drum that serves as a garbage can. From above come the cries and shouts of the gathered in the tabernacle.

On awakening the next morning I watch as Angel and Clementino, two older boys, strip the bark from the sapling that stands right outside my window. The long blades of their Bowie knives gleam in the sun as the peelings pile up at their feet. Soon the trunk is smooth as a bone and sticky with sap. They have stripped the tree because they felt like it. The camp girls look on, while behind them, in the meadow, the old women tending to the laundry shake their heads.

"I should send you both home for such destructiveness. Do you not know the meaning of life, that a tree is a living thing? Do you not know that I planted that tree so it would grow and give the cabin some shade? You must both go to your room," red-faced Pastor Lysenko says.

The children plead with Pastor Lysenko not to send Angel and Clementino home. I too would be sad to see them go, though I am also sad about the tree, which will now have to die, and painfully, like a man skinned alive. And what will happen in twenty years? Will no trees be left? Will they be gone, along with the railroads, without which I cannot live?

There was a railroad running through the Catskill Mountains, but now they have taken away the tracks and the ties so only the roadbed is left. They went and took it away before I could see the trains moseying along the ridge above the cabin and the main house and the tabernacle in the dark of night, the light of the engine shining on the trees. Because the good is always taken away from you before you arrive or just after you have arrived and even had a chance to think of it as good. There is some disappearing machine going on—disappearing this, disappearing that.

"I don't want that man talking bad to me the way he do," Puerto Rican Angel says. "He don't be making a good life for himself talking bad to a Puerto Rican." We are in the night now, after the service and the prayer rail. Angel's words take him out of the cabin, Clementino following behind and the spring door slamming shut after them.

"Ooh, there's going to be trouble now," Peanuts squeals, as Angel and Clementino disappear in the direction of the ridge. When they return, Angel says he has beaten a porcupine to death with his garrison belt. Quills are still stuck in his belt to prove it. "The porcupine was messing with me," Angel says. "It showed no respect."

Angel and Clementino are gods of a dark and vengeful kind. They go where no one else can go with the finality they claim to have brought to the poor porcupine.

Pastor Lysenko does not send them home the next day. He says to them, "I forgive you for your wickedness."

During nap time I say to Peanuts, "Peanuts, let's go exploring."

"But we're not supposed to. That would be wickedness," Peanuts says, even as we ease out the spring door and down the hill toward a white house that has been sitting unused, weeds growing high all around it. Inside, the rooms are bare. A chandelier dangles from the ceiling fixture. We climb the stairs. An old iron bed has been left behind. Dust motes float in the warm afternoon air. I begin to laugh. Peanuts begins to laugh. The laughter buckles our knees and doubles us over. Peanuts staggers over toward the window, using the wall for support.

"Johan, Bob is standing on the cabin porch. He's starting to come down this way." His laughter gone, he bolts down the stairs. Panicked, I follow after. Bob will block us from getting out the front door if we don't move fast. He mustn't trap us inside. As I continue my downward path, I reach out and give a torn piece of wallpaper the yank it deserves. Our flight path takes us out the back door.

That evening we are called to the dining hall by Pastor Lysenko.

"Children, children. Be seated," he says, pacing back and forth, his hands behind him. Vera sits across from me. She looks so innocent. They all do, even Angel and Clementino.

"Children, you are my good children, are you not? Say to me, 'We are your good children.'"

"We are your good children," the chorus comes back.

"Of course you are my good children. I needn't even ask. I *know* you are my good children. How do I know? Because you love Jesus. Yes, my children, you love the Lord. And how do you suppose I know you love the Lord? I will tell you, my children, how I know. I know because you seek the Lord. Each night you cry out for the Lord at the prayer rail in our little tabernacle. That is how I know. I see your beautiful, tear-streaked faces, and know that the Lord is working in you and that you are being washed in the blood of the Lamb. I see Reuben and Eddie, and I see little Alma, and it does my heart good."

Alma is the prayer girl. No one prays as fervently or as loud as she does. And Reuben and Eddie have only called me Flathead once since they promised not to, and the next day gnashed their teeth in front of me that they had backslid that one time.

"But there is one I don't see at the prayer rail. Not once have I seen him there. Do any of you know of whom I speak? Do you know, Alma?" When Alma shakes her head, Pastor Lysenko pats her cheek, smiles, and continues down the line. He is so very soft and gentle with the children. He repeats the question to Reuben and Eddie and others, before coming to Peanuts. "Peanuts. Such a nice name. Do you know who it is that is never seen at the prayer rail? Tell us, Peanuts. Be the good boy that you are are and say who it is we do not see at the prayer rail." Pastor Lysenko has cupped the back of Peanuts' head with his hand.

Peanuts looks over at me and quickly turns away.

"Yes, that is the one, Peanuts. Our boy of no faith, who cannot bring himself to the prayer rail even once. Now tell us, Peanuts, the way in which he led you astray and into sin this afternoon. Don't be afraid."

"I don't know."

"You don't know? You don't know it is a sin to destroy property, that it is not Christian and God will not love you for it? You do not know it is a sin to tear wallpaper? You know, Peanuts. Of course you know. You are my good boy, at the prayer rail every evening. Tell us who ripped the wallpaper."

"Johan ripped the wallpaper."

"And why did he rip the wallpaper?"

"I don't know."

"The wallpaper just happened to come into his hand? You know better. It is because this boy is destructive. It is because he throws stones. It is because this boy is ungrateful." And it is true that I throw stones. Just the other day Pastor Lysenko sent me to my room for throwing a stone at a tree even as I stood only a foot from him. And this after sending me to my room two days before for the same thing.

And so Pastor Lysenko turns to me, as does everyone in the dining hall, and I am in the place where I have been before with Sister

Mary Christabel and Bob Pellalugra. The shame place, where I must stand trial. "Do you not love the Lord?" Pastor Lysenko asks.

"I don't know the Lord," I say.

"Do you not want to get to know the Lord?"

"I want to go home."

"The Lord is your home. That is why you must come to the prayer rail, as the other children do. Because if you come to the prayer rail, then you will have no need to go to homes that are not your own. You will not have the destructive urge to do harm to property that is not your own. Do you understand what I am saying?" Pastor Lysenko had continued pacing up and down the dining hall as he spoke, but now he stands directly in front of me, his round face flushed and sweaty.

"Maybe," I say.

"Maybe? The boy says maybe? What have I been telling you in that tabernacle all these nights?"

"I don't know."

"Children, I need for you to leave now. I must be alone with this boy."

As the dining hall empties, I see Vera. She looks disapproving, as if she too sees that I have been bad. Better to be beaten with the others in the room, as I dread being alone with Pastor Lysenko. But he gets right down to business. He gives my ear the Bob Pellalugra twist, and yes, he has his tongue between his lips, though his lips are thin, not thick, like Hannah's, and his eyes squint. Just as my tears are about to come, he lets go and stands back, heaving from his exertion.

"I will drive the devil from you. I will beat you so he flees. In the name of the father, the son, and the holy ghost..." Pastor Lysenko stomps on my sneakered foot with the heel of his leather shoe, causing me to howl and drop to the floor. "I'm sending you home. Now go to your room. Go, I say. Get up. Get up now." He pulls me up with his hands under my armpits, but I drop to the floor again like a sack. He lifts me once again and this time I hobble away.

The boys and girls are milling outside. "Ooh, you really got it," Peanuts says.

Momma, you must come for me. The food is stinky and I have pain all the time that you are not here. There is a screaming in my chest for you that will not stop.

I had begun my letter to Momma, but now there is no need to finish it, as I will be going to Momma and she needn't come for me. But then Pastor Lysenko comes to my room. "If there is one more incident, just one. No one destroys my property. No one."

In the morning my foot is still sore, but by evening I am once again outside. While waiting for the supper bell to ring, I stand to the side of the main house, pick up a flat piece of shale, and throw it sidearm. My target is the gnarled bark of an apple tree, but the shale curves wide of the trunk and down the hill toward the dry pond.

Outside the main house Alma, the devoted prayer girl, cries out, her arms spread and her tear-streaked face raised to the sky, "They are burning. They are all burning. My family is burning." Pastor Lysenko and Bob Pellalugra and his wife June and many of the children are now forming a circle around the weeping and wailing Alma, but she is beyond any comfort they can provide.

"Call a fire engine. Can someone not call a fire engine? Hurry. Run to the phone," I shout from beyond the circle. How can they not call for the fire engines knowing Alma's family will soon die in the flames, as where else can such a fire be raging but in the building back in New York City where they live? What is wrong with the fire department that the trucks are not coming? Does no one see that the entire tenement is ablaze, with flames shooting out the windows? Oh, the heat of those flames. But what is the use? The fire engines and the big hook and ladder truck will race and race in their commotion way through the streets, but too late, too late, as everyone is always too late. And now the fire will spread to Momma. Flames will engulf her too, and if it is not flames, then there will be violence that will come to her, and I don't want to be there to see it, ever. Better to run away because the city is too dangerous and the building that Momma and Auntie Eve manage is too chaotic and there is no hope of order. Let me just bolt into the woods until the fire is spent because I cannot stand the prayer girl Alma's screams. But it won't do to leave the fire engines in the firehouse. No, they have to make the commotion run even though there is no hope.

On the ridge where Angel took his belt to the porcupine I sit on a log, looking down through the trees at the circle obscuring Alma from my sight, waiting for her cries to cease and for word that all hope of saving her family has gone and that their flesh has been burned from their charred bones, because only with death is there no hope and no anxiety about trying to get there in time to save Momma.

In the morning, the boys are kissing the girls and the girls are kissing the boys back and once it starts, it does not stop. First it is one girl and then another.

The camp I had wanted to leave, I now never want to leave.

Darkness falls and voices rise in song in the cool mountain air: "Shall We Gather at the River," "In the Garden," "Blessed Assurance." Pastor Lysenko, his tie loosened and his jacket removed, has found a rhythm with his fiery words. His round face slick with sweat, he beckons the boys and girls to the prayer rail, that we may kneel and acknowledge our sinfulness and invite the Christ Jesus into our hearts. But the dark night is suddenly calling. As if on an unseen signal, we bolt out the door, leaving behind the startled adult remnant. Down through the high grass and into the meadow we streak, screaming and shrieking under the full moon, boys falling on the rubber-lipped girls, all of us kissing and kissing some more while after us come Bob Pellulugra and his wife, thwacking the bushes and filling the air with angry threats, and behind them Pastor Lysenko himself, in a more pleading tone, saying, "Children, children, come home to the Lord. Come home to the Lord," while from the tabernacle atop the hill floats the sound of adult voices singing "Bringing in the Sheaves."

Boys in street clothes playing a pickup game. The catcher has a mask but no chest protector for the hardball heaves from the lanky pitcher. No pretty ballpark with dugouts and a scoreboard and a manicured field as down in Missouri, not in Riverside Park.

Atop the batting cage, right over home plate, perches Frenchie the Algerian. As batters step to the plate, Frenchie drops shavings of dry ice and smiles as the batters wince. They look up, angrily, but then quickly look away, as if they know about his power to pluck out their eyes with his thumb or do even worse. Now a bare-chested kid with a huge, anvil-shaped head steps in and goes into a crouch, bat cocked, handle aligned with his ears. Suddenly he drops his bat and swats his neck, as if stung by a bee, then looks up and sees the smilingly malevolent face of Frenchie the Algerian. But this boy is not like the others. His face, with its permanent scowl, makes him appear older than the other kids, and his hairy, muscular body is more developed than theirs. Enraged, he scales the batting cage. As he does, Frenchie scurries down the other side, picks up a bat, and awaits his pursuer near the pitcher's mound. But the man-boy has no dawdle gear in him. Not even Frenchie the Algerian's bat is a deterrent. Frenchie swings and misses and Man-Boy belts Frenchie a shot to the head that separates him from the bat. Two more blows send Frenchie tottering around the infield before he collapses out by second base. For Man-Boy the game is over. He finds his shirt and walks off, his head back at a forty-five degree angle to the sky.

"Fucking Sean. Don't be fucking with The Head. Know what I mean, Jim?" So a skinny boy says.

"Best believe I know what you mean." another says. "That boy don't *play*. That boy is *serious*."

Oh yes. Oh yes.

The Broadway Presbyterian Church offers vacation Bible school and a musty smell, but the more compelling sound is the basketball that booms in the gymnasium below. Screens have been placed over the stained glass windows and the pastor has been asked to leave for putting a monkey in the trunk of his car. So it has been reported.

And that block just north of my own has other features, like the Wentworth boys, Eric and Jeff, who read and read and for whom the world is waiting. The quality of their beauty is there in the names they have been given, and so I am shy enough among them that I can only say hello.

And in the building on the southwest corner of Broadway where they live with their mother (no father has been allowed into the house) a woman, old and white, leans out of her window on the floor above and shouts down to the street that she is dying and yet never felt so good.

And across the street, by the Esso filling station and garage, zoom zoom Bobby Cassandro has a look of joyful delirium as he banters with the uniformed attendants. Bobby Cassandro has done no harm to the earth in being born simple, and so the attendants are tender with him in their manly way. How cool the garage feels. How appealing is the smell of rubber and gas and oil. Bobby tears around the block, making the vroom vroom sound of a car engine as he goes. No one will ever kill him dead without having to answer for it.

Columbia University has guards in mailman gray to patrol its walkways and secure its premises from the non-university horde.

In years past we have fired roman candles in their direction as they approached to send us on our way. There is one coming now up the Low Library steps, past the spewing twin fountains on the plaza. We do not say, "Chickie, the fuzz, chickie the fuzz" but remain in place. Jerry Jones Nobleonian stands firm. Johnny Donatelli too.

"His name is Louie. He's queer. He likes to suck boys' dicks," Johnny says, of this old man with the slow-motion way of walking. Johnny does not know the gift he has made and never ever will; it is for me to conceal the fireworks going on within.

Nighttime brings thunder and bolts of lightning. The heavens open and the earth is one big flood. I do not need a boat for where I am going, but walk on sneakered feet. The great Butler Library on the Columbia campus is closed; its books are not for you to know till morning comes. Herodotus. Demosthenes. Plato. All the names chiseled in the masonry above you will have to wait to discover.

In the distance, domed Low Library stands above Alma Mater. Angled brick footpaths and a set of steps will take you there. Louie stands alone at the top of those steps, his bald head a beacon.

Slowly along the footpath between the east and west lawns Louie approaches and turns the lock in the library's formidable brass door, then holds the door open and nods. I need no words of invitation to dart through into the darkness, my sneakered feet making a sound of squishy wetness on the marble floor. And now does his flashlight lead to an inner sanctum, another door where the marble ends and a carpet begins. We are in an office with a desk and a banker's lamp and a shelf of books. Now do my shirt and jeans come off that I may lie down on that carpet, my full nakedness exposed by the beam of Louie's flashlight.

Louie loosens his black belt, causing his pants to fall down all around him. What a heavy blanket is his weight.

Louie has coins for me when he is done. Two quarters does he give me to remember him by. Through the darkness he leads with his flashlight. It is good when the confines of the library have fallen away and I can run to the freedom I now am seeking, running far,

far from Louie and who he is and who I am that I am with him. My insides burn and burn. Now is my flesh dependent on the cleansing I am seeking. Now must I throw the coins where no one will know they have ever been a part of me. Now must I be behind another closed door to wash away my sin.

PART 2

A NEW START

From the yard below, near and yet far away, come screams and shouts and the frequent sound of a ball bouncing off the chain-link fence or a thud when it impacts flesh. Dodge ball, my classmates are playing, as the sun overhead burns bright in a cloudless early September sky. If I am not with them during morning recess, it is only that I need to be alone. A new school. A new uniform. I am afraid but also excited. A change has come over me. I am more within myself, quieter. I do not have to act out for Johnny Lacy and Edward Macy. They do not own me, nor do the nuns.

Momma listened when I said I needed more structure than could be found at the chaotic Molodon School if I wasn't to fall and fall and lie dead at the very bottom.Miss Iris, the headmistress, who wears her gray hair in a bun and tucks her used tissue up the sleeve of her lacy blouse, could have said no that rainy, late-summer day Momma brought me for the interview. She ticked off the titles of a number of books: *The Count of Monte Cristo, The Man in the Iron Mask, Penrod, The Ox-Bow Incident*. Had I read any of them? I shook my head no.

"And what exactly have you read?" Miss Iris asked, her eyes sharply focused behind bifocals she wore attached to a loop around her neck.

"*Batman. Superman.*"

"Comic books?"

"He is a good boy," Momma felt prompted to say. The interview was not going well. Already three other schools had rejected me. And why wouldn't they, given my expulsion and dismal reading habits.

Some days later I was sent to see a Miss Sokol. I went alone. There in her Riverside Drive apartment she asked questions and had me repeat back to her a series of numbers. The second part was harder. Illustrations were shown me of black and white blocks in certain patterns which I was asked to duplicate with the blocks set out on the table. There followed a puzzle made up of wooden pieces I was asked to assemble. Stymied, a feeling of rage overcame me. Miss Sokol was trying to hurt me. I wanted to smash things and smash her and smash myself.

"That's a very difficult one," she said, assembling one set of pieces into the figure of an elephant. Her words, which were meant to comfort, were not persuasive. She had seen what I had seen. I was not good enough and had never been good enough. I was as meager mentally as I was physically. The experience shook and shamed me, that Miss Sokol should see me as I truly was.

Nevertheless the school accepted me. Girls were in the majority, at least in my grade. I gave myself that as the reason.

⚘

"I read at least five books a week," Miss Flowers, the English teacher, says. "If you are to be la crème de la crème, then you too must read. You must develop a passion for literature. You must hear the prose of our great writers singing on the page. But you must not read *The*

Catcher in the Rye. It is beyond the bounds of decency. It is the work of a fraud, a writer with a conspicuously inferior mind."

Miss Flowers gives vocabulary tests and spelling bees. Words like *zephyr, obsequious, diphtheria.* We learn the difference between *compliment* and *complement.* There is *there* and there is *their* and they are homonyms.

Sometimes Miss Flowers disappears, not for a day, but for several weeks. A nervous breakdown, it is whispered. Miss Flowers alone somewhere in a room and shaking, like an out-of-control machine with no off switch. It vibrates so violently its bolts come loose. A room in which she sits looking different, disheveled and hardly human. So I imagine this nervous breakdown of Miss Flowers. And the scary thing is that it could happen right in front of the class.

That would not be a *halcyon* day, not for Miss Flowers, not for anyone.

Tiny Mr. Pappas maintains a peacock strut, wearing a different jacket for every day of the week and jackets of varying weights to match the season. And then there are those days when he appears before us in an elegant suit. Always do his ties glow against a backdrop of shirts that are one day green or yellow and the next red or royal blue or luminously white. His personal grooming is perfect: lustrous black hair neatly trimmed and parted, white teeth that glisten, and skin smooth and bronzed in even the harshest winter weather. Mr. Pappas is a man of order, applying a careful selection process even to his shoes and socks.

"The word you're looking for when you see me is *natty,* as in 'Isn't Mr. Pappas a natty dresser?'" So Mr. Pappas says, his eyes sparkling. "I come from Pawtucket, Rhode Island. How many of you know that Pawtucket was the site of the first factory in this country? Not one of you? Then we have a lot to learn."

Our American history textbook sings a song of endless progress. Lexington and Concord and Minutemen. Bluecoats and Redcoats and Hessians. The Erie Canal and Antietam and Gettysburg and Bull Run. Washington and Jefferson and Lincoln. Such a loud and happy song in my ears that I am an American boy.

Mr. Grody has a silver flask he nips from behind closed doors. So the rumor has spread. The smell of alcohol competes with wintergreen on his breath. His skin is inflamed and a permanent quiver afflicts his face and hands, a problem that is especially noticeable when he tries to write math figures on the blackboard. But Mr. Gladwell will not have things flying apart in his class. A smart tone of voice from Ogden Connifer sends a piece of chalk whizzing at the rude one's head. Order and respect are due. Let the class be aware it is dealing with an incendiary device, Mr. Gladwell is saying.

"Quiet. Mr. Shaky's coming," a boy named Freddy Snyder whispers, his words greeted by laughter.

Mr. Shaky. Mr. Glug Glug.

Mean. Mean. Mean.

"Pride goeth before the fall. Do you know what I mean when I say that about your sister Rachel, my little Flathead?" Naomi asks.

"No," I say, wary as to what is to come.

"Your sister learned she would not be graduating with honors. Her studies are all she has. She has no friends. She has no man. Mother says I am the instrument of Rachel's demise. She says I got her started on amphetamines. Do you know what amphetamines are, little Flathead?"

"No," I say.

"Amphetamines are God in the form of a pill. They make you feel like God should make you feel but doesn't have the time to. I take them during the day and go way, way up and have a few drinks at night to cushion the fall."

※

The family sings "Happy Birthday." Even Naomi and Rachel sing "Dear Johan," not "Dear Flathead." A lemon coconut cake, soft and moist and with that tart lemon flavor. Socks. A tie. A shirt. Gifts did they have for me. A shower of blessings, I hear myself say.

"What do you want to be when you grow up?" Rachel asks, inviting me in with her question.

"I want to be a skin diver," I blurt, thinking of Lloyd Bridges, the star of *Sea Hunt,* a series about underwater adventure.

"Aren't all men skin divers?" Rachel's quickness and smiling ferocity startle. I know but don't know what she means.

※

If I have been disruptive and unruly before, here at Claremont I will be as buttoned down as the white Oxford shirts I wear each day to school. It will not do to continue my old ways. Watchful eyes are upon me. There must be no wrong moves. No more throwing erasers or spitballs or instigating classmates to run helter-skelter through the streets of Manhattan in flight from the nuns.

In textbooks I write "Johan is great." The words demand to come out. During English class I show the inscription to Cassie Whitlock, seated at the next desk, who covers her mouth to muffle her laughter. After the class, she does not say, "What did you mean writing such a thing?" or "That is amazing" or anything. There is only that gasp.

※

Tall and lanky and swaybacked Ogden Connifer has a bullet head and buzz-cut hair. He does not write in his books that he is great. He simply says, with a smile that reveals his horse teeth, "I am the brightest boy in our grade." He is a boy sizzling with his own excellence. Ogden is the son of a professor of humanities at Columbia University, and so can recognize intelligence when he sees it and do what he wants with any blocks or puzzles Miss Sokol throws at him.

On school day mornings Ogden Connifer stoops to pick up trash from the sidewalk. Used tissues, discarded magazines, candy wrappers—he deposits this litter in a nearby garbage can, and shows no self-consciousness as he goes about his tidying task, paying no mind to those who put their laughter on him. He has his vision of a world where order reigns to hold onto.

Ogden lives on Riverside Drive, in walking distance of Columbia University, in a building that is known for its order. Some other classmates have East Side addresses—Fifth Avenue, Madison Avenue, Park Avenue, Sutton Place—and surely order reigns in their buildings too, as they have fathers who are doctors and lawyers, fathers who walk with one hand in their pockets, as do the fathers of Johnny Lacy and Edward Macy.

When asked where I live by a schoolmate, I say the Upper West Side, stricken with terror too strong for the power of reason: the unsightly apartment, the spectacle that Naomi and Chuck make of themselves, the religiosity on full display with that verse of scripture on the side of the building. No and no and no again. There is a line that must not be crossed. Never. Ever.

While I am grateful that the school has possibly lowered its standards to accept me, how is it that at St. Andrews, the curriculum required French and Latin, whereas Claremont has no such requirement in its lower school? And everyone has heard of Trinity and Collegiate, two famous prep schools only blocks away, but who has heard of

Claremont? Have I boarded the Texas Special, which runs on 027 gauge track, while others are all aboard the glorious Santa Fe and speeding along on Super O?

"Science has proven that a kiss takes five minutes off a human being's life. But who could possibly care?" So says Gresham Dodger, tall and handsome, who has laid claim to Susan Springer, the prettiest girl in the class, as his very own, because Gresham Dodger, like Johnny Lacy and Edward Macy, is in the claiming class.

Gresham Dodger's family owns a brownstone somewhere close by. He has an older brother Calvin who is now at Harvard and another older brother Colin who is studying at Yale. And his father is an inventor with many patents in his name.

Charles Blatner is not Gresham Dodger and will never kiss Susan Springer. Charles Blatner is a bottom dweller. He tells me that someday he will go to the Bronx High School of Science, a special public school for gifted students who score high on the entrance exam. Over and over does he tell me this same thing. The face he shows me is that of an old man with a sprawling nose and small, angry eyes too close together. Flecks of food, caught in the massive wiring in his mouth, can be seen as he speaks. Like a small, pugnacious dog is Charles Blatner.

A nobody has found a nobody.

"What's the matter? You don't believe me? Just because you're a stupid blockhead doesn't mean everybody is."

My fist strikes Charles on his right ear, just as Gresham Dodger appears in the doorway. Seeing the shot I have given the now howling Charles, whose hand has gone to his smarting ear, Gresham rushes over. From his greater height, Gresham shouts down at me, "We don't do that here. We don't do that here." Some great moral outrage seems to propel his words, as if he is seeking to angle them into my consciousness. The intensity of his gaze and message prevent me from any argument. Gresham Dodger is instructing me. He is saying that wherever I have come from, I am not there now. Gresham Dodger is my teacher. He has not spoken to me before, and he will seldom speak to me again. But he is speaking to me now and I must listen. I must mend my ways.

Now when Momma calls me into the bathroom and closes the door, it is not to look into my mind and open my hand for the money I have taken but to pull from her stuffed red leather bag an envelope and remove from it my report card. "English, A. French, A. History, A. Math, A-. Do you see the joy you are bringing to me, my son? Do you?" Momma says, reading from the watermarked stationery.

It is not for me to stay in that confined space, amid the sour-smelling towels. I must break away and be alone with my joy. I must not have it shared too long with anyone, not even Momma.

A classmate with a full moon face bearing the heavy weight of sadness has, in a soft, shy voice, invited me to her party. Because I cannot say no, I say yes to Susan Piner's invitation, though the alarm bell is ringing loud within me. If I go to her party, then she will have to come to mine, and that can never be. But it is more than that. Susan Piner has asked me to join in her sadness that we have niceness and amiability to offer the world and nothing more. For this reason too must I stay away.

Friday is Human Day, when I can be free of the navy blue blazer and charcoal gray slacks that Momma has bought to cover my bones, and the girls can be free from their white blouses and plaid or gray skirts. School lets out at noon, and I can go to Johnny's Pizzeria on Broadway and Ninety-fourth Street for a chewy slice. Or while the weather is still warm, I can order a ham and American cheese hero, with lettuce and tomato and mustard, at the Ta-Kome Deli on the northwest corner of One Hundred Fifteenth Street and Broadway and walk down to Riverside Park. There I can sit on a hillside and drink my Coca-Cola and eat my hero sandwich with no book to read or person to talk to as an intrusion on my happiness. There I can just sit and soak in the greenery and the river beyond and the blue sky and brilliant sun, knowing that a railroad of America is under this park and that I am part of something bigger than I can ever know.

Later in the afternoon, I head downtown on the subway to the tabernacle for Friday afternoon Bible school, as Momma still wants nothing to take me away from the Lord.

"Nothing," Momma says, and says it loud.

And in this time, Momma also says, "You must promise me not to breathe a word, but Hannah is big with child."

"But who will the father be?" I ask. Hannah goes about as if she has a pillow under her dress.

"Do not ask such a question of me, and especially do not ask such a question of Hannah. Hannah is very private. You must respect that. You must."

"But Momma, where is the baby going to live?"

"The baby will live where he or she can breathe, the way that all babies should be allowed to live."

"Live and breathe where, Momma? Hannah lives in a single room."

"Have you not heard a single thing at the tabernacle all these years? Have you not heard 'Away in a manger/No crib for a bed/The little Lord Jesus/Lay down his sweet head'?"

"But Momma, Hannah doesn't have a manger. She has a room."

"Do you not see how the Indians live in our building, sometimes four to a room? Is two the same as four?"

Momma, so full of her own understanding.

"His name is Moses," Hannah says. "Do not call him Mo or anything short of his full name. Is that understood? And if you touch him, touch him respectfully. I will be watching, even when I'm not there. I think you know what I mean. And if I have power, you have no idea the power he will wield and the smacks he will deliver when he is of age. Remember my words, Johan. Remember them. My son's time is coming and no one deprives my son."

The baby boy is silent and assessing in his mother's arms. No gurgling tot is he. I feel the two of them drinking in my fear and Hannah thinking, Just when you thought my power was waning, suddenly it has grown.

"Why do you say these things?"

"Why did you have to be born with the fresh mouth that you have?"

"What fresh mouth?"

"Are you scared now? Are you?" Hannah asks.

I need not answer what she already knows.

Jerry and his family have moved out of the hotel of the Negroes. They have gone twelve blocks to a fifth-floor apartment in a walkup building. ACademy 2-5565 is the number he gives me should I wish to reach him. If there is brutality on his block, it does not live in his building. The remorseless violence of the street sings its sudden shrieking song, knives and baseball bats used to perish foes from the earth, some of it in full sight of Jerry, sickening him to a place where he can barely speak. "I mean it was like he was swinging at a fastball, taking a real hard cut. And not once, but over and over. I don't know, man. I don't know." Jerry crying at the horror of what he had seen after one man wielding an Adirondack Slugger trapped his victim and did his obliterating thing as we walk in the refuge of greenery in the lower drive of Riverside Park.

But now, fast approaching in the company of a large friend, is the man child with the hammer head who pulverized Frenchie the Algerian down on the baseball diamond the year before, making clear that it is he in whom all power resides. As if words can be dispensed with, we wrestle with the two of them. Rolling down the hill we go, where the man child easily pins me. But no pummeling action follows. He does not cave in my chest or my head and speaks no words, as if only shyness can follow such an impulsive physical act. His friend has made quick work of Jerry as well. And then they are gone, just like that. Gone.

"Was that a dream?" I ask.

"That was real, man. That was real," Jerry says, brushing the dirt from his clothes.

Luigi Santibelli has also gone away, vacating the basement shop where he had been the sun itself. He says he is done with the "old pussy," as he continues to call Auntie Eve. He is not Tall Tommy or Little Tommy or any of the other men in the single rooms whom Momma and Auntie Eve call upon to keep the building standing. He has found a store over on Eighty-fourth Street and First Avenue with a living space at the back.

Luigi's face shows darkness, not the light, when Luke and I stand in the doorway of his new home and workplace.

"I'm-a busy now. I no got-a the time."

"But we just came to say hello," Luke says.

"I tell-a you I no got-a the time," Luigi says, his face transformed by anger.

We walk south, down toward Seventy-second Street. "He didn't have to talk to us that way," Luke says.

"But he did," I say.

"All I'm saying is that he didn't have to talk to us like that."

"He was busy," I say.

"He wasn't busy. He just hated the sight of us."

"He liked us when we were kids. He doesn't like us so much now that we are older."

"What?"

"I think so. I think that's what his face was saying."

"Yeah? His face can talk? What kind of shit is that?"

"I don't know. That's what I saw."

"You saw. You saw. Fuck him. I'm hungry. You want to grab a slice of pizza?"

"Yeah, I'd like some pizza," I say.

"Let's get some pizza," Luke says.

"What kind of name is that, Manootdjian?" my classmate Freddy Snyder asks in that first year. Thick glasses. A nose like a parrot's beak.

"My father is Armenian."

"What's that, Armenian?" His voice booms. His smile is incredulous.

"They're just people."

"People, did you hear what Manoo just said? Armenians. They're just people. Are they like Indians? What are they?" Freddy Snyder laughs and laughs, showing all the wiring in his expensive mouth.

"Just told you," I say.

"What kind of answer is that?' Freddy continues.

"Leave Manoo alone," Gresham Dodger says.

"But I was just asking him a question."

"No you weren't."

The rubber basketball bounces off the perforated metal backboard and through the net-less rim. From the same spot, at the top of the key, I give several head fakes before launching, but the next four are all off-line. I am number 44, Jerry West, of the West Virginia Mountaineers—Zeke from Cabin Creek—but Jerry West's shots generally hit nothing but net.

Beyond the chain-link fence, cars rip past on the West Side Highway and a tanker has dropped anchor in the Hudson River, where used rubbers float at full extension in the polluted water.

Five full-length asphalt basketball courts have been laid out, and on the farthest one I watch as another boy shoots baskets. Even from a distance I recognize him as from the grade below at the Claremont School. Waves of fear pass through me at the sighting of the boy, and yet my feet take me in his direction, one court after another.

He is a handsome boy, his hair shaggy and blond and longer than Momma will ever let mine be. Tall and gangly, he is brave to wear shorts and expose such white, skinny legs. We play a game of Horse and a game of one-on-one. Neither of us has a jump shot; we can't elevate beyond the thickness of a Manhattan phone book. When we part ways, I cling to a small sense of superiority, having come out on top.

We meet some days later on the same court. "So where do you live?" Tom Smits asks.

"Not so far from here."

"Where is that?" By now Tom has disclosed his Riverside Drive address, making him, in my mind, another boy with an immaculate apartment. And there is a second home, in upstate New York, and the position his father holds as the head of the history department at Brooklyn College. And there is his mother, a doctoral candidate in comparative literature at Columbia University, and his younger sister, blessed with a photographic memory.

"A few blocks. Near Broadway."

Fall and winter come, driving us indoors. Weekday nights we go to Madison Square Garden, down on Eighth Avenue and Fiftieth

Street, to see pro basketball doubleheaders. When the visiting Boston Celtics take the court, my eyes are on Bob Cousy, number 14, with his behind-the-back dribbling and full court passes. Or on Tommy Heinsohn, the Celtic forward with the flattop haircut, who releases his jumpers from over his right shoulder, contemptuously slinging the ball at the basket. The Celtics wear kelly green, the Knicks anemic white with orange trim. I see Cousy and Heinsohn and Frank Ramsay and Paul Scharman, and then I see my fear: Negro Bill Russell, their goateed center, and the Negro guards Sam and K.C. Jones. The Negro Boston Celtics will someday outnumber the white Boston Celtics, as someday Negroes will outnumber whites in the general population, with all the consequences that will have for me personally: unbridled anger and endless beatings and the mayhem of welfare hotels rife throughout the city. "The Jones Boys" must never surpass little Bob Cousy.

"Bill Russell is the Celtics' most valuable player. He could play with four dwarves and they would still win," Tom Smits says, after Russell deflects a shot by the Knicks' skinny forward Kenny Sears out toward Sam Jones, who races down the court and banks in a jumper.

"Russell doesn't score," I say, of the towering Celtics' center with the number six on his back.

"He doesn't have to. He controls the entire game. Defensive rebounding, outlet passes, shot-blocking that moves the Knick's offense farther and farther from the rim."

Tom Smits does not count the number of Negroes in the starting lineup of the Boston Celtics or identify with the whiteness of his skin and the blondness of his hair or harbor in his bones the fear that *they are coming, they are coming.*

A haze of cigar and cigarette smoke hangs over the arena, stinging our eyes and fouling our clothes as we watch the stars at night: not only magical Cousy with his behind-the-back passing and set shot but on other weekday nights Wilt the Stilt and Paul Arizin and Elgin Baylor with the beautiful name and the twitch in his neck who can hang suspended in the air, and Bob Pettit, who never makes a wasted move from his post-up position, and Hal Greer and Dick "fall back, baby, fall back" Barnett and Dolph Schayes. And we see the complete stiffs too, like Ray Felix, the seven foot center for the New York Knicks. And the names of the players—Zelmo Beatty and Sihugo Green, and of the teams—the Chicago Bulls, the St. Louis Hawks, the Minneapolis Lakers, the Detroit Pistons, the Cincinnati Royals, the Syracuse Nationals, formerly the Rochester Nationals.

And it is Tom Smits who has brought this thing into my life that is not shoplifting or riding the subways all day long.

But the clock runs out, ending our focus on the action on the varnished hardwood floor far below, and now it is only Tom and me, my fear growing as the subway makes one local stop after another. Things would be easier if Tom got off at One Hundred Third Street rather than One Hundred Tenth Street. He would have one less block to walk, since he lives on One Hundred Sixth Street. But he doesn't. He just has to hang on, as if he senses my discomfort. Surfacing on Broadway, I avoid looking up at the verse of scripture on the wall of the building so he will not look up as well and make an intuitive connection between me and my family and the sign. And when, to my horror, I see Naomi and Chuck coming out of the nearby bar, I just say a fast goodbye and we go our separate ways.

"You do have a telephone, don't you?" Tom says.

"Sure. Sure I do."

"So what's the number?"

"UNiversity 4-5783."

"Aren't you going to ask me for my number?" Tom says.

"Sure. I'll ask for it."

"Well?"

"Well, what?"

"'I'll ask for it' isn't the same thing as asking for it."

"Okay, so what is it?"

"ACademy 2-9947."

Just because I have the number doesn't mean I have to use it.

"It is that nice boy Tom on the phone for you," Momma says. Tom in my life makes her heart happy. She wants me out of immigrant shadows and in the bright sunlight of America, and Tom offers proof that I am moving in the right direction. A small, harmless breach, I tell myself, Tom Smits calling. After all, he can't see into my home through the telephone. But I do not like Tom's calls. They do not cause my heart to swell with happiness. All I feel is fear and tension lest Tom hear my family in the background and ask sharp, probing questions or crush me with mocking laughter, as I suspect Tom's real purpose to eventually be.

If I cannot give Tom my apartment, so Tom can go hah hah hah, I can give him indoor basketball courts when cold comes to drive us from the outdoor courts in Riverside Park. But a problem exists here, too. The gyms I know about are at Columbia University and Teacher's College and Riverside Church, north of where I live. It will not do to meet Tom Smits at the halfway point between our two buildings *(Not so far from here. I live not so far from here.)* That would mean meeting south of where I live and then walking north with him past my block. Such reckless stupidity could only be re-warded with Tom Smits laughing at Momma in her funny men's shoes and rubber stockings and looking down at Naomi and Chuck, who might well be drunk, and—no, no, we must not have this. We must not have this, as Momma says.

And so there is nothing to do but to meet on the safe ground of Chock Full O' Nuts on One Hundred Sixteenth Street and Broadway, because nobody but nobody can laugh at Chock Full O' Nuts, seeing that Columbia people go there all the time for their nutted cheese sandwiches and on Fridays tuna fish sandwiches and clam chowder soup, and those wonderful cream pies the chain serves all days of the week except Sunday, when they are closed. Chock Full O' Nuts has no blemish of family upon it. It has no mismatched furniture you can point to and put your laugh upon. It just has the order and the cleanliness of its ways.

"The heck with Chock Full O' Nuts. I'll come over to your apartment. We'll meet there," Tom says, unwilling to pretend he hasn't seen my fear.

"I'll meet you there," I say, meaning Chock Full, as if I hadn't heard. Because to have heard is to engage Tom in a discussion, and there is nothing to discuss. Nothing.

In a building on the Columbia campus we descend to the basement and pass through a maze of long, narrow passageways lined from floor to ceiling with thick horizontal steam pipes wrapped in padding cinched with metal bands. Now and then a worker appears in dark blue work pants and shirt or we hear the shouted voices of workers, but no adult voice barks, "Hey, you two, where do you think you are going?" And yet to know that any moment one sharp command can bring to an end my dream of making a gift to Tom Smits of the part of my world that is respectable and that will not unleash the hah hah hah.

Through a small door we pass. Far below lies a tightly organized space with dark green generators and ramps and walkways. Down the enclosed spiral metal staircase we go. The generators whir with frightening power as we come to another door. There, on the other side, lies a gleaming hardwood floor and fiber-glass backboards and hoops with white nets, not unadorned metal rims, attached to them.

"Amazing." Tom marvels, from the place of generosity that he possesses, and I bask in his approval, even as I sense that Tom's way is not to be in violation of the law or to trespass on private property. And so there is this qualm that I have led Tom Smits where he truly does not belong.

Alone, with only the sound of our squeaking sneakers and the bouncing ball echoing off the floor and the backboard, I can dream of one day what might come to be.

"The underground man. That is what I am going to call you from now on," Tom Smits says.

"At this very moment, under one of the world's great oceans, is a tunnel being built to facilitate the cardinals in their exultant trek from their Vatican home to the seat of power in our great nation's capital. So, my brothers and sisters, I ask you: Will we beat back this iniquity through the interdiction power of Jesus or will we live in enslavement to the forces of darkness operating from Rome?"

Interdic-*shun*. Je-*sus*. As if Pastor Odachenko would live for all time in those two syllables.

"I am not political," Ogden Connifer hisses. I have asked him which candidate he favors, Richard Milhous Nixon or John Fitzgerald Kennedy.

"Don't you know the cardinals are coming? The tunnel is being built and they may be walking through it right now?"

Ogden Connifer shows me his smiling contempt. He is telling me something, as Gresham Dodger told me something. He is telling me to look that I might see the chains that have me bound. And if only for a moment I do, I do, that a presidential campaign should cause such fear in me and none in him.

The Hotel Commodore rises down the block from where the trains run forever into and from Grand Central Terminal. Jerry and I take the subway to Times Square and the one-stop shuttle that never fails to reach its destination beneath the terminal. The New York Central is Republican. The granite structure of the terminal building is

Republican. And the store at street level below the Commodore has Republican operatives who have stocked it with the buttons and badges of Republican power.

With flashers pinned to our jackets alternately showing the faces of Nixon and Henry Cabot Lodge, his running mate, we stand among the tall buildings with badges for the men in wool overcoats and fedoras as they rush with their attaché cases toward the terminal in a end-of-day exodus. Richard Milhous Nixon, from Yorba Linda, California. Henry Cabot Lodge, born in Massachusetts, with roots in our Colonial past. Harvard. A man who has to be the best of the best, with that distinguished gray hair.

Some toss coins in the basket and even dollar bills, awakening in us a hunger for more. We head uptown, along rain-slick Madison Avenue, and move indoors, to the Roosevelt Hotel, on Forty-fifth Street. Through the ornate lobby, thick with bellhops, we head to the mezzanine, where men in suits and women in evening gowns lounge on plush chairs, to the plainer upper floors. Silver-haired men answer our knocks, men here with their wives from Ann Arbor, Michigan, and Wichita, Kansas, and Shaker Heights, Ohio, eager to step out and experience the Great White Way. Into their pockets they reach for coins and draw bills from their wallets in exchange for the badges we offer, hasty transactions so as not to throw off their evening plans. One saying, "Honey, do we have any change lying around for these wonderful kids? Never mind. Here, guys, take this."

That night, our pockets bulging with coins and dollar bills, I have to hold my pants up as we head home.

On the northeast corner of Amsterdam Avenue a black and white sign hangs over a diner: "Hamburger, 5 cents." It is a sign for me to keep my eye on, as it says that economy exists. The people who go there have poverty in their bones, and knives emerging heated from their boiling veins. The brownstones and other small buildings all along the side streets from Broadway east to Central Park house them. It is an area in which I must mind my Ps and Qs, make emotional adjustments to reduce the threat of violence, and feel only anger for those of my male classmates in their crested blue blazers who invite the wrath of the neighborhood with their raised voices and brash ways, ignoring the reality that they must recognize the threat to be safe from it. To walk about free and uninhibited is grounds for punishment. The danger level is especially high when passing the public junior high school just across the street from Claremont.

"Yo, pussy. Yo, faggot. You looking at me wrong, baby? You want a punch in the mouth? You want to come over here and suck my dick? How about you give me five dollars or I cut your heart out? Yeah, you motherfucker, with that box for a head."

This is the school that Jerry Jones-Nobleonian attends, and there is no Gresham Dodger to say, "We don't do this here. We don't do this here."

A box for a head? No one makes mention of my head at the Claremont School. Not one word. Still, I continue to sit in the back row as a precaution, lest others behind me study my head and note the flatness of the back of it and think of names to call me. It would not do to have to feel their eyes upon me and be unable to think of anything but their fixed focus. A hand mirror gives me a view of it as I stand in front of the medicine chest mirror in the bathroom at home. As flat as the sheerest cliff. I stare at the beautifully shaped heads of the other boys. Even Charles Blatner has a nice round head. Every time I hope to see something different, but the flatness remains, harshly uncompromising.

As the end of eighth grade nears, school yearbooks are issued. The captions under the photos all begin, "We wish for him" or "We wish for her." For Gresham Dodger the wish is for a dazzling career as an artist. For Ogden Connifer, the wish is for a professorship at Yale. For Susan Springer, the wish is that she share the secret of her beauty. For Johan Manootdjian, the wish is that he receive the missing part of his head.

So they saw and they knew. All along they saw. All along they knew.

Part 3

Johan Meets Jane

Chapter 1

The spring day when a new chapter in his life was to begin Johan turned the corner onto Amsterdam Avenue and saw the man-child Sean in the bright afternoon light with a finger in Scully's face. "You got something to say, you fat fuck? You want your ass kicked in front of all your friends?" A thrill of terror shot through Johan seeing the veins like bulging cords in Sean's thick neck.

"I'm sorry, man. I'm sorry," Scully said, his wise guy stuff gone and all that fat shaking like jello inside his size extra large red and white LaSalle High School cardigan. Scully had gone belly up.

The basket of Sean's balloon-tired delivery bike held a carton of groceries. He pushed the bike off the stand and pedaled across the avenue and up toward Morningside Drive, his head tilted back in an angle of triumph.

"What the fuck is wrong with you, Scully? You got some kind of death wish?" Kevin Donnelly stood just over five feet. Even when he cursed, he sounded kind and gentle, a soft-spoken sadness being in his nature. "He yells out, 'There goes the Headmobile,' as Sean is riding by on his bike," he goes on, for Johan's ears. Kevin took a heavy drag on his Parliament. He made the tip glow. Kevin was fourteen and looked eleven. Tiny pools of spit formed around his sneakered feet on the cracked sidewalk. Smoke. Spit. Smoke. Spit.

Some of the kids said Sean's head was shaped like a hammer. Hammerhead, they called him, but never to his face. They could afford to sound on Johan's head. Squarehead. Blockhead. They knew there would be no reprisal. Sean was something else. Sean had the power to take you down in both fists and he had it in his will, which paid no mind to your larger size and strength.

Sounding. Your momma goes down for wooden nickels. Your momma wears combat boots. Always something about mommas.

"Fuck you." Sullenness had entered Scully's face and tone.

Luis was right on him. "No, man, Sean's going to fuck you. He's going to fuck you up bad." His words were hard, emphatic, like the pitches delivered by his strong right arm. He and Kevin were classmates at Bishop DuBois High School. Scully could say fuck you to Kevin, but not to Luis. Luis was big and broad-shouldered and tough.

LaSalle and Bishop DuBois and Cardinal Hayes and Power Memorial and Xavier and Archbishop Molloy. A Catholic world of mass and confession and the Baltimore catechism and the punishing hands of the brothers and nuns.

Sean hadn't looked at Johan, and yet Johan felt as if Sean was looking at him the whole time. Was it really three years before that Johan had witnessed Sean scaling the batting cage in Riverside Park in pursuit of Frenchie the Algerian on that rocky baseball field in Riverside Park? Sean was a part of him now though they had never so much as spoken to each other.

A balding man with a red nose and broken blood vessels in his meaty face stepped out of the grocery next door. Quart bottles of beer clanked in the big brown bag he carried as he slowly climbed the steps of the gray stoop and disappeared into the tenement. Every day was the same thing with Scully's father after his shift as a city bus driver. Soon his pudgy twelve-year-old sister and his sumo-wrestler-sized mother headed up the steps.

"Damn, Scully, your family got some serious bulk," Jimmy Riley said.

"Fuck you," Scully replied, not in anger, almost lazily.

That afternoon they played stickball against a windowless wall of the nearby hospital, food fumes from the kitchen blowing out of a metal vent. The game ended when Scully smacked the Spaldeen into the grounds of the rectory of the Notre Dame Church, the pink ball lost somewhere under the English ivy.

It being Friday, he was free to stay out with his friends into the evening playing ringolevio. One team hunted; the other hid, so as not to get caught and stuck in jail.

"Your ass is mine," Luis, the jailer, shouted, seeing Johan sprint for the jail trying to free Scully and Kevin, and moments later it was true. Johan's ass was his, or his chest was, as Luis clamped him in an iron grip.

"Damn, you're all bones," Luis said, causing Johan's face to turn red. Luis telling him what he already knew—that there wasn't enough of him.

Afterward, they sat on the steps of an entrance to the Columbia University campus. If Scully's stoop was their second home, then Columbia was the third. "A gift from the class of 1929." So it was written on the arch above the gate. That was a long time ago, 1929. Thirty-three years. The gift could only mean those college years the alumni spent there were special, golden, like the gold lettering on the arch. And why not? To be enrolled at Columbia was to take your place with the gods. It meant to be chosen. It didn't matter that they wore those silly freshman beanies as part of their orientation. They were in. *In.*

A girl stepped out of the hotel across the street wearing cutoff jeans and a pink top. Johan followed her with his eyes as she headed toward the corner of Amsterdam Avenue under the sodium vapor lights of the new, sleek lampposts the city had been installing. She had come into Jimmy Riley's line of vision, too. "Hey, baby," he shouted. You could count on Jimmy Riley to say something like that.

"What you going to do if she answers you?" Luis challenged. "You ain't got no words for her. You low on charm and looks and savoir faire."

"I let this do the talking," Jimmy said, his frail body shaking with manic laughter as he grabbed his crotch.

Jimmy hadn't meant to be taken seriously. Didn't Luis understand that? Luis, who was now blowing perfect smoke rings from his Winston, didn't have to put him down with his brutal truth. Why couldn't Jimmy be left alone to imagine himself as a Romeo? Even if Jimmy Riley tried not to show it, the hurt was there. Johan felt safe while playing games with them; sitting around was a riskier matter.

He looked toward the hotel, hoping to see her return. Minutes later there she was, walking slightly pigeon toed into the hotel clutching a bag of groceries.

"You want to fuck her, Johan?" Scully's blunt question was like being struck a blow. Johan's face reddened. Sex was not a subject he could speak about easily.

Scully ran his hand hard over the back of Johan's head. "My man Flathead is horny."

"Sure he wants to fuck her. Right, Johan? You want to stick your skinny dick in her. You're going to go home and jerk off over her, aren't you?" Philip Malloy was a bit crazy. The other day he just missed Scully's head with a full swing of a stickball bat. It was best to be careful with Philip, as it was with all of them.

Jerry Jones-Nobleonian began to laugh, as Johan could depend on him to do when someone was riding him.

"What are you laughing about, Jerry? Where'd you get skin like that? Someone dip you in lye?" There was ugliness in Philip, that he would speak like that to Jerry, or anyone.

"No one dipped me in lye," Jerry said. "I had an allergic reaction to penicillin, that's all."

How far would Philip go? Would he start in on Jerry's woolly hair and broad nose? Would he force Jerry to explain that his real father was Estonian and that he was not run over but "runned over" by a Soviet tank during the takeover of the Baltic countries during World War II and that the Negro man his Estonian mother lived with was not his natural father?

Scully laughed, clearly enjoying Philip's cruelty.

"What are you laughing about, Scully? Look at Scully's pants. Tell me you don't see a come stain there."

"Come on, man, that's dried milk." Now it was time for Scully's face to redden again.

Jimmy Riley returned slugging from a twelve-ounce bottle of Pepsi and beaming. He seemed to have recovered from Luis's harsh words. "You see that girl I shouted to? I go, 'What you doing tonight, Babes? Let's you and me go down some alleyway.' So she goes, 'Your cock ain't big enough to make the proposition even interesting.'" Jimmy laughs in his wild, self-deprecating way.

"Let's go, boys. It's time." Louie stood at the top of the steps in his gray uniform, and jangled his keys, one of which would lock the gate.

The group moved on. "I hear he's an old faggot who likes boys," Philip said, in that hard, disparaging voice of his.

"Johan heard the same thing. Right, Johan?" Scully again.

"Your fat fucking mother heard the same thing," Philip said, and waved goodbye. He lived on Morningside Drive, in a solid and well-maintained building bordered with hedges and a flowerbed in spring and summer. There was nothing of the squalor of the tenements on Amsterdam Avenue on his street. Just beyond his building and down a deep drop was Morningside Park. Only the ignorant or the very foolish wandered its footpaths, as brooding Harlem was further to the east. The morning sun shone on his building. If he went about in oxblood loafers and tweed jackets and khaki pants, it was because his father did not drive a bus or walk the beat with a nightstick and a holstered gun. His father owned a bar and grill. In an earlier time his father was a prize fighter, a middleweight with a thumping right who still enjoyed coming out from behind the stick to bang with unruly customers.

If the night was over for Philip, it wasn't for the rest of them.

"Let's go visit Fritz," Jimmy Riley suggested, and so they wandered west across Broadway, past a row of fraternity houses from which poured loud music, Friday and Saturday night being party night. Halfway down the hill leading to Riverside Drive, they entered a single-room occupancy with a Rooms to Let sign hanging out front.

Fritz was short and balding, with only wisps of red hair remaining. He worked as a butcher at the meat store a couple of doors down from Scully's stoop. Johan liked to watch as Fritz sent his cleaver through the bone to sever the chops and then trim the fat with a sharp knife on the chopping block before wrapping the meat in thick butcher paper.

"Are my little boys here for pussy? Is that why they have come?" Fritz was like a lynx or some other clever little animal. He stared with piercing eyes through wire-frame glasses.

"Damn straight," Luis headed for the stack of *Playboy* magazines at the foot of Fritz's bed.

Louie. He has stayed in Johan's mind. And the girl, too. Did she really say that to Jimmy? Did girls care about the size of a boy's penis? It didn't seem possible that she had said those words. And yet, suppose she did?

"Hey Johan, look, for God's sake. It won't kill you," Luis said. Several issues of the magazine lay open on the floor to the centerfold. But his eyes remained averted from the airbrushed photos of the naked women.

"What's the matter, Johan? You don't like the girls? You're not different from us, are you?" First Philip. Now Fritz.

"Why doesn't everyone just leave him alone?" Kevin's defense was only further cause for embarrassment.

He waited for the shackles of self-consciousness to fall away so he could leave. Only some need for concealment had caused him to come in the first place. He knew where he wanted to be, and everything in him was screaming to get there. He stepped toward the door, grateful for the power of the *Playboy* women to distract his friends.

Louie was just coming out of the main entrance to the library. That jowly face and thin-lipped little mouth. He looked around, and seeing no one, motioned Johan inside.

The thud of his heavy belt buckle as it fell to the floor of the carpeted office. The smell of sweat and cigarettes. The sight of his polka dot boxer shorts. The thrill as Louie directed the beam of the flashlight over Johan's naked body. The feel of his cold mouth. The way Johan came, almost immediately, as he often did.

Through the bars of the gate Louie had earlier unlocked, Johan saw the girl emerging from the hotel. Their eyes met and she waved and went on her way, disappearing around the corner. Her smile. Her wave. Some crazy excitement, some new longing was wild within him now.

All three bulbs of the pole lamp were burning. Luke stood naked, staring into the full-length mirror, his feet spread on the black and red squares of the linoleum they had bought a couple of years before to try to improve the room. Johan went to his desk in the corner. Everything was there: the black-and-tan algebra book, the thin blue French text, the Kittredge paperback copy of *Romeo and Juliet*, his three-ring-binder looseleaf with subject dividers.

He understood to leave his brother alone. He thought of Luke's trances as like sleepwalking, which he heard were dangerous to wake a person from. Besides, they never lasted any longer than Momma's spells down at the tabernacle. Was his blood good or bad? Pressing his nose into his forearm would tell him. His neck and back were cratered with acne, as was his face, which he now inspected. Luke virtually bathed in Phisohex, for all the good it did. Phisohex for his face and body and Wildroot for his hair. He moved on to his teeth, knocking his uppers and lowers together a few times to test their soundness.

"Were you with Nancy?" Nancy Becker was Luke's girlfriend. Her family's apartment was Luke's second home.

"No. She's got this tutor who helps her with analytic geometry a couple of nights a week. Winston. You remember him, right? He threw you out for derailing his train set. But she needs to bring her math grades up if she wants to get into a good college, she says. She's pretty smart, you know. I could tell, back in ninth grade, that she was going to be something, even when she had all that wire in her mouth. I'm able to recognize stuff like that. Not everybody can do that. Right?"

"Right," As if Luke was some talent scout who had discovered a young Mickey Mantle or Roger Maris. Johan was uncomfortable when Luke leaned on him, as if he was being forced to say what he didn't truly believe lest Luke be hurt or grow testy. Nancy Becker was preparing for the future and Luke was not and someday she would hurt him. That is what Johan dared not say.

"They have this beautiful apartment on Riverside Drive. You should see it."

Often Luke would tell Johan about Nancy Becker and her family's beautiful home. What about you, Luke? What about you? So Johan would think but also not say.

Luke turned on the radio. An old Elvis song, "Love Me Tender," was playing. "It's late, Luke. Turn it down. Momma's sleeping," Johan said, even as the sound placed him under its spell. Luke only laughed.

Mr. Manootdjian was now standing in the doorway, his eyes ablaze. He reached for the knob and turned off the radio. "What is the meaning of this?"

"Nothing." Luke was a mixture of sullenness and fear.

"What is nothing? You wake the whole house and that is nothing?"

"I didn't wake the whole house. You're just coming in." It was true. His father was still in the suit he wore to work that morning and to his church service afterward.

"Are you trying to provoke me?"

"Leave me alone."

"You are sick, maybe? You would like to be put in a hospital for crazy people?"

"No. I want you to hit me. Come on over here and hit me." Seeing Luke naked, his right arm cocked and his hand balled into a fist, Mr. Manootdjian backed out of the room.

"Like everyone has to live in terror of his big fucking hand," Luke muttered, sitting on the bottom bunk.

Johan's antennae were up now, as they were every night when his father returned home.

In the bunk below his brother soon was snoring lightly. Minutes later there was another sound, that of the door opening and footsteps coming closer in the dark. "No," Johan shouted. "No."

Mr. Manootdjian's fist made a thudding sound on Luke's body under the blanket. Luke woke up screaming.

The light had come on. "What is this? Tell me please what this is. Tell me." Johan's mother stood in her white terrycloth robe holding her chest, as if to stop it from heaving. "Do you wish to kill me? We cannot have this violence. Do you not understand, any of you?"

Mr. Manootdjian was gasping for breath. He was not young. Sixty. Old to be a father. Old, period.

But no one died. No one. Sleep came. It really did. But before it could, Johan watched the lights from the cars down on Broadway sweep along the ceiling. His mind moved past the stuff of family to thoughts of Louie, and how he had been dirty but now was clean after washing himself. His thoughts turned to the girl and the thrill it summoned when their eyes met through the bars of the gate.

Chapter 2

Monday morning came. Johan rode the subway two local stops to Ninety-third Street. Pain found him and only grew worse as he stepped onto the platform. He paused and rested his head against a steel pillar. He had abandoned his mother. He had left her all alone, and now she was weeping without a soul to comfort her. For some time he stood there, struggling against the impulse to run home and make things right for her. It was like that every school day morning; a force field would present itself that he had to struggle to push through. And yet, once within the confines of the school, the pull of home would lift.

"So what did you do this weekend, Manootdj?" Even shorter than Johan, Freddy Snyder had a booming voice that brought the whole room into the conversation. A good athlete in spite of the thick glasses he was required to wear, he played guard along with Johan on the junior varsity team.

Fear quickly consumed him, as it did with any questions that involved his personal life. "My family and I went to see *Splendor in the Grass*," Johan blurted, remembering having seen the name of the film displayed on the marquee of the Nemo Theater on One Hundred Tenth Street that morning. His intention was to cast his family in a worldly light. It wouldn't do to share his parents' religiosity with Freddy and expose himself and them to ridicule.

And yet ridicule awaited him. Freddy's mouth hung open, exposing the thick embrace of the metal around his upper teeth. "You saw *Splendor in the Grass* with your family? With your family? Are you kidding me? People, did you hear what Manootdj just said? He went with his family to see *Splendor in the Grass?*" Freddy gave every word of the movie the full measure of astonishment he felt it deserved. There seemed to be no room for silence or restraint in him. And in drawing in the rest of the room, Freddy seemed to prove that their classmates were a monolithic entity from which Johan was permanently separated.

"Let Manoo see what he wants to see." The boy who came to his rescue was named Lance. It was said that he had a musical gift. He was also handsome, with long brown hair that fell over his forehead, and he was at ease with the girls. Though they would never be friends, he felt liked by Lance.

For the rest of the day Freddy's amazement lived in Johan's mind. Stupid, stupid, stupid. How could he have guessed so wrong in trying to make himself and his family presentable? Within the confines of the school, he felt reduced, cowed, able to offer nothing more than an amiable smile.

By the open door to his homeroom he stood after lunch. The voices of several girls rose in jubilant song, tunes to which they knew all the words. Diane Coleman and Robin Abel—both of them tall and slender and smart—were among them. Despite the gaiety the room felt dangerous and off-limits, as if the singing could cease at any moment and mockery begin, but he needed his Latin book for the next class. Maybe he could just slip in and out. As he moved along the perimeter and reached inside his desk, the singing stopped. He had almost made it to the door when Diane Coleman shouted out, "Hi, Dreamboat," prompting huge laughter.

In the last class of the day, Miss Simpson, her gray hair pulled into a bun, led a discussion of *Romeo and Juliet*. "Take thou some new infection to the eye/and the rank poison of the old shall die." Such was Benvolio's advice to Romeo, lovesick over Rosalind. How sad that Romeo should be in such pain. He thought of Nancy Becker's domination of Luke. Nothing of the kind would ever happen to him, Johan assured himself, as he quickly headed home to change out of his uniform and then made a beeline to Scully's stoop,

But the girl was not there that afternoon nor in the days that followed. A week later, when he had stopped looking past Scully and Luis and Jimmy Riley and the rest of them in the hope that she would materialize, there she was, stepping out of the Hotel Arizona, as on that first night.

"Where's your gang?" she said.

"I don't have a gang."

"Sure you do. "

"That's no gang. They're just friends of mine."

She wore her strawberry-blond hair in a bowl cut and her green eyes sparkled.

"Well, one of them has a fresh mouth."

"That could be."

"What do you mean, 'That could be.' He does."

"Do you live here?" Johan pointed to the hotel.

"Oh, no. My father has me come down a few afternoons during the week to buy groceries for my grandmother. She's got a room here. I'm just going to the store for her now."

"Come down from where?"

"Who wants to know?"

"Sorry," Johan said.

"Just kidding. One Hundred Twenty-second Street."

"That's not so far."

"Well, I have to get going," Jane says.

As she walked off, Johan called out. "Maybe I could walk you home tonight." The words were just there.

"I like that idea. I head home about eight o'clock."

That evening, by the unused tennis court next to Butler Library, Johan took her hand. As they proceeded along the brick footpath, he was afraid to turn his head, as if the spell would break if he looked at her. With every second that passed his self-consciousness grew that his hand was locked on hers.

A construction site awaited them down a long set of stairs near the north end of the campus. A gray plywood fence had been erected around the site. In this dark and desolate area of the campus Johan paused and kissed the girl. Her soft lips parted slightly, and he felt the tip of her tongue.

"I want to marry you someday," he blurted.

"Slow down," Jane laughed, emphasizing both words and deepening his shame.

Now a light was shining. The beam held steady on their faces. "Lonely over here. A good place to get in trouble," Louie said, looking old and fat, before continuing on his rounds. His gumshoes fell silently on the pavement.

Beyond the confines of the Columbia campus the gingerbread-colored buildings of Teachers College softly spread along the two-lane cobblestone street. Everywhere the institutions of the gifted, and on their fringes the dwelling places of the remnant.

"This is me," she said stopping in front of a five-story walkup building two blocks north.

"I'll see you soon, I hope," he said.

"Not if I see you first." She headed up the stairs of the stoop and disappeared down the narrow hallway. It was an expression he had heard before, without quite knowing what it meant.

As he climbed the hill toward Broadway, he read out loud the names carved in the porticos of the old apartment buildings--the Delaware, Simna Hall, Marimpol Court, Reldnas Hall—trying to block out the painful blunder. *I want to marry you someday.*

In his room that night he closed the door and listened in the dark to the radio. Luke was still out visiting with Nancy Becker, and so he lay on the bottom bunk as a song from the musical *Oliver* came on the air. "Where Is Love?" a boy sang in a plaintive voice. The song washed over him; warm tears streamed down his face. Did love in fact fall from the sky above or appear from under a willow tree? Oh, the words weren't important. It was just the plaintive voice. Even as he lay there, he sensed something excessive in his nature. A thirst or a hunger, it was, something sickly that rendered him helpless.

And perhaps Luke sensed the same thing. "Are you OK?" he asked, opening the door and turning on the light.

"I'm fine," Johan said, drying his face on his sleeve and climbing up into his own bunk.

"You are about to be in the red," Miss Timmons said. A small woman with frosted white hair, she ran the school cafeteria. He had come to her on the checkout line with a hamburger and half-pint of milk on his tray.

"I'm sorry?"

"In the red. Do you not know what that means? Have your mother make out another check. You need some good food to put some meat on those bones."

She spoke with a half-smile on her face that was not really a smile at all. And her mention of his mother's name was paralyzing. He did not want his family on the school premises in any way.

In the afternoon Ron Reisman, a boy from one of the upper grades said, with an assassin's smile, "I'll bet you don't weigh more than fifty pounds." Johan had no defense in the face of the perceived meanness of the older student and went numb. Of course he had been right to make his knife thrust. A missing part of Johan's head and a body he shouldn't be seen with in public. Johan smiled to cover his hurt. It was all he could offer anyone at this school.

And there was Mr. Horvas, the school librarian, with that per-- manent expression of peeve on his handsome face, as if the world itself was an affront and worthy of low-grade outrage. "He says it's a good book, and he's only read fifty pages," Mr. Horvas sneered, to a pretty blond girl in one of the upper classes, having heard him reply to Freddy Snyder in the school library that he was liking *Of Mice and Men.*

And of course Mr. Horvas was right. How stupid to imagine he could offer an opinion on a book after fifty pages. How even more stupid that such a thing had never occurred to him.

"The Duke of Earl" came loud from the radio ("And I, I walk through my dukedom, nothing can stop me, the Duke of Earl"). "You boys a little young for the suds," said the checkout man, as he bagged the six-pack of Rheingold, throwing in a church key as well. "You both be cool now," he says.

"Duke, Duke, Duke, Duke of Earl," they sang, trying to approximate a royal strut, as they headed down the hill and into the park.

Johan had never bought beer before or even tasted it. The idea had just entered his mind. It would take him higher than he had been the night before, higher than he had ever been, higher than the stars that were out on this spring night. They took the stairs down to the lower level of the park. On the Jersey shore the Spry sign glowed a constant red.

"You see what Ellie did last night? A homer and a double. Ellie's good too, isn't he?" Jerry said, Ellie being Elston Howard, a catcher and sometime first baseman and outfielder for the very white New York Yankees. Jerry was looking for a Negro face to light up his life, he said, without saying it. Mentioning Ellie was as close to saying he too was a Negro as Jerry could come. Johan did not challenge Jerry to tell the truth when he talked about how his real father was "runned over" by a Soviet tank while defending his homeland. Lies had to be allowed for. You had to place soft protective padding around them. And anyway, Johan had his own lies, his *Splendor in the Grass* lie and his "My family lives on the Upper West Side" lie. Jerry had placed his lie about his father in Johan's protective custody. *Ellie is good too, isn't he?* It was like crying to be seen and heard and *valued*.

"Ellie's real good," Johan said, though when at the ballpark, his focus was on Mantle, as if a cone of light embraced him in the out-field or standing at the plate in a coiled stance with that big number 7 on his back, or on Roger Maris, as he used to think of Duke Snider more than Willie Mays before the Dodgers and Giants left town.

Below, through the tangle of brush on the other side of the fence, cars with their headlights on sped along, their tires making a spanking sound as they hit the cracks in the road. Beyond was the river, with its filmy, sewage-filled water, and on the other side, the Palisades.

Couples strolled along the footpaths, under the long branches of scaly plane trees in full bloom. Suddenly the earth trembled. From below came the loud rumble of a freight train. And yet the urge was no longer there to run to the tunnel and wait in ambush with a supply of rock ballast to boom off the rolling stock of the New York Central.

"You remember that girl the night we were playing ringolevio?"

"What girl?"

"You know. The one Jimmy Riley claimed said something to him."

"Oh yeah. That girl."

"I walked her home," Johan said.

"Oh yeah?"

When he pressed the church key against the top of the can, beer foamed out of the triangular hole. The beer had a metallic taste, like coins in his mouth.

"I kissed her. She let me."

"She got a girlfriend? Maybe she could get somebody for me."

The beer had induced no journey to the stars and beyond, as he had hoped; rather, it had rendered him sodden, he realized, as they climbed the hill out of the park. And yet, he and Jerry had finished all six cans. Despite his mother's warnings and the taste and the effect, he had found a new friend, though not one to rival the hold Jane Thayer would have on him, at least not in those high school years.

Outside Johan's building a tall Negro man stood with his arms crossed. With him was a woman with a frizz of brownish hair and glazed eyes, her massive breasts threatening to burst her tight blouse.

"Where you been, boy?" Jerry's father said, ignoring Johan.

"We were in the park," Jerry said.

"You were in the park. You were here. You were there. Everywhere you were, but not with us," his mother said.

"Let's go home now," Jerry's father said, taking Jerry in hand.

In the lobby Naomi sang "Over the Rainbow" to an audience of tenants who came and went, none of them stopping so much as to pause, as if they didn't have the time for a twenty-nine-year-old woman seeking attention for her small gift. Her husband, Chuck, who sat in a stuffed chair, was more appreciative of Naomi's offering, if belligerently so. "Your sister has a great instrument. She could be somebody." The familiar pint bottle of wine in a green bottle rested by the side of the chair. He looked and sounded aggrieved.

A feeling of rage and injustice seized Johan that they should be there at all, making a spectacle of themselves. His anger was directed at his mother as much as at them for her laughter, for saying he didn't know what it is to was have children, her prayer being that one day they would all be together in heaven. It was for sure they were not here on earth.

"Hello, brother," Naomi called out.

He waved and kept moving.

"Snotty brat," Chuck snarled, as Johan began to climb the stairs.

"You watch out for my husband. He's a real man."

Staring into her pert, pretty face he would feel joy but also regret that he was only meeting her now. Why couldn't he have had this happiness sooner? Not that it could ever have been, since she and her parents moved around the Midwest before coming to New York City. Even so, he had the feeling that they were born to be together. But there was no need to tell her so. He didn't have to make the same kind of mistake twice.

"Hey babes, what you doing with that goofball?" Jimmy Riley shouted, in that vaguely Negro intonation he, blond and pale, could lapse into, seeing Johan and Jane together. Jimmy's surprise, and that of all the neighborhood kids, only increased his joy. He was the kid who couldn't look at *Playboy* centerfolds with the other boys, and yet here he was with this pretty girl.

"My man Flathead has got himself a girlfriend. Fucking Flathead!" Scully called out, for all to hear, as confirmation that Johan was being seen in a new light.

Good. Let them all call out. Let them all shout.

Chapter 3

"It is a man named Sean on the house phone. He is calling from the lobby and asking to speak with you. I don't like for people to call you at night. Who is this man?" His mother stood in the doorway of his room, where he was doing algebra homework. He was in the B section of Mr. Arbuckle's class, not the A section where Diane Coleman and Robin Abel and the smarter kids could be found. He was afraid of algebra and the feelings of barely controllable anger, mostly directed at his mother, that came over him when some of the problems stymied him—that same depth of rage as he experienced during the intelligence test.

The worldliness of the world had come in its darkest form, his mother was saying.

"He's not a man," Johan said., putting down his pencil and leaving the room, as if it wouldn't do to keep Sean waiting.

"I want you to see a movie with me tonight. Get down here."

"I don't have any money," he said, trying to ignore the gruffness in Sean's voice and afraid for some reason to tell him he had homework to do.

"That's okay, because I'm paying."

"OK," Johan said, throwing himself upon the night and the anarchy looming.

Mrs. Manootdjian stood in the vestibule between Johan and the front door. "Johan, who is this person? Why do I not have a good feeling about him? What does he want with you?"

"He's from the neighborhood. He wants me to see a movie with him." There was no need to tell her he had not exchanged two words with Sean nor had he any idea how Sean came to know where he lived.

"I say to you that I do not like it. What is this night that calls and calls my children and never quite returns them? What is it, I ask you, if not the work of Satan?" There was vehemence in his mother's voice now.

He understood his mother's concern. He had his own. His homework was incomplete. He was deviating from the straight line he was trying to walk so he wouldn't fall into his old ways at the Episcopal school. And yet. And yet.

Sean's appearance startled. Gone was the five o'clock shadow. Instead of jeans and a T-shirt, he was wearing a gray suit with a black turtleneck and black shoes with a high shine. If it weren't for the enormity of his head, you would say he was handsome, like a male model in one of those shirt ads.

On the corner Sean flagged a cab, with authority, as if he had been doing it his whole life, and from the back seat gave forceful directions to the driver. The smell of the leather upholstery mixed with the cologne Sean was wearing. As the cab streaked down Broadway, a feeling came over Johan that grew only stronger throughout the evening; he had been transformed into a pretty, refined girl asked out on a date by a brute. Sean's violence was palpable—it was there pulsating in his powerful body—and yet it pleased Johan to think that he could somehow tame him.

"If you're wondering how I found you, your friend Jerry told me where you lived," Sean said, as the cab passed through Columbus Circle and approached Times Square.

The blaze of lights on both sides of Seventh Avenue served as a distraction from the painful image of his mother blocking his path. The strip was a feast of movie marquees and huge billboards advertising American commodities—Hygrade's Franks, Nescafè, Canada Dry, Four Roses— all competing for the eye's attention.

"Keep the change," Sean said, peeling off a ten-spot from a roll of bills and handing it to the hackie.

A red carpet had been unfurled in front of the theater, and soon they were inside, settling into soft seats.

"You want something?" Sean asked.

"No, I'm OK."

"I'm buying. Tell me what you want."

So he told him, and Sean returned with two big boxes of popcorn and sodas.

"I brought some money. I can pay."

"This is on me," Sean said, as if the matter wasn't for discussion.

"Thank you."

"You're welcome," he said, and Johan could only wonder if Sean was mocking his fearful politeness.

Since being dragged from the Nemo Theater by Hannah, Johan had been to movies in neighborhood theaters, but on screens far smaller than the one before him. As the pleated curtain slowly opened, the lights dimmed, and music poured from the speakers to mark the beginning of *Lawrence of Arabia*.

The film was as endless as the desert locations, T. E. Lawrence and his Arab band sweeping across the white sands of Arabia to battle the ruthless Turks. In one scene, Lawrence, disguised as an Arab, was captured by the enemy and kept in captivity overnight.

"You know what they did to him?" Sean whispered, leaning into Johan with a laugh of barely repressed hysteria.

On the return trip home, the cabbie played the staggered streetlights on Amsterdam Avenue just right, speeding uptown without stopping. The big face of a public clock showed the time to be 11:30 pm. How dark and quiet the streets were along this lonely stretch. He had never been out this late before with homework undone, not since coming to Claremont. As the cab approached Ninety-third Street, Johan stared out at the quiet block and pictured the brownstone buildings of the Claremont School and thought with a sharp pang how much the school meant to him. He must never fall behind. Never.

"I see you in that uniform sometimes. You go to some private school?" The question sounded like an accusation.

"Yes."

"So where is it?"

"We just passed it," Johan said, as if the exact address would allow Sean to barge into the heart of his dream.

The cab left them at Sean's apartment building, across the street from the Cathedral of St. John the Divine, dark and gloomy, its three massive doors closed for the night. Again Sean flashed a thick roll of bills. Not the kind of money you earned pedaling a grocery bike.

"There's plenty more where that came from," Sean said, seeing where Johan's eyes had gone. It would not do to tell Sean that he was less interested in his money than he might think.

"I want to see more of you," Sean called out as Johan headed down the long side street to Broadway. He turned back to see Sean laugh loudly, his head thrown back, before strutting into his building.

I want to see more of you. Such power the words had, in spite of Johan's strong reservations, to create an inner glow.

His mother sat at the dining table, reading from her Bible in her white robe.

"Do you know the time, foolish boy? Do you?"

"I'm sorry."

"Is this what you do to me? Do you not know the trouble that I have? Do I have to have more? Where did you go with that man?"

"To a movie," he said, trying to steel himself against her pain.

"I cannot take anymore of this."

His mother looked old and careworn. There were kids in his class with parents younger than the age his mother was when he was born.

"It was just this one time."

"One time. One time. It's what all my children say, before I lose them to the filth of the world."

He lay in bed with the crushing weight of his mother upon him. He had not made things right for her; he had only added to her pain. He would be very good from now on. So much depended on being so.

But his mother did not die during the night from sorrow, just as she hadn't when he said he could not bear attending church anymore the year before and stopped going. Whatever she might say, she was not of one mind about the world. She had a mother's understanding that she couldn't shield him from what was out there, as she couldn't shield any of her children.

She seemed happy at the breakfast table and his life did not fly off the rails because he was out late the night before. In study hall he managed to finish his algebra homework, and later there was a big red "A" atop the paper he wrote on "Romeo and Juliet" for Miss Simpson, and so he was on a straight line again, with no disorder in sight.

Once again he saw that he could compartmentalize his life and succeed. He needed only to be polite and amiable with his classmates and teachers, and the door to a bright future would remain open.

When, out of the blue, John Edel approached that day and said, "You're a really good student," Johan stammered and could say nothing intelligible. John Edel was established in his mind as one of the very brightest boys in the class. But perhaps John Edel hadn't approached him on the spur of the moment. Had Johan not overheard his name mentioned as Freddy Snyder spoke with John Edel only moments before? And had not John Edel glanced his way as they spoke? "He could use a few friends. Do him a favor and talk to him," he could easily imagine Freddy Snyder saying to his good friend John. And to approach him with a compliment about his mind. John Edel had a good mind. and Johan did not have a good mind, at least not a mind like John's, and so the time could only come when John Edel would see that Johan was not a good student, and what kind of friendship could that be, one founded on Johan inevitably disappointing John Edel, who earned straight As with the smallest of effort, whose knowledge of science and mathematics and literature and history seemed to antedate the books that were assigned each year? Maybe such knowledge had been with him since birth. And it was the same with Ogden Connifer and the new boy, Bert Bach, whom Diane Coleman and Robin Abel and all the girls found as cute as his name. Bert a chunky kid with a snout for a nose. "So cuddly. Such a teddy bear," the girls squealed.

That afternoon, he found himself briefly alone in a classroom with Diane. Not knowing what to say, he mentioned having seen Ogden picking up trash in front of the school that morning. "It's kind of an unusual thing to do," Johan said.

"Not half as unusual as the shape of your head," she said. Speechless, he met her blow with a weak smile and moved away to nurse his wound. He had brought it upon himself. It was the price he had to pay for gossiping. Still, for her to talk that way. He would have to be even more careful in future. No one must get in. No one.

The store wasn't much: a narrow space with floorboards worn below the nailheads, a skimpy assortment of canned goods on dusty shelves, and a produce section with wilted heads of lettuce and rubbery carrots and bananas with spotted skins. Sean stood behind the counter operating the slicing machine. The whirring blade shaved one slender piece after another off the big slab of boiled ham. He paused to adjust the knob for thicker cuts and then resumed until a substantial pile had accumulated. He then stuffed the meat, along with a helping of coleslaw, between the halves of hero bread, but not before slathering the bread with mustard and mayonnaise and popping a piece of stray ham in his mouth.

Johan had hurried up the long block from Broadway to Amsterdam Avenue to be there, as if not to be there was to not be in life at all.

"I'm Lawrence, and I go to the desert because it's clean," Sean bellowed, before tearing into the monster sandwich.

A man in need of a shave came from the back of the store. A soiled apron curved around his big belly. "What is this? A fucking restaurant?" he barked, seeing Sean's snack.

"Fuck you and all your guinea ancestors, Funelli," Sean barked back. "I'm a growing boy. I've got to eat."

"You know what you can eat," Mr. Funelli said. He grabbed his crotch through his apron and his bulging eyes lit up.

"You believe this degenerate bastard?"

Sean and Mr. Funelli were putting on a show.

A woman with a full figure entered the store. She wore a pretty pale green dress.

"Good afternoon, Mario."

"Good afternoon, Miss Prescott, how are you today?"

"Marvelous, Mario," she said, in a big stage voice, and ticked off a list of cold cuts she would need. "Can I expect the order within the hour?"

"You sure can, Miss Prescott," Mr. Funelli assured her.

"Ciao," she said, and swept out of the store.

"I'll take this one myself," Mr. Funelli said. For the next few minutes he put together her order in a small box, which he carried out to the bike and placed in the basket. Then he jumped on the seat, sinking the balloon tires under his heavy weight, and flashed them a loony grin as he pedaled away.

"He thinks he's going to get laid, as if she's interested in the big jerk," Sean said, and started singing "A Foggy Day in London Town," stopping after a few lines. "Someday I'm going to blow this joint," he announced.

"How are you going to do that?"

"Believe me, I have a plan."

Johan saw his need to be special. It was the same thing he saw in himself sometimes.

Jane entered the store. She wore a red barrette in her hair. Johan felt obliged to introduce her to Sean.

"We've met. I'm always coming here for things for my grandmother."

"Nice to see you," Sean said, though not sounding as if it was so nice.

She came back with a bunch of carrots from the produce bin. "They're starting to get soft. Do you have anything fresher?"

"That's what we got," Sean said, going hard on her.

"Well, I guess they'll have to do."

Sean snatched the five-dollar bill she placed on the counter, rang up the sale, and gave her the change without a thank-you.

I walked with her around the corner to her grandmother's. "Is he really a friend of yours?"

"Sort of. Maybe."

"How old is he?"

"A couple of years older. Why?" Mr. Funelli labored past on the bike, the basket now empty.

"Just wondering."

He didn't say anything about the movie. It seemed best to leave things there.

"Mommy, I saw Johan with a girl today," his sister Vera said.

"Is that right?"

"And they were holding hands."

"My Svenska was holding hands with a girl?"

"Pam and I saw them with our own eyes."

"My, oh my," Mrs. Manootdjian said.

Vera was with her girlfriend Pam Becker, the two of them in their St. Andrew's blue jumpers, when Jane and he ran into them.

That night Luke said, "Mother is really relieved. She wasn't sure about you, if you want to know the truth."

"What do you mean?" Johan said.

"You know what I mean. She wasn't sure you like girls."

It was OK being a question mark. It really was, so long as the question was not in his mind.

There were miracles in this world. The real kind.

Miracle number one. He had been with Jane for a month and she hadn't yet told him to get the other part of his head. Obviously she had seen the flatness of the back of his head with her own eyes, but when they kissed she sometimes also touched the back of his head with her hand, and so she had felt that surface flat as a board. And though his whole body froze in anticipation of the mockery to come, not a single such word did she utter. Not one single Flathead or Boxhead did he hear from her lips.

Miracle number 2. He could show Jane where he lived—if not the apartment, at least the lobby.

"Who put this up?" she said, pointing to the stern verse of scripture in the picture frame:

> For God so loved the world, that he gave his
> only begotten Son, that whosoever believeth in
> him should not perish, but have everlasting life.
> —John 3:16

"My aunt," he said, nodding toward Auntie Eve, who had stepped out of her ground-floor apartment, whirled around in a full 360 degree spin, and shot off toward the elevator, her chin leading the way.

Mrs. Manootdjian followed Auntie Eve out of the apartment. Johan introduced Jane to her. Mrs. Manootdjian didn't ask where Jane lived or what her father did for a living or whether she had any brothers or sisters. "And do you go to church?"

"I go to Sunday services at the Riverside Church."

"I see. Is that an interdenominational church?" Mrs Manootdjian asked, though she knew quite well that it was.

"Yes," Jane said.

Interdenominational. He heard his mother thinking the word meant it was a church for the faithless serving up some dilution of the Christ Jesus message. His mother further thinking that the word meant a place where evil could flourish in the service of the Antichrist to come and that it was no place for a true believer.

Mrs. Manootdjian fished in her bag. "May I give you this?" She handed Jane a religious tract in screaming red ink.

"Thank you," Jane said.

That same afternoon Jane met Naomi and Chuck. It was only a matter of time.

"Trying to get away, brother? Don't want to acknowledge your big sister?" Turning her attention to Jane, she said, "He likes to think he's better than us. My mother calls him Svenska pojka, because she says he's got a lot of Swedish blood in him and he has that blond hair. He doesn't know what a singer I could have been. Do you know who Judy Garland is?"

"Sure. She was in *The Wizard of Oz*," Jane said.

"That's right. I could have been another Judy Garland. Someday Johan will know what failure looks like. He thinks he's different from the rest of us and will get away, but it's only a matter of time before he finds he can't get away because some of us just weren't made for this world, isn't that right, Flathead?

"We should go," Johan said.

"You see. There he is rushing off, as if he has someplace to go and he has no place to go. But you don't look like the kind of girl who needs to rush off. Chuck and I are going to the Moon Palace for dinner. Chuck is the man of the house and is taking me out. We both get beef and green peppers, with a bowl of white rice. It's so delicious. And then we get orange slices and a fortune cookie, too. My last fortune read, 'You have really fine star.' Don't you think that means something?"

"Sure. Everything means something," Jane said.

"But do you suppose they really meant, 'You are a really fine star'? Don't you think that's what they could have meant?"

"Maybe. Whoever writes those fortunes might not speak English as a first language."

"Are you saying they are just making up those fortunes? Is that what you are saying?"

"Not exactly."

Affronted, Naomi said, "Chuck, we should be going."

"You and I are going to sit down and have a man to man someday." Chuck was wearing a white T-shirt with wine dribble on it and looked bleary-eyed.

"That's really your sister?" Jane asked, as Naomi and Chuck walked away.

"One of them," I said.

"Wow. She's so much older than you." Jane says. "How many others are there?"

"A few. And I have a brother."

"Are they all like her?"

"Not exactly."

"Well, your mom's sweet."

"She's kind of religious."

"I understand that."

Johan didn't ask Jane what "that" was. And he didn't ask her if she had any thoughts about the name "Flathead" either.

He followed Jane into the hallway of her building and toward the rear, where they kissed at the foot of the stairs, stopping only at the sound of the front door banging open. A slender, black-haired woman appeared wearing a long wool coat excessive for the warm spring day and a pair of sunglasses. She held a brown bag cradled against her chest. The smell of alcohol was strong on her breath. "Come along now, Princess. No loitering in the lobby." Her voice was soft, unlike her words. She mounted the stairs without pausing. On the floor above, a door could be heard opening and closing.

"My dear drunken mom," Jane said, before following after her.

Chapter 4

The softball rose in an arc and then downward toward home plate, like all the upperclassman's underhand deliveries. As big as a melon the lob looked, but Johan's bat made contact only with the air, as it did with each futile swing in his following turns at bat. The strikeouts were not in line with his image of himself on the diamond.

As he dragged the canvas bat bag along the footpath back to school, he felt a big hand on his shoulder. Mr. Sadowski, the varsity basketball coach and tenth grade biology teacher, was staring down at him from his great height, a half-smile trying to form on his serious face.

"I want you to come out for varsity basketball next fall. I'll be expecting you," Mr. Sadowski said. His short sleeve shirt revealed powerful, tanned arms. A scar ran the length of his left forearm. It was said that Mr. Sadowski served in the Korean War and suffered horrible wounds, such that he had to wear sweatpants, not shorts, during practices on the basketball court. He was different from the other faculty members, it seemed to Johan. He had been close to death; he had surely seen more of the darker side of life than the other faculty members.

"Sure," Johan blurted, casting a fearful look up into Mr. Sadowski's sincere and open face and the mashed nose that looked to have been broken more than once.

"I'm counting on you," Mr. Sadowski said.

It was not for Johan to tell Mr. Sadowski of the basketball fantasies his few words triggered, the twenty-foot jump shots Johan routinely sank. Nor was it for him to share, beyond his imagined court heroics, the emotional fireworks summoned by Mr. Sadowski's invitation.

Johan saw himself coming close to Mr. Sadowski and then running away or completely ignoring Mr. Sadowski, punishing him severely by his absence and pretending the man did not exist. *I'm counting on you.* Did Mr. Sadowski not know he took those words everywhere? Did he not know what it meant to be wanted by a man?

"Is it true you're a Negro?" The boy spoke in a whisper, as if afraid of being heard, his hand over his mouth as a muffler, or perhaps to shield Johan from his bad breath. Or was he ashamed of his buck teeth?

"What?"

"Your nose and your lips. Everyone says they're so big." Jackie Maltor, a sophomore, chuckled, as if he had said the funniest thing ever. He was no one Johan liked very much. He had an ugly way of playing basketball, backing in on you and using his elbows till he was just under the basket for an easy turnaround shot.

"Who is everyone?"

"Just everyone." Jackie Maltor went on with some more of his silent chuckling.

If it had been Jackie Maltor alone, with that stupid curl hanging down on his pimply forehead like a question mark, but *everyone?*

In his room that night, he stood in front of the full-length mirror, as his brother often did, inventorying his features: blond hair, brown eyes, white skin. His nose was in fact big—not as big as his father's, but not small either—and his lips were full. He tried compressing them, but then they just returned to their normal size. Holding a hand mirror while remaining in front of the larger mirror, he examined the back of his head, shifting the angle in the futile hope that instead of the flat plane he would see the sweet roundness that so many boys were blessed with, but when the flatness failed to yield, he put the mirror down. "Flat-headed underweight Negro," he whispered, smiling a big, wide smile.

Mr. Horvas, the librarian, had been asked to fill in as homeroom teacher for that day.

"Thought I'd read you some real literature. Not that Alfred Lord Tennyson crap they feed you here," he snarled. There was a tremble in his thin upper lip and cold anger in those pale blue eyes dotted with pinprick pupils. The lines he read lashed the class to attention:

> "I saw the best minds of my generation destroyed by
> madness
> starving hysterical naked,
> dragging themselves through the negro streets at dawn
> looking for
> an angry fix,
> angel-headed hipsters burning for the ancient heavenly
> connection
> to the starry dynamo in the machinery of night..."

Mr. Horvas, when he finished reading the long poem, glared at the students in his corduroy jacket with elbow patches and gingham shirt and knit tie, as if had just proven himself an angel-headed hipster too. It was clear Mr. Horvas's anger had a life of its own.

Jackie Maltor's sister, Lisa, was a senior at the Claremont School. When she was not at the school she was often at The End Bar, on Broadway, and there she drank with the Columbia boys, throwing back her head and laughing fiercely. "She has more dates in a week than some of these skanks have in a year," Jackie Maltor said, his eyes momentarily ablaze with angry pride. Jackie Maltor was an outsider; his sister, too. They were not the core of who and what the school was. Jackie Maltor's hand over his chuckling mouth could not hide this fact.

Lisa Maltor was drawn to Mr. Horvas ever since he gave her a personal reading of *Howl*. Lisa would be seen hovering near him in the school library, where he practiced the art of whispering in her ear while his eyes were fixed on the person he was whispering about. Or maybe he was not whispering at the person he was looking at, but only wanted you to think so. Always was Mr. Horvath seeking his own supremacy. And then the day came when Lisa was seen no more and it was rumored that she had grown big with child, and then Mr. Horvas too was seen no more, as it was also rumored that he was the cause.

As the end of the school year approached and with thoughts of summer vacation in his head, Johan sat at the back of the room as Mr. Arbuckle, a piece of chalk in his hairy hand, put algebra aside to speak about the challenges ahead. "As juniors you will take a standardized exam called the Scholastic Aptitude Test. There are two parts, verbal and math. The aptitude test only takes three hours, but don't let its length fool you. With college admissions officers, it counts as much, and even more, than your grades over all four years of high school. What is more, you can forget right now about studying for the SAT. Basically, it is an intelligence test, and you either have the ability to do well on it or you don't."

Beyond the iron bars of the ground-floor classroom was the schoolyard, where the branches of the honey locust tree were in full bloom. The day was as sunny as Johan's thoughts were now dark, having heard Mr. Arbuckle place an insurmountable barrier against his future.

You are born with it or you aren't. That's what Harvard-educated Mr. Arbuckle was saying. Johan thought of stooped Ogden Connifer and John Edel, already a little man, and cuddly Bert Bach and pretty, confident Diane Coleman in Mr. Arbuckle's other algebra class. His path would not be theirs; a greater fork lay up ahead. In listening to Mr. Arbuckle hold forth on the SAT, he also heard another voice, one which came from deep within, that said, "You're not going anywhere, Flathead. Nowhere at all."

Johan woke the next morning to the sound of Luke groaning on the floor. Johan called down, but Luke did not respond. On the floor beside his brother was an empty aspirin bottle.

"Could you come, Momma? It's Luke," Johan said, having run to the dining room.

"What is it, Johan?" She put down her cup of coffee.

"I don't know. He's just lying there, on the floor." He was aware of his father all the while. His brittleness. His disgust that his time with Mrs. Manootdjian should now be interrupted. His temper.

"Lying there?" His mother trying to comprehend.

"What is this, my son, that you come to us this way in the morning?" Were his father's words kindling for the roaring fire to come? His father was being inconvenienced, but would he be made to get up?

"Momma, it's bad," Johan blurted. Mrs. Manootdjian responded by rushing off to Luke.

"Such trouble, that boy. Your mother cannot even sit in peace and have her breakfast." Mr. Manootdjian stayed in his chair. He had not been made to get up. He had not gone and kicked Luke in the face for aggravating him.

His mother was bending over Luke when Johan returned to the room. "What have you done, you foolish boy?" Seeing the aspirin bottle, she said, "Good Lord. Call for an ambulance."

"He has some sickness in his head. I will pray for him," Mr. Manootdjian said, after the attendants finally came and carried Luke out on a stretcher. In the emergency room his stomach was pumped and within a couple of days he was released.

Nancy Becker. She it was who brought his brother low when she showed an interest in another boy, she having all the clobber power that women were born to have.

Chapter 5

When summer vacation began, there was Chock Full O'Nuts, with its red and blue and green menu board in the shape of a house and the big windows that looked out on Columbia University and Barnard College. Over coffee and orange juice and a sugar doughnut, served him by a solemn-faced Negro woman, he read in the *Daily News* about the fleet feet of Maury Wills and Willie Davis and the power hitting of Tommy Davis and the mound mastery of Don Drysdale and Sandy Koufax. The Dodgers were pulling away, and his world was as right as the bright sun in the blue sky.

At the bottom of One Hundred Sixteenth Street, past the massive apartment buildings on either corner of Riverside Drive, Jane Thayer waited for him at the entrance to the park. On the lower level, a four-foot fence stood between them and Dead Man's Hill. He climbed over and Jane followed. At the crest of the hill, surrounded by foliage, stood a wire cage, enclosed at the top, and big enough for two people to stand in. In the center was a water bowl fixed to the cement floor. Was it a bird bath? He didn't know. It was a mystery from another time.

"Let's go in," he said, and closed the door behind them.

"Now let's go out," she said.

"We can't," he said.

"What do you mean, we can't? Let's go."

"We're stuck. There's no way out."

"Stop being a jerk. I don't like it in here."

"Liking it is not the point. Once you're in, you're in. You stay until they come and take you away."

"Who are *they*?"

"They? People who stick their feet out and trip you and knock you into a ditch. People who get themselves in front of you and then stall you. You mean you don't know who they are?"

"You can have your *they*. I'm getting out of here." She opened the latch on the door, stepped out, and showed a triumphant smile. "Well?" she said, their faces separated by the wire now.

"Goodbye, Jane. They've got me. They're taking me far, far down." He let his voice trail off.

"Look. Cut this crap out or I'm leaving."

He did as he was told so they could have their splendor in the grass. Kissing and more kissing. Endless kissing. The kissing taking on a life of its own.

"I love you," he whispered. They were not extreme words. They were not the same as saying, "I want to marry you someday." She was not like his older sisters. She was perfect. She was as normal as her name.

Then she had to go and touch the back of his head. Only then did his heart almost stop. His old fear had been triggered that she would suddenly see him as he was and in astonishment be driven to say, "What is the meaning of this flatness?" before running away. Had she not heard the names that he had been called? Had she not been listening?

They were faithful to Dead Man's Hill throughout the summer. Only when it rained and rained and turned the hill soggy did they stay away. He lived for morning sunlight and *The Daily News* and the Los Angeles Dodgers and Chock Full O'Nuts and then Jane Thayer arriving from One Hundred Twenty-second Street to lie with him on the grass for a couple of hours so they could have their splendor, and Freddy Snyder had no power to stop or shame him from doing so with his laughing thing.

There were men who came to Dead Man's Hill as well. They did not go without notice. Spies. Love spies. They knelt in the tall grass and were heard moving in the brush before they were seen. When Johan looked up, they would duck. When he returned his attention to Jane, they rose once again out of their crouches. They were men claimed by their loneliness, men who, wherever they went, they went alone.

To see them was to see some aspect of himself, the younger boy who would stare for an hour out the window hoping to glimpse a female tenant half-naked in her bra or shed of her bra in her room across the courtyard. The men were only doing what he and Jerry had done, watching as the Columbia men lay in the grass with their Barnard girlfriends. They were some part of himself he could not repudiate, so long as they were not dangerous. Nor could he deny that some sickness was attaching that their presence should excite him.

He had read about these men in the pulp pages of the pornographic novels, those with full-color covers of women in erotic lingerie. He would remove them from the racks in the luncheonette and slip them into the centerfold section of the *Daily News*, terrified that Lev would nab and humiliate him for his theft. There was Frankie, who would stand before the mirror admiring his giant cock with only one goal for the day: to find a woman to satisfy his every sexual fantasy. They were not books on the summer reading list or for reading on the Broadway bus but for reading behind a locked bathroom door.

She had bounds she kept him within, braking his hand when it moved too far up her thigh or toward her full breasts. To his left, a man with a folded newspaper under his arm withdrew behind the thick trunk of a tree, again leaving Johan to wonder that some excitement should attach to noting the presence of peeping Toms and sensing the corruption that lay within himself.

Like a weed he grew that year to an even six feet, the added six inches only stretching him thinner. Chock Full O' Nuts presented a bruising reality. The mirrored back wall reflected back to him his Adam's apple bulging enormously from a sliver of a neck and his overall gauntness. He told himself that the pitiless fluorescent lighting was responsible for the unappealing reflection. And yet how substantial and even beautiful some others were when he saw their images in the same mirror. Oh, you knew you were really something when you looked good in a Chock Full O' Nuts mirror.

"Hey look, here comes lover boy," Scully announced, holding a broomstick that served as a bat.

"Where the hell you been, man? Do I have to go and kick your ass to get the truth?" So Jimmy Riley demanded to know, going chest to chest with Johan, but his tough talk Johan understood as only a comic expression of joy, the direct expression of affection being too embarrassing. But Scully, with that Porky Pig body and sly lynx face, was another matter. Scully had all that weight and the malevolent intent to place it on top of you.

Luis drew a box with chalk to represent a one-size-fits-all home plate on the windowless wall of the Interchurch Center. Across the street rose Riverside Church and beyond stood Grant's Tomb. Mornings on Dead Man's Hill with Jane; afternoons on this strip of One Hundred Twentieth Street with the boys from Scully's stoop.

And if now and then cars came along and disrupted their game on the lightly trafficked street, where was the problem? They had everything they needed for their happiness on the asphalt playing field: ball, bat, smokes, bottles of Pepsi, and each other.

Rob Koley was on the mound. His skin, even in winter, held the sun, and his deep-set eyes, ringed with darkness, showed a fire burning. He was from a country called South Africa, another world, and lived with his mother in a single-room occupancy. Though foreign-born, he took to baseball. He pitched out of a neat, compact windup and threw a curveball that broke sharply.

"You're out of your fucking mind. That pitch was a strike. Where are your eyes, man?" He came forward holding the ball in his hand, eager to show Scully the chalk mark where the Spaldeen had hit the corner of the box. You got used to Rob Koley having fits, choking on his indignation, veins bulging in his thick neck and his voice getting squeaky high at the raw deal life was handing him, as you got used to the ring of spit at his feet after each drag on his Marlboro.

"Hey guys, you hear what Koley just said? His mother is on the corner and goes down for wooden nickels."

Rob's mother was tall and blond. Mr. Funelli, the grocer, was often heard to say he would gladly deliver groceries to her door. "You fat slob, Scully," Rob shouted, and threw a high hard one, the Spaldeen bouncing off Scully's forehead.

"Your ass is mine," Scully said. Rob easily ducked the broomstick Scully slung at him. Like a rotating blade, it sailed over his head and landed on the other side of the street. But Scully was not done. He made a berserk rhino charge. Despite his pounds he moved with surprising speed and knocked Rob off his feet. It took Luis to pull him off.

"Like a fucking elevator she goes down," Scully went on.

"Fuck you, Scully. Your mother's so fat she can't fit in a fucking elevator. She's so fat no one wants to fuck her, except you," Rob Koley shot back, the two of them held apart by Luis.

"Oh, shit. You see what I see. Scully's ass is sticking out of his fucking pants. Look at that big fat ugly ass." Jimmy Riley was doubled over with laughter.

Sean appeared around the corner, walking with a swagger, a black San Francisco Giants cap with an orange beak and lettering askew on his huge head.

Another game got underway. Sean didn't so much throw the ball as heave it. His pitches came in on a straight line and were easy to lay wood on. Luis threw flames. His ball hopped and dipped as it exploded into the box.

But Sean could swing the bat. Coming out of a low crouch from the left side he sent ropes in all directions and home runs high off the wall of the church across the street. Not even Luis, who pitched for Bishop DuBois High School, could get much past him.

Johan managed to slam one of Sean's pitches into home run territory to fuel his fantasies, but Scully, undeterred by his ripped pants, brought him back to earth. "Hey, which of you is the bat?"

Scully's words hung out there, stopping time. Johan felt the eyes of others on him. Shame robbed him of his tongue. Stripped naked, he had no defense but silence.

"The Giants are going to catch that team of yours," Sean said, that same afternoon, blowing smoke from his Philip Morris in Johan's face. He had come to know Johan was a Dodgers fan. Johan understood the Giants to be brute and savage strength. They were the tiger leaping on the back of the zebra and sinking its teeth in its prey's neck.

Things had changed since Sean invited him to the movies. He was showing a gruffer side. Inwardly Johan trembled at this threat to his fantasy world in which the Dodgers, behind Koufax and Drysdale, reigned supreme. He did not want to be beaten by Sean. He did not want him on top, not even in a proxy war. The Dodgers were Koufax, his left knee grazing the mound as he delivered, the top button of his uniform shirt undone and his fastball accelerating through the strike zone and his curve swooping in at the batter's head and breaking on the black part of the plate at his knees. They were mean Don Drysdale, number 53, coming from third base with his sidearm delivery to claim the inside of the plate and keep the right-handed batters honest. They were Maury Wills, agitating the pitcher with his arrogant strut off first. They were fleet Willie Davis in center field.

"That's right, baby. They're going to fuck those pussies up. My man Juan Marichal. He's got five kinds of fastball like you wouldn't believe," Luis chimed in, simulating, or trying to, that high kick of

Marichal as he came toward home plate with the pitch but unable to raise his leg higher than his hip.

Sean had a history with the Giants, going back to the Polo Grounds on One Hundred Fifty-fifth Street, and the fact that the franchise fled New York for San Francisco at the end of the 1957 season did not change things. The Giants were formidable. They were Juan Marichal, but they were also Willie Mays and Orlando "Baby Bull" Cepeda and Willie "Stretch" McCovey. And they were the Alou brothers, slap-hitting Matty and power-hitting Felipe, with the twitching neck.

"Look at him smiling," Sean said to Luis. "But we know he's shitting a brick."

It was like that sometimes with the kids from Scully's stoop. He wanted to be friends with them, but he wasn't entirely sure it was possible. And yet there seemed no place else to go.

The room had grown cloudy from cigarette smoke that Friday night, and the beer and scotch were going fast. The street below looked far away, the strollers small as specks. Two blocks north and on the other side of Broadway the illuminated verse of scripture on his family's building glowed in the soft summer night, the gothic lettering and the pastel colors and the classical columns that framed it giving the mural a kind of beauty.

Through the partially open door of Kevin's room could be seen a woman enter the apartment. Haggard and gray-haired, she used the wall as a support to slowly make her way deeper into the apartment. With her free arm she clutched a brown bag and her pocketbook. In a boozy voice she called out, "Hey, Hank, are you coming or what?"

"I'm coming, for Christ's sake. You left your damn key in the lock." A gangly, stoop-shouldered man carrying a bag with clanking bottles soon followed after.

"Sometimes things get fucked up," Jimmy Riley said.

"Ain't nothing fucked up. Why you want to sound deep when you ain't deep?" Luis went.

"I didn't say I was deep. I said things sometimes get fucked up."

"You fucked up. You fucked up on beer and Scotch."

"Fucking right I'm fucked up, and I'm going to get fucked up some more."

"How about you, Rob? You and that mother of yours fucked up?" Scully goes.

"The only thing fucked up here is that big fat fucking ass of yours," Rob goes.

"How about I sit my big fat fucking ass on your little fucking face?" Scully goes.

"That ain't going to happen here, Scully," Kevin goes.

"A man has a right to ask for respect in his own house," Luis added, in his I'm-not-playing voice.

"How about you start wearing your mother's bra. Your tits are big enough," Rob goes.

"How about I wear your mother's bra instead? Or how about I wear Jane's bra? You think Jane would let me wear her bra, Johan?"

"Come on, Scully. That ain't right, asking Johan shit like that about his girlfriend," Jimmy Riley said.

"I'm not asking to suck her tits. I'm just asking to wear her bra."

"Damn, Scully, how about letting me suck your fucking tits. You got bigger ones than anyone," Jimmy said.

"You can suck something else, the same thing the Head gives you to suck," Scully shot back.

There were stories about Sean and some of the neighborhood kids, stories that Sean himself had spread about kids visiting him while his parents were out.

"Ain't no one wants to suck your ugly little dick, you best believe," Jimmy went.

Johan had moved away from the window and onto the floor, where he lay missing the softness of Jane. His friends made a summer night in Manhattan feel like the winter coldness of Siberia, but he had the beer and the scotch to keep him warm and ease the feelings of discomfort, which had no place in Kevin's small room, where everyone was at risk of exposure. No, it was best that they not see him for the outsider that he was.

He was in a time in his life when he did not know the cost of being lost in the endless softness of Momma and without the bracing firmness of the father who says, "You, you're coming with me. I will have you listen to something other than the cries and whispers and longings and sorrows of women. I will pitch your ear to the sound of the lion as well as the dove. I will freeze your face with ice where it has been burned by fire."

Such seemed to Johan to be the attendants at the Esso gas station and garage. To step inside was to receive refuge from the summer heat and embrace the masculine smell of oil and gas and rubber. The man-sized boy Bobby Cassandro emerged, revving his imaginary engine. Vroom, vroom, came the roar of his engine before he tore off, his right shoulder lowered and his head leaning forward. The two attendants had followed him outside and watched him disappear around the corner. To Johan, it was clear that they still had love in their hearts for him. He had never heard them talk down to Bobby Cassandro or in any way make fun of him. They had claimed him as one of their own.

It was outside this garage the following week that Jane said to Johan, "I'll be going away this weekend."

"Going away where?"

"To New Jersey with my church group."

She belonged to a Friday night social group at Riverside Church. It was where she went without him, and where he understood not to follow.

"Why?"

"Because I want to. It will be fun."

"What kind of fun?"

"Boating. Swimming. Lots of stuff."

Jane Thayer had knocked him down. It had never occurred to him that they would ever be apart.

"Can I call you?"

"No, you can't call me." She laughed. Then, seeing how worried he looked, she added, "It's only for the weekend, you know. It's not like I'm going away for a year."

But that was the point. It felt like a year. It felt like forever.

The weekend came and he drank beer with the boys on the lawn of Columbia University. As usual, Scully rode him, tuned in as he was to the pain, the unrelenting anxiety, Jane's absence had summoned. Not for a minute would it leave him until the beer began to bring a measure of relief. He poured out more and more from the quart bottles into a paper cup. Soon Scully's grating voice pounded less in his ears. The voices of the others—Jimmy Riley and Luis and Jerry—seemed farther away.

"Damn, Sam. Who drank all the fucking beer?" As if from another world, Luis's voice came to Johan. By then, he was some yards away, on his knees and leaning into the hedges that bordered the lawn. So sick. Oh, Jesus, he wouldn't ever again….So much vomiting. On and on. How good to just lie there in the cool grass when it stopped. Someone—it could only be Scully—saying Jane wouldn't be kissing him now.

In the morning the pain found him. He lay holding himself tight, trying to squeeze the anxiety out of him. Luke was away, doing construction work on the school's property in Westchester. Just as well, as it would not do to be lovesick in the same room with his brother.

That evening he sat at the fountain in the Whelan's drugstore, sipping a vanilla coke in a glass of crushed ice, his eye on the Coca-Cola clock. How slow, how deliberately slow, the hands moved. Unable to wait any longer, he rushed for the phone, enclosed himself in the booth, and spun the rotary dial.

Jane's mother answered. "Well, hello there, Tiger. No, Jane is not back yet, but we expect her any minute. You just hang on." There was playfulness in her voice.

The counterman wore a bowtie with his tight white shirt, from which he looked about to burst. A white paper hat sat jauntily askew atop his head. He brought Johan a second vanilla coke. "Jimmy," his nameplate read. He seemed to come by his smile easily, as if it was natural to his being. "Are you here again, woman? Is it that you like me some little bit?" he said to a plump Negro woman. He too was Negro and from one of the Caribbean islands, his accent suggested.

"You go on now and get me a cup of coffee and never mind about liking you," the woman scolded, and he only laughed. How? How could such a happy disposition be, Johan was left to wonder.

He had resolved to let another half hour pass but within twenty minutes the phone booth called him back. Through the glass panel of the closed door he watched his sister Naomi shuffle over to the pharmacy counter. She had been thin and pretty, but now her face was puffy and her body bloated. And that shapeless blue dress. He groaned inwardly as if the very sight of her was repugnant. Why, when he felt most vulnerable and needy, did she have to appear? The sight of her brought fear that her future could be his if he wasn't careful, that he too would be stashed in some room in the building and grow older. Once again he saw the building as a death trap and his family as a death trap. He turned away and fed the phone and spun the rotary dial.

"You are a passionate and impetuous young man, are you not? You just put your ardor on hold. The damsel will be arriving soon, no doubt."

Her mother was laughing at him, and Jane was delaying her return on purpose simply to thwart and humiliate him. When, finally, he did reach her it was if his abject dependency had been revealed for Jane and her parents to see. Even so, he felt the need to press her to see him, though her parents wanted her to spend the evening with them after having been away for two days. Reluctantly, she said yes to Johan, but only after supper, which her mother was then preparing.

That evening they sat on a bench in the quadrangle of the Jewish Theological Seminary on Broadway, down the block from her building. Once more, as he had on the phone, he told her he had missed her, but filled with anger when she didn't say the same.

"I've been thinking maybe we shouldn't see each other anymore," he said.

"What's the matter?"

"Nothing's the matter. I've just been thinking about it."

"You've just been thinking about it?"

He walked off, hoping to give her some of the pain she had inflicted on him, even as he knew she hadn't been doing anything to him at all. Within a few blocks he paused, the fear spreading that he had driven her away, necessitating yet another phone call. "I'm sorry," he said.

"It's all right."

"What's that mean, it's all right?"

"Really, Johan, it's all right."

"Do I have to die? Is that it?"

"Stop being so dramatic."

"You think I'm being dramatic?"

"You're being something."

At home that night he couldn't be sure his apology has been enough. He needed some reassurance.

"Please. No more calls."

Later, he lay in bed imagining a conversation in which Mrs. Thayer, in a motherly moment, said to Jane, "Perhaps there is something wrong with him. Perhaps he is not quite right for you."

❧

Even as they passed did Johan mark those days of summer special, a time of innocence. He did not know that he would never again lie on Dead Man's Hill with Jane, that those months were a closed chapter, or that they would grow more special in his mind with the passage of time. He had not yet read Wordsworth's *Intimations of Immortality* and what its lines, including "Splendour in the Grass" were conveying.

<h1 style="text-align:center">Chapter 6</h1>

He flipped through the bulky textbook: phyla, bacteria, proto-zoa, chloroplasts, mitochondria, meiosis, mitosis? Lab work? Messy, gruesome dissections? What world was this where order did not prevail? No one must threaten his dream. No one. There would be no easy A, only a hard-won C. No one must be allowed to blem-ish his virtually perfect record. And no one must be allowed to see the meager quality of his mind.

And there was Mr. Sadowski, the athletic coach who had dared to show an interest in him the previous year. To learn now that Mr. Sadowski would be teaching tenth grade biology was more than his mind could tolerate. Mr. Sadowski wore shirts with frayed collars and dull ties and ill-fitting suits and had to work a summer job doing construction. But it wasn't only the obvious paucity of mate-rial blessings; the same poverty of mind that afflicted Johan surely would be apparent in Mr. Sadowski. Surely Ogden Connifer and Bert Bach and John Edel and Diane Coleman and Robin Abel would put their laughing thing on poor Mr. Sadowski as he fumbled his way through each class. To witness such humiliation of a man who had come to mean so much to him would be unbearable.

And there was Jane. The course would require too much of him. He wouldn't have as much time with her.

His mind was a torment: one minute he had decided to stay with the course; the next, he had decided to ditch it. It went that way for a week.

"If you withdraw from the class, you'll only be taking four courses? Your classmates will be taking five? You understand that, of course?" Miss Redding, the assistant to the principal, said when Johan went to her the following week with his decision. She had a Southern accent and her every sentence ended with a question mark. Johan made an effort to keep his eyes on her face, not her ample cleavage.

"Yes."

"Why would you drop this course? You know that a science course is required for you to go on to college?"

"I have to."

"Why do you have to?"

"I just do."

She pulled his folder from the file cabinet and made a note. "Don't start running from challenges," she said, lifting her eyes from the folder and dispensing with the question marks.

The barrier had been removed. So he thought that afternoon as he headed for Scully's stoop. There had been a scare, but now all the lights on the road ahead were shining green. Still, four courses, when Diane and Robin and John and Ogden and Bert were taking five. It was something not to think about, as were Miss Redding's sharp words.

"It's Patty Joyce and Chao," Kevin announced, as if the main event of their lives was about to arrive.

Two boys approached, moving at a fast clip. One was stocky and blond, the other thin and dark skinned. The pair turned into the liquor store two doors down from Funelli's grocery. The next minute they were burning rubber back down the block, Patty Joyce holding a bottle of whiskey by the neck. Down past the Cathedral of St. John the Divine they sped to their home base in Manhattan Valley, where the Irish and the Puerto Ricans dominated.

"Damn. That Joyce is crazy. He has it made with a full basketball scholarship to Xavier," Kevin said, referring to a Catholic high school in lower Manhattan, while outside his liquor store, the owner, a small man wearing a blue smock, stood fuming.

Johan imagined them on some rooftop breaking the seal on the bottle and chugging the alcohol. Oh, to have that kind of talent to be reckless with.

"You like to kiss. I can tell. You have nice full lips," Mr. Funelli said to Johan that afternoon, as Johan headed for the back of the store.

"He can use them for more than kissing," Sean said. Johan caught his drift and remained silent. It would not go well to counter Sean's words. It would not go well at all.

Kevin and Luis and Jimmy Riley also entered. Mr. Funelli followed as they moved to the rear, clustering near the leaky toilet.

"Any of you touch that bottle and you're dead. Got it? That is vintage wine," Mr. Funelli said, pointing to a bottle on the shelf and scowling.

"Telling us not to drink his sorry-assed wine," Jimmy Riley said, after Mr. Funelli had returned to the front of the store. "Are we going to listen to that fat fool?"

Johan reached for the dark green bottle and pulled the cork. Could wine taste so salty and bitter? He quickly spit it out as Mr. Funelli came running to the back of the store. "You're not going to kiss for a while now, are you? You don't want to be kissing with your mouth smelling of piss," he said, as Jane entered the store.

"What's going on?"

"Your boyfriend didn't tell you he likes to drink piss?" Mr. Funelli asked.

Confusion showed on Jane's face, so Jimmy told her.

"I don't believe it."

"Yeah. Ugly old Funelli's piss, too," Jimmy went on.

"Yuck," Jane said.

Two men were playing a match on the enclosed clay court just beyond John Jay Hall on the Columbia campus. John Jay. Alexander Hamilton. So much history. They look tanned and fit in their tennis whites. Not many extended volleys. Probably professors to have the use of the court. Those big foreheads and powerful, well-shaped heads. Another world, the world of strength and fitness and intellect.

"You like them, don't you?"

"Who?"

"You don't know?" he said.

"I said who."

"You know who. Just tell me the truth. It's OK." His voice steady and reasonable.

"Look, cut it out."

"The truth is important."

"Your being a jerk is what's important," she said, before tearing off across the campus.

That evening he placed several calls to her home from the luncheonette. All three were needed, not merely to make up with her but to reach that perfect level of harmony, anything short of which was too uncomfortable to bear. But Miss Redding's comment, as piercing as an arrow, was harder to move beyond. He hadn't the right stuff to stay the course, just as he hadn't at baseball camp. He would have to live with his weakness, his cowardice. And Mr. Funelli with his mean little prank, humiliating Johan in front of Jane. He thought of Luigi and his warning not to sit in the chair he had just upholstered. Well, at least Mr. Funelli hadn't cracked him in the head with a frying pan.

"Not good. Not good," Lev said, lifting his eyes from the newspaper he had spread out by the cash register at the luncheonette.

"No. Not good at all," Johan agreed. The Dodgers were faltering and the Giants were closing fast. Don Drysdale was having his best year, Maury Wills was closing in on one hundred stolen bases, and Tommy Davis, from Boys' High in Brooklyn, was hitting a ton, and yet they couldn't shake the Bay Area beasts in those unfriendly orange and black caps. That right-hander of theirs, Jack Sanford, was a mediocrity on an amazing roll, and there was the insolent supremacy of Marichal, with his high leg kick and five varieties of fastball, and the hugeness of Willie McCovey along with the power of Orlando Cepeda and the all-around brilliance of Willie Mays.

There was that recurring dream from Johan's childhood, in which he made eye contact with a figure far off in the distance. Though he could tell instantly the man meant him harm, fear rooted Johan to the spot as the man drew near. So it was with the pennant race. Accompanying the collapse was the harsh, jeering laughter of Sean, as if he had known all along that the Dodgers—and Johan—would crumble. As if he was saying, "I'll let the Dodgers and you preen for a while, but in the end I will run you both down. I will always run you down,"

So when Billy Pierce threw so viciously hard and fast from the left side in the first playoff game—so hard and fast for a thirty-five-year-old supposedly past his prime—and just shut the Dodgers down completely, and it was so hard for LA to pull out the second game, Johan could only sense with increasing dread that even the two-run lead the Dodgers took into the ninth inning of the final game would not save them because the power and inevitability of the Giants—of Sean—was real. As he sat at home watching Stan Williams of the Dodgers walk across the winning run on TV, he heard Sean's mocking laughter from a block away.

"What a bunch of pussies that team of yours is. You got beat. You got whipped," Sean said, that same day.

"It would have been different if Koufax hadn't been injured," Johan lamely offered.

"All you've got is excuses. You got your ass whipped. That's all." And then, in a lower voice, penetrating and knowing, punctuated by another burst of laughter, he added, "And there's more ass whipping to come."

Johan could not deal with Sean with words. He would have to do so with distance.

The man was not any man. He had eyes that started a commotion going within Johan when he stared in that signaling way before disappearing around the corner. Johan counted to ten before he too turned the corner, ignoring Harry Frug's "Hiya, Johan, how ya doing?" as he stood outside his radio shop. Now was not the time for dawdling if all was not to be lost.

The man stopped to look back before disappearing down the hill. Shortly, Johan found him waiting, keys in hand, on the front steps of a walkup building.

The carpeted stairs creaked as they mounted them before entering a high-ceilinged studio apartment, where Johan lay naked on the man's bed. When the fever passed, Johan saw that the man was overweight and had hair on his shoulders and back as well as his chest. He saw too that the man's feet were big and that bright red pimples dotted his rear end.

Over the next month Johan was to spend a number of afternoons in the man's bed. Always when the thought came, he had no power to resist. He was eager for the sex and the release it brought and tried to block out the hairy body and pasty skin and those pimples. But he did see these things more and more, and the sexual frenzy became a low fire and then the fire was banked and there was only the frightening loneliness of the man's company. The man and Jane. It was the difference between a cold cell and a warm room.

His name was Allan Fletcher. He taught English literature at the Columbia School of General Studies while working toward his Ph.D. at the same university. So he told Johan.

In the aftermath of each encounter Johan disappeared the sex from his mind; it was a thing apart from Jane that he just did. If his mind told him to go and his body told him to go, then how was he not to go?

What bothered him was telling Allan that he hoped to attend Princeton, the kind of talk that made him turn his face to the wall in shame, his words having rendered him more naked than the removal of his clothes. It was not good to not know your place, having heard Mr. Arbuckle's pronouncement about the SAT.

There came a time when the sex did begin to bother him. Not the sex itself, but what it signified for him and Jane. "Am I going to be this way forever? Will it get stronger in me so that I won't be able to be with girls?" Now the fear had grown that, like an undertow, this sometime urge would take him far out in cold ocean waters and far away from Jane.

Allan did not put any tormenting laughter on him, as Sean might do. "You will go along for months without thinking of homosexual sex and then you will be standing in the lobby of a hotel, say, and you will make eye contact with some man, and the desire will be instantly in you again and you will act on it, and then some more months will pass and there will be no more of that desire until the next time."

Until the next time. Johan pictured Jane and him married and staying at a hotel. One afternoon, he encountered someone in the lobby. That look was exchanged and he went to the man's room, and then he returned to Jane "until the next time." A cry of resolve rose in him. Nothing but nothing must come between Jane and him and their future together. Nothing.

"I know where there is a whorehouse, Johan. Do you want to go? They have some of the very finest women in the city at this establishment," Jerry said.

"Finest women? Establishment?"

"That's what I was told." Jerry fanned his hand to show his excitement.

"How much?" Johan heard himself ask.

Though it was a school day evening and he had homework, it did not seem within Johan's power to resist the opportunity, if that was what it was, anymore than it had been to resist engagement with Allen Fletcher. A door opened and it was for him to walk through it.

Someone had to be present in the renting office during the day to sort and distribute the mail to anxious tenants, handle queries from prospective tenants, and receive and record the rent payments. It was not work his mother cared for. She needed to be free to show rooms to those in need of lodging and to assist with the washing and distribution of bedding and towels. She wasn't someone to be tethered to that small, confining space eight hours a day. And it was hard to imagine Auntie Eve, given her age and level of distraction, handling the position. It took a person of a certain temperament such as Alice Greene possessed. There she was now, slowly and methodically writing out a rent receipt, receiving payment, and giving back change to a tenant in the queue.

"I would like my post, please. Patel, in 9C4," a sari-clad woman said, speaking that precise foreigner's English that could be heard all throughout the building. The red bindi in the middle of her forehead signified she was married.

Mrs. Greene stood and peered into the boxes on the wall into which mail was sorted, and extracted the letters for the ninth floor, flipping through the pile carefully and giving each envelope her full scrutiny. Other tenants followed, Pakistanis and Indians and Nigerians wearing heavy coats as a buffer against the fall cold. Returning from jobs or school, they were anxious to have their mail before the office closed. What they were hoping for were personal letters that arrived in the colorful air mail envelopes. They were far away from home.

Soon Mrs. Greene emerged to close the window from the outside, inserting a folded matchbook cover into the crack to keep the window from swinging open. She then returned to the office and latched the window from the inside.

But then another tenant, a bearded Sikh wearing a white turban with his business suit, rushed up and banged on the window. "Singh, in 6C1. My post, Miss, please," he thundered. In a moment Mrs. Greene appeared with a few letters for the man.

Again the light went off and she appeared again, this time in her wool coat and with her bag in the crook of her arm.

"Good evening, Johan. How are you?"

"Fine, thank you."

"Your mother says you are doing so very well in school. She's very proud of you."

"I'm doing OK."

"Do you know my neighbor's boy Errol?"

"I don't."

"He has won early acceptance to Brown University."

Mrs. Greene lived in the embrace of order and related easily to success. Her husband, equally petite, was a physician. This quality of fineness she was imbued with was there for everyone to see. But it wasn't right that this fineness should be there on the premises of the building. It wasn't fair at all that she should have to witness the failure of the Manootdjians.

As if she could read his thoughts and feel his uneasiness, Mrs. Greene searched his face boldly through her pince-nez glasses. The process of reevaluation was underway. Somewhere within her she had to know. She had to. It wasn't fair that she should pretend that she didn't.

"Well, I will be going," she said.

Johan followed her path out of the lobby, noting the small steps she took and how she paused at the framed verse from the Gospel of John. He then watched as she looked both ways before crossing the westbound street and entered the house of order.

Jerry was late, but then he was always late, as if it served some purpose known only to him.

"Stay here," Johan said.

"You got some kind of plan? You got something going on so we can meet these fine women?"

Johan left the building and passed through the street-level gate down the stairs to the yard. Through the screened window he saw his mother and Auntie Eve standing at opposite ends of the mangle and holding taut the ends of a washed and dried sheet, which they fed between the canvas-covered rollers until it dropped, pressed, on a long board. They then took the ends of the pressed sheet and came together, matching the ends and then folding it once more. They then continued the process with the next sheet. Behind them, dirty linen sloshed around in the perforated steel belly of the big washing machine, the two drive wheels and the axle rotating in one direction for a few minutes, then reversing. And there was the racket of the giant extractor, as it wrung water out of the dripping laundry before its transfer to the drier.

The laundry room. It was where his mother and Auntie Eve most liked to be. It calmed them to make things white and like new again.

Back upstairs he sent the elevator to the top floor. "I'm going in through the window. When I tap from the inside, let me know the coast is clear to come out."

He flicked the latch on the office window with a thin piece of cardboard and was quickly up and through. In the dark he lowered down onto the roll-top desk that dominated the tight space and struck a match. Opening the side drawer of the desk, he helped himself to three twenties from a thick envelope by the gray money tray. As he was about to tap on the window, he heard the elevator door open.

"Is that you, Jerry?"

"Hello, Mrs. Manootdjian."

"Are you waiting for Johan? Is that why you are here?"

"Yes, I am. He just went upstairs for a minute."

"But it is late. It is a school night."

"We won't be gone very long. We are just going to see a friend down the block."

"Is it that strange man Sean?"

"No, not him."

"Tell me, Jerry. Do you attend church?"

"Oh, yes. Sometimes I go to the Presbyterian church on the next block."

"I see. But do they preach the true word of God? Do they tell you that Jesus is the way, the truth, and the light, that no man cometh to the Father except through Him?"

"Oh yes, they're very good. I wouldn't go to them if they weren't serious. Myself, I'm a serious person about religion."

"That is very good, Jerry. Very good."

Mrs. Manootdjian's mind was working. Johan could feel her doubt about this church, and in the silence that followed could also sense her coming closer as he squeezed far back in the kneehole of the desk. Now she was pulling open the sliding door. She was no one to fool with, not with her special powers. She knew the ways of the mind and the way into the mind. If her special powers were on, he must die on the spot, and she would die as well. Her heaving heart would burst. The smell of sulfur from the match permeated the space. Surely she would smell it and grow suspicious. But no, he remembered, the strong yellow soap powder used in the basement laundry room had destroyed her sense of smell. She was seated now; her rubber stockings and low-cut black shoes were only inches from his contorted, six-foot body. Any second now, she would say, in a quiet voice, "I know you're there, Johan." But no, she turned off the light and slid the door closed.

A hard rain had begun to fall; the vehicles tearing along Broadway sent up plumes of dirty water. They turned east on One Hundred Tenth Street past the gloomy mass of the Cathedral of St. John the Divine. The rain poured down on the trash cans lined up against the wall of the small building they came to and pooled on the dented lids and soaked the stuffed brown bags outside the cans. The rain was just falling in a cold, relentless way. Wet and dripping, they climbed to the top of the first flight of stairs. Jerry's knock brought a man to the door. A bushy mustache dominated his face. "What you want here?" he asked, in a heavily Spanish accent. His eyes showed wariness. Johan looked back down the stairs to the broken pane of glass in the front door. The odor of dead rats came from the walls.

"We came for women. We have money," Jerry said, and the man stepped aside.

The living room served as a waiting room. A red light burned in the ceiling fixture. The parquet floor was badly scuffed; the fireplace was in disuse. Across from them sat a thin man with a hacking cough.

Soon a dark-skinned man emerged from a long hallway and left the apartment. The mustached man motioned to the man with the cough to follow him down the hallway, then returned and motioned to Johan and Jerry as well. Their wet sneakers squeaked as they followed after him. On either side of the hallway were rooms. In one, the door partially open, a naked and overweight woman sat on the edge of a bed stroking a Negro man's penis.

The room Johan was led to was lit by a pitiless white ceiling bulb. In the middle of a queen-size bed lay a heavy, middle-aged woman with sagging breasts and stretch marks. Johan recoiled inwardly. The faint mustache, the wrinkled skin, the huge, hairy patch—he wanted to flee.

"Here," she said, tossing him a rubber from the table. Her smile revealed a gold front tooth. He sat in a chair to the side of the bed, holding the packet,

"You come here." To his ears it sounded like "Joo come here."

"Yes," he said, but stayed seated.

"What is the matter? You no like your mamma? Mamma telling you to get out of those wet clothes."

He did as she said, then placed the lubricated rubber on his limp penis and climbed onto the bed. With eyes closed he sank into her. It was over fast.

Standing with his back to the woman, he used a tissue to remove the rubber.

"You a nice boy," she said.

The brown bags had come open in the downpour. Coffee grinds, grapefruit rinds, tin cans, banana peels, had tumbled out, the rain continuing to hit the refuse very hard.

He lay in bed that night, his mind playing back the thievery, the betrayal of his mother and the prostitute. Where would it end? But life was calling to him in the way that it could. If schoolmates were not inviting him into their lives, there were other avenues for exploration. Anyway, the moral consideration wasn't the main thing. He hadn't been caught. He told himself he needn't worry about his mother. God was her cushion from life, her reality. Did she not say as much, that her only prayer was that they all be together in heaven? Whatever disunity there was down here, whatever heartbreak, maybe did not matter. Her eyes were on the finish line.

"You have a call from that man Sean again. He is down in the lobby," his mother said. That word "man" and that word "again," as if he had been calling every night. Even so, her opposition to "that man" had become less vocal. And in fact, he had come calling. Several times. He had a need for the bright lights and big events, for the world that Pastor Odachenko denounced. Just some weeks before he took Johan to see his first Broadway show, *Stop the World! I Want to Get Off.* Anthony Newley sang a big, passionate number called "For Once in My Lifetime," and it still reverberated, with all its pathos, in Johan's consciousness. And then there were the flashing skates of Andy Bathgate at Madison Square Garden as the New York Rangers took on the Chicago Black Hawks with Bobby "The Golden Jet" Hull and Stan Mikita one night down at Madison Square Garden. Johan learned about slap shots and icing the puck and the blue line, and watched the Zamboni smooth the ice between periods. And there was that big roll of bills Sean flashed, the way he always did, and his references to the big bets he had placed. "Five hundred dollars. I'm out five hundred dollars if these fuckers lose," Sean said. And of course Johan had to be careful to hide what he saw, that all Sean's money talk was a failed attempt to make himself a figure of importance.

But on this particular night they were not going to a movie or a show or Madison Square Garden. "You're coming downtown with me. I'm gonna rent me a room," Sean said, bending the English language to his own needs the way he bent the world.

Sean flagged a cab, which they took to Forty-ninth Street and Eighth Avenue, and stopped in at the White Tower down the block from the Garden. "Give me three, and heavy on the onions," he barked at the counterman moving the hamburgers around on the grill with his spatula, the world outside obscured by the fogged windows. The small space was crowded with men eating in their coats. Sean splattered the burgers with ketchup and washed them down with two big Cokes. "Gimme two more," he ordered, his mouth half-stuffed with the remnants of the last one.

As they headed west, away from Broadway, the warm lights of clubs housed in the basements of residential buildings beckoned them down the stairs to a world of cool jazz and sultry female singers.

"This may be our place, baby," Sean said, stopping in front of a building with a "Rooms Available" sign hanging above the entrance-way. Inside, behind a Dutch door, the top half of which was open, sat a skinny older man in his untidy office. He had long, uneven sideburns and a giant Adam's apple bulging from his reedy neck.

"What can I do for you two?"

"I'm looking for a room. That's what you can do for me," Sean said.

"And will you be the missus of the house?" the man asked, addressing himself to Johan. When he didn't answer, the man turned to Sean. "What's it take to get her mouth open? Do I have to guess?"

Sean's gruffness gave way to hysterical laughter.

"Allow me to introduce myself. My name is Desmond. But you can both call me Des, as in Des-ire," he said, in a suggestive voice. Standing now, he struck an akimbo pose. He then led them upstairs through a dimly lit corridor into a room with a lumpy double bed and a dresser and a view, through the dirty window, of a brick wall. "Would you like to stretch out, Sweetheart?" he said, patting the mattress.

Again Sean erupted in laughter.

"Are you looking at my pearly whites, dear? No need to worry. No lover has ever yet complained of my bite."

Johan had been staring not only at Desmond's rotting buck teeth but his purplish gums and slobber lips, wondering how it was that this unshaven and extremely ugly man in oversize jeans could have the odd effect of making him feel desirable. He suspected that he was essentially harmless, simply desperate for attention. Even so, a feeling of entrapment began to grow standing under the bare bulb hanging from the ceiling and imagining the rootless occupants of such a seedy residence.

A loud, popping sound came from the courtyard. Desmond opened the window and stuck his head out. "Stop throwing that fucking garbage into the courtyard or I'm calling the police, you scumbags," he shouted to the air-mailer.

On the street, Sean said, "I'm moving up, baby. I got me a room. And I'll be talking to Frankie boy Sinatra soon about business."

"What kind of business?"

But the time for singing had come, Sean treating startled passersby to a few lines of "April in Paris," then followed with a few more of "I've Got the World on a String."

In the back seat of a cab heading uptown, he whispered, "Now it gets serious. I'm going to have a few parties. Invite some of the boys."

Johan thought of some of the boys he might mean, like Jimmy Riley and Kevin and Rob Koley.

"Maybe some night I'll take Jane down here. I'll bet a stiff cock would split her wide open." He erupted now not in song but hateful laughter. If Johan was disturbed by Sean's venom, he didn't show it or offer any protest. His silence would have to speak for him.

Sean wasted no time. There was to be a card party down at the room that Friday night. "Don't come unless you expect to lose some money," Sean warned everyone on the block.

Johan told Jerry about the card party.

"There's someone you've got to meet," Jerry said. "His name is Lenny from Long Beach. This guy is fantastic. He can do anything. I'll go to this party if he can come, too."

"That's his name? Lenny from Long Beach?"

"That's right. Lenny from Long Beach. Out on Long Island. He's my best friend. I'll come to this party on the condition I can bring Lenny with me."

"Sure," Johan said, having no reason to believe it would be a problem.

"You don't know how good this guy is. He can take a car engine apart and put it back together again practically blindfolded. Sometimes his old man treats Lenny with no respect or tenderness and kicks him out of the apartment, so he has to go and live with his moms out on Long Island. But for right now he and his old man are doing OK. I'm going to bring him down to Sean's room so you can see what quality is all about."

Mrs. Greene stepped from the building, having completed her office shift. She smiled and crossed the street.

"Are we going to do it again?" Jerry asked.

"Do what again?"

"You know. The office."

"No."

Looking back the break-in seemed like such an underhanded thing to do, and the close call with his mother only added to its awfulness.

"Why not?"

Jerry's question made clear to Johan that including his friend had been almost as big a mistake as the act itself.

❧

"Hey, where do you think Sean gets the dinero to rent a room, anyway?" Luis wondered, as he and Kevin and Jimmy and Johan exited the subway at Fiftieth Street and Seventh Avenue.

"Tips. He makes a lot in tips," Jimmy said, cracking himself up with his own joke.

They stopped at the White Tower for a bag of hamburgers and asked a man heading into a nearby liquor store to buy a bottle of scotch with the money they gave him. "Some nights we all need a little something, don't we, boys?" the man said, and some minutes later emerged from the store and handed them a fifth.

Sean was dealing cards to Scully and Rob Koley when they arrived. "You guys in?" he asked, before they had taken off the coats.

Soon Jimmy was shouting, "Hit me again, motherfucker. I'm going to ruin your ass," and laughing his crazy laugh that told you his whole plan was only to ruin himself.

"Oh, this sucks," Kevin said, getting his third bad hand in a row.

Kevin and Jimmy could handle loss. It wouldn't mean a whole lot to them. Luis was another matter. He had a competitive streak and too much pride to lose easily. If he was a real sore loser, there could be a scene. It felt like things were slipping out of control. Soon he would have to run away. He could hear his mother: "We cannot have violence. We cannot."

When Johan got blackjack and won the bank, Sean bought it back from him for ten dollars. "I'm taking you all on," he said, and snapped at Kevin and Jimmy for taking their time deciding whether they were good or taking another hit. His hair glistened from the gel he had applied and he must have taken a bath in cologne, so strong was the smell. He wore dress slacks and leather shoes and a fancy black silk shirt. In manner and dress he was showing them he was something more than a delivery boy pedaling a bike with fat tires.

The small room was hazy with cigarette smoke by the time Jerry arrived. His friend Lenny had Elvis Presley hair and a tan, though summer was long gone. "This is Lenny from Long Beach," Jerry announced.

"Hey, man, I'm Jimmy Riley from Manhattan," Jimmy shot back, cracking himself up again.

Like Sean, Lenny was all in black, the sort of outfit that would have made a skinny person like himself look emaciated, Johan thought. But Lenny had the body to meet the challenge of filling any shirt or pair of pants well.

Jerry had been beating the drum for Lenny not only to Johan but the whole neighborhood, telling one and all what a great lover and fighter his friend from Long Beach was, and how he could kick ass with one hand behind his back. As Lenny went around the room shaking hands, Johan could only be afraid that Luis and Scully and the others would find him less than the god Jerry wanted him to be. And suppose he didn't fit in? Lenny didn't look like the kind of guy to be sitting on Scully's stoop.

"You want in?" Sean spoke in a gruff voice to convey he was all business.

"Yeah. Deal me in," Lenny said, seating himself between Luis and Jimmy and placing on the table a pack of Luckies and his Ronson lighter. He was good with the smoke. He blew it out his mouth in a controlled stream and sucked it up his nose and could even send delicate rings drifting around the room. He won some hands and lost some hands, and Sean showed him not even the slightest friend-liness, as if he was leaving the nice stuff to everyone else. If anything, Sean seemed to grow worse, snappier and more intense.

Johan had started strong but soon was cleaned out, as if by Sean's force of will. "What's the matter, Pussy? Things not going your way? Pussy going to start crying?" Like bullets he fired the words.

It seemed to Johan that everyone in the room was witnessing his humiliation. He grabbed a can of beer and drank it quickly, then filled a paper cup with scotch. It burned going down, but not even a second cup was enough to burn away the shame. It was like he was naked before Sean and all of them and had nowhere to hide.

A key turned in the lock and Desmond crashed through the door. His face was unshaven and what hair he had stood up wild and uncombed on his head. "Am I late for the party?"

Luis jumped up, his right hand in a fist and his arm cocked. "Who the fuck are you, Champ? I'm about to cave in your chest."

"What the hell's the matter with you, coming in here like this?" Sean stood up from the table.

"Oh, honey, don't be talking to me in that rough way. Use your velvet tongue instead. It feels so much better," Desmond said. When Sean started toward him, Desmond split back out the door.

Jimmy lay laughing on the bed. "Who's that evil-looking man? Is that your boyfriend, Sean? Ahhahahahahahaha."

Desmond was a welcome distraction, but Johan, needing something more to show he was recovered from his blackjack defeat, impulsively lobbed a piece of hamburger bun toward Jerry, seated across the room. But if he meant the toss as a friendly gesture, a way of connecting after feeling so alone, Sean saw it otherwise. "Now I'm going to kick your ass," Sean said, punching him to the floor and continuing to pound him.

"Hey Sean, Sean. What's the matter with you?" Luis's voice sounded far away. It seemed forever before Sean was pulled off him and the punches stopped.

"Maybe you live in a fucking pigsty, you stuck-up private school bastard, but you don't come around here and throw food in my place."

But then there was a gentler voice, again as if from far away. "Man, he didn't do anything that bad," he heard Kevin say.

"I want that prick out of here unless he really wants to get his ass kicked."

No, no, just let me stay here, Johan thought. His eyes remained closed. There was safety in darkness. He could even try to believe nothing had happened. But soon hands grabbed hold of his arms and pulled him to his feet and his eyes opened to the harshness of the light as Jimmy placed his coat around his shoulders. Johan tried to smile. He hoped his smile spoke for him. He hoped it told them that what happened had no meaning for him and was no big deal at all.

"Are you all right, man?" Jimmy asked, having followed Johan out into the hallway.

"I'm fine. Really,"

"Look. Maybe you want someone to go home with you," Kevin said. It wasn't good, all that concern. They could get angry at all this attention they had to pay him. He just needed to get away.

On the subway, he tried to maintain the same smile as if Sean was among the other passengers gloating over his victory. Johan must not feed that gloat with any look of hurt. He remembered the satisfaction on Hannah's face after she had done her smacking and more smacking. But his smile began to fade. He had been steam-rollered by Sean, starting with the San Francisco Giants overtaking the Los Angeles Dodgers, and then Sean beating him at cards and after that beating him physically. He told himself he would never be around Sean again, that he just wouldn't, even as a voice whispered that he was silly to think he had the power to stay away.

"What on earth? Who did this to you? Who?" Mrs. Manootdjian stood over Johan.

"No one did anything to me."

"Do not give me your lies and evasions. Tell me now. Have you been with that man? Has that man done this to you?"

"What man? I haven't been with any man."
"Your eye is blackened."
"I had an accident. That is all."
"That man is your accident," Mrs. Manootdjian said.

Chapter 7

Mrs. Manootdjian was happy for Johan when Tom Smits called. Tom Smits was normal, as Horn and Hardart was normal. She knew normal when she saw it, and even if she had never seen Tom Smits, she *felt* his normality, being that he was from the Claremont School and not whatever hellhole Sean had crawled out of.

For a while Tom Smits and Johan had the university gym to themselves, but other kids entered one evening. He recognized them. Tough kids. And there were a few girls with them, and some of the boys and some of the girls went under the stands so they could be alone together and have a private place for what they needed to do. LaSalle Street boys and girls, Johan thought of them as. A white boy was among them. Because in New York City, people had faces you sometimes remembered without ever having spoken to them, as if there was a part of you in which they were meant to live, though for what purpose you couldn't say. And with that sometimes came the sweet ache, as when Patty Joyce and Chao sped from the liquor store with the bottle they had boosted.

And it was for these kids to fight with fists and then with bats and then with chains and knives and zip guns because they were needed when it was clear that other groups of kids had done them wrong with displays of spoken or unspoken attitude requiring them to show that they weren't playing, man, they just weren't playing.

A man-child entered with his stone ditty bop walk signifying his own stylized truculence, his dread-inspiring vibe sufficient to silence the raucous sound of the boys and girls. "Poppy's here. Poppy's here," one whispered. But Poppy paid them no mind. He walked out on the court from under the basket and crossed the half-court line and said to Tom, as if Johan was not present, "Listen up, Bones. I gots to get me some of this. I wants you to plays me. I wants you to beats me. Because if you don't beats me, then I gots to beats you." Poppy wore khaki pants and low-cut black sneakers. He wore a white T-shirt. He had close-cut black hair. He had a face that was not meant for smiling.

It was neighborhood news that a cold rain had poured down on Poppy's life. He had hurt some people with knives. He had stabbed them in the chest and in the back for not having enough money when he held them up or for giving him a wrong look. He had been away to reform schools, but he always came back. He did not carry books or keep normal hours.

Johan was afraid for Tom, afraid that he was not understanding the mean power of Poppy and might react with anger if Poppy elbowed him in the face or gave him a forearm whack underneath the basket, or just gave him clobber because Tom wasn't wearing the right expression.

Poppy reached into his back pocket and took out his blade, a blue-handled stiletto, the kind you saw displayed with the blade open in Times Square shop windows. He placed it tenderly on the side of the court. "I wants to play light. I don't wants nothing holding me back," Poppy said. Seeing Johan's fearful focus on the knife, he said, "Listen up, Bones. I don't wants for you to be looking at my thing or touching it. Don't makes me repeat myself."

Tom looked at Johan, as if to say, "Where am I?" but when the game began he did not hold back. He did his back-into-the-basket move and fake-one-way, then wheel-for-a-hook shot move. He hoisted his I-can't-get-off-the-ground jump shot while Poppy played with a sullen dignity, as if performing some intricate dance step to the staccato beat of his dribble. He let loose with left-handed jump shots on a flat trajectory. Some banged hard off the rim and some were all net.

When Tom missed a hook shot and Poppy put in the rebound from under the basket, Tom raised a squawk. Poppy should have taken it back behind the foul line before shooting. Poppy fixed him with a baleful stare. He finally said, "I gots mines. You gots to get your owns, Bones" before stepping back for a corner jump shot that hit nothing but net.

"Game's over, boys and girls." A guard stood at the entrance and tapped his nightstick on the stairs leading down to the court. Johan and Tom grabbed their coats and the ball and fled, as did the other boys and girls, but Poppy pocketed his blade and headed slowly toward the guard and his nightstick and his uniform. The guard was not anymore banging with his nightstick. He was not saying "Boys and girls." He was not saying anything. He was just watching Poppy, the way the world was compelled to watch Poppy.

The driver was an SRO type of man, Johan thought, sitting just behind the emaciated and unshaven man as his school mates boarded the bus. Would Freddy Snyder hurt the driver's feelings with some insensitive remark? But no, the driver was invisible to Freddy and Lance and all of them. There was a whole world they did not see, and why should they, as it was not theirs? Soon the driver pulled the halves of the doors together and drove north toward Morningside Heights on Amsterdam Avenue, Johan willing the driver to hit all the lights and speed past Scully's stoop. When he braked at One Hundred Fourteenth Street time seemed to stop. The whole gang was out there: Scully and Luis and Kevin and Jimmy and Philip, the kid with the sharp mouth. And there was Sean carrying a box of empty bottles down to the grocery store basement. A small life it suddenly seemed, kids hanging around the stoop of a rundown building swigging from bottles of soda, smoking cigarettes, and dotting the sidewalk with small islands of spit. And there was Jane turning the corner and heading toward them. Even from her, for a moment, he could feel some distance.

The gym was in the basement of the Riverside Church. From the end of a long corridor, beyond the locker room, came the booming sound of a basketball being dribbled on the hardwood floor calling to them with the promise of losing themselves in play. Nearer to the court, having shed their uniforms for gym shorts and a T-shirt, came the sound of squeaking sneakers.

The basement also featured a bowling alley and a spacious room where the Friday night social group, of which Jane was a part, held dances. He told himself that if he imagined the worst happening, Jane and Scully and the other kids showing up at the gym and witnessing his extreme thinness, then it was less likely to happen. That day his privacy was even more important, as he had the misfortune to be assigned to the skins, not the shirts. How well built the other players looked under the pitilessly revealing gym lights. Even Mr. Arbuckle, who often joined them for these scrimmages, looked great in his tennis whites.

Mr. Sadowski put them through fifteen minutes of exercises—jumping jacks and wind sprints and sit-ups and pushups—before they could scrimmage. The talent pool at the high school was slight. There weren't ten boys who could control their dribble while running up and down the court. Tom, from the ninth grade, his classmate Freddy Snyder, and Johan were the only three non-Juniors or Seniors to try out for the varsity.

"Johan, get your hands up on defense," Mr. Sadowski barked. Did he not know that to lift his arms was to give fuller exposure to his ribs? And yet, at the end of the scrimmage, Mr. Sadowski patted him on the back and said, "You'll be starting for this team next year." Suddenly, his future was in front of him again.

"Wait for me," Tom Smits said, as Johan tore from the locker room. They walked through the Barnard College campus, passing the tennis court. Behind them was ivy-covered Millbrook Hall and ahead a deep hole in the ground, the site of the new library. And then there was the big wrought-iron gate at 117th Street leading onto Broadway and the forest green wood fence that served as a barrier between the campus and the street.

Johan had hoped to drop away from Tom Smits before they came to his building, but the block where he lived was now looming. Harry Frug's appliance store was closed as was Mr. Berger's hosiery shop, and neither his sisters nor Luke called out to him, nor did his father or mother and Auntie Eve, nor Jerry Jones-Nobleonian nor any of the gang from Scully's stoop. There was no calling out of any kind as they came to One Hundred Tenth Street, three blocks past where his building stood.

"I'll see you," Johan said, asking only that no further smart thing fly from Tom Smits's mouth. But Tom Smits had the smart thing ready anyway. "Where did you say you live?" His smile was one of deep amusement.

"Around here."

"Around here?" He laughed and shook his head.

From the fruit and vegetable store came Mrs. Manootdjian, carrying a small bag of groceries. With her free hand she waved, and so Johan had no choice but to do the same. And if he had been hoping that Tom had not seen this mutual display of recognition, it was a foolish hope. And so, as Mrs. Manootdjian went on her way, Tom pounced. "Who is that old woman with the funny shoes? Tell me it is not your mother."

Without answering, Johan tore across the street, dodging cars and buses and trucks, and sought refuge in Whelan's Pharmacy, where he spun the rack containing paperback novels, seeing without seeing for a few minutes, until he could be reasonably sure the coast was clear and it was safe to head home without the bloodhound Tom Smits behind him.

Chapter 8

Johan could remove himself from Sean physically, but he couldn't remove him from his mind. Sean had used brute force to pound himself even more into his consciousness. Strangely, there arose, beyond the humiliation, an element of satisfaction in knowing that he had engaged with Sean's power and survived. A new level of intimacy with him had been reached.

Scully's stoop was calling. He heard it calling. There was no need to remind himself of the distance he felt when seeing it from the school bus. His love was there, on that strip of Amsterdam Avenue, from the pharmacy on one corner to the florist's shop on the other. It was where he must go to feel good, even when it made him feel bad. He was missing his life when he was not there. Besides, if he did stay away, Sean might think he was ashamed to show his face.

"What do you do in that room, anyway?" Jane asked.

"Sean likes to play cards."

"You shouldn't have to get a black eye from playing cards."

"That's the way he plays cards. From blackjack to a black eye."

"He's dangerous. Don't you know that?"

"You're dangerous," Johan said.

"You wouldn't mind if I borrowed Jane for a night, would you, Johan? I'm having a party. How about it? I know she likes me. You can always tell these things." Philip Malloy took a few practice swings with the taped store-bought stickball bat. Philip had seen what all of them had seen. He had no fight in him.

"I don't know about that," Johan said.

"What's that mean? I want to go out with your girlfriend. You have a problem with sharing her?" There was only numbness where anger should have been and the feeling that Philip had the force of inevitability and could sweep him out of the way like a fallen leaf.

"Damn, Philip, leave him alone. Show some respect," Jimmy said.

"Respect my dick," Philip replied, grabbing his crotch before speeding away to catch a bus.

"Damn. I would have caved in his chest, he talked that way to me," Luis said. Cave in his chest? Put a hole in his chest? What was this language of grotesque violence that it should be part of everyday speech? And yet in his thoughts that night Johan imagined just such a thing.

In the winter darkness the lights in the university buildings gave a warm glow. Snow had fallen, crowning the tops of the hedges lining the campus walkways and blanketing the south lawn and muffling all noise but the crunching sound their shoes made on the snow underfoot.

"Tell me how you're interested in them. Tell me." Because he could not name his nemesis and make him any more real than he already was. She would know, and even if she didn't, it was only a matter of time before she did.

Jane came quickly to attention. She had heard him speak in this tone of voice before. "Cut it out, Johan. Cut it out."

"Who is it, Jane?" Because once the soreness started, it had to run its course.

"I don't know what you're talking about." Her raised voice signified she was leaning toward the histrionic for the sole purpose of attracting attention and humiliating him. That wasn't right. It just wasn't right. With his open hand, he slapped her face.

"You bastard." She held her struck cheek, her eyes flashing fire, and took off.

Two students speaking softly passed by. Others followed. The campus did not rain down its scorn. And yet punishment awaited. He had crossed a forbidden line. He had struck a girl. This he understood, as the snow fell and fell to the earth, so eager to soil it.

"Oh, hello, young Romeo…No, she can't…No, I couldn't say…Yes, of course I'll give her your message." Mrs. Thayer with the velvet voice had smoothly dispatched with him.

He was back on the line within a half hour. "Another day, Sport." A masculine voice this time. Her father. *Sport.* The word like a hard jab to his chest. Her father knew. Jane had told him. Mr. Thayer was banishing him forever.

Within minutes he was seeing Mr. Thayer's words in a different light. He hadn't expressly forbidden Johan to call. Though the thought of hearing one more "Sport" from her stern-voiced father was terrifying, there was the chance that Jane would pick up the phone herself.

The third time was not a charm. "Lights out, Sport. Lights out." Mr. Thayer slammed down the phone.

Unable to sleep, he wandered through the apartment and found his mother at the dining table. She was in her robe and reading from the Bible. "What is it, my son, that you are still up?"

"It's nothing."

"You can tell me. Is it your girlfriend? I won't breathe a word."

"No."

"Has she upset you?"

"Stop."

"I will give you something so your night will not be sleepless."

She went off to her closet in the hallway, the one she kept under lock and key. She returned with a slender yellow capsule in the palm of her hand. "Here. Take this with a glass of water. But you must lie still in bed so it can take effect."

Minutes later all was miraculously light within him. The darkness and the fear had been dispelled. A brimming confidence had replaced the woeful insecurity. He would call Jane tomorrow and they would be back together. At school he would chat easily with Bert Bach and John Edel and could even imagine approaching Diane Coleman or Robin Abel. There would be no terror, no lack of confidence, no sense of separation from anyone.

In the morning he awoke to pain as raw as the night before. He didn't care about Mr. Thayer and his "Sport" stuff or Mrs. Thayer and her velvet voice. He must speak with Jane. He must regain his life. And there she was on the line, and there he was with words of apology just pouring out of him.

"I understand."

"Can I see you later?"

"I don't think so."

"Why?"

"I have other plans."

The phone went dead.

In English class he stared from the back row at Robin Abel, her black hair in a bob, and wondered, in horror, how he could have imagined speaking with her when he could barely say hello. If, in the dark, the pill had expanded his horizons, in daylight he had contracted back into his normal frightened self.

"Did I tell you? I'm going out with Jill this Saturday," Lance said to Freddy Snyder in the hallway afterward.

"Maybe we could double-date. I have a date with Sharon," Freddy Snyder says.

Jill. Sharon. *Date.* Such an unbelievably cold word. A word that meant you saw someone once and then discarded her for someone else. A word that meant unbearable change. The pain. Never again must he have such straying thoughts. Never again. Always and forever must he commit himself to Jane.

"Get your damn hand off my leg, you faggot," Scully said, in a carrying voice in the darkened theater that Friday night.

"Ain't nobody wants to touch your ugly leg, my man," Jimmy said, in an equally carrying voice, as the coming attractions were shown on the movie screen.

On the refreshments line, an idea came to Johan. He could have Jerry call for him. "All you have to say is that I was hit by a car."

"Could you lend me some money for popcorn and a soda?"

Johan forked over the money.

"Oh man, she ain't going to go for that," Jerry said, as he started in on the popcorn.

"I'll hold the popcorn. Just go call her."

"Is this Jane? A friend of hers. My name is Jerry Jones-Nobleonian…Yes, it is a very distinguished name." Jerry cupped the receiver. "Her moms is going to get her," he whispered. "Hello, Jane? This is Jerry. I just wanted to tell you some bad news. Johan got runned over by a truck and he's in bad shape at the hospital….No, really. It's no lie. He got runned over real bad."

Jerry put the phone back on the hook. "She hung up, man. She says it's all a bunch of your horseshit and that you put me up to it. It don't sound too good for you, man."

The wall clock in the theater glowed in the dark. Within ten minutes he was back at the same phone booth, this time alone.

"Well, what do you want? Are you going to live or die? Tell me the hospital where you are staying and your room number so I can send flowers," Jane said.

"I miss you."

"Poor baby." She laughed and hung up.

The facial contortions of Jack Lemmon. And pixie-faced Shirley Maclaine. *The Apartment,* the movie was called. But that laugh of Jane's meant more than anything on the screen. It meant she was happy to have heard from him. Drawn from his seat back to the booth, he called once more.

"Fuck off, creep." No laughter at all in her voice this time.

Another week went by. He hadn't died. He hadn't died at all. The phone booth was not calling to him the way it had. And he was living somewhat beyond the sadness of the crime he had committed in putting his hand to her face.

League play began. Mr. Sadowski called him from the bench. The red and white uniform, the organized competition, the refs in their striped black and white shirts and with their whistles, the small crowds—it was all a thrill. But his time on the court went by so fast. He wanted to play all afternoon and into the evening. Still, he scored on drives and shots from the corner, compensating for a lack of jumping ability with quickness and agility. Never mind that they lost. His performance, and the pat on the back from Mr. Sadowski, were sufficient cause for intoxication. Listening to Murray the K's swinging soiree on WABC that evening, he imagined love and admiration pouring down on him from the stands as he did things that had never been done before on a basketball court.

At the next practice session, he was once again grounded in reality when he collided with Ron Reisman under the boards, his bony hip making a hollow sound as it knocked against the senior's elbow. The action stopped as Ron gave him a look that said, "You and I both know you have a body to be ashamed of," a look Johan deeply received, Ron being the same older boy who had suggested that Johan couldn't have weighed more than fifty pounds.

The big marquee jutting out onto Eighth Avenue, the Nedicks and its hot dogs on toasted buns, the smoke-filled grandstand and those steep steps, the roaring crowds, the vendors hawking food and drinks, the darkened arena and the lights trained on the hardwood floor—Tommy "Ack-Ack" Heinsohn slinging jump shots with contemptuous confidence and Bob Cousy, his rooster head always up as he dribbled, and Bill Russell, at center, intimidating Bob Pettit, the high-scoring forward with a twenty-foot jump shot, and the other St. Louis Hawks—he loved those nights at Madison Square Garden.

But he didn't love Tom Smits, not when he said, "You're bright. You should go to a school like Brown or Penn," as they stared down at the court. Did Tom Smits not know what Mr. Arbuckle had to say about the SAT?

Then there was the night that Loyola Chicago took the court with four Negro starters. They had Les Hunter at center and Vic Rouse at forward. They had deadly Ron Miller and racehorse Jerry Harkness as starting guards. Loyola Chicago ran right over its slow and clumsy white opponent, as Tom bet Johan they would, once again showing no fear about Negro advancement. Tom Smits did not know what unappeasable Negro anger was, how they punched and punched and when you fell down they punched some more. Tom Smits laughed as Loyola Chicago humiliated the white boys. He just laughed and laughed, leaving Johan no choice but to punch him in the face. Tom Smits had beaten him, and now he had to beat him. Johan ran from the Garden and all he had done, but before he was home, the rage had given way to shame. He had wanted Tom Smits to know only his smiling and amiable ways. He had not wanted Tom Smits to see what Gresham Dodger, who was no longer at the school, and Jane Thayer had seen.

Vera did not deny their mother or the family. How such a thing could be Johan could not say. There she was sharing what passed for their sofa with a girl whose long, silky blond hair had the light of the sun in it.

"Hi, Johan," Vera said, in the teasing way that she could when with a girlfriend. "You remember Pam, don't you?"

As the girl stared at him, he heard her unspoken scorn for the way they lived. It was all he heard.

"We're going over to the diner. Want to come?" Vera asked.

"OK. Sure," he said, before he could say no.

The crew had drifted down from Amsterdam Avenue to hang around outside the diner. "Hey, look at the girls Johan is with," Scully said, loud enough for Johan and Vera and Pam to hear.

"Hey, my man, why don't you introduce us to these fine-looking girls?" Jimmy called out, as they entered the coffee shop.

"That's my brother's gang. My brother is a hoodlum," Vera said, as they took a booth.

"A gang sounds very romantic. Is your gang anything like those in *West Side Story?* My parents took Nancy and me to see the play," Pam said.

West Side Story. Her question froze him. It felt like a test.

"No," he said, not wanting her to know he had never heard of the play. "And my sister is just kidding. That's not a gang. They're just some kids from the neighborhood."

"No, I'm not kidding. He's unbelievable. You don't know some of the characters he hangs around with. There's this one guy who looks like he's thirty-five. I call him Watermelon Head because his head is that big."

"He doesn't look thirty-five," Johan said, though he couldn't say exactly how old Sean looked.

"You know what he did to get thrown out of St. Andrews? He threw toilet paper at the nuns. And at camp he was always crying to come home."

"Were you always crying?" Pam Becker put her big blue eyes on him.

"No. Not always."

"He bawled like a baby. No one knew what to do with him."

"Were you unhappy there?" Pam asked.

"He missed our mother. He's a little mama's boy, though he tries to hide it."

Johan was unable to speak.

"He's got this other friend. I see them together sometimes. He's tall and real cute. I keep asking Johan to introduce me, but he never does," Vera said. She was talking about Tom Smits.

"Why don't you introduce her?"

"I don't know," he lied. It would not do to say he was not good enough for Tom, and neither was she. It would not do to open himself to more of Tom's ridicule when he found out about the family.

"Look. Isn't that your girlfriend? Aren't you going to go over and say hello?"

Jane was sitting several booths down with Philip, the kid with the smart mouth.

"I don't think so."

"You broke up?" Vera went on.

"I guess."

"What did you do to her?"

"I don't know. Nothing."

Back in his room he stared through the screened window across Broadway, the diner in full view. Though it was a half hour before Jane and Philip emerged, he maintained his vigil, following their path until they were out of sight. Then he lay on Luke's bottom bunk curled up in the fetal position and moaned softly.

"Are you having trouble sleeping again? Of course you can have a pill," his mother said, when darkness came.

He had been doing so well before seeing Jane. And now, with the pill in him, he began to do well all over again. The pill just melted all the pain away, and made him hope daylight was a long time coming.

In the morning the orange snowplows were out, heralding their arrival with the click-click of chains on their huge tires so that the snow that fell and fell could not keep the cars and trucks and buses from coming and going and coming and going.

Two kids stood at the top of a snowdrift and let fly with hard-packed snowballs at a southbound bus. A woman jumped back in her seat, startled, as the snowballs slammed against the window of the bus. The boys raised their arms in triumph, as he would have some years before.

The weekend had come and that evening the diner was calling to him.

"My younger son came down from Ithaca to see me. He's doing swell. Did I tell you? He's a straight A student at Cornell, and he's majoring in chemistry. He's got the right stuff. I don't know where he got it—not from me—but he's got it. He took the test for the Bronx High School of Science and got in. He got a perfect score on the math part of that test. What's it called again?" Ralph, the counterman, flopped the wet rag over and leisurely wiped around the cake stand and the condiments.

"The SAT?"

"That's it. The SAT. And now he's on a full scholarship at one of the best colleges in the country. The other one, he's a shmegegge, if you ask me, driving a cab and with no thought of the future. You look like a smart boy. You think you'll get a perfect score on that test?"

"I wish." He could see from Ralph's grin that he didn't think so either. Ralph had a sad, slow way about him and bags under his eyes.

"He's spending time with his mother during his college break. She lives on Mosholu Avenue. You know where Mosholu Avenue is?"

"No."

"The Bronx Zoo is nearby. You've never been to the Bronx Zoo?"

"No."

"My younger boy used to live there. He knew all the animals. You know what a dromedary is?"

"A dromedary?"

"How are we going to get you into college if you don't know what a dromedary is? It's a kind of camel."

"Oh, that's right," Johan said, feeling his ears turning red.

"How come I don't see you with that girl anymore, the pretty one?"

"I don't know."

"So what do you know?" Ralph didn't wait for an answer but went off down the counter with his rag, where a customer was waiting.

"Johan?"

He turned on his stool. A girl with red hair stood facing him. "My name is Frieda. I'm a friend of Jane's. Can I talk to you for a minute?"

"Sure." The thought that Jane had told her about the slap made him uneasy.

"Jane misses you. She really wants to see you again."

Her voice was solemn, embarrassingly so. He had a feeling that such words went against her grain, that she was a mirthful girl and he was not worthy of such an avowal, especially from a pretty messenger. Still, the message elated him.

"Are you kidding? Him? Philip? I saw him that one time. Who was that girl I saw you with at the diner?"

"You mean my sister Vera?"

"The girl with the blond hair.»

"Oh, her. She's just Vera's friend."

"What's her name?"

It wasn't for him to ask why she wanted to know, not when he already knew. "Pam," he simply said.

Chapter 9

A untie Eve placed boughs of holly in the lobby, and even a small tree with lights, but a grinch swiped the tree and the stand as well, leaving only the bed of snow, and so Auntie Eve had to get a second tree, and all that went with it.

The Manootdjians had their own tree, a Douglas fir, decorated with ornaments and electric lights and a star. Underneath the tree were small gifts, lumpy and hastily wrapped.

Mrs. Manootdjian cooked a turkey, as she had for Thanksgiving, and the apartment filled with its strong, delicious smell. There were sweet potatoes and gravy and stuffing to go with the turkey, and the dinner would not have been complete without tart Ocean Spray cranberries and gallons of apple cider and soft, sweet pumpkin pie.

Mr. Manootdjian said grace. "Dear Lord, we thank you for our many blessings, for this food on the table that my beloved wife has prepared, and for all the good she brings into our lives…." It went downhill from there. He grew emotional and started to weep as he struggled to thank the Lord for having led him to Mrs. Manootdjian.

"Hayk, we must finish. The food will get cold," she whispered.

"Praise Jesus. Thank you, Jesus," his father said, as he slowly lowered himself into his chair at the head of the table.

Auntie Eve did not join them. She had her island of aloneness on which she stood, Johan picturing her by herself, as he often did, on a dark and cold Stockholm night under glittering stars. It gave him hope to picture her like that.

And his sister Rachel was not there either, but her absence was different from Auntie Eve's. It was a howl of loneliness and lostness from some crummy room in a hotel for transients.

Nor was Naomi, for she had committed herself to her husband Chuck, whom Mr. Manootdjian forbade to enter the apartment, lest Mr. Manootdjian be made to get up by Chuck's drunken and ceaseless provocations. But their daughter Jeanne was present. In fact, she had a small room off the living room in which to stay so she didn't have to share a room with her mother and father and endure the purposelessness of their days and nights.

And Luke was present, and Hannah as well with her two-year-old, Moses. And though she said that night, as she was often to say, "Nobody deprives me and my son. Nobody," it was not received as holy writ, as her life was marked with deprivation and the shame that burdened not only her but others among the Manootdjians.

Afterward Mrs. Manootdjian spoke to Johan, out of earshot of Jeanne, saying, "It has been the life's work of Naomi to drive your sister Rachel down from the heights she aspired to and reached. You must know that there is malicious intent in this world and it comes often in the form of these pills the psychiatrists, such as the ones Naomi has been in the care of, dispense. Naomi gave your sister Rachel these pills and then led her to the bottle. The world has now claimed your sister Rachel, as a wolf snares the lamb, and is doing terrible things to her, but the Lord has vanquishing power over Satan's domain and we will all be in heaven together, my son. All of us. Of this you can be sure. Because the Rapture can be delayed, if we are to be a slave to time, but never cancelled. Tell me you understand these words I speak. Tell me."

"I understand," Johan said, the turkey having made him drowsy and ready only for sleep.

The school was not content with the brownstones that housed it and the beautiful yard where, in warm weather, the children played dodge ball and read on benches under the beech and honey locust trees. During the holiday season there was a relocation. No more ivy-colored walls. No more two-stop subway rides on the IRT West Side local. No more unfriendly public school eyes upon them as they emerged from their school for the privileged wearing their preppie uniforms. The school now had a more prestigious address on the East Side, one where sleek, chauffeur-driven cars would not be in conflict with the tenement surroundings.

Human Day had been eliminated. Students were no longer free to wear casual clothes in place of their uniforms on Fridays. Furthermore, anyone found smoking within three blocks of the school would be immediately suspended.

As Johan waited at One Hundred Tenth Street for the Number Four bus ("What's yellow and green and comes in bunches? The Fifth Avenue Coach Line bus") at 8:30 that morning, there, crossing Broadway with long strides, was Tom Smits.

"I guess One Hundred Tenth Street is going to continue to be our meeting spot," Tom said.

"I'm sorry for what happened at the game," Johan said, thinking of Gresham Dodger.

"That's all right. I always knew you were a real bruiser." Tom laughed.

Along the northern perimeter of Central Park the crowded and overheated bus crawled, the fare box making a periodic commotion as it sorted the coins. The driver turned down Fifth Avenue. Mount Sinai Hospital, the Museum of the City of New York, the Metropolitan Museum of New York. Johan realized the advantages of having a school on the other side of Central Park, its fields covered with snow and the trees in their winter bareness. The compartments of his life could be kept more easily separate; each passing street put more and more distance between him and his family's building.

Just down the block from the quiet formality of the Frick Museum, between Fifth and Madison Avenues, a five-story former mansion now housed their school. There was no yard to flee into and in place of creaky wooden stairs, a marble staircase to the upper floors—or an elevator, should you choose. The fluorescent lighting gave the halls and classrooms the brightness of a supermarket.

"You didn't know we were moving until last week? You didn't know? How could you not know? The move has been talked about for months. People, listen to this. Manootdj didn't even know that we would be here until his parents got a notice in the mail. Can you believe it?" Freddy Snyder's voice registered his disbelief.

"You be careful, Freddy. Johan has a gang. He's going to sic it on you," Lance said, as he had before.

"Do you really have a gang?" Freddy asked.

"No."

"Say, Manootdj, what kind of name is that anyway? You told me once. Is it Persian or something?"

"There is no Persia, Freddy. I think it's called Iran," Lance said, winking at Johan.

"Well, okay, but one of those countries. You know what I mean."

"Nobody knows what you mean." Lance laughed.

New location or not, he would have to be careful and say nothing that would call unwanted attention to himself.

And yet, what a perfect world, he thought, as the day progressed. Jane and he would finish high school and then he would go off to college and she would too. They would be in different states, but not so distant. And maybe he would see some other girl and she would find a boy to be with, because they were supposed to live a little before they got married and settled down. Still, they would love only each other. Their love would be preserved and when they graduated, they would resume all over again, and go on as if there had been no interruption at all. Though he hadn't talked to Jane about the matter, he was sure the future would work out just that way.

In French class he stole looks at Robin Abel several rows ahead. She too was perfect, every strand of her hair always in place. Well, not quite perfect. There was the minor eruption of acne on her right cheek, but even that somehow added to her luster. And those long legs sheathed in black tights she wore with her gray skirt. Other days it was a plaid skirt. And sometimes there were those knee socks. She read *Paris Match*. She read Albert Camus in French. She knew the plusque parfait perfectly.Diane Coleman was seated in the same row as Robin. Her hair was strawberry blond and she had a mildly freckled face. She too read *Paris Match* and Camus in French and knew the plusque parfait perfectly. She had been Coleman the last two years, and before that she had been Gaynor.

Then Bert Bach and Robin smiled easily at each other and once again he was restored to sanity. ("Did you hear what Flathead went and did? Did you hear he went to Robin and asked her for her phone number? Have you ever heard anything funnier in your whole life?")

Old Mlle. Gallimard—it was whispered that she was almost seventy—walked between the rows of desks, and stopped at Johan's. "Lisez cette maxim, en Anglais, s'il vous plait." There was a slight quiver in her heavily rouged and powdered face as she spoke.

"Whom one has ceased to love, one cannot love a second time." They had been reading the maxims of La Rochefoucauld.

"Parfait," she replied. He felt warmed by her response.

But as the day went on, the maxim stayed in his consciousness, and the following day as well. Some unsettling and unasked for truth has been presented and was now ripping a tear in his world. How was he supposed to stay with Jane and live at the same time when the Frenchman was saying that once Jane and he went off and led separate lives during college, they could not get back together again. Life would have moved them permanently apart. All those happy days and months spent with Jane, with the future promising nothing but the same, and now some aphorist from the eighteenth century just came along and canceled that happiness?

Once again he overheard talk of dating. Yes, Bert Bach would be going out with Robin Abel that weekend and Diane Coleman had been seeing a freshman at Columbia. How heartless. Where is the love and warmth in such experimentation? He would not hurt Jane with that kind of coldness.

The future must be held on to and made to stand still. But however he tried to fit Jane into it, the construction fell apart. The future was now pain, a problem without a solution.

The cafeteria was in the basement and awash in fluorescent lighting. Lonnie, a boy from the grade below, approached the table where Johan sat alone. His movements were spastic, one of his legs angled inward and slightly buckled. His face contorted as he opened the container holding his half-pint of milk. On his tray was a gloppy egg salad sandwich, some of the egg falling from between the slices of bread as he lifted it to his mouth. He masticated with his mouth open, globs of yellow stuck in the heavy braces on his teeth. They ate in silence.

Mr. Horst-Lehman, the Claremont principal, also taught sophomore English. The tailored suits and jackets he stood before the class in suggested a wardrobe even vaster than Mr. Arbuckle's. He was a heavy-set man, his face jowly and dotted with warts and moles, and his pointed tongue slid lewdly and with regularity from between his thin lips. His readings from *Henry IV, Part One*, animated the play. The theme of redemption stood out for Johan. As the play opens, Harry, King Henry's son, spends his time in a tavern with Falstaff and Bardolph and other lowlife wastrels, in marked contrast with Hotspur, the son of the king's rival Northumberland. How amazing to read of Hotspur as "the theme of honour's tongue," a warrior who could ride his horse "on the perpendicular."

"Johan, it's awfully stuffy in the room. Would you open the window a crack?" Mr. Horst-Lehman paused to ask. With uncontrollable self-consciousness, as if all eyes had been drawn to him, Johan rose to perform the task.

"That is, if he is able to. We're not exactly looking at Hercules," Mr. Horst-Lehman chuckled, eliciting loud laughter from the class.

When the handle of the casement window wouldn't turn, Johan's face turned even redder.

"Is virility incarnate having a problem?" Mr. Horst-Lehman asked, with mock sincerity, to more laughter.

Finally, the crank yielded and Johan returned to his desk with a smile meant to show he hadn't been hurt at all by Mr. Horst-Lehman's jabs.

"Some of these cretins can't write a line of iambic pentameter," Tom said, as they waited for the bus at the end of the school day. Was he talking about Lonnie, the spastic boy, Johan wondered, but did not ask. He could only be grateful Tom didn't challenge him to prove his knowledge of meter.

The bus pulled to a stop at One Hundred Tenth Street and Broadway.

"What do you say I come home with you now? We'll watch a little TV."

"No. Not today."

"Look. I'll bring over our TV if you don't have one."

Johan left him with the same smile he had shown Mr. Horst-Lehman and his classmates. But the smile quickly vanished. Had Mr. Horst-Lehman been waiting all along to crush him, knowing he and his family were not Claremont quality? And what was he to do about Tom, with his ceaseless mockery? Alone, anger took him over.

Winter turned to spring. Scully's stoop had begun to call.

"Yo, my man is back," Luis went, giving him a rap on the arm.

"Yo, Flathead," Scully went.

"Yo, private school punk, where you been? Do I have to kick your ass for disappearing?" Jimmy Riley went.

But Philip went, "You manage to get your dick in that girl yet?"

Johan saw blazing hatred in Philip's small eyes. He saw Philip's barrel chest and thick legs. The butterflies started to flutter. He was there only a minute and about to get in a fight he would quickly lose.

Nearby Sean was carrying soda bottles down to the basement for sorting in wooden crates. Back and forth he went between the basement and the store.

"I guess Head's having a hard day. He sure is blowing awfully hard," Philip said, in a loud voice. "Get it, Scully? Blowing hard?"

"Oh shit, your ass is grass now, my man." Luis said. Philip turned in time to see Sean charging and grabbed a piece of plywood with a long nail in it. He swung at Sean's head and missed. Several hard shots to the face later and Philip was on the pavement. He staggered to his feet, his hand cupped over his bleeding mouth. Blood stained his striped oxford shirt and khaki pants, which were torn at the knee. Jimmy tried to help, but Philip stiff-armed him out of the way and ran off across the avenue holding his mouth in a rage of humiliation.

"Damn, fucking Sean," Luis said, reminded that Sean could and would move against anyone.

He has an animal's instinct and ferocity, Johan thought, once again thrilled by Sean's power though it had been used against him only months before.

"Do you still not talk to Sean?" Jane asked.

"I've been keeping my distance."

"He's so violent." She had heard about Philip and the beating Sean gave him.

"Philip is a wise guy. He beats up on people with his mouth. He'll also whack you in the head with a bat when you're not looking."

"I guess that's why Sean beat you up, too, huh?"

"That was different."

"Whatever Philip said, it doesn't give Sean the right to do that to him."

"I guess not." She made no mention of his violence toward her.

"You seem to still like Sean," she said.

He could have said the same to her about Philip, from the way she was defending him.

"Does he still have that room downtown?"

"I guess so."

"What do they do down there, anyway?"

"They play cards. They drink beer and whiskey."

The quizzical smile on her face suggested something more might be going on. Johan offered no more information. He was OK with the idea that some element of mystery attached to his life.

The playing field needed some care. Portions of the outfield showed bald spots and the infield looked hard and untended to. The field seemed to sit there neglected, as did the Cathedral of St. John the Divine itself, of which it was a part, with its unfinished tower. He thought back to his years at St. Andrew's and the commencement ceremonies held at the cathedral and to the nuns going about the streets like flocks of urbanized penguins. He had been unruly, incorrigible. It was only right that he had been expelled. It was very much warranted.

Someone was calling to him from a distance. Though he recognized the voice instantly, he only slowly turned to acknowledge it, as it was one thing to warm to Sean in his mind but another altogether to interact with him. And there he was, leaning bare-chested out the third-floor window of his family's apartment on the opposite corner. If Sean had any similar inhibition, he roared past it. "I got me tickets for the Mets and Braves tonight. You coming?"

No auxiliary verb. No need for one. Everything from Sean was urgency. And yet, in his semi-naked pose, he projected not so much power as vulnerability. How easy it would be to reply with a no or simply not respond at all and close the door on him with finality. But how unkind it would be to reject him, how painfully sad and hurtful.

"Sure," Johan called, ignoring the small voice within counseling otherwise.

An hour later their cab pulled up at the Polo Grounds, at One Hundred Fifty-fifth Street. Batting practice was underway, and in the twilight Sean and Johan ran down balls hit into the stands along the first base line, managing to grab a few in the scramble that ensued with other fans at the sparsely attended game.

Their seats were directly behind home plate, with a view out past the pitcher's mound to the locker rooms under the Rheingold sign beyond vast center field. The ballpark had been unused since the Giants left town, but now the Mets were playing there while a new stadium was being built in Queens.

"You want something, you just say. It's on me," Sean said. The smell of ballpark franks had made him hungry, and Sean shouted out their orders in a voice as loud as those of the hawking vendors.

"I'm doing good, man. I'm on a fucking roll. I'm like Frankie boy. I'm like a fucking chairman of the board." Sean made no mention of the incident in the room or the one with Philip. The reality was there, too big to be spoken of.

From delivery boy to chairman of the board.

In the second year of their existence, the Mets were still a ragtag expansion team, and the Milwaukee Braves were not the pennant-winning team they had been some years before. But they had Aaron and they had sweet-swinging Eddie Mathews and they had southpaw Warren Spahn with the elegant lefty windup and delivery. Since the Dodgers and Giants fled after the 1957 season, Johan had dreamed of the return of National League baseball, and now here it was. Not that it was the same. It could never be the same: Johnny Podres jumping ecstatically into the embrace of Campy after shutting down the Yankees in that seventh game in 1955, and the Duke, with all those consecutive forty-homer years in Brooklyn. But he was a different Duke now, an old and part-time player not in Dodger blue—and not even number 4 on his back but number 28.

That night, as the cab climbed Coogan's Bluff and sped down Broadway, Johan could be comforted that while Sean could arrange these lavish evenings, he needed Johan more than Johan needed him.

"Keep the change," Sean said, handing the hackie a twenty, then turned to Johan. "I'm headed up to Boston in about two weeks to see Fenway Park. You coming?"

Sean had been on his good behavior. Why disappoint him or make him angry? Why not just go along for the ride? Unable to say no, he said yes.

"But Johan, this is very good. An A in history and an A in Latin," Momma says, in the privacy of the bathroom. She had seen what Johan had also seen on the report card—a B+ in geometry and a B in English. He had fallen and her words were not enough to lift him up because they conveyed that she realized he had fallen. It had taken a while for Mr. Horst-Lehman to see beyond Johan's blond hair to his Negro nose and lips. Mr. Arbuckle had aided this reevaluation by informing Mr. Horst-Lehman of his low mathematical aptitude, his inability to grasp theorems involving rectangles and parallelograms and rhombuses and the rest of it. They were catching on. And, of course, there was the weakness he showed in dropping the biology class. There was no need to tell his mother. Her ears were too tired of the language of defeat.

When you have tooth pain, you treat it yourself if you know what is good for you. You do not go to Dr. Millsley and allow him to send pain shooting through your body when his slow drill strikes a nerve. You remember that childhood experience of sitting in his chair in Rockefeller Center and stay away. You pack aspirin into the hole in the molar on the lower right side of your mouth. That way the aspirin can take direct action against the pain by attacking it at its source, whereas if you swallow the aspirin it goes to all different parts of your body and what good is that? And after you take the aspirin, you lie still on your bed and moan softly, so you and no one else can hear.

After three days of this misery, Johan surrendered to a neighborhood dentist, and when he left her Claremont Avenue office that school-day morning with the cavity filled and walked up toward Broadway, he could be proud that he hadn't continued to run and hide.

Only 8:30 am, according to the wall clock in Chock Full O' Nuts. His lip felt fat and puffy from the Novocain, making the coffee hard to sip. There was still time to make his first class if he hurried. He could put a stop to this indulgence with Sean and say no, he didn't want him in his life. He could say to himself if not to Sean, "You are not good for me. I want to be with those kids who frighten me because of their abilities and all they represent. I want to be pulled into their light and not into your darkness." All that he could say simply by leaving right then.

And even if he was late for his first class, an emergency dental appointment was a legitimate excuse. But then, wouldn't it be better to let the day go and start fresh the next morning? There was something not right about coming in late. No, get back. Get back now. In a moment of clarity, it was all there. He remembered his mother ironing his shirt for him earlier in the morning. Didn't she want the best for him? Hadn't she worked so hard? Hadn't she suffered enough disappointment from her children?

He pictured Ogden Connifer, lanky and pimpled, sitting in Latin class, his spine curved, easily translating a passage from Caesar's Gallic campaign. He saw John Edel confidently offering some insight on *Crime and Punishment,* which they were now reading, and Mr. Horst-Lehman nodding in approval. He saw all his classmates within the walls of a sanctuary whose doors would close on him if he was not there in the next half hour.

In the grip of anxiety he pushed through the revolving door only to lock eyes with Sean across the street. Frozen by his stare, he stood in place as, Sean, mindless of the traffic, streaked across Broadway.

"Was my man splitting? Boston, baby. We're bound for Boston." Before he could respond, Sean had flagged a cab and he too was in it.

It wasn't too late. He could jump out at any stop light, but paralyzing indecision born of fear kept him in place. And it was the same at the Port Authority Terminal. Breathing in the exhaust fumes, he passively moved forward with the line and handed the driver the ticket Sean had purchased for him. Soon the big Greyhound was cruising through the gritty streets of Hell's Kitchen and heading north out of the city.

"What's the matter? You going to cry over being away from that snotty school? This is school." Sean laughed loudly and pulled on his Philip Morris, then contentedly let out a stream of smoke.

Gray clouds had settled in, and soon a steady rain was falling as the bus reached the interstate and continued to fall hours later, when the bus pulled into a depot near Kenmore Square.

"We're not going back. We're going to stay another day so we can see us some baseball," Sean said, crushing Johan's unspoken hope that they would just turn around and head home. On a back street, away from the major hotels, Sean found them a small rooming house.

"Where is your luggage?" the woman at the front desk asked.

"We don't have any luggage," Sean said.

"You'll have to be out at ten o'clock tomorrow morning unless you want to be charged for another day."

She showed them to a room with an alleyway view and beds with mattresses no thicker than the weekday *Times.* The rain having stopped, in wet socks they headed to the Boston Common. They came to the bridge spanning the Charles River, where rowing crews practiced on the water.

Back in downtown Boston, Sean grabbed Johan's arm. "It's them. It's them. Luis. And there's Brooks." Sean was feverish with excitement. And yes, Luis Aparicio and Brooks Robinson, the left side of the Orioles' infield, were standing outside their hotel, one sharp-featured and the other round-faced. "And there's Mikey and Stu," he went on, meaning Mike McCormick and Stu Miller, pitchers who had come to the Orioles from the Giants in an inter-league trade. He spoke as if he was on a first-name basis with them. Johan stared at the players on the red-carpeted stairs with envy, not because they played baseball for a living, but because they were where they were supposed to be. For a moment he saw the horror of vicariousness, of rooting for teams and individual stars while neglecting his own life.

"Is this Mrs. Manootdjian?" The operator asked, that evening.

"It is I."

"I have a collect call from Johan. Will you accept the charges?"

"Johan?"

"Me. Your son. Remember?"

"But Johan, where are you?"

"I'm in Boston."

"You are in Boston?"

"Ma'am, do you accept the call?" the operator interjects.

"Yes, of course."

"I know it's crazy and you won't believe me, but I came up here to see a baseball game. We're going to have to stay over, but I'll be home by tomorrow night. I promise."

"We? Who is we?"

"Sean." Johan immediately regretted that he hadn't lied.

"It was he who put you up to this, is it not?"

"We just wanted to see a baseball game."

"There are no baseball games in New York City?"

"We wanted to go someplace different."

"Where on earth are you staying?"

"We got a hotel room. Sean looks older than he is."

"You are telling me something I do not know? What ails you? Do you know that the school called this afternoon when you did not show up? I have been worried sick. First it is one and then it is another and all of you going on in your willful ways without a thought of me."

She had begun to cry. At that moment he remembered all her tears over the years, and the resolutions they had prompted in him to do better.

"I'll be back by tomorrow night. This won't happen again. You'll see."

Sean lay on his bed smoking a cigarette, one arm under his head. "What's the matter, baby? Miss Mommy? This is only the beginning. Next I'll be going to Chicago and Pittsburgh and Philadelphia and Houston and Los Angeles and everywhere else, too. I'll be seeing Willie and Juan at Candlestick. I'll be seeing Gordie Howe on his home ice in Detroit. I'll be seeing Frankie boy out at the Sands in Las Vegas. Because I'm going places, not like those stiffs you hang around with on Scully's stoop. I know how to make things happen. You're a sarcastic son of a bitch behind that smile. You don't even have to say anything for it to come out."

"That doesn't sound right," Johan said.

"Whose idea was that religious sign on the side of your building, anyway?"

"It was Jesus's idea."

"What the fuck are you talking about?"

"Just that."

"What do you mean, just that?"

"Jesus even had it painted, too."

"Jesus had that fucking sign painted?"

"Sure he did."

"You talk some sick shit."

"The truth is not sick shit."

"What kind of religion is that you belong to, anyway?"

"Pentecostal."

"Penta what?"

"The Holy Spirit that descended to earth after Christ's ascension to heaven. It can be in anyone, even you. A lot of hellfire and brimstone."

"Like that movie with Burt Lancaster. *Elmer Gantry*."

"Sort of." There had been ads all over the subway. *Elmer Gantry is coming.*

"Private school. Pentecostal. Everything about you has to be different." He lit another cigarette with the one he'd smoked all the way down. "All those priests and pastors and ministers are like that Elmer Gantry guy. I don't care what the religion is. They're all on the take."

Johan listened to Sean's self-serving cynicism as the rain again began to fall and beat against the window. The world was full of lies, his own included. With the light off, there was now only the glow of Sean's cigarette. He could feel the current of Sean's thoughts, as if they were a palpable, threatening thing.

"You don't have to pretend you're sleeping. You don't have to pretend anything. I know who you are. I've always known who you are. You want me to come over? All you got to do is say yes. You want that, Johan?"

Sean was reading him in the dark, listening for weakness in his silence, his breath. The springs squeaked in Sean's bed. The light from the cigarette moved closer.

"I'm here, Johan. I'm right here."

There was really no power in Johan to deny him. Not even the darkness could conceal this fact.

They woke late the next morning and found a nearby diner. The man behind the counter was unshaven. "How you want those eggs?" He spoke gruffly, and Sean replied in kind. The stench of old grease spread as the grill heated up and flies buzzed the fatty strips of bacon that Sean had ordered with his eggs. At the end of the counter were dirty dishes in a gray bin. It took everything for Johan not to flee into the street. He had a cup of coffee and orange juice and toast without butter.

"You eat like a fucking girl," Sean said, as he began to attack the eggs sliding around on his plate. Soon everything was gone, even the mound of blackened hash browns and the yolk, which Sean sopped up with a slice of white bread. Nothing can hurt me, he was saying. Life itself was there to be devoured.

The sun had come out and the day was warmer, stiffening Sean's resolve to stay and take in the game that afternoon. They killed some time wandering about the downtown area and the footpaths in Boston Common.

The dimensions of the Polo Grounds were weird--you could hit a 251-foot home run down the line--but Fenway was also irregular, with the giant green wall just beyond the infield in left field and a big net on top of it. The ballpark's light towers rose above the surrounding buildings.

By the second inning, Sean was nodding off in his seat, his head and upper body listing into the aisle. Several times Johan shook him and Sean straightened up only to slump again. He also began to drool.

"Let's get out of here," Sean said. He was unsteady on his feet as they headed for the exit. From the ballpark came the short-lived roar of the fans. A base hit? A home run? Who cared? Now famished and miserable, Johan once again imagined his well-fed classmates moving ahead with their lives.

"I'm broke," Sean said. Johan picked up the coins that had fallen from Sean's pocket. A street vendor hawking Red Sox pennants and caps gave Johan directions to the turnpike, and some blocks later, he stood off the ramp with his thumb out while Sean lay in the grass.

A Volkswagen van pulled over. "Is your friend all right?" the driver asked. Sean had fallen asleep in the rear seat, his head against the window.

"He's just tired. He had a long night." They had lucked out. The driver was headed for New York City. They were going home.

"But Johan, what is the meaning of such a thing? Did you take leave of your senses?"

"I made a mistake. I know." Johan said. He tore into the chicken breast she had served him.

The front door opened. His father was just coming home from his evening church service. How good that his mother kept his father out of his life, a decision she had made long before, knowing as she did what Mr. Manootdjian could do if he were made to get up.

Chapter 10

That spring, when warm weather came, they did not lie on Dead Man's Hill, but sought a more private space, or Johan did. Down past Dead Man's Hill and the tennis courts Johan led Jane to the knoll above the railroad tracks where once he had gone with Luke and Tall Tommy. A thicket of prickly shrubs met them as they inched down the narrow dirt path created by others making the same descent.

"Here?" she asked, when they came to a small clearing sufficient to lie down. Johan saw on her face a look of concern.

Above, cars raced along the exit ramp. Below a southbound freight roared toward the tunnel as he unbuttoned her blouse and fumbled with the clasp of her white bra. "I'll do it," she said, sitting up and loosening the bra effortlessly.

Rustling in the nearby brush came to his ears and then again. And though he did not hear it a third time, it was there in his mind, growing and growing. This was not Dead Man's Hill. This was an isolated and suddenly dangerous space. "We've got to go."

"Why? What's happening?"

"Please." He did not want his life or hers to end. He knew there were knives in New York City with their names on them.

Run, Johan, run. Run from the er-re-ra man. Run from all the harmful elements of the universe. Run with Jane Thayer down the exit road to the viaduct, past the meat-packing plants and the garages to the laughable safety of Broadway.

✣

Sean was not riding his delivery bike in triumph. He was not bellowing "A Foggy Day in London Town" or going to war with Frenchie the Algerian in Riverside Park and leaving him unconscious on the baseball diamond or applying superior force to the face of Philip, causing him to run home for the relief he could find with blood flowing from his ruined mouth. He was not walking with a strut as if by gait alone he could transcend the world and circumstances he had been born into and elevate into the realm of *class*. He was not a Celtic warrior riding into battle bare-assed on a bareback steed but an invalid in a hospital gown lying weak in an adjustable bed in a semiprivate room in St. Luke's Hospital only a short walk from Scully's stoop and Funelli's grocery.

After the Boston trip Sean had shown up at the emergency room with yellow skin, where he was diagnosed with hepatitis. Johan thought of the greasy spoon, remembering the stench of old grease and the flies on the bacon, but no one could say for sure that was the cause.

It was something to see powerful Sean in the loose-fitting white gown with a V-neck that revealed his hairy chest and an identification band around his thick wrist and the nurse bringing him a tray of food and instructing him to sit up and eat. The illness that had laid him low had also humanized him. The lion was in need of people's care. He was being made to see where his power ended.

Sean's father came to visit. He was a small man with the face of a scowling cat. That Sean had a connection to this older man, who worked at the northern tip of Manhattan in the subway yard, was another source of wonder. Sean and his father were the same, and yet they were obviously different. And yet it was all about Sean. Johan sensed Sean watching him, even when he wasn't, and Johan was watching him as well, no matter where his eyes were turned.

"You go over there and lie down," Sean's father said to Jane during her one visit. He spoke to her in a raspy and commanding voice as he pointed to an empty bed, and it was Johan's concern that she would go up against him with some smart words that would spark his anger.

"Fat chance," she laughed, and no storm followed.

Then came the afternoon when Sean soured on Johan, seemingly out of the blue, and with Scully and Luis and Kevin Donnelly and Jimmy Riley in the room. Sean saying, "You just come here because you don't have anywhere else to go. Beat it."

The hepatitis had diminished his strength but not his voice. "You heard me. Beat it." And so Johan did, smiling, as if no such words had been spoken, just as he had at the downtown room where he had received Sean's punches. Only in his aloneness later that same day would he allow his hurt and anger to show.

"Your hands cold?" Sam, the manager, of the TasteRite Supermarket, asked. He wore a gray smock over his white dress shirt.

"No," Johan answered.

"Then get them out of your pockets."

Johan restocked the shelves with goods taken from cardboard boxes and sorted the empty soda bottles into their wooden cases down in the basement, bringing order where there had been clutter. And then there were the deliveries he got to make, streaking down the hill to Riverside Drive on the wagon bike and pushing it back up the hill because he didn't have the leg strength to pedal his way to the top. It made him happy to be working. It gave him a sense of purpose. He had his mother in his mind's eye. He felt her approval all throughout him that he was not like floundering Naomi.

Meats were stored in the freezer, and Sam sent him down to the basement for a box of franks. But the heavy metal door closed behind him with authority, and try as he did, he could not open it. Within a minute, amid the hanging sides of beef, goosebumps had formed on his arms. A rat the size of a cat emerged from under a shelf. The rat had it worse. Its coat was covered with ice. No darting and leaping for this rat. It could only inch forward toward the door, where it too awaited liberation.

But suppose there was no liberation? Suppose the afternoon passed and Sam emptied the cash registers and turned out the light and called it a day and Johan was left all alone in the freezing cold with the rat?

"Caramba," a Mexican worker exclaimed, a half hour later, jumping back when he opened the door and the rat tottered out. The store cat jumped too, clear atop a stack of boxes.

It was her birthday and in her blue leather diary, with a gold lock, he wrote "iwtmys." How safe he felt knowing she would never guess its meaning. But she had only studied the entry for a few seconds when she said, "I want to marry you someday," her laughter evoking shame in him once again that she should see him in such an available light.

Luke was working hard that summer. He had not gone to the country place of the Episcopal nuns up in Brewster, New York. Instead he had been painting, coating the walls of the rooms she rented with the pale green that she favored over colors that shouted or walls painted a chalky white. Europe was Luke's goal with the money he was earning. Europe would be the college he was not attending that fall.

"Nancy really loves me. She said so," Luke told him on the warm, late August night before he was to leave as they walked in Riverside Park. Nancy Becker would soon be up at Vassar, where his sister Rachel had been but was no more. Johan said nothing but feared that Nancy would be putting a hurt on his brother sooner rather than later. Hadn't Luke's pain over a temporary breakup with Nancy led him to swallow a bottle of aspirin?

Across the road stood St. Andrew's, the former mansion, a freestanding marble building. Johan remembered the second-floor bathroom, from which he had tossed the toilet paper at the nuns back in sixth grade, and the wide stairway his mother had climbed to take him away, and the garden path he had walked after cleaning out his locker the next day.

"Remember when you were going to get working papers and a job and save up money so we could live together in our own apartment? That was one of the places where I wanted us to live," Johan said, pointing to a fairly new apartment building of blond brick on the opposite corner. "It still makes me happy just to see it. It's like the building glows."

"It's just a building. Anyway, you'll see. I'm not going to be like Hannah and Naomi, that's for sure. You won't find me rotting away in one of those rooms I've been painting."

Farther south they came to a bridge over a roadway leading to and from the West Side Highway. Twin lamps stood on granite bases at either end of the arcing bridge. At the first lamp Luke stopped and struck a match.

"Tell me what you see in there," he said, holding the match between the base of the lamp and the retaining wall on which it rested.

"It looks like two pennies."

"Yeah. We put them there the other night. They're like a wish. You know, that we'll always be together."

Seven blocks later Luke stopped again. "Look over at the corner windows and count up five flights and three windows over. What do you see?" He pointed to a block-long building that followed the curve of the road it rose above.

"I see a window with no light in it."

"That's right. That's her room." Luke pointed to a darkened window.

Pennies under a bridge lamp and a dark window. His brother had found his Riverside Drive apartment, if only for a while, but it had not been with Johan.

The cobblestones were slick from the downpour, the cab fishtailing around the curves of the West Side Highway as if racing over greased glass. From the exit ramp Johan could see the freighter still docked at the pier and wondered how such a small vessel could make an ocean crossing. The dark clouds increased his anxiety.

"Hey, here he is. Look, I want to give my little brother hope. I want to show him we can get away. Right, Johan?" Luke had his hand around a Heineken's bottle in his cabin on the vessel.

Langley Farmer had come down to see Luke off, as did Judson Iorg, another classmate of his brother's. Long gone into the past was that shit-smeared sneaker with which Johan had fouled his immaculate apartment.

"I guess so." The big brother stuff was embarrassing. The silence that Langley and Judson maintained told Johan they thought so too.

"Where will you go when you get there?" Judson was skinny and jug-eared.

"The first thing I'll be doing is renting a motorbike in Rotterdam. After that, I don't know. Just drive around, I guess." He made the motorbike sound more interesting than the trip itself.

"But where are you going to drive around to?" Langley asked.

"I have these relatives in France and Sweden. I'll go see them. You poor guys will be in college while I'm floating around Europe and Scandinavia."

Mr. Manootdjian had only given Luke his sisters' address reluctantly, and with a warning not to "aggravate" them during his visit. From Marseilles Luke would go on to Paris, and then to Sweden to visit some of their mother's remaining relatives.

Luke pried off the cap on another bottle of Heineken's. "Nineteen cents on this tub. Can't beat that. Come on, Johan. Have one. It's on me. This is a party, for God's sake."

The beer had a friendlier taste than the city beers Johan drank with the boys from Scully's stoop. Before leaving he had a second.

That night he pictured the freighter heading out of New York harbor. He imagined the vast Atlantic overpowering the ship and claiming his brother. In bed he held himself tight so he wouldn't shake apart.

Chapter 11

His junior year did not begin well. An incident occurred that would stop him in his tracks when memory presented it. The incident seemed, in his darker moments, to have exposed his essential nature.

On the landing just outside the apartment door sat Vera and her friend Pam Becker as he returned from school. "Hi, Johan," they said, practically in unison, highlighting their bond and his aloneness. He heard their laughter as mockery, a gauntlet he must run.

His mother was having her afternoon coffee at the dining room table. "How was your first day at school?" She was frowning.

"Okay." He was anxious to change out of his new white button-down shirt, as the collar was chafing his neck.

"We cannot have this," his mother said.

"Have what?"

"The two of them sitting out there like that. It doesn't look right."

"Have you told them not to?"

"Of course I did."

"I'll take care of it," he said, resolved to not let Vera think she could intimidate him and distress his mother.

They were still on the landing, their knees up. "Get inside. Momma doesn't want you sitting out here like this," he said, rushing his words.

"Momma doesn't want you sitting out here like this," Vera parroted, causing Pam to laugh. He grabbed his sister's long brown hair. "You jerk," she screamed, as Johan dragged her inside the door.

"But what is the meaning of this?" Drawn by the commotion, his mother had come into the living room.

"You said you wanted them inside."

"Yes, but we cannot have this kind of violence. We cannot have it."

He retreated to his room, where the disgust and revulsion Vera and Pam were surely feeling found him. They had seen him behave like his father, and what could be worse than that? He had been made to get up. He had been *aggravated*. And like his sister Hannah, too. He had dragged Vera inside the apartment just as Hannah had dragged him from the movie theater. Hairs were growing everywhere, all over his face and back and arms. It was now for Johan to turn his face to the wall so no one could see.

⚘

"You're Puerto Rican and you're Irish," Ralph, the counterman, said to Luis and Jimmy, before turning to Johan. "But you I don't know. That nose tells me you're Jewish, right?"

"Yeah, but what's his head tell you?" Jimmy cracked up at his own joke.

"So? Are you Jewish or goyim?" Ralph asked.

"I'm not Jewish," he said. He didn't want Ralph testing him about what *goyim* meant so he could just about say he was stupid, as he practically did the last time, when he was talking about his Ivy League son.

"So what are you?" Ralph shot back.

"My father's Armenian." Then he quickly added, "But my mother's Swedish."

"Hey, Mr. Kemal, come over here a minute. I want you to meet someone." Ralph called to the owner, who stood at the cash register.

"You know what this skinny blond kid here is? He's an Armenian," Ralph said.

Mr. Kemal assessed Johan with a shrewd smile. "Since when does an Armenian have blond hair?"

"He must get that from his mother," Ralph said. "He says his mother is Swedish."

"In addition, you are too tall to be an Armenian," Mr. Kemal said, as if Ralph hadn't spoken.

"My father is tall."

"There are no tall Armenians." Mr. Kemal himself was short and stocky. He dragged on his unfiltered cigarette and drew the smoke up his nose. "I am Turkish. Do you know who the Turks are?"

"Sure."

"Then you know that the Turks and the Armenians are good friends. We have many Armenians in our country."

"That man was fucking with you," Luis said to Johan after Mr. Kemal had returned to the cash register.

"Not at all. He was giving you a history lesson. History is important. And it's all in the eye of the beholder. That's what you need to understand." Ralph went off down the counter.

"Ralph is a strange motherfucker. That's what I need to understand," Jimmy Riley said.

"Have I not told you before? You're very fortunate to have a father. The Armenians were a persecuted people. They were practically destroyed by the Turks. If it wasn't for a Turkish servant who risked his life when the authorities came to their house to take them away, they would all be dead. The servant had them hide in the basement while he spoke with the Turkish authorities. You must understand that thousands and hundreds of thousands of Armenians died at the hands of the Turks." So Mrs. Manootdjian said.

"When did this happen?"

"That would have been during World War I."

"How old was Daddy?"

"He was young. Like yourself now. He was just a boy."

"But what happened after the authorities left? Didn't they come back?"

"God was looking after your father."

"And God wasn't looking after the others who perished?"

"We do not question God. We do not."

❧

Vera had the capacity to surprise. Less than a month after the hair-pulling incident she said, "Pam's dying to go out with you."

"Come on." He did not say that Pam Becker, an arty girl enrolled at a prestigious school, was too good for him, or that she had only recently witnessed him act like a brute.

"What do you mean, come on? Call her. Go ahead," Vera said.

And yet, within a few hours, his thinking shifted. Perhaps a girl like Pam could have an interest in him. After all, she was Nancy Becker's younger sister, and Luke had been good enough for her to see throughout high school. But the night had given him a confidence the morning never did. He woke to terror, remembering his call to Pam Becker the previous night. Not only had he betrayed Jane Thayer, but he would be engaging with a girl in a league not his own.

That same day, Mr. Arbuckle said, during math class, "It's nothing to lose sleep over. If you have the stuff to do well, you will. It's really as simple as that. Go out to a movie and have your Friday night fun and take your mind off it." It was Friday. The PSAT was scheduled for the next morning. Mr. Arbuckle was only repeating what he had said in Johan's freshman year.

❧

"I've already seen it once. Olivier is so passionate, so dynamic. So *brooding*. You'll be thrilled. You've read the book, of course?" Pam Becker said as they left her doorman building to see *Wuthering Heights*.

"No. I haven't," he was forced to say.

"You must. You *must*," she said, grabbing his arm if only for a moment.

On the subway he looked down at the white sweat socks he was wearing with his gray wool school pants. White socks made his legs look thicker, he was sure. You had to be built like Lenny from Long Beach to wear black socks with dress slacks. Luke said there would come a time when Johan wouldn't be caught dead in white socks. It hadn't happened yet.

That scene on the landing kept flashing into his mind. Did Pam not remember that he tried to drag his sister into the apartment by her hair? Did she not see that beneath his pleasant, amiable smile he had become just like his father?

"Tell me the truth. Did you and Luke try to throw Vera into the incinerator in your basement one night?"

"What? No. Never."

The movie played at the Baronet, on Fifty-ninth Street and Third Avenue, across from Bloomingdale's. The theater was new, with soft, upholstered seats and a giant screen. Halfway through Johan placed his arm around Pam's shoulder, and was too embarrassed to remove it. The darkness made him do it. In the darkness you were supposed to touch a girl.

"Wasn't it wonderful? Wasn't it profound?" she asked afterward.

"It was real good." In truth much of the drama on the English moors was a tangled mess in his head.

Feeling mentally suspect and seeking to bolster his status in her eyes, he said, as they reached her building, "I'm going to meet a friend at a Columbia University fraternity party." The lie just popped out of him.

"What a wonderful, exciting thing to do," she said, with the enthusiasm she displayed for everything. "But come up for a cup of tea before you go. My parents are away for the weekend."

The apartment had a stillness to it. Soft lighting. A real sofa. Not a thing out of order. A Johnny Lacy/Edward Macy kind of apartment that left him in a state of defeated wonder. They weren't a few minutes in her kitchen drinking tea when a key turned in the lock and Nancy Becker appeared. With her was a bearded man wearing a Columbia T-shirt under a red-and-black checked lumber jacket.

"Johan, is that you?" Nancy shrieked. He had seen her enough to recognize her, but she was no long lost friend.

The evening was all wrong somehow. He was seeing Pam Becker on the sly, when he already had a girlfriend. And now he was in the family's kitchen with her and her sister and her sister's new boyfriend when there was the PSAT the next morning.

"How is Luke? Has he written?" Nancy asked.

"Not yet."

"Luke doesn't trust himself to be able to put things on paper." She turned to Jim and said, "We're talking about a high school friend of mine." Jim sat with the thick fingers of each hand interlocked on the table and simply nodded.

"I guess I better go," Johan worked up the courage to say.

"Johan has been invited to a fraternity party at Columbia tonight. Isn't that wonderful?" Pam announced.

"Well no, not exactly," Johan said.

"But you have been. You told me." She turned her big blue eyes on him.

"Well, sort of," he mumbled.

"Say hello to the boys at Delta Epsilon Psi." Jim offered a wry smile.

At the door Pam said, "It was just a wonderful evening."

Wonderful. Thrilling. What about fantastic? Had she said superb? He reeled out of the building and up Riverside Drive. Their words—Pam's, Nancy's, Jim's—burned in his ears. He sped up, trying to leave behind the scene of humiliation and every memory attached to it.

The windows of the fraternity house had been opened and the loud sound of the Four Seasons poured into the street, followed by the Chiffons, singing "He's So Fine," the music promising a good time was to be had inside.

Jane would be home now, after an evening with her church group. Now, when he thought of her, she seemed kind of dreary in comparison with Pam.

Among the Columbia students were a few neighborhood kids. Like weeds among the roses they appeared. The free booze and the cachet of the Ivy League had drawn them to the Friday night bash. The frat boys had rounded up some local girls from the nearby bars.

Johan poured a foamy cup of beer from a big metal keg, drank it fast, and then poured another. He followed with a cup of scotch and club soda. Unlike the beer, it burned going down. He quickly followed with a refill, afraid that the liquor would be gone before he had had enough. The alcohol now in his bloodstream and the pounding music summoned a painful desire for achievement, recognition, stardom, something.

"Are you here at the college? You look a little young," a tall, thin girl with her blond hair in a ponytail said over the music.

"No. But maybe someday. I'm a basketball player. I think I can win a scholarship to Princeton, or some school like…"

A bull-necked man in a pale blue Columbia football jersey placed a powerful forearm around the girl and moved her away.

Johan pushed his way out onto the street. Though it was only on the next block, his building seemed far away. A feeling of wooziness had begun to come over him.

"How the hell are you, Johan?"

Chuck was on duty, sitting in a far corner of the lobby with his legs spread and a bottle of wine at his side. His boozy, mean voice boomed across the big space.

"Fine." Johan was desperate to speed past.

"You're fine, huh? You're always fine. Come over here, for Christ's sake."

Johan leaned against the large antique table, a thick slab of glass protecting the surface. Behind the table a large porcelain vase stuffed with rhododendron leaves rested on the marble ledge of the big chicken-wire window looking out on a small yard.

"So what grade are you in?"

"Eleventh grade." The wooziness was increasing.

"You good in math?" His voice sounds like a drill.

"Not really."

"I was taking calculus when I was your age. A whiz is what I was. I'd be a professor right now if the head of my department hadn't taken a dislike to me and cheated me out of my doctorate." He stopped and stared at Johan in a penetrating way. "You've been drinking. Jesus. You're drunk. I can see it. I hope you throw up your fucking heart, you wiseass punk," he called out, as Johan retreated.

He woke the next morning to sunlight pouring through the window. His mouth was dry. It took a minute to realize he was in Luke's bunk and still in his clothes. The room smelled of vomit. He remembered the walls spinning around and around and putting his foot on the floor to stop the motion and praying for the endless vomiting to stop.

The alarm clock said 10:35 am. The PSAT was well underway at the Claremont School. He sat up. His head hurt. He held it in his hands.

"The spelling part of the test was really tough, wasn't it, Johan? That word *diphtheria* was a real killer, wasn't it?" Diane Coleman's penetrating voice carried over the din in the school cafeteria as he passed the table where she sat with John Edel and Bert Bach and Mr. Arbuckle. He turned and showed her his smile. He wanted her to see that her words had no effect on him, that her knife had missed his heart.

But Diane Coleman had not missed his heart. She knew her way to it. He was but a thing of transparency for her to play with. He sat alone with his back to her table, her allusion bringing into current time, as if years had not passed, Miss Flowers' spelling bees, which featured words such as *diphtheria,* and in which he excelled. She was saying that simple things like spelling bees he could show up for while shunning rigorous exams like the PSAT. She was obliquely saying he was a coward, and not merely a coward but a stupid coward.

That afternoon Mlle. Gallimard stood over his desk in French class, her puffy, rouged cheeks quivering. She had asked a question he did not understand.

"Vous n'etudiez pas, Johan?" He shook his head and she turned away. Diane answered her question promptly. Diane, who read *Paris Match* and Camus in French. He stared, unsmiling, in his back row seat, as she basked in the glow of Mlle. Gallimard's approval.

That Friday, as always, school let out at noon and he rode home on the Fifth Avenue bus, changed out of his school clothes, and had a Chock Full O' Nuts lunch—clam chowder soup and a tuna fish sandwich and an orange drink and blueberry cream pie. When he walked out, he could almost feel substantial in its brutal mirrors.

As he turned the corner headed for Scully's stoop, Jimmy Riley was approaching. He did not have the laughing thing on his pale face. "Did you hear? They shot Kennedy," he said, and headed off before Johan could think to reply.

Death. Whole minutes slipped away with his mind on something else, only to return to the fact. A great weight of grayness had descended.

Because her church social had been canceled, he and Jane headed down to the Riviera Theater on Ninety-sixth Street and Broadway. Scully and Luis and Jimmy were there too. And though the men who stood over the urinals too long in the men's room were present, it was not for Johan to dawdle with them on this night.

Jackie Maltor, from the Claremont School, was also at the movie theater. He lived down on Riverside Drive at One Hundred Fifteenth Street. Jackie didn't scare Johan in the way that Tom Smits did. It did not bother his mind that Jackie might see him with Jane and his friends on this night. Jackie had no social status that he needed to be intimidated by, having a sister such as he did who had fallen and fallen in spite of her beauty. Besides, he was as much an outsider at that school as Johan was. And remembering the rumor communicated back in ninth grade by Jackie to Johan that he was a Negro and the way he had of covering his mouth when he laughed to hide his prominent gums or to shield others from his bad breath had made Johan not like him very much.

Jackie was not alone but with his cousin from Alabama, a tall, lanky older kid named Eustis who wore a sleeveless black T-shirt, jeans with a studded black garrison belt buckled on the hip, and stomp boots. On his forearm was a large tattoo of a bowie knife.

"I'm glad someone found a way to shoot the mother. We've been wanting him done for some time where I come from. He was a nigger-loving mother, and I'm only sorry it wasn't me who pulled the trigger." Jackie Maltor's cousin said these things at the refreshment stand, where Johan stood with Jimmy Riley waiting to get popcorn and soda.

"Damn, man, you should get some toilet paper and wipe your mouth after shitting out of it," Jimmy said, and took off before Jackie's cousin could grab him.

Was Eustis just a big country stupid who thought that dressing tough was being tough? Did he not know that there were in New York those with no play in them who could hurt you to the point of finality whether you were decked out in tough clothes or not? Johan could only wonder.

Outside, after the movie, Jimmy shouted, "Hey, shit mouth, how you doing?" to Jackie's cousin, standing only a few feet away under the marquee. Eustis pulled off his garrison belt. "If there's anything I like more than fucking, it's to bash northern white trash. Come here, Twiggy, and let me hurt you beyond your heart's desire."

"Hurt me, motherfucker. Hurt me," Luis said, taking off his coat and tossing it to Jimmy.

"This is too good for a Spic," Eustis said, handing the garrison belt to Jackie before moving in on Luis, who popped him twice on the jaw and sent him backward into a parked car, where he slowly slid down to the sidewalk.

In the dark that night, John Kennedy's face grew bigger and bigger. Johan wanted to take it into sleep with him, but in dreamland instead were men with flashing knives poised to do violence to each other.

The following week Jackie Maltor invited Johan to his apartment after basketball practice. His parents were away. Johan was afraid his redneck cousin would be lurking, but Jackie assured him Eustis had gone back to Alabama, taking along a black eye and fat lip and a deep hatred of Puerto Ricans to add to his long list of prejudices.

For the first time he was in the apartment of a Claremont student, there on the tenth floor of one of those tall doorman buildings on Riverside Drive with a huge marble lobby and an atmosphere of resounding tranquility, as if each spacious, well-appointed dwelling was a place of stunning order. He had been here with Jerry some years before for trick or treating. Another time they had overturned a fire extinguisher on one of the landings and fled down the back stairs as foam spurted from the nozzle. It was not for him to tell Jackie Maltor such a thing about his vandalizing past.

The invitation warmed him toward Jackie Maltor, who might have been handsome were it not for those crooked and prominent front teeth. Jackie had not gotten the wire, unlike many of the Claremont students. Dental and facial correction were big at the Claremont School—buck teeth got straightened and big noses were made smaller. But it wasn't long before his newfound appreciation of Jackie vanished.

"I head out to Long Island just about every weekend with a friend of mine and make it with a different girl each time. My friend has a car. He screws his girl in the front seat and I screw mine in the back seat," Jackie said, chuckling with his hand over his mouth.

Johan knew nothing about that region of the state, except that it appeared on the map as some narrow appendage. The Long Island Railroad. That he knew from passing through Penn Station. A commuter railroad, not a real railroad. Nothing like the Pennsylvania Railroad, which crossed state borders. And yet, hearing about Jackie's sexual exploits, he now did know something about Long Island, that it was an emotionally cold region where no happiness was to be found. He couldn't help imagining Jane among those girls he and his friend had their way with before abandoning her on the side of the road and leaving her to cry and cry.

"A little vermouth. A little vodka," Jackie said, offering Johan a concoction in a stemmed glass. The drink tasted sweet and went down easily. It even had an olive. Jackie quickly refilled his glass as a feeling of euphoria came over Johan. The refill went down easily as well. Minutes later he staggered into the bathroom where he vomited before passing out on the tiled floor. How long he lay there he didn't know. Jackie shook him awake. "Oh Jesus. You stink," Jackie's laughter was a constant that afternoon.

The streetlights were now on as Johan staggered up the hill toward his building. He thought of homework undone and of Jane but more of the bed that soon would be his to lie down on. In the lobby he stumbled and fell and was slow to get up.

"Oh dear. Is he going to be all right?" Mrs. Greene was just leaving the renting office.

"He's just piss-eyed drunk. That's all it is. He does this all the time. He just has to learn how to handle the stuff." Like Mrs. Greene, Chuck seemed far away. "Come on. Get the hell up, and stop disgracing the goddamn family," Chuck said, as he pulled Johan to his feet.

"Must my son be bad before he can be good? Must he go down before he can go up? Must he search before he finds? Have I not told you about my father, my son? Have I not told you that my mother would send me out into the snow to find him and to smash the bottle against the rocks? Have you not read in the book of Proverbs that wine is a mocker, strong drink is raging?" So Mrs.Manootdjian spoke to him that night.

Chapter 12

The first league game was against Thoreau, a school with a similarly small enrollment as Claremont. The team relied on a 6'4" forward, a ringer from a school with a strong basketball program that he was expelled from. The boy, if he was one, had a powerful physique and blew past the skinny Claremont defenders for savage dunks that left the wooden backboard trembling. Other times he gunned from twenty-five feet out. From near and from far he did his destruction while wearing a fixed, cool expression.

In the next game an undersized guard was unstoppable as Abel Academy routed Claremont for a second league loss in a row. The kid shook free for one twenty-foot left-handed jumper after another.

"I can't understand it. That team was shorter than us, had a cross-eyed forward, a center who couldn't jump, was even uglier than us, and still won. Unbelievable," Tom said, in the locker room afterward.

If Johan was bothered that the team was performing so feebly, the disappointment was softened by being the leading scorer for Claremont. His personal success on the court fed fantasies of adulatory fans chanting his name in arenas across the country. He had a selfish streak it was best to keep well hidden.

But then Claremont turned it around, winning its next three games against good teams, and Mr. Sadowski didn't leave the locker room wearing a look of disappointment. But there was, for Johan, a problem. Tom dominated the offense and pulled down more rebounds. Johan didn't know how to arrange his face so his distress doesn't show.

Then one afternoon it happened, as it had to, and Johan understood that he deserved it for not having held in his mind that afternoon the possibility of it happening in the first place. During the scrimmage there came a shout from the balcony. "Yo, look who the fuck is here, guys. It's my man Johan." Staring down were Scully, Luis, Kevin, and Jimmy Riley.

"What a funny-looking basketball team," Jimmy Riley laughed, in his Jimmy Riley way, falling all over the balcony.

"Are they friends of yours?" Mr. Sadowski turned to me.

"I sort of know them." He could feel the other Claremont kids staring at him.

"Hey Muscles, Jane know you look like that under your clothes?" Johan didn't need to look up to know that was Scully.

"Leave now," Mr. Sadowski roared.

"Johan's gang," Lance said afterward, in the locker room.

"Boy, where did you say you live?" Freddy Snyder asked, with his usual astonishment.

"One Hundred Tenth Street," Johan said, unable to remember what he had told him before.

"Johan's the only person I know who has a different address every time you ask him," Tom chimed in, from the next row of lockers.

Although he had resolved to not to show his face after his friends' invasion of the gym, Johan's feet took him back to Scully's stoop that Friday night. He had no place else to go. It was for him to face their mockery once again, and they did not disappoint.

"Damn, now I know why you've been afraid to take your shirt off. You're all bones," Luis said.

"Jane digs him for his he-man chest," Scully added.

"Where is Jane?" Kevin asked, in a kinder voice.

Johan explained that she had her Friday night social group up at Riverside Church.

Though it was a cool fall evening, they pooled their money for quarts of beer, which they poured into paper cups on the Columbia

University lawn. After several cups the burn of his companions' words began to fade and mercifully, their focus was elsewhere than on his meager chest. Luis, in the grip of emotion, had a story to tell.

"The principal, he was going to call my parents because I had been fighting with this chump. I went down on my knees to Brother McNeese in his office and said, 'Puh-leese don't call my father because he'll kill me. Puh-leese.' He could see I was trembling and he let me slide. Because my father, man, he don't play."

Johan was near tears listening to Luis's story. Luis, powerful as he was, had someone who could put fear into him and to whom he could defer. The same feeling that visited Johan when Sean had to submit to the nurses and doctors in the hospital came to him now. How happy he was for Luis that he had a father who meant so much to him. What a wonderful thing, even if it probably made him a little stupid, too. Because fathers had a way of making you stupid.

"Fucking Johan. You drink all the fucking beer again? What the fuck is with you, man?" So said Scully after Luis had finished his story.

"Sorry," Johan said.

"Sorry? Damn. You just about drank it all," Kevin said.

As they headed toward the exit, there was Jim, Nancy Becker's date those weeks ago, climbing the stairs. Jim's eyes found his before Johan could look away. Jim gave a smile of recognition.

"What you smiling at, chump?" Luis demanded.

"Your fraternity brothers?" Jim said, addressing Johan.

"You know this chump?" Luis demanded of Johan.

"Sort of." Johan trembled at the threat of violence.

"Damn. You know some fucked-up people," Luis said. "I was about to cave in the motherfucker's chest. What's that shit about fraternity brothers?"

"Just some joke. He was teasing me, not you," Johan said, Jim having moved on.

"Best not be teasing me. I'll put out his fucking lights."

Yes, yes. Cave in chests. Put out lights. Do whatever you want in your mindlessness. So Johan thought, as he headed home past the blaze of lights along frat house row.

Mrs. Jacoby was like a cartoon character with her overbite and puppy dog eyes. She spoke in a raspy voice, covering European history from the Middle Ages to the Napoleonic wars with enthusiasm, but her real passion, beyond the Edict of Nantes or Cromwell, seemed to be hope, specifically in regard to college. "All I mean to say is that you don't have to enroll directly in an Ivy League college. My high school grades were only so-so. I wasn't ready to go away to some prestigious college right out of high school, emotionally or academically. And so I spent my freshman year at Brooklyn College, where I earned straight A's, and that was my ticket to Wellesley. The point I am trying to make is never give up—never."

What Johan heard was Mrs. Jacoby trying to convince herself more than the class of her own worth.

Beyond personal narrative, Mrs. Jacoby had assigned each student a topic that required outside reading. The student then was to present his or her topic to the class. Every week a different student took his or her turn at Mrs. Jacoby's desk, not merely giving the report but fielding questions from the class. Bert Bach had discussed the causes of the French Revolution. Ogden Connifer reported on a biography of Martin Luther. Diane Coleman had much to say about Joan of Arc. And now Johan had been assigned a lengthy biography of Henry VIII.

The due day for the report rushed toward him. All he could do was step off the tracks so the laugh train, the mockery train, the We Wish for Him the Back of His Head train that Mrs. Jacoby had set in motion did not destroy him.

"Can you tell me why you did not show up for class with your presentation?" she asked, the following day.

"I was feeling sick."

"Is that all it is? You were feeling sick?"

"That's all."

"There's nothing more?"

"No." Her show of personal interest only fed his self-pity. He felt a mad destructiveness taking hold. Let the wrecking ball come in. Just let it.

"I'll tell you what. I'm going to give you a month's extension. How's that?" Mrs. Jacoby says.

Extension? He was not seeking an F, but he didn't want the assignment hanging over him either.

"Sure," he said.

The day that the PSAT results arrived, Johan heard numbers like 70 and 72 and 73 for Bert Bach and John Edel and Ogden Connifer. He heard the number 68 for Diane Coleman,

The PSAT. The dropped biology class. And now his failure to stand before them in Mrs. Jacoby's history class. He smiled his way free of the cafeteria and took refuge in a bathroom stall, where he placed his forehead against the wall, feeling the coolness of the tiles.

During English class, he stared at Sheila Lichton, a girl with a bad case of acne and a look of defeat on her pie-shaped face. She suddenly dropped out in the middle of ninth grade but returned the following year. There was talk that she had gotten pregnant. The scorn others showed her was inevitable; such punishment had to be the penalty for falling behind and showing your weakness. Sensing his gaze, she turned and offered a tentative smile. He smiled back and turned away, not needing to be reminded that he too was in the loser's circle.

A thin blanket of snow had settled on the pathways and lawns of the university campus. As they walked along, Jane hummed "Silent Night." Maybe her choir group was practicing Christmas carols. He did not know and he did not ask. Her humming sounded hostile and pompous, as if she was trying to be annoying, the proof being that self-important and earnest look her face could assume. She was also trailing just a step behind to add to his irritation.

"Is there something you want to tell me?" She had left him no choice but to launch another investigation.

"What's your problem, mister?" She had learned well to be alert to the warning signs.

"Who is it you're after now? Philip again?"

"That's right. I want Philip. I want Scully too. And Kevin and even Sean. I want them all," Jane said, a terrible fire coming from her mouth.

Just like the year before, he slapped her, only this was a hard slap that turned her head. Her cheek against his hand felt good. She reacted with a gob of spit to his face.

Such a warm glow coming from the lights in Butler Library, he thought, as she ran off. He was going to get it good now. Real good. A posse of the righteous riding hard to give him the beating that he deserved for hitting a girl, *a girl*. Standing right there at the scene of the crime he sought to disappear within himself, so when the posse arrived, a stranger could say to them, "He went that a way."

Since the fall a man named Henry had been coming around. He was a tall Negro with pomade in his hair and a Howdy Doody smile and a big gap where his front teeth should be.

"How old are you, man?" Jimmy Riley asked.

"How old do you want me to be?" Henry replied.

"What kind of answer is that?"

"The kind of answer your question deserves."

"What's that on your cheek?" A red and swollen abscess had developed on the left side of Henry's face.

"I'll tell you if you let me see what's on your cheeks."

"I didn't say *cheeks*. I said *cheek*."

"You mean you want to show me one without the other."

"Damn, Sam."

"Henry's the name," Henry corrected, telling Jimmy and all of them, with his humorous manner, that he lived where their questions could not reach. He was telling them what it meant to be him, a Negro man, in that time.

Henry was going with a freckle-faced white girl named Louise from the project on One Hundred Twenty-fifth Street. She was seventeen and plain and afflicted with a sad expression. No one, not even Philip, attached the word *skank* or any other such derogatory name to her, so strong was the power of her sadness.

Louise had a brother, Donnie, and if she could exist only in shadow, he was the sun itself. Radiantly blond and beautiful, and filling his clothes so well, he made you want to go out and buy the same jeans and flannel shirt in the foolish hope that you would look just like him if you did. Donnie was going steady with a neighborhood girl named Maria, from down on One Hundred Eleventh Street. She wore his blue varsity jacket with "Stuyvesant" in white lettering on the back, the name signifying the kind of mind he had that he had gained admission to this elite public high school. She was petite yet big-breasted, with lustrous black bowl-cut hair, and big eyes that saw right through to your heart's desire and registered the level of excitement her presence had brought you to.

Mention of Donnie caused Henry to roll his eyes and smile like the cat that had eaten the canary. "Yum! Yum!" was what he said, going so far as to lick his full lips. And maybe the fact that he didn't say the same about Louise said it all. Or maybe nothing here said it all about the boys and more than boys who gathered on Scully's stoop and did the ordinary and not so ordinary things they did on the streets of New York City on the Upper West Side of Manhattan in the early 1960s.

Mrs. Thayer saying, her voice as velvety as ever, "Your darling's return is imminent. Yes, of course, I hear the urgency in your voice, your young passion. You can be sure I will be your faithful messenger."

Mr. Thayer saying, "No more calls tonight, old sport. No more calls tonight."

And though Mr. Thayer's iron firmness drove Johan from the phone booth, an hour later he was back again, having reassessed the situation. But the line was busy, and stayed busy. The Thayers were learning how to deal with the likes of him.

"Why you in that phone booth so much?" Lev asked. "You have so much the important business?"

"Yes. The important business."

"Sleep. Sleep is the important business. And food."

The school day dragged by. His classmates were monsters of good purpose, shooting up their hands so they could shine. When the final bell sounded, he fled back uptown. Holiday decorations had appeared in store windows and Christmas trees were lined up on the streets, young men in heavy coats and watchman's caps eager to sell.

That afternoon he sat on the rim of one of the two fountains on the esplanade above the Columbia mall. Two men hurried past bronzed Alma Mater, her arms upraised and a book in her lap. As they came near, he heard them laughing—hard, intelligent male laughter, as cold as the wind that flapped the flags of the university and the United States on the two flagpoles.

Behind them there was Jane. On the mall, wearing her green parka. And not alone either. The blond boy, Donnie, glorious in his varsity jacket, was walking with his arm around her. And there Johan was, seeking to summon the mask of indifference to his face, should Jane turn and see him.

That night, in the dark, while lying down, he listened to his breath. Breathing in. Breathing out. Such a gentle sound, in contrast with the vehicular flow below. In his breath he sought to stay for the refuge it provided from that other world. And then, no, no, all over again there was Jane, and there was Donnie, and there was the cold wind rushing in. And then there was his mother with the sleeping pill. Oh, the mercy that the tiny yellow capsule showed and the sense of well-being it brought.

"Donnie broke up with his old lady. She be going with some other guy, so he don't have an old lady. Jane and him making eyes at each other when you're not around, so now he got your old lady. Are you going to be a man and kill him, or are you just an old pussy? That's the question." Jimmy Riley did his crazy laugh in the presence of Scully and Kevin and Luis.

"Yeah, here's what you do. Tear off your shirt and show him your manly chest. That should scare him off," Luis said. Johan retreated into Funelli's grocery, where on the radio Frank Sinatra was singing "The Wee Small Hours of the Morning."

"So what do you think about your old flame going out with the gorgeous one? Did my man think he'd be her only one?" The bout with hepatitis had not softened Sean.

"I'm OK," Johan said.

"You don't know how sick and feeble you look, champ. And you thought you were such hot shit bopping around with your girlfriend."

Hot shit. It was just the way some people spoke, he told himself. The snow was falling heavily. Already pools of slush had formed where sidewalks met the street. The cold water seeping through the canvas and the air holes of his sneakers saturated his socks as he trudged up Broadway. His hand went to the small square package in the pocket of his parka. He touched it lightly, fearful of messing up the gift wrapping and the neatly tied bow.

Just before closing he had rushed into Tillman's, on One Hundred Tenth Street, and bought a silver-plated bracelet while a recording played of Nat King Cole singing about chestnuts roasting on an open fire.

At One Hundred Twenty-Second Street, the gothic buildings of Union Theological Seminary just behind him, he paused to watch a northbound subway roar from the tunnel and onto the el. As if it were a talisman, he again lightly touched the small box before proceeding east up the hill to its crest, then allowed downhill momentum to lead him on even as a voice within was saying no, no, no.

Outside Jane's building he began his vigil, staring at the colored lights blinking on and off in the ground-floor window of an apartment across the street. A police car climbed the hill, the chains on its tires clicking on the cobblestones. An old couple, walking arm in arm, made their way slowly up the steps, and brushed the snow from each other's coats before entering. Soon after, two screaming boys ran out, banging the door behind them. Snowballs they packed and hurled at each other as they headed further down the hill toward Amsterdam Avenue. A half-hour passed. Johan's nose ran steadily, exhausting his supply of tissues.

"What are you doing here?"

She stood looking down at him from the top of the stoop, her voice loud and stern, her hands in the pockets of her parka. It was an I'm-not-afraid-if-people-hear-me voice.

"I wanted to give you this," he said, pulling the box from his pocket. His words sounded nothing like those he had rehearsed, fear taking all the life out of them.

"Look, Johan, I don't want a Christmas present from you. How about just going away? That would be a great Christmas present to me."

He stood paralyzed by her vehement rejection.

"You are just a selfish bastard who would give me a gift to make me feel guilty and for no other reason. Now get lost. I've got to go around the corner to the store. Please be gone when I get back."

All holiday cheer gone, he reached out and slapped her, wanting to stop her ugly words, her ugly mouth.

"Bastard. Fucking bastard. My father will kill you."

Her father? Her father? At the top of the hill he heard a chorus of seminarians spreading yuletide cheer with "Hark! The Herald Angels Sing."

Donnie had organized a tackle football game. Its roughness was reason enough to stay away from the playing field in Riverside Park on a cold, clear Saturday morning in January, and besides, where Donnie went, Jane was sure to follow. And yet the park called him deeper and deeper into it. From the top of the stairs, he stared down at Donnie, his blond hair a beacon, standing in his football pants and a red jersey. He looked like a powerful young god preparing for battle, his helmet in hand. Shoulder pads and a pair of black cleats for traction on the snow-covered field completed the uniform.

Johan had told himself he would come near yet remain apart. But after several minutes, the field called him downstairs to its level. And now even the sidelines didn't suffice, his need to belong drawing him to the poorly equipped pool of kids from which the two teams were being chosen.

Among the last picked, he looked out from the huddle. There, arriving, was Jane with her girlfriend Frieda, the two of them staring out at the field. Some plays later, the huddle broke and, Johan ran a button hook, catching the ball chest high. The goal line was his to cross when Donnie submarined him. Over his padded shoulder he went before belly-flopping onto a mound of hard-packed snow inches from the end zone. The wind driven from him, he struggled to his knees, gasping for air.

Some minutes later, when able to, he staggered off the field, his arms pressed against his abdomen. "My hero," Jane said.

The world seemed a long way off as he lay in bed for the rest of the day. He had lost. He had gone where he didn't belong. If others were blessed with toughness he didn't possess, then so be it. The bed felt soft and warm, better than the cold, hard world. His breath had returned. That was the important thing. He had that for company.

Chapter 13

The man sat reading at a desk outside the door to the auxiliary gym to ensure only university students entered. But he didn't turn Johan away. Some wordless communication between him and the man compelled Johan to put aside his basketball plans as students in shorts and T-shirts came and went. The boom of basketballs on the hardwood court carried through the wall.

"That's a big book," Johan said, seeing the fat Penguin copy of *David Copperfield* on the man's desk. "I have three days to read all of it," the man said.

"Isn't that a lot?"

"These are the things that are expected of graduate students here," the man said, guiding his black frame glasses back up his nose with his index finger. He spoke in a murmuring and earnest voice.

Johan followed him into the stairwell, where they did not stay long. Afterward, he wrote out his name and phone number on a matchbook cover.

Johan visited Quentin several times at his studio apartment. He was a big man but he was not rough. He did nothing hurtful.

Because Jane Thayer was not gone from his thoughts, Johan asked Quentin to go to a movie with him that Saturday night on the chance that Jane would be at the theater with Donnie and the boys from Scully's stoop. Johan wanted to be seen in the company of this older man so Jane could know that he had important things going on in his life.

And because all of them were there in the theater being their noisy selves, Johan positioned Quentin and himself on the aisle several rows below so they would be in their line of vision and maybe even rival *Irma La Douce* for Jane's interest. But when he looked back her way, hoping for some show of curiosity if not distress in Jane's face, all he saw was Donnie smooching her.

Following the coming attractions and before the feature could begin, Jimmy Riley started up. "Yo, Johan, who's that man you're sitting with? The two of you look *strange* together." Quentin showed no sign of agitation. He just slid his glasses back up his nose and drew on his Pall Mall.

Johan headed for the men's room a few minutes later but instead left the movie theater and then darted down a side street. He did not stay to a predictable course. There were doorways to duck into and trees and parked cars to hide behind as Quentin might be following behind, with the question "Why?" written all over his big face. The ache he felt for Quentin he could not hide from but there was no going back.

Scully threw a party that January, his parents being out. The kids on Scully's stoop did not have parties. They just hung around the stoop or sat up in Columbia University or in the park. But Scully was trying something new, and Johan had to look at him a different way, that he could do a thing like that.

Scully invited the O'Donnell sisters, Mary Marie and Cathy Cathleen, from One Hundred Eleventh Street between Broadway and Amsterdam Avenue. And Luis came, and Jimmy Riley, and Rob Koley and Kevin, too. And Philip showed up, with Mary Ellen Fitzkelly, another neighborhood girl. But Sean was not to be seen. No, no. He was out there doing his mystery stuff, robbing the Catholic Church or whatever. He had no time or inclination for a party like the one that Scully was throwing.

"Hey, man, you sure live in a shit hole," Philip said, the whiskey speaking for him. Philip's words were like a slap to Scully's face the way they brought him to attention.

"Your moms," Scully said, feebly. He did not want any more acid from Philip, who had not learned anything in the time since Sean punched him in his mouth so Philip had to run home with his hand over it.

The beer and the scotch and Frankie Valli singing "Big Girls Don't Cry" turned on Johan's lights. Now he was staring at Mary Marie. She wasn't Jane, but she was smiling at him, a nice open smile. Scully moved in on Mary Marie before Johan could approach. He seemed to know how to take the lead in a slow dance without getting his feet all tangled up with Mary Marie's, who looked dreamy-eyed in his arms. Then it was Ben E. King and the Drifters singing "Save the Last Dance for Me," but Marie had gone on to dance with Luis. When the time came for her to rest her tired feet, Johan, drunk now, said, "You are the best, the very best. Can I walk you home?"

"Well, that is sweet of you, but I don't really think so. I will be going home with my sister," Mary Marie said.

"I could walk with the two of you."

"Thank you, but no," she said, less genially. It was only an awkward minute before Scully came to claim her once again.

Johan used the banister to steady himself as he made his way down the steep stairs to the sound of the Drifters singing "Up on the Roof." On the dark street he spoke nonsense syllables to ward off the humiliation he was feeling. He wondered, not for the first time, about the bonding element of Catholicism, and why the religion had the coldness of the winter air on his face and in his bones as his building came into sight.

The black watchman's cap pulled tight over his brother's head made him look older as he came down the ramp from the freighter.

"Good luck, Luke," some guy called to him before getting into a waiting car.

"That's Rolfe and those are his parents. He's been studying philosophy at some German university. He's really smart. I drank Heineken's with him all the way across the Atlantic. Dirt cheap."

He had rented a motorbike, as he said he would, and drove up to Nice, where he visited with his father's sisters. "They're a strange pair. Very frightened and suspicious. They dress in dark clothes and keep to themselves. All day they're peeking out from behind the curtains in their apartment window, like they're watching for something." Uncle Sixten, Mrs. Manootdjian's brother, was more hospitable, but neither Sixten nor his wife could comprehend why anyone would travel such a distance to see them. They were farm people who were up and about before sunrise.

A biting wind was blowing off the river that evening. Luke had pulled out a letter from Nancy Becker as they walked in Riverside Park. Holding the letter with both hands to keep it from flapping, he read aloud one sentence under the light of a lamp. "'I love you but I'm not in love with you.' What's that mean to you?"

Johan thought of the La Rochefoucauld maxim and of Jim, Nancy Becker's friend. "It means something has changed," he finally said, afraid anger would replace vulnerability on his brother's face. They came to the bridge where Luke and Nancy had left the pennies. Luke didn't mention the coins or check to see that they were still there. He did look sore, as if Johan had written the letter and was to blame. He folded it carefully along the creases and returned it to his coat pocket as they headed home.

"Blue Moon." It was the song Johan thought of in relation to his brother, or the part of it where the moon saw Luke standing alone without a love of his own.

"Hey, look. I'm not going to be here forever. It's just for a little while, until I figure out what I want to do. It's like not even being in the building. You know what I mean?"

Mrs. Manootdjian had given Luke the apartment next door, where once upon a time the singer Miss Resnick had lived.

"Right," Johan said, as Luke scrutinized his face.

Luke scraped the walls before priming and painting them. Then he sanded the floors and applied two coats of polyurethane, turning the old wood golden. He wanted to make things right for Nancy Becker. Luke had been to her home many, many times. Now she was coming to his. A big night was brewing.

"Mom, could you cook up some of those Swedish meatballs?" Luke said, and instructed her to fuss over the dinnerware to ensure the plates and cups were matching. Mrs. Manootdjian carried the food she had prepared next door on a tray. In that way Nancy Becker did not have to see the circumstances of the family apartment. After the entree, roast beef with baked potato and creamed spinach, Momma served them some of her specially made spice cake and cups of coffee. She had this sweet smile on her face, as if all she was there for was to make them happy.

Nancy wore her hair in a bob that showed off her slender neck. Luke had never seen Nancy looking finer. She stayed the night. That was a first. They had never gone all the way before. As a bonus she reached orgasm.

"She told me I made her feel like a real woman," Luke said with pride the next morning, after Nancy had left. Things were not as she had hoped at Vassar. She threw a chair through a window because of the pressure of exams and was talking about dropping out to become a Woolworth salesgirl. Luke did not sing "Big Girls Don't Cry" to Nancy Becker.

"Dig this. She says we have to get married. What do you think?"

Think? Was his brother going to put her right there in that apartment so they could become a younger version of Chuck and Naomi? Would they go around the corner to the luncheonette for their late afternoon morning coffee before heading down to the Earvin Bar on One Hundred Tenth Street to get soused several evenings a week?

"I don't know," Johan said.

"What do you mean, you don't know."
"I don't know."
"You know."
"No, you know."
"What do I know?"
"Whatever it is you know."

Luke signed up with an office temp agency. In jacket and tie, he rode the rush hour subway to midtown Manhattan, where he spent the day in an office building stuffing papers in filing cabinets while pretty secretaries ignored him, reserving their attention for handsome bosses. His weekly paycheck was a measly sum after the agency took its cut.

The jukebox at Flynn's, across the street from his building, was loaded with Jerry Vale and Mario Lanza and Frank Sinatra and Tony Bennett, and there was a miniature bowling game Luke liked to play. And Wally, the bartender, treated him real well. Around closing time he gave him a free scotch on the rocks.

"He doesn't do that for everyone, you know," Luke said. Wally was not one to play around with. He wore bright shirts with the short sleeves flipped up to show off his huge biceps. Luke had seen his takeout power in the way he dealt with a couple of rowdies and smart mouths short on respect.

And the place had a waitress named Peggy. Luke liked to order the shells with clam sauce and a little salad, and Peggy gave him extra bread. One night after her shift was over, she took off her apron and she and Luke danced and continued the party back at his place. She had blond hair with black roots and stretch marks from the three kids. Luke had never been with a woman who was a mother before. It was different, that's all, he said.

"Why don't you introduce me to your friends sometime?" Luke asked, having seen Johan with the kids from Scully's stoop.

"What do you want with them? We don't do anything." Luke was older than his friends. How could he hope to fit in? It took Johan down a sad road to hear his brother speaking from his loneliness.

"Forget it."

"No. We don't have to forget it."

"I said forget it." Luke gave his right forearm to his nose and kept it there a while, to signify the conversation was over.

"Going my way, Sonny?"

When Johan turned he was met by the megawatt grin of Lenny Cerone, at the wheel of a white four-door Bonneville with whitewall tires and red leather seats. Next to him sat Jerry Jones-Nobleonian.

"Didn't I tell you he was the very best? Didn't I?" It didn't sound like a question.

"Don't be throwing no hamburgers at me," Lenny said, with a smile, referencing the downtown room where Sean had beat Johan.

"Oh shit. Oh shit," Jerry said, in gleeful support of Lenny.

"Where have you been? I haven't seen you since that night," Johan said to Lenny.

"He had a falling out with his old man here in the city. So he went back out to Long Beach to live with his moms. But she was not respecting him or herself, and that shit is hard to put up with. There's only so much a man can give and a man can take. So he's back here giving it another go with his pops. That's the righteous truth," Jerry said.

"Wow," Johan said.

"Wow, what?"

"Just wow. That's all," Johan said, as Luke came out of the building.

"I want you to meet my best friend, Lenny from Long Beach," Jerry said to Luke. "You see this Bonneville right here? Lenny owns it, and that's no lie."

"Hey, that's some nice set of wheels you've got," Luke said.

And Lenny said, "It's four on the floor and blow it out your ass all the way."

"I'm looking to get a car myself, or maybe a motorcycle, so I can get out of the city when I want to. You know what I mean?" Luke said.

"Fucking A I know what you mean. You've got to have some freedom in this life. Come on, man. You want to go for a ride? I'll take you where you want to go," Lenny said, on the winter day that Luke fell in love with him.

"Sure. Let's go for a ride," Luke said.

"You coming? There's room," Lenny said to Johan.

"Not today." Johan saw no point to telling Lenny about the rampaging cars of New York City when Lenny already had one.

Frieda Heinz, Jane's friend, had calculation occupying her mind and lust in her heart when she saw Lenny's wheels and the body and face that he was displaying. She saw him to have leader of the pack quality and could give herself to no other.

Luke's apartment is where Lenny took Frieda so he could know her and she could know him. But Lenny's love was not a constant love. It did not provoke loyalty of the tongue or the heart. Lenny sounded on the girl he now was going with, though it was Jerry Jones-Nobleonian who was the instigator of Lenny's jibes. The Fisher truck company was going strong and had a reputation for vehicles that were built to last. "Body by Fisher" was an emphatic statement of its excellence. Now when Frieda was not on the scene, Lenny and Jerry would say "Body by Fisher" and add "face by accident," and then do their laughing thing. It was not laughter that came spontaneously but was more mechanical and forced laughter that had Jerry's jealousy and pain that Frieda should be on the scene in the way that she was.

Luke had no sounding he wanted or needed to do about Nancy Becker, whom he held in a status above his own. It was not for him to violate himself or her in that way but to live out the slow death of what they had in silence. If he was unhappy away from her, he was even unhappier when they were together. Apart from her, he could tell himself that they might have some future with each other, but he couldn't do that when in her presence. The thing between them was dying.

The thumping bass came through the wall. Though it was bedtime, the Manootdjian family was treated to the noise machine of the Dave Clark 5 and Mitch Ryder and the Detroit Wheels. Mrs Manootdjian did not pound the wall with her shoe for silence as she had done when Miss Resnick occupied the apartment. No. In her robe she let herself into Luke's apartment, where he sat on the floor between powerful speakers. She was like a mime, her words virtually inaudible. The more upset she grew, the more he laughed, as if it gave him pleasure to see her undone, but his smile disappeared when Johan turned off the stereo.

"Don't mess with my music," Luke said.

"She needs to sleep."

"I said don't mess with my music, Momma's boy."

"Luke, be reasonable. We cannot have this," Mrs. Manootdjian said, but Luke was not listening. He had gone into his forearm with his nose. He had gone where he needed to go.

Lenny Cerone did not always dress sharp. Sometimes he got into the dirty, wearing an old T-shirt and torn jeans and a red bandanna around his scalp so he could go under the hood without his hair falling into his eyes and tend to the malfunctioning carburetor or misfiring pistons. Lenny Cerone did not need books or the measuring device of the SAT or the plusque parfait or the Edict of Nantes or the wine-dark sea. He had the knowledge he was born with and that no learning could add to.

But Mrs. Manootdjian was no fan, seeing him bent over the engine of his big Bonneville or escorting Frieda, with her flaring nostrils, up to Luke's place to do the hanky panky. "We cannot have such a thing. He looks like a hoodlum. What will the tenants say? Have you no common sense?" she demanded of Luke. But it was like with the music. He had no choice but to live in the pleasure places his life had long been taking him toward. Mrs. Manootdjian saying, "Like dirt beneath their feet they treat me, every last one of them. As if I am filth they can dispose of. Thinking that I do not see, when I see everything. Everything."

At the Bronx bowling alley, not far from Yankee Stadium, Kevin rolled a slow ball, finishing with one leg scissored behind the other. The black beauty started at the edge of the lane and curved gently into the head pin. Luis threw hard and straight and down the middle, as if impatient for that satisfying collision of pins, and got a lot of difficult splits. Jimmy Riley threw a lot of gutter balls. Scully was a machine, with strike after strike.

Jane Thayer had come along. Her ball rolled lazily down the lane and often found the gutter. Johan paid her little attention. The fever had broken. The music pumped him up. His ball seemed to roll down the lane a little faster when the jukebox played "Heat Wave." That song just owned him where some, like "Surfing Safari," did nothing for him or his bowling ball.

Then Jane Thayer smiled at him. With that smile she was saying it was time once again for him to be with her. And so, though they had come separately, they left together ahead of the rest of them. On the way to the subway they passed Yankee Stadium, still in its winter rest before the fever of summer. He did not ask Jane about Donnie. He knew without asking that Donnie has gone back to his girlfriend Maria and her dark beauty. He was just grateful that Jane had taken him back and that they could kiss that night in the hallway of her building and he could walk home that night with his feet off the ground.

Chapter 14

"I gave you this long extension in the hope that you would see your way clear to complete the assignment. Can you explain why you haven't followed through?"

Mrs. Jacoby still had her kindness and her concern, but she was now showing her teeth. It was hard to sit with her. If only she would once and for all release him from her care so the wrecking ball could come in. When he did not speak, she said, "Do you understand that if you don't complete the assignment, I have no choice but to give you a failing grade?"

"Yes, I understand. You must. You must."

Claremont played a varsity game against New York Friends, a Quaker school, that afternoon. The Friends' center, no more than five and a half feet tall, was a human pogo stick with his huge vertical leap. In one stretch Friends ran off sixteen straight points, putting the game out of reach by halftime.

Tom Smits has been scoring with ease. The entire first half was just one big swish time for him—hook shots and what passed for jump shots and tap-ins and driving layups. There he was, struggling back up the court after a bucket, leaning forward with his jaw out and his padded knees pumping awkwardly. At halftime, all Johan could focus on was that he had not scored a basket. Once again it was a lesser matter that his team was getting trounced. All he saw was that Tom was winning and he was losing.

When the team left the locker room and returned to the court, he quickly dressed and raced into the street, then disappeared down a flight of stairs into the subway, where he stared out the rear window of the last car. "Find me now. Find me now," he thought, as the train left the lighted station behind and entered the dark tunnel.

The news trucks had made their nightly drops downstairs and his father was accounted for. He had heard him, with all the agitation his footsteps summoned, enter the bedroom he shared with Johan's mother. The apartment would be Johan's now, he thought, as he left his bed and poured a glass of milk in the kitchen. But within a minute his parents' bedroom door opened and footsteps approached. It was his father, not his mother, who appeared, tying the belt of his brown robe as he stepped into the kitchen.

"Are you still up, my son?"

"I'll be going back to bed soon." His father looked ancient, his face fallen and his nose spread over his face and his chest plate visible in the V of his robe. Over a dish of crumbly bleu cheese from the stash he kept in a brown bag in the refrigerator, he sat in his corner of the dining room with a pamphlet from his shelf of religious material. The room felt cold to Johan without his mother. Unlike her, his father seemed all about God and nothing about people.

"Have you been a good boy today? Have you made your mother proud?"

"Yes," Johan lied.

"Never do anything to upset your mother. Your mother is our salvation. She is the rock on which we stand."

From the other side of the wall came the lonely, piercing sound of a saxophone. "What is that, please?" His father's voice radiated displeasure.

"I'm not sure." Johan spoke as if the sound had some inexplicable source.

"Could it be him?" His father arched a thick eyebrow.

"Who?"

"Who? Who else but the supremely worthless one next door would I be talking about? You will go to my cretinous son and tell him to turn down his sinfulness? You will tell him this?"

Johan had to knock repeatedly to get his brother's attention. On entering a strange smell hung in the air. It came as no surprise to Johan to see Lenny.

"Take a drag on this. It'll do your head some good," Lenny said. He offered something too skinny to be a cigarette.

"What is it?"

"It will take you where you don't even know you want to go." Lenny said, holding out the joint.

"Go ahead. Stop being so serious," Luke says.

"No. Not tonight. Daddy's upset. He wants you to lower the volume."

"What else is new?" Luke said, even as he turned down the sound.

Mr. Manootdjian was still in his corner and the music had grown faint.

"You won't do things like this, I am sure. You will do well by your mother and me. I have confidence in you," his father said, turning back to his reading.

"Yes," Johan said, as he felt he had been saying all night.

Mr. Arbuckle gave a surprise quiz in intermediate algebra the next morning, rat-a-tat-tatting the blackboard with a new stick of white chalk in posting the theorem: if $a + x = b + x$, then $a = b$ and $-(-a) = a$. Then he folded his arms and smiled, as if his only purpose was to thwart Johan, who had no hope of solving the problem.

After the class he ran into Tom in the boy's room.

"What happened to you yesterday?"

"I wasn't feeling well."

"Jesus. So you just walk off at halftime? We came within two points of winning."

He was more used to Tom being sarcastic than disappointed. The news that it had turned into a close game only worsened his feelings toward him.

"That's too bad."

"You really need to get with it," Tom replied, and pushed past him.

In homeroom he lifted the top of his desk and reached for his French text, then slumped in his seat, imagining Mlle. Gallimard's rouged and quivering cheeks as she stared at him with Gallic scorn for showing up with homework undone. A solution came to him. Why not skip the class? For that matter, why not take off the whole afternoon?

Lunch-hour din from the cafeteria carried out into the hallway as he passed by. How good to be apart from all that social racket and by himself, he thought, as he entered the locker room the next door down.

"Close the door and sit down." Mr. Sadowski was leaning back in his chair with his feet up on the desk and his jacket off. The white shirt he wore with his loosened red tie was slightly wrinkled from prior use. A food tray with the remnants of his brown bag lunch rested on the gray metal desk. Of course. Mr. Sadowski was like him, as uncomfortable at the Claremont School as he was. When had he ever seen him eating with other faculty members in the cafeteria?

"Do you want to tell me what happened yesterday?" The soles of Mr. Sadowski's scuffed black shoes were worn. His feet were as big as those of Johan's father. City sophistication would never attach to Mr. Sadowski; he belonged to the hardscrabble region of the South he came from.

"I wasn't feeling well," Johan said, settling on a kind of truth.

"And you felt no responsibility to tell me?" Mr. Sadowski spoke firmly but without anger, his voice a low and sincere rumble.

"I wasn't thinking."

"I thought you had come a long way since ninth grade. You seemed more relaxed and a part of things. And if you fill out a little more and work with weights over the summer, there's always the possibility of an athletic scholarship. You have real ability to play college ball, and your teachers speak well of you. Is something bothering you that you'd like to talk about?"

He had no business saying that. It was not right to talk about possibility. When things were done they were done, and the thing to do was to keep them done unless cruelty was your intention.

"Everything is fine." He said the words with the finality the situation deserved.

"You have a good record, but your teachers at the last faculty meeting said your grades were beginning to slip noticeably. Mrs. Jacoby and Mlle. Gallimard were concerned. If there's anything on your mind, you can see me at any time. Understand that I'm always available to talk to you."

"Thank you."

"I'd like to see you come back to the team. In fairness to the others, I'd have to keep you on the bench for a couple of games."

The bell rang for the next period. He stayed behind after Mr. Sadowski left, grabbed his parka from the locker, and exited through the side door, climbing the stairs to street level. He walked quickly, trying to outrun his talk with Mr. Sadowski and expel his words and attention, all that caring manliness that shook him so he couldn't so much as think. But one thing he could think, and more than that, *know*, as he passed a fur-wrapped woman walking her toy poodle on a long leash, was something Fifth Avenue face Mr. Arbuckle, with his theorems and rat-a-tat chalk, would never know, that sometimes the best addition was by subtraction.

The trees in Central Park were still bare, the only sign of spring a softness in the air. Tired-looking horses clip-clopped along pulling hansom cabs and their tourist cargo and nannies pushed strollers with bundled babies in their care. One minute at the school with no thought of leaving and the next he was racing up the avenue, with angry thoughts he couldn't outrun of Mr. Arbuckle purposely confusing him with complicated theorems and axioms and postulates.

Thwarting him, just thwarting him, the way his mother used to stall him, just stall him.

The Bethesda Fountain terrace was deserted and the lake still frozen. He climbed the stairs to the bandshell. He remembered the flying tackle by the plainclothes detective that had brought him hard to the ground after he had knocked over the overflowing garbage can. From another chapter of his life the incident seemed.

Splendor in the Grass was playing at a West Side movie theater. He stepped into the darkness, leaving behind the Claremont School and its demanding teachers and rich, snobby students for a couple of hours in a cushioned chair. No censorious and controlling older sister to clamp her hand on his shoulder and drag him from the theater like an angry and avenging Fury. No Freddy Snyder to mock him and his family, as he did for mentioning the film back in ninth grade.

But really, the story wasn't right. It just wasn't right that the teenage lovers Deanie and Bud, who kissed and kissed and kissed some more and would have kissed even more and gone all the way if forces, meddling and hurtful forces, hadn't interceded and separated them so that when they came back together they couldn't stay together. And no, no, it wasn't right that he should have to hear

> though nothing can bring back the hour
> of splendor in the grass, of glory in the flower;
> we will grieve not…

From the sundial on the Columbia mall that afternoon, he watched a couple of students turn their heads as Jane approached, noting with excitement as well as fear their reflexive response to a pretty teenage girl. When she drew even closer, he noticed something else. Her eyes were red and puffy from crying.

"Did something happen?"

"Dear old Mommy was blotto again and throwing around her accusations about how my father doesn't sleep with her because he's sleeping with me. When I told her to cut it out, she slapped me in the face. I'm so sick of those two. She's drunk within three hours of getting up and he spends more time with his mother than he does with her. I just can't wait to get out of there."

Her description of the clash summoned the same distress as when he witnessed conflict at home. And now he had to worry that she would link him with her mother because was he not a slapper, too?

They headed down to the diner. Jack Jones was singing "Wives and Lovers" on the jukebox. Jack Jones was always singing "Wives and Lovers" on the jukebox. Something about how she had to fix her hair because wives can be and have to be lovers too when their husbands walk through the door.

"You know, someday I think we're going to get married, don't you?"

"I guess so."

He went on in spite of her unenthusiastic response. "Well, since that's going to happen, I was thinking it would be okay if we went all the way now. I mean, if we're getting married anyway, why shouldn't we?" He gripped the sugar dispenser, running his hand down it, fearing her fury.

"I need time to think about it," she said.

Married. Sadness overcame him just saying the word. He saw an ironing board. He saw curlers. He saw the world leaving him behind. The word stripped him of his youth. He left her that afternoon feeling dishonest, as if he was pretending to believe in something he really didn't.

It had been a day for ideas, or impulses, and now he was visited with another. That evening he spoke with his mother. Could he have a room outside the apartment, like Luke? It didn't have to be big. It could be the smallest room in the building.

"But why? Is there something wrong where you are?"

"It's just that it's sort of noisy sometimes. I'd like a quieter place to study."

"That is so even though Luke is no longer there?"

"It's a little hard to concentrate."

"Of course we can find you another room, if that will help you with your schoolwork."

Even as he spoke a wave of guilt and shame washed over him that he should practice such deception on his mother, who wanted only the best for him. It was everything not to go to her and say he was fine where he was in the apartment. But images of Jane disrobed in a room beyond the apartment won out.

In the morning he dressed, fully intending to make his brief truancy a thing of the past. But his feet led him to the subway and Times Square. Preparations for The World's Fair were underway out in Flushing, Queens. He would visit the site, which was scheduled to open sometime that spring, but not even glimpses of the massive Unisphere and pavilion after pavilion of futuristic buildings as the train approached Flushing Meadow could lift him from the sinking sense that he was on a train to nowhere. There came strongly the feeling that there was nothing out there for him; it was all in the confines of the Claremont School. Had he learned nothing from the dismal excursion to Boston with Sean? But there was no going back, not when he was now behind in all his classes. What advancement could he hope for with failing grades for the semester?

He headed back to Times Square. In the steep balcony of a twenty-four hour movie theater, fallen from the grandeur of its stage-show prime, men sat scattered, some snoring, their legs over the backs of the chairs in the next row down. Pale overhead lights exposed the debris under the seats and in the aisles—waxed paper cups, popcorn tubs, candy wrappers. Soon the lights dimmed and a film called *The Days of Wine and Roses* began. Jack Lemmon, a public relations guy who drank a lot, fell in love with Lee Remick, a secretary at his office. A teetotaler, she took him home to meet her father. In one terrifying scene, Jack Lemmon writhed, suffering delirium tremens, on the floor of her father's greenhouse, having torn apart flowerpots in a mad search for the bottle he had hidden. By now Jack Lemmon and the secretary were man and wife, and she had begun to drink, too.

The movie was frightening, but it would be heroin, if anything, that hooked him, not alcohol, like it had hooked those nodding junkies on the street, men and women standing in place with their heads hanging and their knees buckling and their torsos twisted. And there wouldn't be any such descent into alcoholic madness for Jane either. She was the real focus of concern. No, she would not join the women who walked the streets at night, having fallen from life's favor. She would not end up in some seedy bungalow with only her bottle, although without him she might. How anxious he was to save her as he left the movie theater.

"I've been thinking about what you asked me," Jane said that afternoon as he feigned distraction, flipping through the jukebox selections at their booth in the diner. "I mean, it is true that we are going to be married, even if not right away. And we do love each other."

Married. That word again. Sincerity did not entirely become her.

"I mean, we are going to get married, aren't we?"

"Of course we are," he said, while saying nothing about his truancy.

"Look, Johan. You even have a new desk to study at, and a beautiful new sofa that converts into a bed," Mrs. Manootdjian said, showing him the narrow room he could now settle into. Simon Weill had purchased the sofas and desks in quantity. Whether it was new furnishings or a new elevator or a new washing machine for the basement laundry or any other large transaction, Simon Weill saw to the purchases. It was for Auntie Eve and Johan's mother to collect rent money and do the tenants' laundry and manage the work crew who painted rooms and replaced fuses and otherwise maintained the building.

His mother's humble desire to please made the monstrousness of his deception almost unbearable. It was everything not to confess and beg her forgiveness. But he held back, fortified by reasoning that told him it was his life, not hers, that he was ruining.

That first night in his new room he thought of Luke in his suite of rooms and Naomi and Chuck in their room and Hannah in hers. Perhaps Naomi too believed, when she and Chuck took that room upstairs, it was simply a matter of time before she moved away. Perhaps Hannah thought the same thing. Suppose ten or twenty years went by and he was still there. But then Jane entered his mind and dispelled such thoughts as he fell asleep picturing her lying beside him, just the two of them behind a locked door at last.

As the days passed, it seemed strange that the school did not inquire about his absence. Had it gone unnoticed? All he knew was that his truancy was gaining an irreversible momentum. Each morning, he maintained the charade of normalcy, leaving home in his uniform for a day of solitary exploration, which generally meant returning to those movie theaters along Forty-second Street where he could escape reality for a few hours. There was suave, heroic James Bond in *Dr. No* engaging with bikini-clad Ursula Andress as she emerged from the aquamarine Caribbean like a glistening goddess, and the sinister machinations of Dr. No and SPECTRE, his organization committed to evil. And there was *Hud,* which made Johan inwardly groan with admiration and envy that Paul Newman could fill his jeans so well as he leaned his psychic weight upon Patricia Neal before he so much as even touched her. And there was Tippi Hedren, in *The Birds,* to fall in love with, too. That a woman could call herself Tippi, so light, before landing on you with her weightier surname.

⚘

"What'll it be?" The name tag on the woman's white smock said Rosie Sullivan.

"I'd like a box of prophylactics," Johan said, rubbers sounding too descriptive.

"What kind of prophylactics?" It was a word she took her time with.

"What kind have you got?"

She recited their names, in a voice loud enough to reach the ends of the store. Trojans. Ramses. He kept his eyes fixed on the colognes and perfumes in the glass case.

"Ramses, please," he murmured, not knowing one brand from another.

Jane was out front of the building, surrounded by Lenny and Jerry and Luke, as he arrived with his purchase. In that moment he hated the very sight of them, and hated them even more when Lenny said, "You don't mind if I borrow your girlfriend for a while?"

"Hey, don't do anything we wouldn't do," Jerry called out.

Upstairs, he waited in the public bathroom down the hall while she undressed. She wanted it that way, she said. When he returned, she was in bed, with the covers up to her neck.

She placed her hands on his chest to stop him, though when he finally succeeded there was no cry of pain. The rhythm that developed and the release that followed were pleasurable, and more than that, but somehow the aftermath was even more remarkable, the hours he spent in wonder that he had actually been inside her and that they had done *it*.

A shout rose from the street."Yo, Johan." Luis. But how had he found them?

Then it was Kevin. "Hey, Johan. We know you're up there. Jerry told us where we could find you."

"Hey, my man, get your ass to the window before I come up there and whip it good," Jimmy Riley called up.

"We've lost him," said Kevin.

"Yo, Johan, I'm going to whale on your ass for this," Jimmy promised, in that strange way he had of offering threats that came across as an expression of love.

Soon the street fell quiet, the sound of a basketball bouncing off the pavement growing ever fainter.

He touched her down below. "Not now. I'm sore," she said.

"There is a parents' meeting tonight at your school that I must attend."

Three weeks had passed since his truancy began.

"Did you not hear me?"

"I did," he said.

"Your teachers speak so glowingly of you."

He imagined her face when Mr. Horst-Lehman or some other faculty member told her of his absence. He hasn't been at school? But how can such a thing be? Her face stricken with worry and pain. Leaving the school crushed, in tears, humiliated, and feeling the whole weight of the world upon her and nobody to turn to, not his father, who didn't even know what school he was attending or what grade he was in. All she would have was God, and on the long bus ride home she would question him with hot tears streaming down her face, asking what she had done to deserve children such as these: an oldest daughter who was prideful and disagreeable and lazy; a second daughter who took pills and drank and slept away the day and who had married a drunk; and even Rachel, with her fine mind, going crazy with drink and disappearing after dropping out of that fine college she had worked so hard to get into; and now her sons turning out to be worthless as well. She would feel all these things and he would have to die for having failed her.

He returned to Forty-second Street, where *McClintock* was playing. Big John Wayne could not only not sling lead in the Old West but court a woman the likes of stormy Maureen O'Hara. He then wandered down to Battery Park, at the tip of Manhattan, and rode the ferry out to Staten Island. The water was rough, the winds strong. Forces were at work in nature to sink the vessel. Land was unsafe and water was treacherous. Where was he to go?

Evening came. He pulled back the shade. Under the glare of a streetlamp stood Luke with Lenny and Jerry beside the Bonneville. Luke's white dress shirt, the kind he would wear to St. Andrews School with his blazer and tie, was hanging out of his pants. It was something to notice, along with his idleness.

When the knock came, he was lying on the convertible sofa. He stubbed out his cigarette and opened the window. If she smelled the smoke, so be it; he didn't want her to see him with a lighted Marlboro.

"Can you tell me why?" she asked, in a quiet voice, locking the door behind her. She wore her light brown dress with polka dots, the one she also wore on church day.

Nothing came to mind, not difficult classmates or anything else that might win her sympathy or understanding. There was nothing to put in the way of her inevitable sorrow.

"So you wish to do like the others, is that it? You also wish to disappoint me? Can you not at least answer me?"

"I couldn't be there anymore."

"Why didn't you at least tell me? Why did I have to find out in such a way?"

He couldn't answer.

"Are you having trouble with Jane?"

"No."

"So you went and deceived me. You tricked me into giving you this room. You did not want it for your schoolwork at all. You were not even in school when you came to me. How could you do something so low?" She began to cry.

When she left, he smoked another cigarette. If there was fear and guilt, there was also something else. His mother's tears were dangerous. He was in need of protection from them.

She came back that night. When there was conflict, she always came back. "It is I," she said, knocking on the door. She paid attention to language. She knew her predicate nominative.

"But can we not be reasonable? What will you do?"

"I don't know."

"But can you not tell me if there is something that upset you?"

"No," he said.

He counted it as something that her eyes were dry when she went away again. She would adjust, as she always did. She already had. She had her God to see to that.

From the window of the bus, the park had a bleakness to it as the city slowly transitioned from winter to spring. A solitary Parks Department worker poked here and there with his gaff, spearing pieces of litter and depositing them in the canvas sack slung over his shoulder. Maybe he too could work for the Parks Department. Didn't he love walking the footpaths of Central Park and Riverside Park? He could sit on a bench in the warm sun having his lunch and do his part to maintain order on the grounds. Or seeing the familiar sight of a UPS driver in a chocolate brown uniform carrying an armful of parcels into a Fifth Avenue building, he wondered if such a thing could be his in the future as well. No mystery of pi. No SAT. A simple life that yet would save him from the rooms his siblings had surrendered to.

"What's the matter, Johan? You been sick or something?" Freddy Snyder spoke at his ear-piercing volume.

"Yeah. He's sick of all your questions," Lance said, winking at Johan.

Always the same shtick with Freddy and Lance. With or without words they communicated.

At the lunch hour, Mr. Arbuckle turned and made eye contact with Johan at a nearby table. Mr. Arbuckle then got up and joined him.

"How are things going?"

Johan felt for Mr. Arbuckle, having to leave the company of Diane Coleman. He was the kind who would be uncomfortable extending himself outside the winner's circle. And why not? People should be with their own. Problems began when you tried to mix things up. Probably Mr. Horst-Lehman had prodded him. Mr. Arbuckle had big dark eyes, like the man in the black topcoat in the Times Square bookstore some years before. And those big lips. Surely Mr. Funelli would say of Mr. Arbuckle that he too liked to kiss.

"Things are okay."

"One thing my father told me was that no matter what situation I found myself in, I had to keep moving forward. Keep driving, he said. Life demands toughness. We all have difficulties we must overcome."

"Yes," Johan said, glancing over at Diane Coleman as she sipped through a straw from her half-pint of milk. But her eyes on his forced him to look away. They defeated him every time.

"It's best to make life as tidy an affair as possible. Unhappiness can be an indulgence and is controllable if we really try. Is there anything you would like to ask me or say?"

"No. I'd just like to thank you for talking to me."

"Remember that I am here any time you need me."

When the bell rang signaling the end of lunch, Johan left the building. The street was calling. The park was calling.

"He'll see you now, Sweetie," Miss Redding said, bathing Johan in her soft Southern voice as she held open the door to Mr. Horst-Lehman's carpeted office. Behind a huge desk he sat, bifocals halfway down his mottled nose. The rich black suit and dazzling yellow tie he wore only added to his commanding aura.

They were not alone. It came as a surprise, not a happy one, to see Mr. Sadowski also present. He wore a lesser suit of mailman's gray and scuffed black shoes.

"Mr. Sadowski would like to say a few words to you," Mr. Horst-Lehman said, a faint note of condescension in his voice, as if poor Mr. Sadowski wasn't capable of more than a few words.

"I just want to say you have your whole life ahead of you. You'd be far better off going through with the school year than withdrawing. It keeps you on the right track."

He was terrified of hurting and angering Mr. Sadowski, who talked so earnestly, and who meant so much to him, and yet the words came out anyway. "I can't stay," he said, lowering his eyes to the carpeted floor.

"Where will you go?" Mr. Horst-Lehman asked.

"Go?" He didn't understand Mr. Horst-Lehman's question.

"You would have to enroll at Commerce High School." Johan recognized the name of the school. Jerry Jones-Nobleonian was now enrolled there. How special Claremont had made him feel. How much he was now giving up. But when something was ruined, it was ruined.

"Okay," he said, unable to hide his disappointment. He hadn't thought of going to another school at all.

"Perhaps you would be more comfortable with the level of competition at such an institution. If I may say, I think your real problem is your fear of competing. You're not exceptionally bright, if intelligence tests are any indication of the caliber of one's mind. And I see you failed to take the PSAT this past fall. Maybe it is a fear of finding out the level of your abilities that is the real issue here."

The words stung, but inwardly he accepted the truth of what Mr. Horst-Lehman said. He was only confirming what Johan already knew.

"At some point in your life you will have to develop a backbone," he went on.

"Yes," Johan said. A backbone.

"You take care of yourself, Sweetie," Miss Redding said, offering him a smile on his way out.

He was woken by a knock on the door. Still in his flannel pajamas, he let her in. She put down the schoolbooks clutched against her chest and undressed. Her shyness was gone. It was nothing for her to undress in front of him now. It was like that many mornings; waiting until afternoon was just too hard.

They caught the IRT local to Sixty-sixth Street, where he coaxed her off the train and into a dank-smelling underpass connecting the uptown and downtown platforms. Against the tiled wall he pressed her and they kissed, long deep kisses, then disengaged at the sound of footsteps in the echoing passageway. Down the stairs came an old man with a cane, his gait agonizingly slow. Impatiently Johan waited for him to pass.

Another set of footsteps followed. Quicker steps, of someone in a hurry. A voice, a familiar one, boomed. "Way to go, Romeo." Lance flew past, with a grin and a wave, before disappearing.

"Do you know him?"

"Just someone from Claremont."

By now she knew. It was nothing to her that he had left Claremont. The future was not really her concern, not in the way it had seemed to be for Johan.

He delayed mounting the stairs to street level, hoping that Lance would have caught the crosstown bus so he didn't have to ride with him across the Central Park transverse to his stop on Fifth Avenue, from which he would walk the few blocks to Claremont. Mortifying thoughts flooded his mind of Lance informing Freddy Snyder and Robin Abel and Diane Coleman and the rest of them that he had seen Squarehead kissing his girlfriend in a subway underpass. He tried to block the humiliation with baseball images from the previous year, the overpowering left arm of Sandy Koufax delivering high heat and curveballs impossible to hit.

He would be more careful in future on this, his new route. He would stay out of the underpass with Jane. He must never go where Claremont could be found. He must remove the school entirely from his life, as he had the crest no longer stitched to the breast pocket of his blazer.

Far over, by the East River, stood the Ridge School in a tired-looking brick building. He assumed it took in cutups and dull souls like himself, those cast away by more rigorous schools. At the lunch hour he sat nearby, in a small, cheerless park, and ate his store-bought ham and cheese sandwich, the school having no cafeteria. The day was gray and the playground empty of screaming children on the seesaw and slide and swings.

The Frenchman's maxim was back. How was he to go away to college? Would she not die? Would he not die? Maybe he could find a college close by and see her on weekends? But no plan for the future seemed to hold. If he could only call her now, or better yet, be with her and protect her from lurking danger. Someone could be plunging a knife in her chest or pushing her off a subway platform in front of an incoming train. He buried his face in his hands. The world was a very dangerous place for Jane Thayer to be.

"It is your friend Tom on the phone," his mother came to his room and said that evening.

Reluctantly Johan went to the apartment and picked up the receiver.

"I've been missing you. How are things going?"

"Fine," Johan said.

"Did you find another school?"

"Sure."

"What's the name of it?"

"Ridge."

"Never heard of it. Are you playing ball?"

"No." He felt no need to tell Tom that the new school had kids who could dunk and that there was no place for him on such a squad.

"Look, I really want us to stay in touch."

"Sure. We'll stay in touch," Johan said.

With the SAT looming, he turned to fantasy, imagining scores like 650 and 625, respectable numbers that would allow him to maintain eye contact with the Diane Colemans and Robin Abels of the world.

On the morning of the test, with two sharpened number 2 pencils in his pocket, he headed for Hamilton Hall. In the auditorium, the proctor handed out the test booklets and offered instructions.

How many numbers are there between 260 and 389? If two circles of radii 4" and 9" have their centers...?

Stymied, he began to skip, desperate to reach the finish line, and sought only those questions he could quickly answer. On the math part those questions were few, and when he backtracked to the more difficult ones, answers still eluded him. A familiar soreness soon consumed him. The sons of bitches with their tricky questions. They wanted to see him fail. He fell back on guesswork, his pencil hovering over the columns on the slick coated paper. If the previous answer had been in Column D, surely the following would have to be in another column. Or no, maybe those Educational Testing Service people in Princeton, New Jersey, were being clever and the correct answer was in Column D again.

That afternoon, the achievement tests in history, French, and English summoned none of the frustration engendered by the math aptitude section earlier in the day, and by evening, his mental land-scape began to brighten. The conviction even came to him that his pencil had been directed to the right answers. Big numbers began to flash before him, numbers his mind could feast on. He really was going somewhere. Life was good once again.

Warmer weather arrived. He sat alone in the park with the *Daily News* and his own thoughts for company, grateful for a break from this shell of a school. Now there were others in the park as well, drawn by the beautiful spring day. An infant beamed on the swing as his mother sent him in an arc back and forth through the spring air. Such a happy sight, a little boy with his attentive, caring mother.

On his return after the lunch break, he saw a cardboard box outside the principal's office. The words "SAT scores" were written in magic marker on the side of the box. Several students sorted eagerly through the booklets, tossing them back until they found their own. The results had come too fast. He left and walked around the block. When he returned, only several booklets remained. There, on a label glued to the cover, was his name. He placed the folded booklet in his pocket and retreated to a bathroom stall, where he read the numbers. There they were, indelible evidence of his incompetence. He peeled the strip off the booklet and deposited little pieces of it in the garbage.

Like a steer wrestled to the ground and seared with a hot poker in those TV westerns, he too had been branded and herded in among the losers, separated forever from the Ogden Connifers and Diane Colemans and Robin Abels. What did it matter if others didn't know. *He knew.* He understood that those numbers would be with him for the rest of his life as the quantifiable measure of his worth.

Chapter 15

"Baby, baby, baby don't leave me." Everywhere he went in the summer heat the Supremes were singing to a pulsing bass, their sound menthol cool and hot at the same time. And Martha and the Vandellas had people dancing in the street—Baltimore and D.C., and Philadelphia, PA, while cautioning not to forget the Motor City. Infectious joy they brought, but he could not soar with their sound, the numbers he had received a constant weight anchoring him to the ground.

He worked that summer as a delivery boy at the BonTon Cleaners on the corner of One Hundred Twelfth Street. Mathematician Charlie owned the establishment. All the correct numbers were stored in his brain pan sufficient that he graduated from MIT and could greet each customer with a self-assured smile that told them who they were dealing with.

A Negro named Derrick managed the store in Mathematician Charlie's frequent absence. He too had abundant brain power, having attended the Bronx High School of Science before dropping out for reasons he did not disclose. Derrick stood short and chunky with an energy that set his being in motion even when he was resting in place, but did pain have a hold on him to make his smile less than what it appeared? Johan intuited the white boy status which Ronnie's smile assigned him and accepted the distance maintained through politeness.

Another Negro, LeRoy, worked in the back. He was taller than Derrick and louder. "That motherfucker come back here one more motherfucking time giving me his motherfucking shit I'm gonna put his sorry white ass in the presser. You dig what I'm saying?"

"Sure. I dig it," Johan said, because LeRoy seemed to be addressing his remarks solely to him, his full and powerful voice impacting like a powerful wave.

"You hear that, Derrick? Motherfucking white boy digs it I be putting his white-assed motherfucking boss in the presser. This motherfucking white boy is all right." LeRoy had a wide mouth in a handsome face from which his sound poured. He lived in the ground of his pain, relieving it with his words so he didn't have to do what he said he would do to Mathematician Charlie, a man too large for the hissing presser unless LeRoy were to bend and fold him or do something else even more diabolical. And so Johan came to love LeRoy as well for his heart pounding with its own goodness, his fiery words but a camouflage, as with Jimmy Riley.

To be with the two Negroes was to be in another world that smelled of happiness and the street and strange pain.

"Why you always leaning like that?" Derrick asked, seeing Johan use the wall next to the automated rack of garments sheathed in plastic for support.

"I don't know."

"We calling you Leaner from now on," LeRoy said. He peeled a ten from the roll of bills he kept in his pants pocket. "Here's what you do, Leaner. I'm feeling the need for a taste. You know what a motherfucking taste is, Leaner?"

"A taste for something to eat?"

"Ain't wanting no motherfucking food. Now you know that liquor store right across the street."

"I know it."

"You go there and get me a pint of vodka. They give you any trouble, just say it's for LeRoy. You go on now."

When he came back, LeRoy cracked the seal and chugged half the bottle. "That's some good shit, boy, some good motherfucking shit." He went back to pressing garments. As the day passed, LeRoy grew quieter. The alcohol had deposited him in the sullen place. Not that he was really drunk. All that heat from the presser steamed the alcohol out of him, big beads of sweat forming on his bare arms and face.

A week later, when the Negroes of New York City went up against the police of New York City for days on end for an injustice they perceived, causing the very buildings themselves to tremble, LeRoy said, "Don't you be going up to Harlem now, motherfucking white boy Leaner. Black man gonna rip your ass if you do." And when Johan's eyes grew wider than they already were with fright, LeRoy could laugh, showing off a gold tooth. "Shee-it," he said, calling attention not to the thing named but some feeling instead that only elongation could convey.

On the days that Mathematician Charlie did not need Johan, there was still stickball. The bats they swung now were thick, store-bought things with taped handles, not broken-off broomsticks.

And there was Lenny, bonded to his Bonneville and Frieda, and the language that he spoke: cams and V-8 and piston rings and divided grilles and quad headlights and twin fins. The Bonneville was now the Moon Mobile, so named because of Jerry's talent for showing his bare ass to selected viewers in other vehicles on the Henry Hudson Parkway. And there was Terry Stafford too, singing that song "Suspicion" about how every time he kissed her, he couldn't be certain that she loved him. So earnestly and fast did Terry Stafford sing.

"I can do anything with you I want."

"Don't say things like that," Jane said, as if she had seen something in what Johan said he didn't want her to see.

"No, no. I have no power," he said, wanting to take back what he couldn't so she wouldn't live with the beast he had had revealed. Those words. They came from a place he did not quite recognize. And yet he did, he later had to realize. He did.

Questions came, in the day and night. How did something fresh come to feel old? How did something pleasurable come to feel painful? How had he come to tarnish Jane Thayer so she would never again be desirable to the world? How, by contrast, did Cathy Cathleen and Mary Marie appear to sparkle and why did he have it in his mind that pristine Cathy Cathleen and Mary Marie and the likes of them would shun Jane Thayer, leaving her all alone? And why was it now painful to be with Jane Thayer and painful not to be with her? Could someone not answer him?

And now there was an external sign of change. The window of Funelli's grocery store was covered with whitewash. Sean was now a checker at the newly opened PriceRite down on One Hundred Tenth Street and Broadway, where the Nemo Theater had been. He would no longer be pumping his balloon-tired bicycle impervious to and disdainful of the traffic coming toward him. Now he was only one of many in a store with wide aisles and bright fluorescent lighting. He would not be helping himself to ham and coleslaw on hero the way he had.

"Looking for your friends?" Scully asked, making it clear he was not one of them.

"I guess," Johan said. It was one of those muggy nights when the air didn't move, as his mother would say.

"Well, they're not around," Scully said, and walked away.

Desperation for the moment blinded him to the reality that he was calling out to his nemesis, and so he followed Scully around the corner and to an entrance to the Columbia campus.

"I was wondering—what I mean is do you mind if I ask you something?"

"Go ahead. Ask me anything."

"It's just this. Jane and I have been sleeping together for a while now. What I want to know is this. Do you think that if we were to stop, things could go back to the way they were?"

"What kind of question is that?"

"It's just a question."

"You really want an answer?"

"I really do," I say.

"The answer is no. Now get lost, Fucko."

❧

"We should give up smoking." Running two blocks left him winded.

"But I like to smoke," Jane said, taking a big drag on her Winston.

"I've got to get free of them." He threw the flip-top box and the ten remaining cigarettes in the trash can.

"What a waste," she said, blowing a perfect smoke ring.

"I can't just cut down."

"The next thing you'll want to give up is sex."

"We should talk about that, too."

"Oh, no." She clasped her hands to her head in mock horror.

"What I've been thinking is that maybe we should meet outdoors."

"We are outdoors." In fact they were sitting on the sundial on the Columbia campus.

"Maybe we should stay out of my room. Do you know what I mean?"

"Not exactly," she said, coolly.

"I mean, we'll just feel better if we do." It wasn't for him to tell her she would be unsuitable for Mary Marie and Cathy Cathleen and outside the circle of respectability if they kept going to the room.

"We'll feel better if we stay away from your room?"

"We are in deep water. We have to get back to shore."

"Are you all right?"

"I am being purposeful."

"Purposeful. Of course. That explains everything."

He was feeling better. Not even the stifling August heat was a bother. Free of the room, they walked in Riverside Park like normal people did so renewal could begin. And when Jane said, over sodas and danishes at the diner, that a couple of girls from her Friday night social group at the church wanted to get together, he thought, "Take that, Mary Marie. Take that, Cathy Cathleen, take that, all you who would reject Jane."

With light having dispelled the darkness, he was prompted to say, "Let's go up to my room."

"I thought your room was off limits."

"Oh, it'll be all right."

She laughed, and laughed even more when he reached for the pack of cigarettes she had placed on the table. "One, just one," he said, even as he was reminded of his father extracting a spoonful of sugar from the bowl over Mrs. Manootdjian's protest.

Back in his room she whispered to him to go slower. She had not instructed him before and he listened. Afterward he lay on his back, saying nothing.

"Are you all right?"

"I'm fine. It's just hot in here." The feeling of suffocation had returned. Everything they had gained they had now lost.

They would stay away from the room for two days and then go back to it. They would stay away for three days, and then go back. Each time the pain returned.

"I have a plan," Johan said.

"Oh, good. I can't wait to hear it."

He tried to ignore the sarcasm in her voice. "We need to decide on how long we can be together each day. Maybe two hours maximum. Does that sound about right?"

"What will that do?"

"That way we don't overdo a good thing and wind up back in the room, because then we would have to start all over again."

"But I like the room. You're not making a lot of sense."

"All the good feeling will come back. You'll see."

"Good feeling?"

"Right. OK. I'm going now. What are you going to do?"

"I don't know."

"You don't know?"

"That's what I said."

"Why don't you know?"

"Because I don't."

"I'll call you later. Okay?"

"Fine. Call me."

"What? I shouldn't call?"

"When do you not call?"

"So I shouldn't call? That's what you're saying?"

"I'm not saying anything. Just go."

"I said I was going."

"Saying is not doing. Now go."

"I am."

"Look, if you're not going, I'm going. Bye. And don't follow me."

As he headed down Broadway, it was everything not to rush back and tell her how much he loved her. On someone's radio the Crystals were singing "He's a Rebel," but there was no soaring with the music. A half hour passed. Walking and his brief time away from Jane seemed to brighten his outlook. Soon he was in a phone booth.

Mrs. Thayer answered. "No, my sweet. I'm afraid the object of your affections is not presently present."

Once again the distance that had been gained had been lost. Worse, it could not start again without his first speaking with her. And the wall clock in the Whelan's drugstore was not cooperating. In fact, it was being viciously balky, the minute hand barely moving. But a solution existed to the clock's cruel dilly-dallying. If he walked slowly back to the phone booth and dialed her number, the right amount of time would have gone by. He didn't have to just sit at the counter and be a complete slave to monstrous time.

"Oh honey, your voice sounds so full of yearning. Where can she be that she is not here for you? How cruel. What torment young lovers put each other through."

When finally he reached Jane, he exploded, as if she had purposely been frustrating him. Then he slammed the phone into the cradle, which required that he call back and apologize, and when that did not suffice, ensure his apology had been accepted with a follow-up call.

※

Coney Island was not his bedroom. The ocean offered a perilous freedom. The sun-worshipers did not rise up en masse off their towels and shower him with mocking laughter. Nor did Jane run for the comfort of a boy with more substance on his frame. Nor were there sideways glances to take in the sorry spectacle he was. This he could say with some certainty as his monitoring equipment was operating full-time.

As he lay slathered in suntan lotion, an image hotter than the sand of Jane naked back in the room formed in his mind. They wore their still wet bathing suits under their clothes on the long subway ride back to Manhattan, the sand grinding into their bottoms on the rattan seats.

"Can I come over and shower at your place?" Jane asked. He was unable to say no. They showered together in the public bathroom down the hall. As she began to dress, he touched her wrist. There it began.

Quickly new pain found him, but that evening something miraculous happened. Right there in the show business column of the *Daily News,* two film stars who had divorced some years before were now, ten years later and after numerous other involvements, planning their remarriage. Propelled by joy, he flew downstairs to phone Jane with the news that the reunited couple had destroyed the pompous French maxim man and his cruel maxim. And the same with that movie *Splendor in the Grass.*

"Jane, listen. It's incredible. Do you know what I just read?"

"Johan, do you know what time it is?"

The hour hand on the Coca-Cola clock on the wall of the luncheonette was approaching midnight. "Sure, but look, this is about two famous people and how…"

"No. No looking. No anything."

In the morning, his elation was gone. He sought out the anti-septic ambience of Chock Full O' Nuts, but two cups of coffee and a half-eaten sugar doughnut later, the anxiety remained crushing. He tried walking the footpaths of Riverside Park. Though that did nothing to lessen his pain, a new idea came to him. And so, he turned and raced off to St. Luke's Hospital.

"Well, what is it?" the emergency room receptionist asked.

"I need to see a doctor right away."

"What's the problem?"

"That's what I want him to tell me. And I want him to tell me to my face, as that is the only way." Surely the doctor would be armed with wisdom.

She cast on him an appraising eye while handing him a form attached to a clipboard. "Take a seat."

A girl holding her hand to her bloody mouth and moaning struggled down the corridor after hearing her name over the PA system. A man with sunken cheeks and the wheeze of an asthmatic sat in a stupor in one of the molded plastic chairs. Soon he too disappeared. Some minutes later, Johan was called to a windowless, fluorescent-lighted room, where an intern in a lab coat soon appeared.

"What seems to be the problem?" He was young and slight, with wispy blond hair.

"I've been seeing this girl. Her name is Jane Thayer. We started sleeping together because someday we will be getting married. It was just like that song by the Crystals. You know the one I mean, that makes you feel so good all over you're practically delirious. Today I met the boy I'm gonna marry, only it was today I met Jane Thayer, the girl I'm gonna marry. What I need to know is whether it can be like we just met all over again if we stop sleeping together? La Rochefoucauld said we couldn't, but I am frankly tired of that man."

The intern said nothing. His eyes were ice blue.

"What I mean is, is there future time for us?" Johan's words were not carrying. They traveled a bit and then fell to the ground like stricken little birds.

The intern broke his silence. "I suspect these things work themselves out."

"These things?"

But the intern had already moved toward the door, which he held open for Johan.

Men and women of quiet purpose walked about the courtyard of the Jewish Theological Seminary, paying no attention to Johan and Jane as they sat on a bench in the entranceway. Lights burned in the buildings. Even on a summer evening there was work to be done. From Broadway came the rumble of a subway train breaking free from the tunnel onto the el.

"Don't cry. I talked to Daddy. He said it was all right with him if we got married when we finish high school," Jane said.

Married? Married? Going to the chapel and we're going to get married?

Times Square. Fifth Avenue. Grand Central. Vernon-Jackson Boulevard. The subway climbed from the tunnel onto the el. Far below was the sprawl of the Penn Central railroad yard, the tracks an intricate web of silver tendrils. Across the river stood Manhattan, the needle of the Empire State Building reaching for the sky.

"Hey, fuck you, you fat fuck. Why do you have to take up so much space?" Kevin squealed, Scully having squished him against the end rail. His smallness was his wound but also his protection, as was Luis. The boys were feeling rowdy.

As the Flushing train reached the Willets Point Station in Queens, the roar of a jet departing from LaGuardia could be heard overhead. A new world awaited. What a thing. Johan had never been on a plane.

Jimmy Riley, Rob Koley, Scully, Kevin, Luis. If he was with his own sex, maybe he would know peace.

Outside the stadium Scully started. "Did I tell you guys about Flathead here? He's going all crazy because he's been sticking his dick in Jane. He's asking me all this weird shit about the future, so I slapped him and he didn't do shit when I did."

Johan punched Scully as hard as he could, right in the mouth. Scully spit out some blood, his face red with rage, and rushed at Johan, whose fist found his right eye, before Scully crushed him into the asphalt with his huge weight and pounded away until Luis and the others could pull him off.

"The next time I fucking kill you," he blubbered, but the restraints held.

The basement-dwelling Mets had fat Jack Fisher on the mound They had pokey Chris Cannizzaro behind the plate. They had hands of stone Ed Kranepool at first base. But the Cardinals were redbirds on the fly. They had fleet Curt Flood and fleet Lou Brock and the nonchalant power of Ken Boyer. And they had Bob Gibson on the mound delivering heat. By the third inning they were putting it to the patsy Mets.

Shea Stadium was a bowl of pastel-colored seats. From the top of the grandstand, the players appeared as specks on the brilliantly lighted field. A steady wind had begun to whip in off Flushing Bay. Though the game was an agony of slowly passing innings, he struggled to stay in place. He had made of the evening an endurance test and decided that failure to stay until the end would bring harm to Jane and him.

But now another idea had come, dissolving all the stress and gloom, as a vendor hollered, "Beer, ice cold beer" and tissue-thin hot dog wrappings blew through the air.

"I need to find the bathroom," he said, during the seventh inning stretch.

"You do that, Champ." Luis's voice sounded cold, dismissive, reinforcing the sense that he had become a stranger among them since he had disappeared with Jane into his room. Free of their judgmental eye after descending the concrete steps, he streaked onto the exit ramp.

On the other side of the door a radio could be heard, one of those gabfests that went on into all hours of the night. Johan knocked softly, and then harder. A lock turned and the door opened as far as the chain allowed. An old woman peered out through the small opening.

"Well, come on in then," she said, unlatching the chain and opening the door wide.

The air in the room felt damp, as if she had just run a bath. He sat in a stuffed chair while she lowered the volume on the radio and poured herself a glass of carrot juice.

"My nightcap," she said. "Now what can I do for you?"

The visit had seemed like a good idea. He would unburden himself as she listened sympathetically and she would respond with wise counsel and comfort and somehow make things right. But now, her hard stare, the bluntness of her question, and the silence that followed all conspired to make him squirm, the unventilated room no more hospitable to confession than the pitilessly impersonal examination room at the nearby hospital where he had sat with the young intern.

"Well?"

"I—I mean Jane and I—have been doing something."

"I'm listening."

"We started…it got serious…for a year it has been serious."

"What has been serious?"

"Sex. The seriousness of sex." He tried to leave it there, but couldn't. "All the way. That kind of serious. Now I don't know how to make her new. I don't know how to make her like Mary Marie and Cathy Cathleen."

"Like who?"

"They're sisters. They don't go all the way."

Her face had a slight tremor that he now associated with the pent-up Gallic fury of Mlle. Gallimard, his former French teacher.

"I've said it before. God made the small town and the devil made the big city."

"Do you think so? The city is all I know."

"You see that door behind you?"

"Yes." He had no need to turn. He knew where the door was.

"Well, you came in through it. Now I guess it's time you went out through it."

She wasn't his mother. She wasn't the forgiving kind. He ran from her aged steel out into the night.

Chapter 16

"I received a call from Miss Redding at the Claremont School. They will be only too happy to have you back. Miss Redding told me so. She seems like such a nice woman, and she's very fond of you."

It was a door he hadn't expected to reopen, and walking through it would bring pain, now that the dream of excellence had died. After all, he ran away when the going got tough. But he missed the comfort that association with quality could bring, along with all the social terror.

"Hey, Manootdj, you're back," Freddy Snyder said for all to hear, that first day.

"Call him Hot Lips. Right, Johan?" Lance winked and smiled.

"What's that about Hot Lips?" Freddy said, but Lance had danced away.

He showed himself as even more self-effacing, understanding that all along Claremont had been putting him in his place. The boy who inscribed the boastful pronouncement "Johan is great" in his seventh grade textbook was now a cowering shell. Sean and Scully had beaten him. Tom Smits had beaten him. The SAT had beaten him. His own mind had beaten him.

The chemistry course, a science requirement which he needed to graduate, was taught by James Janely, a tall, middle-aged man with a receding hairline, a furrowed Beethovian brow, and a large belly that required him to leave his suit jacket unbuttoned. Diane Coleman was heard to say he looked like Rex Harrison and that she would be his Liza Doolittle any day.

In addition to a thick chemistry book, James Jane assigned the class a slender volume titled *The Two Cultures,* by C. P. Snow. Both the author and he, Mr. Janely said, were interested in building a bridge between science and the humanities. His almond eyes shone with good humor as he spoke, in a casual, elliptical way, one hand in the pocket of his wool trousers. For all his intelligence, he was seen as a man in the process of slow disintegration: the redness of his nose and the smell of liquor on his breath said more than any words he spoke.

The chemistry book was terrifying, the information on its glossy white pages an unfathomable mystery, from ions and moles to valences. Sitting in his room with the gooseneck lamp trained on the text, Johan could only wonder if there was a place in the world for kids as dumb as him.

Frank Furr taught junior English and also served as the homeroom teacher for the senior class. He had pale skin, and though just out of Bowdoin College, only a remnant of blond hair remained. Like Miss Jacoby, he offered words of encouragement, drawing on his own experience. "My guidance counselor back in high school told me I wasn't college material," Mr. Frank Furr said that first week, sitting on the edge of his desk. He shared this information as if his presence on the Claremont faculty had somehow proven the counselor wrong.

But suspicion, having been aroused by the confession, now lingered, at least in Johan. What was Frank Furr missing that made the counselor say what he did? Had the counselor seen that Frank Furr was just a low number guy? And why hadn't Frank Furr listened?

What right did he have not to? Why hadn't he just stopped and gone belly up on the world, the way you were supposed to do if a guidance counselor said those words to you?

Frank Furr wore gingham shirts with his tweed and corduroy jackets. He was not to be seen in a white oxford shirt, as such plainness went against the identity he was seeking to establish. He let it be known that he had a wife and was pursuing a master's degree in English literature at New York University (New York University, not Columbia). This much Johan understood—Frank Furr was fighting the verdict that he was not top-shelf.

One morning a white-haired guest speaker addressed the student assembly. Senator Barry Goldwater of Arizona had defeated Governor William Scranton of Pennsylvania for the Republican nomination for president of the United States. The man told the student body why Barry Goldwater would be good for the country.

"This man is a patriot. He believes in America and stands up for this country of ours at a time when it is fashionable to be always pointing out our faults. This man is a great crusader for the American way and a relentless foe of world communism. He has his eye on the evil around us and will deal with it forthrightly." He went on in this way, holding high the banner of Republicanism, the party of brand-name goods, saying not a single good thing about Lyndon Baines Johnson, the biggest Democrat of all, because to be a Democrat was to be an anarchist and to rob the country of what made America the country it was.

Frank Furr, in the question-and-answer period, had no questions but he did have a statement, declaring, "This man Goldwater is a lunatic, an American nightmare. He is warmongering, self-righteous, devoid of compassion. His America uber alles approach will drag us down the path of destruction." So Frank Furr spoke, causing a buzz in the assembly room. Afterward Mr. Arbuckle felt obliged to take Frank Furr aside and castigate him for his loose-tongued ways.

But what was Johan to make of Frank Furr's salvo? What did it mean that Frank Furr was challenging the brand-name hegemony of the Republican Party—what Grant's Tomb with its Republican deceased lying within, or what the Civil War with its Republican president had been? Did he not understand the confusion in Johan's mind in regard to Barry Goldwater and what a Republican now meant?

"Laddie, it will be for you to have many girls in your life, I will allow myself to think," Beatrice, the doctor's Scottish assistant, said, having seen him with Jane Thayer from the window of the doctor's ground-floor office.

"I guess," he said.

"Guess nothing, laddie. Be brave and go out in the world and take what is yours. The doctor will be with you shortly." Every word Beatrice spoke had high energy content and yet brought pain and sadness.

Dr. Pfeffer's office was on the main floor of the house of order across from where Johan lived with his family. In the doctor's waiting room, as in that whole building, you could know a sweet peace as you flipped through back issues of the *National Geographic* and patted the gentle golden retriever and the wandering cats. Dr. Pfeffer had seen enough to speak in a slow and measured way. He was Jewish and he was chosen, having risen above all the quotas set up against innate excellence to graduate from Townsend Harris High School on the border of Harlem in New York City and go on to Cornell University and Columbia University medical school. He had knowledge of the exterminating demons on the European continent and the barbaric cruelty that poisoned minds could inflict. With that understanding was life but the thing in front of him and for the living; he would leave the dead to their own devices.

What Dr. Pfeffer saw he didn't often say, having wisdom to apply as a brake on his tongue. In the long ago, he made house calls on Naomi and Rachel, prompting their wild and laughing insistence on his lewd intent. That Johan's sisters Naomi and Rachel should have thought a man like Dr. Pfeffer would be drawn to them.

Dr. Pfeffer walked a solitary path, with wives discarded along the way. If he needed warmth, he had his pets and Bernice.

"My mother sent me to ask if there is something you can give my brother-in-law to help with his drinking," Johan said, when finally he got to see the doctor. Chuck had been on a long bender and passed out in the lobby that same day.

"Has he tried arsenic?"

"Arsenic?"

But the doctor was now focused on the prescription he wrote out with his fountain pen. Some years before, a car had backed into Luke and injured his knee. Luke asked Dr. Pfeffer how bad the injury was. "How bad does it have to be?" the doctor replied, having his own way of speaking.

"You've got a good pair of eyes and a good set of shoulders. You should join the Air Force," Dr. Pfeffer now said, tearing the prescription free from the pad and handing it to Johan.

Air Force? Johnny Andrews, the Negro boy from down the block, with whom Luke and Johan went to Ebbets Field, had joined but was now dead. His helicopter was shot down in Vietnam. His mother dressed in black and held her silence, a silence loud in Johan's ears when they passed on the street. And his grandfather, with his old and leathery face, had a silence of his own aimed at all ears with the capacity for hearing. My boy is dead and you're alive, their silence said.

Mr. Manootdjian lay in an adjustable bed. A curtain separated him from the other patient in the room, an old woman with a tube in her nose who stared at Johan with eyes of death. His father's face broke apart in a smile. All Johan saw was decay: the sallow skin, the mess of metal the inside of his mouth had become; the clump of hairs protruding from his big ears; the bony breastplate exposed by his half-open hospital gown.

"You are my good boy. You have always been my good boy," he said, after Johan had kissed his unshaven cheek. *Good.* The word so paralyzing.

A nurse arrived to remove the food tray, placing the metal cover back over the serving of chicken and mixed vegetables. "You have to eat more. You're a growing boy," she said, in a commanding voice.

"A what?"

"You need your strength," she replied.

His father had lapsed into a diabetic coma, not for the first time. Tests at the hospital determined he had also suffered a mild heart attack.

"Are you in pain?"

"Not so much, my son. God is good. God is always good."

That word again. Those words. God. Is. Good.

Sean found himself a summer love that carried into the fall. Johnny Joye filled his clothes so well that he caught the eye of all wherever he was seen to strut. He did his business on the street and in penthouse suites and on island retreats as well. He did not go for jeans or Keds but only the finest threads and footwear, including slacks that outlined where he was endowed the most.

New songs were playing—"She Loves You" and "I Want to Hold Your Hand" calling for immediate surrender when Johan heard them blasting on the radio of Lenny Cerone's Bonneville double-parked in front of the luncheonette. Even as the songs were playing did Johnny Joye appear in a short-waisted and collarless jacket of Christmas red, the outfit made more remarkable by the fact that an identical one was being worn by his running buddy, Louie Love, as if they were one half of the Fab Four.

In this time a woman also came into Sean's life, as if he had willed her into being and directed her to his checkout line at PriceRite. Because she was slow to pay, some of the checkers groaned when they saw her on their line. But Sean was accommodating of her dawdling ways. He gave her no gruffness, and took extra care when bagging her groceries instead of dropping big cans of V-8 juice on her eggs or mashing her beefsteak tomatoes under cans of Crisco oil.

"You are a real polite young man. They don't make them like you anymore," she said, commending him in a loud, raspy voice.

Soon he was personally delivering boxes of groceries to Mrs. Louise Dinker, who lived just around the corner from Scully's stoop in a building with a locked front door and an intercom. Over tea and cake, he learned that her husband, a Wall Street stockbroker, had died five years before. Visitors were few, Sean suspected, seeing the dust that had settled on the surfaces.

On his third delivery, Mrs. Dinker said, "My husband was an older man when we met. He had an eye out for younger women. That's why he chose me."

Sean stayed for a while, and as he was leaving, reached into her bag for a twenty. "This is my tip. I'm an American boy. I have to get ahead, right?" he said.

On subsequent visits he continued with his material theme, saying, "What's yours is mine. What's mine is yours. When love comes in the window, you share and share alike." And then he sang for her, turning to his Frank Sinatra repertoire for "Paris in Springtime."

He drained her savings account. He pawned her diamond ring. He badgered her to sell shares of stocks and bonds.

"Now I've got some class. You know what class is, boy?" In this way did he speak to Johan, favoring a word that clanked with non-class in Johan's ears. He bought top-of-the-line luggage for his steady, Johnny Joye, and himself, and together they flew to other American cities—Atlanta and Detroit and Chicago and San

Francisco—in search of sex and bright lights and gambling, en route getting bombed on the booze in those miniature airline bottles. And everywhere they went, Sean showed his class with a fat tip.

A deficiency in class was his one complaint about his steady. "Sometimes he doesn't show me any. We were in Miami a few days ago for an all-weekend party in the best part of the city. There were all these sharply dressed men, right? All these guys with class? And he goes off with the first drooling slobbola to show him any attention. Now that shows me something."

The world continued spinning on its axis that fall, and Sean continued to be born into the life he had willed for himself, and Johan could only hope the thin smile he showed Sean hid the widening chasm between them.

Seeing classmates studying the now familiar-looking SAT booklets in the school hallways, he hurried to the office, fearful that his might fall into someone else's hands. Miss Redding reached down into the box at her feet and read the numbers before handing me the booklet. "Don't tell me you can't do well on these tests," she said, giving him some hope that he had improved.

He found an empty classroom and removed his hand from the numbers slowly, going backward digit by digit. The achievement test numbers were solid if not exceptional and he had come up in the English portion of the aptitude test. The math part was a different story.

"How did you do?" Tom asked, later that day.

"OK," Johan said.

"Just OK?"

"Yes, OK," Johan said, and moved on.

Robin Abel was ecstatic. "I was so ashamed after the PSAT last year. I didn't want to tell anyone how badly I had done. I almost died," she said openly. It was all different now. The stigma has been erased. She had raised her score by 200 points.

In French class, Mlle. Gallimard stopped at each student's desk and asked to see the test results. "Tres bon, Robin," she said. "Merveilleux," she said to Ogden Connifer, blasé about his perfect score. After looking at Johan's booklet, she dropped it on his desk and shook her head. She expected her students to score at least 700 and he had fallen short by fifty points.

The next morning he rode on the bus to school with Tom.

"Since you're so secretive, I asked Miss Redding for your board scores, but she wouldn't tell me. I did happen to see the draft of a letter of recommendation for you on Mr. Sadowski's desk in the locker room. He mentioned your 'tremendous potential.' Unfortunately, he dropped the 'o' in the first word and substituted an 's' for a 't' in the second word. "

Tom and his lacerating tongue. Johan felt pain for Mr. Sadowski. It wasn't right, that kind of mockery. He remained silent and stared out the window. The leaves on the trees in Central Park were beginning to turn.

That afternoon he had an appointment with Mr. Horst-Lehman, who also served as the college guidance counselor. Miss Redding placed a manila folder on his desk. Mr. Horst-Lehman spent a minute reviewing the file through his bifocals before tossing the folder onto a pile on his cluttered desk.

"Have you given any thought to where you might like to go to college?" He pressed his hands together and rested his nose against his fingertips. Johan mentioned Hamilton College, in upstate New York, a school small enough that maybe he could make the basketball team.

"An applicant with your class ranking might stand a chance, but your SAT scores on the aptitude part are insufficient. Maybe you would consider these other schools." He mentioned Muhlenberg, Gettysburg, Franklin and Marshall, and Colby. "We have to know our place in life. That is essential if we are to be happy in this world."

Johan nodded and said thank you.

"Do you remember the Glendocia boy, who played the trumpet so beautifully at the tabernacle?" Mrs. Manootdjian asked.

"I do," Johan said, picturing a fat-lipped boy with a crown of hair as golden as the trumpet on which he played solos for the congregation. He remembered too the velvet-lined case in which he kept his instrument and various mouthpieces.

"He is now at a Bible college in Oklahoma. It would do my heart so much good to see you do the same."

Johan tried to imagine the school's basketball team. Did they kneel and pray during timeouts? Would Oral Roberts be watching from the stands? They didn't talk about tuition. It wasn't the family way to talk about money, although he knew the tuition for him at Claremont was less than it was for others. And college would cost so much more. A feeling of shame came over him. His mother looked so old. He had no right to ask her for anything. And maybe he didn't have to ask his mother for anything. Maybe he could begin to access the money on his own.

It had come to Johan's understanding, though he had no proof, that his mother, on the books, was receiving a paltry wage for her services as the building's renting agent. And since his father surely earned an equally paltry wage as a cashier, additional sums had to come from elsewhere. That elsewhere could only be the rent revenue. If Simon Weill, the building owner, was a crook taking more than his fair share of the monthly income he was entitled to by terms of the lease, then quite likely Johan's mother was finding justification in extracting additional funds for her family. And so, by his own faulty logic, why couldn't Johan do the same?

As a child, he had a number of times entered Auntie Eve's apartment, having borrowed the key to it from his mother's keyring.

Now he came, in the stillness of a Sunday morning, with his own key to her apartment, having found a way to slip the key from his mother's ring and make a duplicate at the hardware store before returning it undetected to the ring. And once again, as he had when a child, he found himself trailing after Auntie Eve down to the subway entrance at One Hundred Tenth Street to fully ensure she was church-bound before turning back.

As he remembered, envelopes stuffed with bills could be found on the floor of her closet between her pairs of shoes. He took a twenty from each of the three envelopes, while his ears remained pricked for footsteps in the lobby. The orange rolls of quarters and green rolls of dimes he left alone. The portrait of a bearded Jesus with shoulder-length brown hair still hung on the wall. Wherever Johan positioned himself, the eyes of Jesus seemed to find him.

Chapter 17

That morning, standing over the bathroom sink, he probed a molar with the tip of his tongue. Dr. Draver, the neighborhood dentist his mother had recommended, had begun a root canal the week before. He brushed gingerly around the lower right side of his mouth. Rinsing caused no pain. Maybe what Dr. Draver said was true and the tooth would hold for the weekend.

Dr. Draver said he had an irrational fear of the drill. She joked that he would break the armrests with the grip he placed on them. "You are too young to be having so much trouble with your teeth and will have to learn to trust," she said when he last visited, with some crossness in her voice. But trust what, the drill not to find the nerve that would electrify his body with pain a thousand times worse than biting down on tinfoil?

Mrs. Manootdjian was at the breakfast table, pouring heavy cream into her coffee. With her free hand she whisked away a roach scurrying over the tablecloth.

"Is your friend Tom from a Christian family?" They were alone. Mr. Manootdjian was out of the hospital and still sleeping.

"I don't know."

"They must be wealthy to have a house in the country," Momma says.

"I guess."

"And what is it Tom's father does?"

"He is a university professor."

"Is that right? And what does he teach?"

"History, I think."

"He must have a fine mind."

"Yes."

"And your friend's mother. Is she educated, too?"

"She is studying for a doctorate."

"A doctorate. What is that?"

"Some kind of degree you get after you have gone to college."

"Then she must have a very fine mind, too."

"Yes. I guess," he said, buttering his toast and trying to chew on one side of his mouth.

"Your father has a fine mind. You know that, do you not?"

"Yes."

"He can speak five languages."

"Yes."

He kissed his mother and said goodbye and headed down to Riverside Drive. Why was he doing this? Why not just spare himself a weekend of agony? So he asked himself as he approached Tom's building. Just keep it safe, the way it should be. Crossing lines was dangerous, like the line he crossed the summer following sixth grade, drawn in spite of himself toward Tom on the basketball court in the park. Now, as then, his feet were moving him along as if against his own will.

"Who are you here to see?" the doorman asked.

"I'm going to see Tom Smits."

His family formed a welcoming committee in the foyer of their apartment—Tom's mother, tall and lanky and in her early forties, radiating a formidably observant power; his pudgy and freckled younger sister Beth; and his father, whose red hair had mostly vanished from his shiny, well-shaped head.

Their smiles seemed to convey expectation as well as welcome, as if they were waiting for him to say something witty or clever. When he could only muster a shy "Hello," they dispersed. He had failed his first test.

Seeing the fine Oriental rug laid down on the sparkling parquet floor and the floor-to-ceiling walnut shelves lined with books served as a reminder of the unbridgeable chasm between Tom and him.

"My father doesn't live with us anymore. He moved out six months ago. He has his own apartment downtown," Tom said, out of earshot of his father, who walked ahead of them toward the car. The news of Tom's parents' separation was jarring, not at all the picture Johan held in his mind of Tom's family. And though it was shameful to acknowledge, a small measure of comfort came to him to learn that things weren't perfect in his friend's world.

As the roomy station wagon speeded up the West Side Highway, Johan noted the neighborhood landmarks—the railroad tunnel that ran under Riverside Park, the single spire of Riverside Church, Grant's Tomb, the pier at One Hundred Twenty-fifth Street, where old men dropped their fishing lines in the polluted water. How often, as a child, he would stare at the cars rampaging along, and now he was himself in such a car, its power ushering him out of a very small world into something larger and grander. Some door was opening, and it would be exhilarating if not for his fear of Mr. Smits, who spoke in a peeved voice.

"Half the faculty signs a protest against our military involvement in Vietnam. A flock of bleating sheep. Not a single one of them questions what it might mean for the rest of Southeast Asia if we don't fight back." Mr. Smits banged the wheel with his hand for emphasis. Mr. Smits's anger was frightening, even if it wasn't yet directed at Johan.

"Sure, Dad. The next thing you know the Vietcong will be invading Australia with their sampans," Tom said, and grinned at Johan as if to say, What am I supposed to do about my foolish father?

"You can believe that is so," Mr. Smits hissed, as Johan himself would have said, had he been able to find his voice. Weren't the Communists relentless? Had Tom forgotten the scenes on TV of the Hungarian Revolution, people being crushed on the streets by Soviet tanks for fighting for their freedom? The Communists had some kind of mental as well as physical strength that the West lacked. They had the power of their terrifying inevitability.

They stopped at a restaurant in a small town on a twisting rural road. The leaves on the trees were turning—scarlet red and bright yellow and dull brown combinations of color on the oaks and maples and elms. The smell of burning wood filled the brisk autumn air as their feet crunched the gravel in the parking lot.

"What a hell of an intellectual conversation this is," Mr. Smits roared, hearing Tom and Johan talk about the Knicks. "When I was your age, I was discussing Dostoyevsky and Tolstoy, not sports. I had read all their novels, could easily identify Beethoven's nine symphonies, and knew every Impressionist painting worth committing to memory and those that weren't." He raised his glass, signaling a refill of his bourbon and water to the waiter.

"All right, Dad." Tom's tone was appeasing, sensing it was time to reel in his sarcasm.

They arrived in the last light of day. The lawn was carpeted with fallen leaves and a massive maple tree stood in front of the white clapboard house and its screened-in porch. Johan settled into an old rocker by the hearth, transfixed by the fire that Tom had made, and left only when Mr. Smits entered, as if they weren't meant to be alone in the same room together.

He had been given a small room at the top of the stairs, and as he unpacked his bag, he heard Mr. Smits down below say, "Tom, you and your friend get ready. We're going to the Baxters in about twenty minutes. There'll be a poker game going tonight."

Johan sat on the edge of the single bed. "Your friend"—it sounded unfriendly. An hour before the house had seemed strange and new. Now it was familiar and safe. He wanted to stay behind the closed door and just lie on the bed with the pretty afghan over him. No more new things. No more.

A dull pain in the tooth began on the short drive to the party. Johan stayed back in the kitchen, with a view of a large round oak table in the living room where the men had gathered for their poker game. He kept his hand against his cheek, as if pressure alone could bring relief. From another world he listened now to the banter, the laughter growing louder as the level in the liquor bottles fell. Such easy intimacy these men and their intelligent wives had. Like his father, the men were professors, Tom explained, all of them on the faculty of the nearby college.

As the pain grew, so did his fury at Dr. Draver. How could the stupid woman let him go off to the country like that for the weekend? He couldn't wait to show her the proof of her incompetence.

"Did you see Bentley's wife?" Mr. Smits said to Tom, on the drive back.

"What about her?" Tom asked, sitting next to his father in the front seat.

"You get in bed with her and you'd better expect a ride."

Mr. Smits spoke as if the experience of riding Mrs. Bentley had been his.

"Dad," Tom said.

"Dad what?"

"I'm not exactly interested in Mrs. Bentley."

'Well, maybe your silent friend back there is."

The smell of alcohol filled the enclosed space.

"Dad, could you slow down just a little?" Mr. Smits had begun to navigate the curves at a terrifying speed.

"It's not my way to slow down," Mr. Smits said.

That night Johan lay under the blankets with crushed aspirin between the gum and the tooth and fell asleep to the sound of an owl breaking the silence with irregular hooting.

In the morning he was made ravenously hungry by the smell of bacon frying downstairs in the kitchen. But to eat meant running the risk of awakening the beast. He dressed and some minutes later found Tom flipping through a copy of *Playboy*. His father had gone off with the car into town, Tom said. Maybe he had gone to get a ride on Bentley's wife, Johan thought.

As if Tom had read his mind, he said, "My father uses this place as a real fucking pad. He brings his prettier students up here."

"How do you know?" With longing he watched Tom demolish his plateful of eggs and bacon.

"Little items, like a pair of panties, under the sofa. Definitely not my mother's, I'll tell you that."

It was painful to think that Mr. Smits had left Tom's mother because she was no longer young and pretty. His own parents would never divorce. Pastor Odachenko called it a sin. "What God has joined, let no man rend asunder," he would thunder.

"Does your father know that you know?"

"I don't say anything. He has a temper, as you have seen. He once chased a motorist who had cut him off for twenty blocks through city traffic, ran him off the road, and got into a fistfight."

"Did he win?"

"He clobbered the poor guy."

They walked to the top of a hill and a sweeping view of cultivated farmland dotted with red barns and white houses. In the crook of his arm Tom carried a rifle. "My father goes deer hunting with it," he said, slipping a cartridge into the chamber.

They stopped to rest at a low fieldstone wall. "You see that gray squirrel? There has been a war going on here for some time between the red squirrels and the gray squirrels. They can't coexist. And the red squirrels are winning. Their strategy is simple. They bite off the balls of the gray squirrels so they can't reproduce."

Johan had only ever seen gray squirrels in the city parks and thought it just as well that he didn't have to witness the red ones practicing their ruthless violence on the gray ones.

"You know, my sister and I have genius IQs. My father got this psychologist friend to test us when we were kids. He was the chubby guy wearing horn-rimmed glasses at the party last night. Probably he gave us a few breaks on the test, but we're smart all right." Tom squinted through the scope at a crow flying over a silo.

Tom and his fractured family belonged to this New England tableau of picturesque farms and rolling hills and faculty parties, like the dominant red squirrels.

The drive home took them through quaint towns with tree-lined main streets and houses with white picket fences and churches with steeples. Mr. Smits had been mercifully absent for much of the weekend, but now, the sustained proximity in the enclosed space of the station wagon seemed to ensure that Johan's luck had run out and he would have to engage with Tom's father. When their eyes met fleetingly in the rearview mirror, it seemed to confirm his fear.

"We'll have dinner now. Maybe afterward this damn traffic will have thinned," Mr. Smits said, referring to the stalled traffic on the interstate, the endless succession of taillights glowing red in the darkness that had fallen.

At another roadside restaurant, Johan buried his face in the oversize menu, seeking refuge from Mr. Smits, who sat opposite him in the tight booth. The waitress was slow to take their orders, and the food didn't fly out of the kitchen once she did.

"Tom tells me that you have had a toothache on and off all week-end. Are you able to eat?" There was asperity in Mr. Smits's tone. His face was flushed as it always seemed to be. He ordered a scotch and soda and then another.

"I'm kind of hungry."

"Your last name is Armenian. Do you eat Near Eastern food at home?"

Near Eastern. That means closer than Middle Eastern? That means Turkey and Iran and what is now Soviet Armenia? "No. Not really." He was not prepared to tell Mr. Smits that his father didn't speak about things Armenian, at least to him, and that the only trapping of Armenian culture was the large rug his father had once hung on the bedroom wall. An oppressive sight, but it had merci-fully fallen down when the supports proved inadequate.

"My mother cooks chicken and leg of lamb and pot roast." Was it right to mention those foods? Were they acceptable? Would Mr. Smits laugh?

"Tom tells me you're rather secretive about where you live. Why is that? Don't you suppose my son should be able to know where one of his friends lives? After all, you know where he lives. It's the principle of reciprocity, wouldn't you say?"

"Oh come on, Dad." Tom sounded embarrassed.

"What's the matter? He seems able to speak. Why shouldn't I ask him a few questions?" Mr. Smits said, while keeping his eyes on Johan. "So where do you live? Tell us."

"Between Broadway and Riverside Drive on One Hundred Twelfth Street."

"Is there a street address, or is mail just sent to 'Between Broadway and One Hundred Twelfth Street?'"

"Sure. The street address is 607 West One Hundred Twelfth Street."

"Well now, that wasn't so painful, was it?" Mr. Smits popped a piece of buttered bread into his mouth. "And what is your father's occupation?"

"He's an accountant," Johan heard himself say.

"What's the name of his firm?"

"Mankin," Johan blurted.

"Mankin. Mankin," Mr. Smits repeated, trying the name out. "Sounds like some kind of hybrid name. Your father must be a partner in the firm."

"Oh yes." Johan pictured his father sitting in his corner in the dining room reading literature from the evangelist Oral Roberts and devouring stinky cheese from the stash he kept in that crumpled brown bag in the refrigerator. He bit into the hamburger, too famished to resist. Soon the ache returned, and became his steady companion for the rest of the trip.

"Where did you say you live?" They had reached One Hundred Twenty-fifth Street and Broadway. Above, a train rattled along the tracks of the el.

"One Hundred Twelfth Street, but you can leave me at One Hundred Sixteenth Street and Broadway."

With the car stopped at the light, Mr. Smits turned, his face ablaze. "Why would you want me to do that?"

"My dentist is on that street. She lives where she has her office and I'm going to see her."

Mr. Smits returned his eyes to the road and drove on. "Of course. How perfectly clear. How silly of me to even ask. Your friend will be seeing his dentist at 9 p.m. on a Sunday night," Mr. Smits said, addressing himself to Tom.

Johan would flee, but his bag was in the trunk.

At One Hundred Sixteenth Street Mr. Smits pulled to the curb. Tom got out with him and opened the trunk.

"My father, the Grand Inquisitor." Tom punched Johan playfully on the arm and gave a helpless shrug.

Johan toted his bag down the hill away from Broadway as they drove off, then paused in a doorway, fearful that Mr. Smits might double back and catch him in his lie. He would live with the pain another night and call Dr. Draver in the morning. Once again his mind flooded with all the accusation he would hurl at the woman for sending him out into the world in such painful disrepair.

Chapter 18

"Well, this is it. Welcome to the Thayer residence," Jane said, with a sweep of her arm ushering Johan into her family's apartment. A musty smell. Cramped rooms. Worn and mismatched furniture. A faded rug on the living room floor and the unsightly bulge of the extension cords running under it. A sofa and armchair raked by the cat's claws. Dusty surfaces. Dirty windows.

A door to one of the bedrooms opened and her mother appeared, one hand to her wrinkled neck and the other around a glass. "Hi there, Handsome. You don't mind if I call you Handsome, do you? Jane never does. Ha ha. Do take off your coat and make yourself comfortable. It's not a Fifth Avenue duplex, but it will have to do, be it ever so humble and all that. Would you care for some cookies and coffee or tea?" Her black hair was streaked with gray and crow's feet showed in the corners of her big green eyes.

"No. I am fine. Thank you." Johan stood dazed by her torrent of self-conscious words.

"Whoops. My competition is giving me the evil eye. Don't do anything I wouldn't do, sweethearts," she said, and withdrew. Jane tapped the side of her head with an index finger and shrugged, as if to say, "What can I do?"

On and off he was still trying to keep Jane out of his room so she could be good as new, and so she had invited him to her apartment for the first time. They weren't on the sofa for a minute before he had his hand up her skirt and she was unzipping his fly, both of them trying to muffle their groans of pleasure. Still, as he hadn't entered her, he could leave believing that he was not using her up and the future was still theirs to be in together.

As Christmas approached, it was working. Redemption was under-way. Jane had gone ice skating at Wollman Rink, in Central Park, with Cathy Cathleen and Mary Marie and some of the guys from Scully's stoop, while Johan stayed back in his room and tried to study. She was being received by those untarnished Catholic girls who faithfully attended Sunday mass. It was as if she had been dropped into the big washing machine down in the basement and deep sudsing action was removing the stain of her involvement with him.

The knock at his door came and there she was, in her knitted cap, her cheeks red from the cold and her white skates slung over her shoulder. What more proof did he need that she had some re-lationship to the world and had not been banished to drown in her own tears? What more proof did he need that they were ready for the room again and the privacy it afforded to do as they needed to do?

He awoke that forbiddingly cold January morning to an inner voice telling him not to go where he did not belong, that there was no basis, other than fantasy, for believing he could gain admission to such a school. Mr. Horst-Lehman was right—his test scores left him unqualified; overall, his credentials were as light and flimsy as the body and mind he lived in.

Outside the darkness was still holding as in the mirror of the public bathroom down the hall from his room he inspected himself in the Harris tweed jacket his mother bought for him. How great it looked in the window of Albee's, down the block. But on him the jacket looked boxy, his reedy neck shooting out of it.

He left the building wearing a beige trench coat and soon the soles of his oxblood-colored penny loafers were slapping against the floor of the concourse in Grand Central Station as he hurried to the gate to catch the 6:55 to Hartford.

As the train left the platform and eased into the tunnel, he thought of the application he had submitted. Under "Interests," he had put reading and sports, listing neither hobbies nor extracurricular activities other than basketball. No library committee, no yearbook committee, no assembly position. Being on a committee meant other kids; it meant staying after school instead of meeting Jane; it meant the dullness of an interminable afternoon when the street was calling. His mood brightened as the train emerged into the morning light and gained speed. Well, the words would come. He would find something to tell the interviewer.

Some hours later he stood on the quadrangle enclosed by gothic, vine-covered buildings. Tall trees bare of leaves rose above them. On the crisscrossing paths an occasional student appeared, the college having emptied out during the winter break. Inside the modern administration building, the corridors lined with bulletin boards, a young secretary with her blond hair in a bow interrupted her efficient typing to check the appointments calendar and asked him to take a seat.

A man in a tailored suit, his Chesterfield coat folded neatly in the chair to his left, sat smoking a cigarette. He looked like the handsome actor William Holden. The shrewdly appraising stare of the older man caused Johan to quickly look away. When the door opened and a tall kid in jacket and tie came out, the man rose and put his arm around him. The admissions officer followed. "You and Jeff look around some more if you'd like, Mr. Gifford." The father waved as he and his son moved toward the door.

The secretary handed the admissions officer a folder.

"Frank Graves," the officer said, squeezing Johan's hand with his powerful grip, and ushered him into his office. "Tell me a little about yourself," Mr. Graves said, after seating himself at his desk with the folder open in front of him.

"I'm not sure what you mean."

"Well, what are your interests? What kinds of things do you like to do?"

"I like to read. I like to play basketball, too." What little confidence he had brought to the interview was now gone. He could think of no way to expand on the simple statement he had made. And Mr. Graves's steel-gray eyes were no help. Though the room was chilly, he could feel sweat beginning to dampen his shirt.

Mr. Graves pressed on. "I see that you changed schools in your junior year, and then returned. Can you explain?"

"Well, I needed to get away. I just couldn't stay there anymore." When Mr. Graves allowed the silence to continue, Johan added, "I was having some difficulty."

"Difficulty?"

"Some difficulty with myself. That's all it was. Somebody was doing better in basketball than me and my girlfriend, I didn't know if we would ever be like new again, and homework was piling up."

Mr. Graves leaned back in his chair. "This is an extremely selective college. We have a large number of strong applicants, even more than usual this year."

"Yes, I understand."

"Thank you for coming," Mr. Graves said, getting up from his desk and seeing Johan to the door.

Johan talked to himself on the way to the train station, seeking to block the waves of humiliation that engulfed him. New York City felt far away, but soon he would be back home.

The basketball season winding down, the news came that it had been arranged for Claremont to play a preliminary game against Earl Academy at Madison Square Garden on a Saturday night. Fans settling into their seats would get to see two very average private school teams go at it prior to the Knicks game against the Philadelphia Warriors. If others saw the game as cause for elation, Johan was simply embarrassed by the thought of such exposure, imagining Richie Guerin and Willie Naulls and the other Knick players standing in the runway in their white warmup suits with orange and blue trim cracking jokes about the skinny white boys running up and down their court.

A person knew when he was deserving and when he wasn't deserving. A person knew when he was fit for exposure and when he wasn't. As the event drew closer, he told neither Jane nor his family. He did not need to grow his shame any bigger than it was. What he needed was for them to stay away from him and him from them so the night would not be worse than it had to be. Claremont faculty and parents as well as students might show up in force and put their laughing thing on his family and Jane should he dare to show anything more of himself than his semi-nakedness in his basketball uniform. Because his family wasn't good enough. Because Jane Thayer wasn't good enough. Because he was not good enough. Was it his fault if he knew that, knew that, knew that?

The evening, when it came, was a blur. One minute he was meeting up with Mr. Sadowski and his teammates under the marquee and the next he was staring up at the empty rows of seats, with here and there a few scattered pockets of relatives and friends of the Claremont and Earl Academy players in the stands. And then the buzzer rang and the game was over and he was being carried off the shiny hardwood court, having banked in the winning shot.

Outside the locker room, schoolmates he had never spoken a word with offered congratulations, as did faculty members. And there was Robin Abel, tall and thin and pretty, her dark eyes shining, saying to him, "I'm having a party tonight. I'd like so much for you to come." And handing him a note. A girl like that. It didn't make sense.

He left without showering, needing distance from the life opening to him for that one bright moment, and now that moment was gone, he was alone on Eighth Avenue, the cool breeze quickly drying the sweat on his face and body. Cars and cabs tore along the avenue looking for someone to hurt and warm air rich with the smell of the underground rose through the subway grates. When he was a safe distance from the scene, and there was little likelihood of laugh hounds following behind, he pulled the scrap of paper from his pocket and stared at the neat rightward-sloping script: Robin Abel, 840 Park Avenue, penthouse A, BU 9-8765. Imagine that. Even her phone number. Along the avenue old men sat on bar stools drinking and smoking and watching boxing ring warfare on TV. His life with Jane felt as dismal and small as theirs.

At Fifty-ninth Street and Columbus Circle, his feet turned east along Central Park South to Fifth Avenue and a line of tourist carriages and the Plaza Hotel, all lit up, and Grand Army Plaza, with its enormous fountain. Soon he went north on Park Avenue on the cold, sparkling night. Seeking to match the number on Robin's scrap of paper with those on the awnings of the doorman buildings that towered over the boulevard, he dared himself to maintain a brisk pace though feeling as if he was fast approaching the edge of a cliff. And now the edge of the cliff appeared, a red awning with the number clearly visible in white. The avenue was quiet, the buildings holding their sense of order, while down below he felt the rumble of a passenger train moving slowly through the tunnel. With each change from red to green of the traffic light he stepped forward, resolved to penetrate the mystery of Claremont social life, only to return to the safety of the curb.

A cab pulled up in front of the building. Robin Abel stepped out of a Checker cab with another girl he did not recognize and two young men in jackets and ties. Another arrived carrying John Edel and Bert Bach, the appearance of these familiar Claremont faces producing a shiver of fear and dispelling the illusion that he could be on the same social footing with her or any of them. She had seen him in his moment of stardom, just that blip of time, which led her to believe he might be worthwhile knowing. She had seen something he couldn't hope to sustain. He moved back from the intersection to avoid detection and headed for the subway and the below-ground experience that would take him home.

With warmer weather the park called to them. They went to it and leaned against the iron fence that served as a barrier to Dead Man's Hill. The trees were now in bloom. Almost three years had passed since they would eagerly climb over the fence for a morning of pleasure. She had grown heavier. Her hips bulged in the jeans that had fit her so well the year before and she had developed the habit of running her hands down her sides, as if to shave off the unwanted pounds. Her added weight was as nothing to the weight of their involvement on him.

"Johan, I was thinking. My cousin Jennie says her family in Mexico City would like to have me down for a couple of weeks this summer. My father said it would be okay with him. Her father's an executive with some big American company. They're pretty rich, and I used to have this feeling that they looked down on us, but maybe I'm wrong. It might be kind of nice to see Jennie."

With every word that she spoke, the weight on him lifted.

"When would you go?" he asked, seeking to mask his relief with an anxious expression of concern.

"Maybe it's the wrong thing to do."

"Not at all. Just remember to come back."

"Of course I'll come back."

There were people who wanted her, people with status. No more dependence on Mary Marie and Cathy Cathleen, who shunned her one day and accepted her the next.

Horseback riding. Tennis. Swimming. Parties. Jennie was completing her first year of college at the University of Texas and would be returning home to Mexico City. She was beautiful and knew everyone, Jane said. It wasn't long before Jane's trip was as worrisome to him as the prospect of their going on in the same way had been.

It happened on the long side street between Amsterdam Avenue and Broadway as he was heading home. There, in his mind's eye, he saw his mother with a detachment and clarity he had not known before. He could leave her. It was nothing more than that. He stopped and leaned against a parked car, pondering this newfound freedom.

❧

"Johan, come on. You're not going to China. You'll be back tonight," Jane said, pulling away after he tried to give her a long kiss.

"You're right," he said, embarrassed, standing in the depot reeking of gas fumes. The uniformed driver at the door of the bus snatched his ticket, as if to register his disapproval of Johan's excess. "I'll phone you when I get there," he turned and said, but Jane had already gone.

Fear found him when the traffic stalled in the Lincoln Tunnel. Suppose the wall cracked and the tunnel flooded? Suppose. Soon the bus was in the ruins of New Jersey—marshland and, in the distance, refineries with clouds of smoke streaming from the stacks. Across the aisle an old man with watery eyes laughed silently, his chest heaving. Had he too seen the inappropriate kiss? *I want to marry you someday.*

Philadelphia was the Liberty Bell and Independence Hall. But really, it was, as Johan turned a corner, the startling sight of Connie Mack Stadium, with its tower and cupola rising casually above the cracked, weedy sidewalk and rundown residential buildings. The perfect symmetry of the arches and columns, the neglected grandeur, the sheer promise of a field of green beyond its magnetic perimeter, brought Johan to a complete stop, as if witnessing some glimmer of the eternal, an ache surfacing for something on the nebulous fringes of memory, some time in the faraway past where everything was in harmony—a summer day packed with people and love and excitement and security.

The groundskeepers lay down white chalk lines and turned the infield a dark brown with streams of water from their hoses. Advertisements for Schmidt's beer, Gillette razors, and Alpo dog food plastered the outfield walls. The Dodgers wore their road uniforms of gray and powder blue, with those fetching red numerals below the slanted name of their new city, Los Angeles. The hometown Phillies wore white pinstripes with burgundy trim.

Don Drysdale came out of his windup with a sidearm delivery, causing some batters to bail out of the box, and now he was off the mound jawing at one who did not appreciate the close shave number 53 had given him. Jim Bunning, the Phillies right-handed hurler, wore number 14, a low number usually reserved for an everyday player. Bunning, stringy and equally mean, matched Drysdale, one goose egg after another going up on the outfield scoreboard.

The Phillies had more than sliver lips Bunning. They had big Dick Stuart. They had little Tony Taylor. They had left-handed power hitter Wes Covington with his slouching stance and jolting Johnny Callison with the big number 6 on his back. And they had Frank Thomas and always dangerous Dick Allen with his moonshot-launching power.

The Dodgers still had fleet Willie Davis. They still had Brooklyn Tommy Davis. They had Ron Fairly and Wes Parker (as smooth as his name) and Maury Wills, with all the infield agitation he could cause when he danced off first base. And behind the plate they had Johnny Roseboro, who knew how to direct pitches to his carefully positioned mitt.

The pull of seeing the Dodgers in a strange city had been strong, overwhelming. Having only gotten to see them that summer day in 1957 at Ebbets Field before they were gone, gone, to Los Angeles, and now here he was with a chance to see them again, in a historic ballpark in a city not his own. But the fifth inning came, and his pockets were empty. Hunger pangs came as he watched those around him devour ballpark franks and the windbreaker he had zipped to the top proved no match for the dropping temperature.

Into extra innings the game went, with neither team having crossed home plate. The fear grew of being hungry and trapped overnight in what he saw now as a strange city.

Through the dark streets he fled to the bus station, where he made a collect call.

"Are you with that man again? Is that it?" Mrs. Manootdjian demanded, remembering Boston.

"I'm with me, Momma. With me. I'll be home. You'll see."

"Do not give me these sleepless nights, son. Do not do that."

On the bus a powerfully built Negro man took a seat across the aisle. As the bus left the terminal, the man turned to him, and said, in a matter-of-fact voice, "Are you spitting at me, man? Is that what you're doing?"

"No."

"Don't be lying to me now so I have to hurt you."

"No. I'm not lying."

"I'll be having my eye on you. Because I can't have you disrespecting me."

The man turned off his overhead light, He was now a pulsing presence in the dark."Oh, Jesus," Johan thought, holding his sides and feeling the vibration of the man all through his being.

Chapter 19

Miss Weston, the music teacher for the upper school, sat alone in the auditorium on the main floor as Johan emerged from the stairwell. She was a familiar face, though he had never spoken with her. She held a negligible place in his mind and surely he did too in hers, as he had no ability to blend his voice with others in chorus or to carry a tune or truly understand an octave or musical notation.

Without introduction of explanation, she said, "I want you to read this passage," trailing her finger down the length of one page and half of the next of a slender paperback. He began reading the English dialect in an even voice, without feeling or real comprehension or curiosity about the content or where this might be leading. His only desire was to get away, and Miss Weston obliged with a perfunctory thank-you, after which he disappeared back into the stairwell.

And yet, the next day, Bert Bach stuck out his hand. "Congratulations," he said, and so Johan shook the small, soft hand of a boy he had been unable to speak to in the course of four years.

"For what?" Johan managed to say, over the vast differences that separated them. Bert had given up the fuzz ball hair cut, but his popularity with the girls would remain if he had no hair, as they were drawn to his mind.

"You've got the part of Bill Walker," he said, smiling up at Johan.

"That's nice," Johan said.

"You do want the part, don't you?" Bert, appearing puzzled, felt obliged to ask.

For some reason, he had thought Bert expected him to be nonchalant. Wasn't that the way intelligent people were? "Oh sure. It's great," he said, hoping with these more animated words to convey the enthusiasm Bert was evidently expecting. He was ready to give Bert whatever he wanted, whatever he needed, paralyzed as he was by the fear that Bert was ready to unleash some mocking laughter. Yet Bert continued to stare at him, as if something remained puzzling about their interaction. Assessing, or trying to assess. That is what chunky Bert Bach's intelligent face showed he was doing before he moved on.

Johan remained in the dark, but not for long. A buzz was going on in the classroom about the senior play, *Major Barbara,* written by George Bernard Shaw. That buzz. The ferocity of it. The *extent* of it. Everyone seeming to have an understanding of what was going on and grabbing for every morsel of what was going on like ravenous sharks, devouring everything the school had to offer and in ongoing dialogue about what that thing was.

Some days later the doorman directed Johan to the eighth floor, where a maid answered the door and later served soft drinks and fruit juice and small sandwiches during breaks in rehearsal.

"Where does it go?" Johan asked, staring at the spiral staircase.

"What do you mean, 'Where does it go?' Haven't you ever seen a duplex apartment?" Freddy Snyder still had no use for modulation.

"Sure. I guess I just forgot."

Freddy smelled vulnerability. It seemed in his interest to do so. "Where were you today, Manootdj? How come you weren't at school?"

"I was home fixing my bike," Johan said, somehow thinking that would sound more interesting than saying he wasn't feeling all that well.

"People, did you hear what Manootdj just said? He didn't come to school because he had to stay home and fix his bike."

"Way to go, Manootdj. What's it going to be tomorrow, a leaky toilet?" Bert Bach laughed.

"Or the dishwasher," Diane Coleman said. She wore a man's shirt of luminous white outside the tight jeans that sheathed her long legs. No one would ever see her trying to shave weight off her body.

This much Johan understood about the character he would play. Bill Walker was a working-class brawler who specialized in what for. Bill came to the Salvation Army looking for his girlfriend, who had done him wrong by running off. Enraged to learn that she had become a religious convert, he grabbed a Salvation Army woman by the hair and gave her a little of his what for and then dished out some more for an older woman, while threatening others with the same. But when he came face to face with Major Barbara, the Salvation Army leader, she bothered his conscience for striking the women.

Major Barbara: It's not me that's getting at you, Bill.
Bill Walker: Oo else is it?
Major Barbara: Somebody that doesn't intend you to smash
     women's faces, I suppose. Somebody or something that
     wants to make a man of you.
Bill Walker: Mike a menn o me! Ain't Aw a menn? Eh? Oo
     sez Aw'm not a menn?
Major Barbara: There's a man in you somewhere, I suppose.
     But why did he let you hit poor little Jenny Hill? That
     wasn't very manly of him, was it?

These and other lines he spoke, and Diane Coleman, her beautiful face lightly dusted with freckles close to his, responded with words of redemption, her orthodontically straightened teeth as white as her shirt. Transfixed, he listened.

Major Barbara: It's your soul that's hurting you, Bill, and
     not me. We've been through it all ourselves. Come with
     us, Bill. To brave manhood on earth and eternal glory in
     Heaven. Come.

As his hand came near the faces of poor Jenny Hill, the girl, and the older woman, Rummy Mitchens, the vise of self-consciousness tightened and he pulled back. Did Miss Weston know about his violence? Had she been there to bear witness on the Columbia campus, or elsewhere, when he slapped Jane Thayer? Did they all know? Was this why he had been chosen?

Miss Weston's coaxing words flew like darts from her gap-toothed mouth. "I know you have it in you. I know you can do it," she said, with a smile and a wink.

To Riverside Church they moved for full dress rehearsals, the stage and footlights and heavy curtain and rows of seats offering tangible proof that something would come of all those evenings in the homes of Diane Coleman and Bert Bach and Freddy Snyder.

"You'll finish my milk, won't you, Johan? You're a growing boy," Diane said to him one afternoon, during a break in the church cafeteria, and slid the half-pint across the table. "The straw's been in my mouth, but you won't mind that, will you?" She winked as he sipped from the straw. She was his age, and yet she was older.

Following the rehearsal he headed back to the neighborhood. From the sundial on the mall of the Columbia campus he watched as Jane, barefoot on the south lawn, chased after a Frisbee tossed by Rob Koley, lunging for the disc as it curved away from her and rolled to a stop in the grass. Feebly she tossed it back, the disc falling far short of where Rob and Scully and Kevin and Luis and Jimmy Riley were gathered. The thought occurred to him to leave, but his feet took him forward, and as he drew near, they stopped their activity and stared.

"Here he is, Jane. Here's your man," Scully said, putting an arm around her.

"Yeah," she said, "my man," the sardonic tone bringing a wall of laughter.

⚘

It was not right to deny his mother on a city street or kill her with neglect at any place or time. He recognized the fear he was captive to of the laughing things out there. It was for him to emerge from the bondage of shame, if only a little at a time. And so he did in inviting his mother. But when Hannah and Vera accompanied her to the theater, some challenge presented itself to his mind that they should be sitting in the audience as well. He could not think of them liking or supporting him. The wall must not come down. It was dangerous to see beyond the darkness to the light when he was invested in injuries and slights that kept him apart.

And Jane. Jane had come too, to the very church where she attended its Friday night social. There she was, sitting with Mrs. Manootdjian and his two sisters.

But his father had not come. He was not a consideration, as he was lost to the men of the Christ Jesus and the garage church in Astoria. And his brother Luke had not come. He too was not a consideration, as he had his own lostness going on. And his sisters Naomi and Rachel had not come, for they were as they were. But let it also be said that Johan had not invited any of them, as shame had not up and left him. It still had visitation rights, and more, and saw to it that, ashamed of them as he was, he was doubly ashamed of himself.

For those of the clan who gathered, were they wearing "Manootdjian" name tags to declare their association with him so Freddy Snyder could go to town on them? But what did it matter? Were the footlights not blinding Johan to the beyond and keeping him safe from any affiliation with kin or friend that might work against his autonomy?

In oversize pants and a loose-fitting shirt, and fueled by hysteria, he shouted out his lines, smacked this one and that one, and for this received a burst of applause. "You stole the show," someone said. They had been only too happy to give him something, like those who called attention to his basketball ability because nothing noteworthy could be attributed to his mind. Thoughts like those went with him into the night.

Ogden Connifer was hosting a party at his family's apartment on Riverside Drive.

"You can't come. It's only for cast members. That's what Ogden Connifer told us," Johan said to Jane, leaning on his understanding of what Ogden Connifer said while not entirely sure that Ogden Connifer said anything of the kind.

"Ogden Connifer? What kind of name is that?" Jane jeered.

"I have no idea," he said, above the post-performance noise of the milling crowd.

"God, you looked so skinny in those pants," Jane said, letting those be her final words.

From the living room window in Ogden's Riverside Drive apartment Johan could see down past the trees of the park to the darkness that had come to Dead Man's Hill. Lance played a medley of songs, drawing a small crowd to the Connifers' grand piano, among them a tall young man in a cashmere sweater with his arm around Diane Coleman. A sophomore at Princeton, someone said. And there were others not part of the cast, let alone the school. Johan had lied without knowing it, but had no regrets. He stood in a corner for a few minutes, not knowing where to put his eyes, and headed for the door.

"He's such a snob," he heard someone say. Was it Robin Abel, talking to another girl. Could it be? No. Laughable to even think it could have been directed at him.

A gauntlet awaited him in the lobby of his family's building.

"Marlon Brando himself," Lenny said, saluting with a raised coffee container.

Luke handed him a paper cup. The wine tasted sweet.

"Hannah and Vera said you were great. I got kind of messed up. That's why I didn't come. You know what I mean?"

"It wasn't a big deal."

"My brother the star. Can't you just see him going far? He's going off to college. Where'd you say you were going?"

"I don't know."

"Why not go someplace like Columbia or Harvard?" Lenny asked.

"Because they don't want him, that's why." Jerry laughed.

"Hey, man, leave him alone. He's doing great," Luke said.

"All this college stuff. Like Harvard is better than somewhere else. It's all bullshit. Like where did Lyndon Johnson go? Some place you never heard of and look at him. He's sitting in the White House. Where did Abraham Lincoln go to college? Or George Washington? I'll bet they didn't even go to college at all, and look what they did. So all this Harvard shit. 'Look at me, man. I go to Harvard.' Like you're supposed to kiss their asses, or something. It's all bullshit, man." So Lenny riffed.

"Pour Johan another cup of wine. He still looks thirsty," Jerry said.

Luke filled his cup again. "Hey, this is the last one. You're drinking all our wine. What are you anyway, an alcoholic?" He laughed.

"Don't be calling him no names. He's a star." Jerry laughed.

A young woman wearing a short skirt and black tights passed them and entered the elevator.

"She's mine, all mine, if she comes back down," Jerry said.

"In your dreams," said Luke.

Johan's personal college fund continued to grow. Every Sunday morning he performed the same ritual, trailing Auntie Eve down to the subway station before zipping back to the building and pocketing a few twenties from her money closet. And this Sunday was no different. From inside her apartment, he listened, with acute anxiety, for footsteps out in the lobby. Hearing none, he opened the door only to find a white-haired man with a mustache directly in front of him.

"You gone and moved to a new apartment?" The man spoke with a Southern accent and in a whispery voice. His eyes and face filled with a laughter you could see from his expression but not hear, even from up close. He wore yellow pants and a bright blue shirt, as if en route to clobber golfballs on some fairway with his mashie and whatnot.

"No," Johan said, trying to recover from his fright and inwardly recoiling at what sounded like an insinuation. He knew the man's name and where he lived: Calvin Crawford, in room 11C4. Though he had never spoken two words to him, he imagined Mr. Crawford as a former riverboat gambler with a hidden past, someone who maybe carried a derringer and was more than willing to shoot people dead with it.

"Hey. What's your hurry?" Mr. Crawford said, when Johan began to head off, as if he hadn't finished amusing himself.

"I'm not in a hurry."

"You ran off like you were in a race." Mr. Crawford shook with more of that soundless laughter.

"Did you want to tell me something?" Johan asked, when Mr. Crawford's amusement went on unabated.

Mr. Crawford pulled himself together sufficiently to say, "Why, you took off without giving me a chance to tell you about a job. Doesn't seem to me that you're very interested, from the way you're behaving."

"I'm interested," Johan said, as Mrs. Manootdjian approached, her keyring jangling. Her arrival seemed to be cause for Mr. Crawford's amusement to grow and grow.

"Good morning," she said.

"Good morning, ma'am," Mr. Crawford replied, as she let herself into Auntie Eve's apartment.

"That apartment is a busy place," Mr. Crawford said, after she had closed the door behind her.

"I guess," Johan said, thinking he had never liked the man just to look at him and now he liked him even less.

"Well, aren't you even going to ask me what the job is?"

"Oh, sorry."

"Go to the bookstore up the block and speak with the owner tomorrow. His name is Hank Kaminski. You can't miss him." The mention of Mr. Kaminski seemed to get Mr. Crawford's silent laughter going again.

Mr. Kaminski stood behind the counter on a foot-high platform poring over a form, now and then checking something off on it with a pen, his glasses atop his head in a cushion of long brown hair. In his other hand, between fingers stained yellow by nicotine, he held a cigarette that was more ash than tobacco.

"Are you Mr. Kaminski?" The question was unnecessary, not only because of the big sign outside that said, "Kaminski's House of Paperback Books," but because Johan remembered the store's grand opening five years before. He had come to the counter with Jim Brosnan's baseball diary, *The Long Season,* and was ten cents short and asked if he could take the book and pay the rest later, but Mr. Kaminski snatched the book from Johan and said, "Come back when you have the dough."

"What do you want?" Mr. Kaminski now asked, without looking up.

"Mr. Crawford sent me."

"So."

"So he said maybe you have a job for me."

"Are you literate?"

Stung into silence by the rudeness of the question, Johan simply stared at Mr. Kaminski. "What's the matter? You don't know what the word means?"

"I can read and write."

"What's your name?"

"Johan."

"You got a last name?"

"Manootdjian.»

"Armenian? Your father hang rugs all over the walls?"

"No." There was no need, given the insulting phrasing of the question, to tell Mr. Kaminski of his father's one failed attempt.

"Are you a thief? If I let you work here, will you try to steal my books?"

"No."

"Be here tomorrow at five o'clock. And be here on time or don't bother showing up."

As he passed by the End Bar several doors down, the smell of meats and beer blowing out onto Broadway through the warm air of the vent, he was seized by a fear that between now and the next afternoon, something would prompt Mr. Kaminski to change his mind.

But Mr. Kaminski hadn't changed his mind. The next afternoon he greeted Johan with a feather duster and said, "Run this over the books on the racks and familiarize yourself with the titles so you can be of some use to the customers." Wire racks of paperback books lined the four aisles and floor-to-ceiling shelves against the walls held others, from the Signet classics, with fetching illustrated covers, to Harper Torch and Doubleday Anchor books aimed at the college crowd. The one concession to hardcover publishing was the Modern Library series, which got a shelf of its own. And at the front of the store were periodicals, quarterlies, intellectual tabloids: *I. F. Stone's Weekly, The Nation, The Observer, The Guardian, Foreign Affairs, The Economist, Partisan Review, Paris Review.*

Johan returned to the counter area sneezing from all the dust he had feathered into the air. "Go get me a container of coffee from Chock Full O' Nuts. Black, no sugar. Don't fool around going or coming," Mr. Kaminski said, handing him a five-dollar bill. Coffee drinking and cigarette smoking. Those seemed to be his two passions, judging from the overflowing ashtrays and the empty black and yellow and white Chock Full O' Nuts containers on the shelves behind the cash register. Unless he had a tapeworm, he couldn't have been much for food, not the way his clothes hung from his frame.

That evening a woman approached the counter and handed Johan a twenty to pay for two mystery novels, but in one fluid motion Mr. Kaminski's skeletal hand swooped down to snatch the bill out of his fingers. Pressing heavily on the keys of the antique cash register, he rang up the sale, making it clear that he alone would handle the money and work the register. If Johan and the woman wanted to know who was in charge, he had just shown them. The woman had a big bust and a small waist. "That one will wear you out. She can go on for hours," Mr. Kaminski said of the customer, after she had left.

"What? How can you know such a thing?" Johan asked.

"I've been around the block a few times," Mr. Kaminski replied with complete matter-of-factness.

Somehow it wasn't for Johan to ask if Mr. Kaminski had been around the block with this particular woman. But his sexual commentary had set him on fire. Mr. Kaminski was saying that women were not necessarily who they appeared to be—that their pleasant demeanor hid their raging sensuality. And there were more dumbfounding assessments to follow. Was it possible that the serious-looking woman who purchased several Jane Austen novels had multiple partners, as did the scholarly woman with the severe expression?

At the back of the store a shelf served as a secret passageway, opening with a push onto a narrow room with supply cabinets and a toilet. Several open boxes, containing copies of Henry Miller's *Rosy Crucifixion* trilogy, lay on the floor. Johan had been restocking the volumes all afternoon. Only the opening of the first one, *Sexus*, in which Tania's privates are described in a graphic way, was he familiar with. He was not the compulsive shoplifter he had once been. In fact, he had not stolen from a store in some years and had no reason to do so now. And yet his terror was no defense against shoving the fat first volume into the front of his loose-fitting jeans and starting a slow, endless walk to the front of the store, where Mr.

Kaminski stood on the foot-high platform behind the register, like a hawk about to swoop down on his pathetic prey.

"Goodnight."

"What's your hurry?"

"It's nine o'clock. I thought I was supposed to work four hours."

"Are you one of those clock watchers?"

"No."

"You're not leaving heavier than when you came in, are you?" Mr. Kaminski's stare was formidable in its penetrating power.

"No."

"Make sure you keep it that way. I have ways of dealing with workers who don't," he said, before turning to a customer.

"You will go, will you not?" Mrs. Manootdjian gave him the announcement of the graduation ceremony she had received in the mail. He glanced at the card, with its fancy italic script, and handed it back to her.

"No," he said, hearing her fearful tone.

"But Johan, how can you not go to your own graduation?"

It would not be like the play. He would have to sit with her. People who, after that day, would be out of his life forever, would see him with her and say, "Oh my god, look at Manootdj. Is that his grandmother? Why didn't his mother come? Does he even have a mother? What? That *is* his mother? Come on now. That woman wearing the men's shoes and the rubber stockings is his *mother*? Damn, if that's his mother, what about his father? What do you suppose *he* looks like?"

Only there would be no looks at his father, for the simple reason that he would not be there. Mrs. Manootdjian wasn't about to divulge that Johan had been attending a private school after keeping it a secret from him all these years.

Johan had knowledge of the Ten Commandments. He had knowledge of "Honor thy mother and thy father." He understood that vileness was rife within him for denying her. And it came to him that it wasn't about his mother and absent father. Did he have to go as the corpse that he was? Did he have to go and see that everyone else had won and he had died so he could die once more?

The next morning, with his mother he arrived at the Barbizon-Plaza Hotel, near Central Park, on West Fifty-eighth Street. On the dais stood Mr. Horst-Lehman, in a silk suit. Something about the future. Something about marching forward with hope and conviction. Behind him sat Mr. Arbuckle, with his glazed and puffy lips. Classmates were called up, in alphabetical order, to receive their diplomas: Robin Abel, Wellesley bound; Bert Bach, headed for Harvard; Diane Coleman, accepted by Sarah Lawrence; Ogden Connifer, Swarthmore.; John Edel, with his ticket to Yale.

He received his rolled parchment, and after the playing of "Pomp and Circumstance," handed it to his mother and headed toward the exit.

"But Johan, where are you going?" His mother looked stunned, but people were too dangerously close. His mother not understanding that the world could not forever be running on Momma time and that he must get away, he must shed this place, these people, this life.

As he neared the door a strong hand gripped his shoulder. Turning, he stared into the big, open face of Mr. Sadowski. Where did he come from that he now stood in front of him in his worn gray suit and dull red tie, imposing, even in a public setting, such unbearable intimacy? And were those tears in his big eyes?

"I just wanted to say that I would be proud to have you for a son."

The words flooded his senses. Nothing was alive in him now but craziness. Witnessing Johan's speechlessness, Mr. Sadowski tore away, as did Johan, in a different direction, streaking past the Grand Army Plaza and the Plaza Hotel and the pungent smell of manure deposited by carriage nags, past too the portrait painters and the zoo, seeking to outrun the stunned, abandoned look on his mother's face and the image of teary-eyed Mr. Sadowski and the bombshell of those devastating words he dared to speak. Proud? Proud? Son? Son? As his flight continued on to the mall and the bandshell, he summoned a nonsense chant —chom whom woona bom—in an effort to expunge Mr. Sadowski's sincere maleness.

At the terrace he slowly descended the steps to the lower level and sat on the rim of the Bethesda Fountain. The several rowboats out on the lake presented a peaceful picture in contrast with the turmoil within. What it was, he couldn't even say, only that there was an ache. Something had been lost. Something had died without his ever having even experienced it. He would never see these people again. The separation had been too abrupt, too violent. He was free, he tried to tell himself, while wondering where in the world there was for him to go and wishing for some way to return and start all over again so he could make it right, because how could you build on something that was so wrong?

Work until you drop. Such was the spartan ethos of Mr. Kaminski, for whom a twelve-hour day was routine. Mr. Kaminski's life was as drab as the soiled clothes on his skeletal frame, and yet he made it seem almost appealing. If, by the end of the day, Johan's legs hurt from standing for eight or ten hours and he had grown tired of unpacking boxes, restocking empty shelves, taking inventory, wandering the aisles with a feather duster, going on coffee runs, or just standing around, by the next morning he was strangely eager for more.

The Communist Party, Quaker relief efforts following World War II, civil rights work—Mr. Kaminski had attached himself to causes and movements in his earlier years, Johan came to learn. Now, in middle age, he was seeking the stability and security he once had no need for. If he had sought to benefit the world, the store was his way of benefiting himself. But it was more than work; interactions with customers and sales reps assuaged his loneliness. Johan sensed an underlying sadness in Mr. Kaminski, that he was not quite the man he had wanted to be, and his wound made his harshness tolerable, a twisted form of affection, to the point where the sight of the stolen copy of *Sexus* in Johan's room became unbearable and he secretly returned it.

"This country never learns. Washington thinks it can stop a peoples' revolution with technology," Mr. Kaminski said, one afternoon, while chatting with a bearded young man who had just come from an anti-Vietnam War conference.

"You should go to Russia if you don't like this country," Johan interjected.

"I should do what?" the man said, with an incredulous smile.

"All the Russians want to do is make a Communist of you. And if they can't do that, they will kill you. You should go to Russia. You'll find out." They didn't need to know that was what his mother said— "Let them go to Russia"—about people who criticized the United States.

"He's young. He has some bad information," Mr. Kaminski said, by way of apology.

"No, I don't. The Communists are coming. First to South Vietnam. Then Australia. Then Hawaii. And from there they will jump to the mainland. They have only one ambition, to put you and me and all of us in reeducation camps."

"Maybe some of us need a reeducation camp." The young man laughed.

"I've hired a reactionary idiot," said Mr. Kaminski.

Jane had met someone, an engineering student at Columbia. She was just sitting on the campus and he came up and introduced himself, she said. "He's throwing a pool party this weekend at his parents' place up in Scarsdale, and he's invited me. His name is Bert. Pretty neat, huh?"

"I guess," Johan said. How long would the party last? Would there be dancing? How many people had been invited? How would she get there? How would she get home? Questions like this he was able to ask. As to what the party meant, that was a question he could not go near. Nor could he ask her not to go. Columbia was Columbia, after all, and if Columbia wanted her, that could only mean the world wanted her, too. The invitation aroused in him not only fear but what felt like painful pleasure.

He imagined them zipping up to Westchester in the Corvette she said he drove, the top down and his chubby arm around her and the wind blowing her hair, as he paced the floor of Kaminski's House of Paperback Books. Would this Bert treat her like the frat boys did the local girls they rounded up at the bars along Broadway for their weekend parties?

Johan paced in his room that evening. Jane described the guy as pudgy, but what did pudgy mean when he had Scarsdale wealth and a Corvette and those Columbia numbers that were the only indicators of success a person needed?

The party was fine, she said the next day. Everyone lounged around the pool for several hours before dinner was served to the ten or so guests who showed up. Bert did no more than hold her hand briefly, drove her home, and thanked her for coming.

Had Bert found her drab? Had he found her uninteresting? Was he disappointed in her figure in a bathing suit? Had her table manners been less than he had expected? Such questions as these Johan asked himself, and took his worried mind into sleep that night.

The songs of summer followed him about. He heard the sullen Stones, how big-lipped Mick Jagger hung on the word "satisfaction," giving it new life, while riding high on the power sound of Keith

Richard's electric guitar. He heard sweet Smokey Robinson and the Miracles sing "Tracks of My Tears." He heard Billie Joe Royal sing "Down in the Boondocks" with feeling and wicked Wilson Pickett sing "In the Midnight Hour," which made him dance in his head. He was brought to tearful attention hearing Sonny and Cher sing "I Got You, Babe" and came to a full stop hearing pissed-off Bob Dylan snarl "Like a Rolling Stone" like the anger angel that he was. And oh yes, he heard the Beach Boys sing "California Girls," but they could not fully pull him to them no matter how many times he heard their clean-cut sound.

With Jane he visited Rockefeller Center, where she picked up her airline ticket at a travel agency near the International Building, on Fifth Avenue, and the huge bronze statue of Atlas, shouldering the earth. Across Fifth Avenue worshipers and tourists flowed in and out of St. Patrick's Cathedral, its thin spires rising into the calm, blue sky.

The gently sloping promenade led to the ice skating rink, ringed by a festival of flags, where in the summer heat waiters in short black jackets maneuvered between tables balancing trays with food and drinks. In the fall, the waiters and diners would be gone and skaters would gracefully circle the ice.

He remembered Dr. Millsley's office high above the street and the fantasy of the dark-eyed man bathing him in a hotel bathroom. How had he grown from a small boy to the tall, skeletal person he now was? It had happened too fast. He was not prepared.

"Will you write?" he asked.

The Aeronaves de Mexico ticket in her bag promised access to swimming pools and tree-lined streets and pleasure-filled days and evening drinks on a verandah; it represented flight from the hot city and its steamy subways cars and huge crowds. People—grown-ups—had arranged for her to be elsewhere. All she had to do was pick up the ticket. It just seemed magical that such connections were possible. By comparison his own family seemed unto itself, with no relations in range, if he was not to count Auntie Eve.

" I'm only going away for two weeks. You're the one who will really be going away."

"I guess."

"What do you mean, you guess? Of course you are. That's what I like about you. You won't allow yourself to be tied to your mother's apron strings, like my father."

"My girlfriend is going away, and I need to be with her when she does," he said to Mr. Kaminski, after his coffee run for him to Chock Full O'Nuts. Today was a *coffee and* day for Mr. Kaminski. He had opted for a nutted cheese sandwich, an excellent choice, though nothing stood up to their Friday sandwich special, tuna fish, which, along with a bowl of steaming clam chowder soup, would bring heaven to earth. Often now Mr. Kaminski told him to get something for himself on his Chock Full runs. If gruff love was not in the air, then it was something close, and not easily tolerable, the stick being the truer and more honest expression of feeling.

"Could you try speaking English, or do I need to send for an interpreter?"

"Huh?"

"Your girlfriend is going away, and you need to be with her when she does?"

"She is leaving on a jet plane tomorrow. I need to say goodbye to her."

"How long is this girlfriend of yours going to be away?"

"Two weeks."

"You're looking like a nervous wreck over her being away for two weeks?" Mr. Kaminski shook his head and laughed.

The next day Mr. Thayer drove a red Simca and whistled madly while zipping over the Triborough Bridge. The noise came to Johan in the back seat of the tinny car as aggressive and excluding and informed by anger.

"Knock, knock," Mr. Thayer said.

"Who's there?" Jane asked.

"Some."

"Some who?"

Mr. Thayer began to sing "Some Enchanted Evening" while maneuvering aggressively between larger cars and highballing trailer trucks.

"Oh Dad, that's funny."

Jane's laughter suggested an alliance of sorts and gave more significance to her choosing to sit up front with her father.

"I'll bet Johan thought it was a real yuck-yuck, too. Didn't you, Johan?" Mr. Thayer sought him out through the rear-view mirror.

"That was pretty good," he lied.

But Mr. Thayer's mind had gone elsewhere. "Listen, big boy, you don't want to mess with this little baby. It's got firepower," he said, addressing himself to the muscular driver sitting in the cab of an oil truck in the right lane.

"Oh Dad," Jane said, once again brought to laughter, forced or real.

At the airport Mr. Thayer kissed Jane and smothered her in a hug.

"Don't do anything I wouldn't do, Sweetie," he said, before retreating to a concession stand and giving them space.

"This is going to be hard," Johan said. Her upbeat mood had separated her from him. He felt only dread hearing the flight announcement and seeing a boarding line form.

"Jesus, Johan. It's only two weeks. What's the big deal?" she snapped, echoing Mr. Kaminski's reaction, and left him with only a light kiss.

He sat up front with Mr. Thayer on the ride back to the city, still reeling from Jane's harsh display of strength. Once again had his excess plunged him into a lake of shame. From overhead came the roar of a low-flying jet. Surely it was Jane's jet, streaking angrily and dismissively through the skies.

A satisfied smile played on Mr. Thayer's face. An unnerving sort of smile. "Feeling okay, Johan?" he asked, taking a break from his annoying whistling. They had come to a stoplight on One Hundred Twenty-fifth Street in Harlem, where some stores remained gutted from the previous year's riot. With ostentatious slowness and a baleful stare, a stout Negro man passed by as if to say that no vehicle had the power he possessed and that the two white occupants were dead if they so much as thought of messing with him.

"I'm feeling fine," Johan said, his attention diverted by a Penn Central passenger train speeding along the el, a blur of glistening steel as it bypassed the station.

"Well, your telephone bill should be lighter. That is, unless you get it in your head to call Mexico City every day." Mr. Thayer chuckled.

Some blocks later, near his building, Mr. Thayer pulled into a parking spot. "End of the line, old sport. End of the line. You don't mind walking the rest of the way, I'm sure. It's not far to the scene of the crime, is it now?"

Johan tried not to think of Mr. Thayer's insinuating words when there were other things, like malfunctioning planes falling out of the skies, to consider, as he lay moaning, on his sofa bed. Hour after hour he listened to WINS, "all news all the time," which had recently come on the air. The endless cycle of reporting had a narcotic effect on him.

"He's lovesick. I told him to get laid and he'll be all right, but he won't listen," Mr. Kaminski said to Mr. Crawford, the man who recommended him for the job and who worked some days but not others. "He thinks he has to be faithful. What he doesn't realize is that she's probably having a ball with all those jalapeño peppers down Mexico way." Mr. Kaminski's ribald slant prompted a look of merriment on Mr. Crawford's florid face and more of that noiseless laughter he specialized in.

Mr. Crawford and Mr. Kaminski made a strange pair, Mr. Crawford spiffy in his creased blue slacks and lemon yellow sports shirt with the alligator over the left breast. Not a hair out of place in that mane of white hair. If Mr. Crawford appeared scrubbed clean, Mr. Kaminski was a model of unkemptness, from his shaggy hair to his dirty fingernails. The casual way that Mr. Crawford moved about the store ensured he would never break a sweat, while those near Mr. Kaminski, intense and engaged, were likely to catch a whiff of body odor.

Like a steamroller was Mr. Kaminski, thinking he could squash Johan's pain with his big laugh.

"Get out there and wash all the windows. And be sure they're squeaky clean. You'll find the supplies you need back there," Mr. Kaminski said, pointing a nicotine-stained finger in the direction of the storage room.

With the sun in the west, Johan rolled back the awning, climbed the ladder, and got to work, soaping and rinsing the plate-glass windows and running the excess water off with a squeegee.

Having a ball. Jalapeño peppers.

"Your window washing stinks. Get out there and do it again," Mr. Kaminski said, the next morning. With the sun shining through, streaks were visible on the glass. But in a friendlier, softer voice, he said at the end of the day, "Work. Just work. It takes care of everything."

One afternoon, walking past, Mrs. Manootdjian saw Johan in the store and waved, and so Johan waved back.

"Is that your mother?"

Because Mr. Kaminski was Mr. Kaminski and not mocking Tom Smits and because there had been too much denying her for too long, Johan nodded, causing Mr. Kaminski to streak out the door in pursuit and lead her back into the store with her arm in his like a gallant, if disheveled, gentleman.

"I've heard all about you, Mrs. Manootdjian, and how hard you work. My assistant, Mr. Crawford, has a room in your building."

"Is that right?" Mrs. Manootdjian said. "My, what a nice store. So many books. You must be very learned."

"Reading is an activity I don't have as much time for as I would like. There are bills to pay. But I try."

"And do you have the Good Book, Mr. Kaminski?"

"The Bible?"

"Yes. In the beginning was the word, and the word was God, and all thought is meaningless without him."

"We have scholarly studies on the Bible."

"Yes, yes, there are the men with the fine minds who strut and preen, but they must be brought low into an understanding of their sinfulness in order to truly see. The world is full of searchers, and a search can only end when the truth has been found. And that truth is in the King James version of the Bible. Well, I must be going. It has been so nice to meet you, Mr. Kaminski."

His mother talking the way she did, leaving mortification in her wake.

"It's easy to see your mother has character and is a worker. Let's see if you can show some of the same drive," Mr. Kaminski said.

Worker. As Johan busied himself unpacking boxes, a customer fumbled for the correct title of a book. "Something about a mockingbird," she said. Mr. Kaminski darted off and quickly returned, triumphantly slapping the Harper Lee novel on the counter. And in that moment a deeper understanding came to Johan of Mr. Kaminski. He was more interested in knowing the titles of his books and their location in the store than in the content between their covers. He was, in essence, a servant to his intellectual masters.

"Were you looking for something in particular?" Several times Johan had gone away and come back to the renting office only to find Mrs. Greene still sorting through the contents of the gray canvas sack the mailman had delivered. He had become like those anxious

428

foreigners who queued up at the renting office window for their post.

"No, not really."

"You'll be going off to college soon. You must be looking forward to that."

"Oh, yes," he said, unable to maintain eye contact with her fixed birdlike gaze.

"And where is it you're going? Did you say Princeton?"

"Colby."

"Colby? Where might that be?" The name brought puzzlement to her face.

"Somewhere in Maine."

"Never heard of it, I'm afraid. Strange. I must have confused you with someone else who's going off to Princeton, or maybe it's Harvard."

The morning came when Mrs. Greene handed him a red-bordered air mail envelope. To his disappointment, a postcard accounted for the letter's heft. The Reforma, said the caption on the back of the card, giving a name to the boulevard on the front where Jane's cousin lived. The letter itself was written on a sheet of lined loose-leaf paper.

The Robertsons have this really neat apartment with a terrace, and they've given me my own room. Jennie has this super boyfriend. He's a medical student at the University of Texas. She's in her second year of college but dates guys older than she is. He's got this white Corvette he tears around town in. Did I tell you she's a model? She's gotten even more beautiful and guys are calling her all the time and she's invited to one party after another. She took me for a tennis lesson the other day. The instructor was a young guy with a mustache and a nice tan. I'm going to need a lot of work, but Ben, that's his name, said I did okay. And then that night we went to a party out in the Lomas thrown by Ben and some of his friends. Boy, that tequila is some powerful stuff, and they sure get wild down here. Some of them just jumped in the pool with all their clothes on. Everyone was real nice except for this jerk who kept insisting that I dance with him when I didn't want to.

Several times he read the letter, the big, forward sloping script pulling him along. She had hit the ground running. Nothing about missing him. His mind fixed on the tennis instructor with the mustache and the pushy guy at the party. Even if the guy had been a crude, he was a persistent crude, and maybe he would wear her down. A widening circle of social involvement awaited Jane, with Jennie leading the way.

You write to me of tennis and of golden tans and parties, but I am alone in my room. After your father dropped me off, I went home and turned on the radio to 1010 WINS, the all-news, all the time station, fearing I would hear that a Mexico-bound plane had dropped out of the sky. You are all I can think about—you and this pain that will not stop. Mr. Kaminski is my only companion. He taunts me all the livelong day. He does not know any other way. Truthfully, I don't mind the verbal beatings he inflicts, as I hear him crying behind his words. You cannot hear that in everyone, but you can hear it in him. Mr. Kaminski has a heart that beats wildly for a love it cannot find. That store is his coffin as well as his life.

"Why would you go to a school in the sticks that nobody has ever heard of and that probably costs a fortune? Did you apply to City College?"

Mr. Kaminski hadn't barged through this door wholly uninvited. Johan had been fretting about the payment coming due to Colby College, money he was not close to raising through his Auntie Eve college fund.

"No, I haven't."

"Why the hell not? It's probably ten times better than this other school and it's practically free."

Johan wandered the aisles, replenishing the racks where stock was low. You got on a track and you stayed on it. The thought of changing his plan created anxiety. August had come; time was running out. That night he could hardly sleep. Suddenly the City College of New York was a viable option. He wouldn't have to relocate or go into heavy debt. He could go to an essentially tuition-free college and maybe get a place of his own, and Jane would come back from Mexico and everything would be all right in his world. Why hadn't he listened to Mrs. Jacoby, his history teacher, and Mr. Horst-Lehman?

The world was not in its proper order in the morning, that Mr. Crawford, on a sunshine day, should be sitting on Mr. Kaminski's stool when Johan showed up for work.

"Is Mr. Kaminski here?"

Mr. Crawford ostentatiously sniffed the air. "I don't think so."

"Will he be coming in?"

"At four o'clock. And believe me, we'll know when he's approaching."

Johan felt the need to hide his revulsion at Mr. Crawford's mockery, as sharing the same space with him was uncomfortable enough without incurring his displeasure. The more Mr. Crawford tried to tear Mr. Kaminski down, the more Johan's liking and respect for Mr. Kaminski grew. Such humble work had to be hard for a distinguished-looking Southern gentleman like Mr. Crawford. Easier to picture him as the owner of a horse farm sipping bourbon on the verandah and looking out at his vast estate than as a lowly bookstore clerk living in an SRO with a public bathroom down the hall.

A woman came to the counter cradling a stack of books, including *Seven Storey Mountain* and *Last Exit to Brooklyn*. Her arrival seemed to have a galvanizing effect on Mr. Crawford. Not generally a speed merchant, he hustled off the foot-high platform and helped her place the books on the counter, then fished a five-dollar bill from his pocket. "Go get me a container of coffee. And get something for yourself, too," he said, turning to Johan.

If it took a thief to catch a thief, then so be it. But he didn't catch him. He just went along with Mr. Crawford's clumsy ruse to get him out of the way so he could rob Mr. Kaminski blind, even knowing the woman's haul of books would come to a painful sum. When Johan returned a bit later, the woman was gone and Mr. Crawford was fuss-budgeting, sorting books into their proper racks not from any mania for organization but to work off his anxiety. A no-sale sign showed in the window of the cash register.

Keeping Jane away from the aggressive guy at the party who wanted her to dance and away from the tennis player with the mustache had required hard mental work, but a corner had surely been turned. Jane had stopped moving outward and meeting more people and slowly recognized what she had in him. Her second letter would prove as much. With the excitement of a dog taking away a big thick bone to gnaw on, he carried the letter Mrs. Greene handed him up to his room. Imagine. A week had passed. Jane's trip was half over.

Dear Johan,

Boy, it really does sound hard for you up there in good old New York City working those long hours for Mr. Kaminski and then going home to your room at night. You should try to get out a little and have some fun. Ben—remember him, the tennis instructor—has a real wicked backhand. Jennie and I went to see him in a professional match and he was terrific. His friends threw a couple of more parties. These people go to parties every night. I don't know how he gets out on the tennis court the next day. They all drink a ton and do a lot of carrying on.

He paused in his reading. The fence he tried to build around her with mental exertion had been a big bag of crap. And she had obviously not read that part of his letter about the pain news of her social life caused him.

Take a deep breath, Johan. The Robertsons have said I can stay down here with them. Daddy will be paying my tuition to a school here in Mexico City. Isn't that great?

The letter fell from his fingers to the floor. He lay on the sofa. A powerful kick to the stomach, it felt like. A blow too big to comprehend.

Later, seeing his mother standing in the lobby, he told himself to say nothing, absolutely nothing, about the news from Jane. And yet the words flew from his mouth.

"Is that so? She likes it so much down there?" A look of surprise and even happiness lit up Mrs. Manootdjian's face. Before he could reply, she said, "I must run," and entered the elevator.

He saw now what he had not seen before. His mother's mind had gone elsewhere. It was not for her to think about his girlfriend or if he went to college or didn't go to college. Whether he was ready or not, the time of his mother's concern for him had ended.

Again all news, all the time. 1010 WINS. The armed robbery of a jewelry store in midtown Manhattan. A rapist at loose in the Bronx. The slaying of a family of four in Mineola, Long Island. The threat of famine in sub-Saharan Africa. Fifteen-minute delays on the Bronx-Queens Expressway and longer delays on the Hutchinson and the Queens Midtown Tunnel and the Long Island Expressway..

"So how's that girlfriend of yours? Hear from her yet?" Mr. Kaminski asked, at closing time. He had already locked the door and was now emptying the cash register. Mr. Kaminski left the drawer open at night so thieves, seeing there was nothing to take, would not break in.

"Yes," I said. All day the store had felt like a refuge.

"There. You see. You got through it. She'll be back in a few days."

"She's not coming back."

"What's that mean, she's not coming back?"

And so Johan told him.

Mr. Kaminski came out from behind the cash register. "Believe me, the pain will pass. You'll get through it." He gave Johan a pat on the back.

The next day was another long shift. At 11 p.m. Mr. Kaminski had him turn off the lights at the back of the store to signal closing time. Johan locked the front door, allowing customers out but no new ones in, as Mr. Kaminski tallied the day's take, which he stuck in a zippered deposit bag.

As he headed for the door, Mr. Kaminski said, "Stick around. We'll go get something to eat."

The Silver Rail had a dining area behind the bar. The sawdust strewn floor. The low lights. The Rolling Stones and Dylan blaring from the jukebox. The happy buzz of the patrons. The slender waitress with her blond hair in a ponytail. He had entered another world, one that, if only briefly, eased his tortured thoughts about Jane.

Mr. Kaminski recommended the steak special, a slab of boneless meat that came with French Fries and a salad. "So are you still going away to that school up in the sticks?"

"Money's a problem." Johan didn't tell him that the deadline had passed for the college's receipt of the first tuition payment..

"You either have the money or you don't," Mr. Kaminski said, smearing butter on a seeded roll.

Johan lifted the pitcher of beer and refilled his glass. "You drink that stuff like it's water. You'll be pissing all night," Mr. Kaminski said.

"Haunted, frightened trees"? "Crazy sorrow"? "One hand waving free"? Who sang lyrics like that?

The tavern ambience seemed to soften Mr. Kaminski. He spoke more about himself over the late dinner than he had in the several months Johan had worked at the store. He was a graduate of Brooklyn Technical High School, one of the city's special public high schools. A low grade in French kept him out of City College; by one point he had fallen below the admission requirement. What an unfair and heartbreaking thing, Johan thought, hearing a trace of sorrow in Mr. Kaminski's voice. But could that be true? Because of one point, he had to wind up working impossible hours in the bookstore he owned? But then, wasn't Johan's fate being determined by his unsatisfactory SAT score?

"Why don't you take her home? Go on. It's the only thought you've had in that empty head of yours since we got here. You think she doesn't know what's going on between your ears? She's a woman. Her senses are on high alert. And you won't win any points with her sitting there like Mr. Above It All. You don't knock on the door, no one answers. Trust me," Mr. Kaminski said, after the waitress had served them.

Back in his room that night the reality of Jane returned and he was reduced to softly moaning while waiting for sleep to take him.

Dear Jane,

You knocked me down completely with your letter. It is only now that I am able to stand and walk around and approximate a sensible person. But I have some news of my own. I too have had a change of plans. I will be staying here in New York City to attend Queens College, which is part of the City University of New York. I applied late to City College and they did not have room for me. But Queens College is a four-year college too, and I will only have to pay $37.50 a semester, not the steep tuition that Colby College demands. This is a good start to my life, whatever the world may say. But just because I will not be leaving New York City does not mean I will not be leaving my room. I must not stay where decay and death abide. Of this I am sure. However, I am not strong enough to live in Queens, where I fear a different kind of death awaits, the death that oblivion consigns, and so I will be in this room until the time comes when I am not. And that time will come, Jane. Yes it will. I struck a blow for my personal freedom in going to Boston a couple of years ago and Philadelphia this year. In so doing I have proven that the cities of America exist in something more than my imagination and are within my range. But do not think that I am changing course because of your decision. It is only that reality has bent me to its will. What I couldn't see before I can see now. My family has no money. We are paupers on Mr. Simon Weill's string. Someday I will fight him, and fight him good. Someday I will be the theme of honor's tongue, like Hotspur, but for now I must languish in the rubble of defeat where my life and my tendencies have landed me. My insides are ablaze with pain at not having you and I feel rooted to this spot where our pleasure and our demise occurred. For now I am being faithful to a time and place that I recognize are no more, but this is the best that I can do. Please do not wound me anymore than you have to with names and places and events. You only make Mexico City sound like a lizard's lair with the tidings that your letters bring.

The approaching fall semester had made the bookstore a madhouse. "Anchor 321….Harper Torch Book 476…" Mr. Kaminski called out, dispatching Johan to various parts of the store to meet the customers' requests. Books sold virtually out of cartons he sliced open with a box cutter. He had been told by Mr. Kaminski to come in early and expect to stay late all week.

"Will Mr. Crawford be here, too?" Mr. Kaminski did not respond.

Several hours later Mr. Crawford arrived, in a pink polo shirt and seersucker trousers and white canvas shoes.

"I'm letting you go," Mr. Kaminski said.

"What do you mean?"

"I won't be needing you anymore."

Johan begin to tremble, as when his father had been made to get up.

"Why?"

"You're lucky I'm paying you at all."

"Who the hell do you think you're speaking to?"

"Get out of my store." Mr. Kaminski somehow chest-bumped the more powerfully built man out the door.

Had Mr. Kaminski caught Mr. Crawford in the act? Had someone seen Mr. Crawford pocketing money and told Mr. Kaminski? Or would Mr. Crawford come to Johan's room in the night and murder him for having snitched, even if he hadn't? For the rest of the day, Johan left Mr. Kaminski to himself, having seen his fire.

The next morning Johan reached under the convertible sofa for the bank passbook and lay back down with it pressed against his chest. Suddenly the path forward to a new freedom and happiness was clear. He didn't have to live the small life he had been living; he didn't have to be a fearful, petty thief.

Again he reached under the sofa, this time for the two keys. One was for Auntie Eve's apartment, the other for her closet. At the incinerator on the landing, he dropped the two keys down the chute. No, they would not be turned to ash, but they would be blackened and shoveled out and deposited with the other garbage in metal cans and then be carted up the ramp to the street. A Department of Sanitation worker would drag the can with the keys to the back of the truck and dump the can's contents into the vehicle's maw. No one would find those keys, or if they did, many were the locks in New York City. Many, many, many. No one would ever ever come to him and say, "Was this your doing?" No one.

He then went to his mother. "Were you looking for me, my son? Is something ailing you?" She asked, as if she had been waiting for him there at the dining room table.

"I don't know."

"Did you come here to tell me something?"

"No. I don't think so." It had been a mistake. To give her his secrets would be to give her himself. He couldn't afford possession of him in that way. He could not have her render him white as the robe she wore. He could not be annihilated in her whiteness.

"You can tell me, Johan. I won't breathe a word."

"I was just a little hungry," he said, as he poured himself a glass of milk from the refrigerator.

"When you are ready, my son, I will be here."

That night, back in his room, he was alert for footsteps, not his father's as in years past, but his mother's soft tread. Lying there in the dark, the possibility grew that she would pass through the wall and pull everything out of him in that coaxing voice. As waves of fear passed through him, he sought comfort in the thought that morning would soon come.

Dear Johan,

I've got news for you, Mr. Self-Pity. You're not waiting for me from any great love. You're just afraid of people and afraid of life. You're afraid to be bitten. You're a private school snob who can no longer afford to be a snob because it's been proven that you're not better than anyone. And when you find out you're not better you run away and hole up in that room. I will tell you exactly what I want to tell you, Mr. Censor. I went to three parties last week and I'm going to four more this week. How do you like that? I guess I'll hear in your next whiny report.

Gusts of wind whipped off the river. The cable wound and unwound around the winch in the elevator shaft. The smell of marijuana was strong as he knocked on the red door and Jerry opened it. "Hey, man," he said.

Two small rooms separated by a beaded curtain. In one room was a stove and a sink and a table. In the other was the living area where Luke also slept.

"Didn't I tell you the penthouse was the coolest place?" Luke said.

The penthouse. A kind of shack with a corrugated tin facade. Up here Luke could almost believe he had nothing to do with the rest of the building.

"It's nice," Johan said, not for the first time.

"Have some grass." Luke offered him the joint but Johan said no. The pungent smell was not enticing.

"Come on. Take it. We got lots more. That's some wrong shit, Jane going off to Mexico on you like that. You can't count on any woman to be normal for very long. Sooner or later they do this strange shit.

You know what I mean? It's like they're born to be unreliable," Lenny said, Frieda having ditched him.

"Did I tell you, man? Lenny and Jerry and me, we'll be going camping up in the Catskills. We're going to get a tent and some gear and load up the Bonneville and take off," Luke said.

"That's right, man. Get some of that fresh country air," Lenny said, before passing the joint to Jerry.

The roof called to him. From the basement incinerator rose smoke and cinders and through the screened chimney. To the south Broadway curved through the tall, flanking buildings. To the west there was Riverside Park, and beyond, the Hudson River and the golden Palisades. To the east were black-top roofs of buildings and more buildings, and the Cathedral of St. John the Divine. And then there was the tall spire of Riverside Church and squat Grant's Tomb and the gray span of the George Washington Bridge, the view north one that often filled him with hope but now just summoned dread, as if the world out there had nothing but pain in store.

Mr. Manootdjian regularly now sat on the traffic island in the middle of Broadway, blissfully unaware of the rampaging vehicles streaking north and south, nor was he drawn by the cooing pigeons at his feet or the idle chatter of the other elderly folks who occupied the long bench. His father said he was happy to be alive but would be happy to die, as his work on earth was done. Much of his time out there he passed with his head bowed in prayer.

Hannah's little boy was now in elementary school. Johan's interest in his nephew and Naomi's daughter Jeanne was not strong. Unhealed wounds in relation to these two older sisters had colored his view of their progeny. Twice in the past year Naomi had overdosed on sleep medications and was sped by ambulance for emergency room care, but she came back from her stays in the psychiatric ward in good spirits, as if she found connection there she couldn't find elsewhere.

As for Rachel, there were occasional sightings. She had a different look now. The braid was gone and she had dyed her hair with henna, turning it a rich reddish brown, and wore it short in a duck's ass. At night she would tear drunk in the dark glasses she had taken to through the lobby and up to the apartment, where she shed angry, bitter tears in Mrs. Manootdjian's arms. Rachel was searching, and as were all her children, Mrs. Manootdjian said. Their various troubles meant that they hadn't yet *found* and would have no peace in the embrace of the world's folly until they did, and that defeat by the world was the necessary prelude to the Lord's victory, as they had to be lost before finding could occur.

Vera had a persevering personality. Strong in her resolve, she was capable of giving others their due, and whatever shame she bore intrinsic to being a Manootdjian, she did not extend that net beyond the border of herself. *Charlotte's Web* had been her go-to as a child and Lucy Arnez her guiding light. Johan had his history with her and that was indelible in his memory bank; if he did not love her enough, it was only that he was unsure of her format, whether under the smile she was friend or foe. It did not help to be so close in age.

When he came home from his workday at the bookstore, Tom Smits was waiting, just inside the lobby.

"So you found me."

"There were several guys standing on the corner. They told me where you live. One of them was your brother. Does he always hang out on street corners?"

Johan led him away from the building to the Turk's diner across the street.

"You didn't return my calls. I must have left five messages for you in the last week." The summer sun had burned away Tom's pallor.

"Things just kept coming up." Johan's mother had given him the phone messages.

"I spent the summer with my mother down in Martinique. It's really been hard for her since my father left. There were men who wanted to make her, but she didn't want to be made. She came back to New York to find the divorce papers waiting for her."

Made? A mother made? From where came the freedom to apply such language to a mother? Johan did not hear Tom's pain. He had no ears for that, given Tom's high numbers, numbers that allowed you to play-act at unhappiness when there could be no such thing for people with his gifts. High achievement *was* happiness. Tom would get his bearings soon and regain his strength. Martinique? Tom and his family belonged to the world. Johan and his family belonged to One Hundred Thirteenth Street.

"Are you still going to that college up in Maine next month?" Not a real college, just a college up in Maine.

"The money isn't there."

"So what are you going to do?"

"I guess I'll go to City College."

"Jesus. Well, it used to have a good reputation."

"Yes." Johan was talking about a college Tom had no respect for when in fact he was not even going to that college but to Queens College, if he was to go to that college at all.

"Let's stay in touch, huh? I really want us to," Tom said. Did Johan hear a tremble in his voice? Did Johan see fear and uncertainty in his eyes?

"Of course."

Dear Tom, I am writing this note so finality can have its place. I am an island country. This you must understand. I do not look on invasion lightly. My guns are drawn and the transgressor will be given a hard blow. Do not assume I am in complete poverty, for my resources are many, even if they have not been called upon and recognized yet. Know this as well: you are a demoralizing eye, of undetermined origin, on my life, and your laughing thing showers down on me from all directions. Do not approach my shore again. My country is not logical in the matter of restraint. It can turn guns on itself as well as the other. Use every one of those high numbers to grasp my meaning. Johan

Seated at his desk and with the light from the gooseneck lamp to read by, Johan checked carefully for misspellings or grammatical errors. He did not want to give Tom more reason than he already had to laugh at him or label him illiterate, the tag he applied to poor Mr. Sadowski. Then he folded the note in thirds and placed it in an envelope, on which he wrote Tom's full name and address in big block letters, so the mailman would not have the excuse of Johan's chaotic scrawl to fail to make good on delivery. Next he sealed the envelope, attached a stamp, and pulled on a sweater, as a fall chill was now in the air. Johan stepped decisively from the room. He must not do the dawdle dance and wait until morning to mail the letter, as delay could prove treacherous to his purpose.

The olive drab mailbox stood right there on the corner. How solid and reliable. Oh what vengeful joy to pull on the handle and drop the letter in the opening. Saying, I will show you who I am and what I am, mister. Now will you finally hear.

"We cannot have it. Luke hangs around outside the building with Jerry and that terrible friend of his." Johan could see and feel his mother's distress.

The trio were outside and did look shabby.

"We're going for a ride. Want to come?" Luke asked.

"Yeah. We'll take you anywhere you want to go," Lenny added.

"And that's no lie," Jerry chimed in.

Lenny wore a red bandanna around his forehead to keep his long black hair out of his eyes. He was jobless and living with Luke. And Jerry had dropped out of high school. Luke stood with his shirt tail hanging out of his pants.

"Not today. Thanks."

"What's this not today, thanks shit. It's a car. What, you don't like cars? They're all around you, man. Wake up." So said Lenny.

They made no mention of their plans for "the country." Johan felt no need to remind them.

In the park he paused to watch toddlers playing in the sandbox with their little shovels and pails, then continued into the lower level. The day was cool, the kind about which people said, "Fall is in the air." Over the iron fence to Dead Man's Hill he climbed. Dappled light filtered through the branches of the trees onto the undergrowth.

The cage called to him. He lifted the latch and entered, then pulled the door closed and secured the latch. Some distance beyond a girl playfully punched her boyfriend on the arm. Johan assumed the boy had been teasing her. They spread a blanket and lay down on it and soon were kissing. The men Johan had seen crouching behind bushes that first summer with Jane—where were they? Was he one of them now? Oh, what did he care? Pressed up against the chain-link enclosure, he felt as much excitement as any he had ever known and could only wonder whether, in Mexico City, Jane at that very moment was engaged in something similar to the scene before him.